KU-483-352

THE GOOD SUICIDES

Antonio Hill

Translated by Laura McGloughlin

BLACK SWAN

TRANSWORLD PUBLISHERS
61–63 Uxbridge Road, London W5 5SA
A Random House Group Company
www.transworldbooks.co.uk

**THE GOOD SUICIDES
A BLACK SWAN BOOK: 9780552778466**

First published in Spanish as *Los Buenos Suicidas*
in June 2012 by Random House Mondadori

First published in Great Britain
in 2013 by Doubleday
an imprint of Transworld Publishers
Black Swan edition published 2014

Copyright © Antonio Hill 2013
English translation © Laura McGloughlin 2013

Antonio Hill has asserted his right under the Copyright, Designs
and Patents Act 1988 to be identified as the author of this work.

This book is a work of fiction and, except in the case of historical fact,
any resemblance to actual persons, living or dead, is purely coincidental.

A CIP catalogue record for this book
is available from the British Library.

This book is sold subject to the condition that it shall not,
by way of trade or otherwise, be lent, resold, hired out,
or otherwise circulated without the publisher's prior
consent in any form of binding or cover other than that
in which it is published and without a similar condition,
including this condition, being imposed on the
subsequent purchaser.

Addresses for Random House Group Ltd companies outside the UK
can be found at: www.randomhouse.co.uk
The Random House Group Ltd Reg. No. 954009

The Random House Group Limited supports the Forest Stewardship Council®
(FSC®), the leading international forest-certification organisation. Our books
carrying the FSC label are printed on FSC®-certified paper. FSC is the only
forest-certification scheme supported by the leading environmental organisations,
including Greenpeace. Our paper procurement policy can be found at
www.randomhouse.co.uk/environment

Typeset in 12/14pt Garamond by
Kestrel Data, Exeter, Devon.
Printed and bound in Great Britain

2 4 6 8 10 9 7 5 3 1

MIX
Paper from
responsible sources
FSC® C016897

For Jan, the youngest of the family

Prologue

A Normal Family

Lola Martínez Rueda, *The Voice of the Others*
Thursday, 9 September 2010

'They were a lovely couple,' say the neighbours. 'You didn't see him much, but he always seemed very well-mannered; he'd be friendly and say hello. She kept her distance a little more, perhaps . . . But she was certainly very devoted to her daughter.' 'They had a beautiful baby,' says the owner of a café close to their home, situated in the Clot district of Barcelona, where a few days before, around ten o'clock, Gaspar Ródenas, his wife Susana and their daughter, Alba, fourteen months, were having breakfast. 'They came many weekends,' she adds. And without my asking she tells me what they usually had: a black coffee for him and white for her, and how beautiful the little one was. Minutiae, of course. Insignificant details and banal commentaries that now, in light of the facts, are disturbing.

Because in the early hours of 5 September, while his

7

wife slept, this 'meek but friendly' father rose from the marital bed, entered the bedroom of his only child, put a pillow over her face and squeezed with all his might. We cannot know if the mother awoke, alerted perhaps by that sixth sense that has disturbed maternal sleep since time began. In any case, Gaspar Ródenas, 'such a well-mannered' husband according to neighbours and colleagues, didn't intend to leave her alive either. Susana died shortly afterwards, from a single shot to the heart. Then, as the canon of the chauvinist killer decrees, Gaspar gave himself the final shot.

The names of Susana and her daughter have swelled the list of women falling victim to those who in theory should have loved them, respected them and even, if we think of the little girl, protected them. Forty-four women have died in the course of this year (2010) at the hands of their partners. Forty-five, with the macabre addition of a daughter. Maybe this case does not conform to the formula we have learned to recognize: a separation under way, reports of ill-treatment. Gaspar Ródenas wasn't – such is the irony of life – a violent man.

The State can, for once, stick its neck out and declare that nothing seemed to indicate that Susana and Alba were in danger. And they are right . . . But that just makes their deaths even more terrible, if possible. Because many of us women already know that mechanisms exist – however scarce and insufficient they may be – to defend ourselves against those men who believe they have a right to control our lives and our deaths. Against those guys who shout at us, put us down and beat us. What we cannot know is how to protect ourselves from the rancour that accumulates in silence, from that mute hatred which suddenly explodes one night and destroys everything.

There is a photo of the three taken just weeks before, on a beach in Menorca. In it Alba can be seen sitting on the shore with a red spade in her hand. She is wearing a little white cap to protect her from the August sun. Kneeling behind her is Susana. Happy, she smiles at the camera. And at her side, with his arm around her, is her husband. Seeing him there, in a relaxed pose, squinting in the sun, no one could have imagined that scarcely a month later this man would use those very hands that are caressing Susana to kill them both.

Why did this thirty-six-year-old man, with a steady, well-paid job in a well-known cosmetics company, with no extraordinary financial burdens and no previous record of any kind, commit murders even more repulsive than others? When did it occur to him to end the lives of his wife and daughter? At what moment did madness overcome him and distort daily reality to the extent of convincing him that death was the only way out?

The answer of his relatives, friends and work colleagues is still the same, although now none of them can believe what they insist on repeating: Gaspar, Susana and Alba were a normal family.

HÉCTOR

1

For the second time in a short period, Inspector Héctor Salgado turns his head suddenly, convinced someone is watching him, but he sees only anonymous and indifferent faces, people who, like him, are walking on a packed Gran Vía and stop once in a while in front of one of the traditional stalls of toys and games occupying the pavement. It is 5 January, the night before *Reyes*, though no one would think so judging by the pleasant temperature, ignored by some strollers conveniently dressed in overcoats, some even with gloves and scarf as befits the season, happy to participate in a sham of winter lacking the main ingredient: cold.

The parade has been finished for a while and the traffic fills the road under garlands of shining lights. People, cars, the smell of *churros* and hot oil, all seasoned with supposedly happy carols, their lyrics dipped in surrealism, which the loudspeakers launch against the passers-by without the least decorum. It seems no one has bothered to compose new songs, so for yet another year there are the same fucking tidings of comfort of joy. That must be what's fucked up about Christmas, thinks Héctor: the fact that generally it always stays the same, while we change and grow older. It seems to him inconsiderate to the point of cruelty that this Christmassy atmosphere is the only thing that is repeated year after year without exception, making our decadence ever more evident. And for the umpteenth time in the last fifteen days he wishes he'd flown from all the revelry to some Buddhist or radically atheist country. Next year, he repeats, as if it were a mantra. And to hell with what his son might say.

He is so absorbed in these thoughts that he doesn't notice that the queue of pedestrians, moving almost as slowly as that of the cars, has stopped. Héctor finds himself at a halt in front of a stall selling little plastic soldiers in bags: cowboys and Indians, Allied soldiers dressed in camouflage ready to shoot from a trench. He hasn't seen them in years and remembers buying them for Guillermo when he was a kid. In any case, the vendor, an old man with arthritic hands, has managed to recreate an exquisite military scene, down to the last detail, worthy of a 1950s film. That's not all he sells: other soldiers, the traditional lead ones, bigger and in shiny red uniforms, march on one side, and a legion of Roman gladiators, historically out of place, on the other.

The old man gestures to him, inviting him to touch the goods, and Héctor obeys, more out of manners than any real interest. The soldier is softer than he expected and the feel of it, almost like human flesh, repulses him. Suddenly he realizes that the music has ceased. The passers-by have halted. The car lights have been switched off and the Christmas lights, flickering weakly, are the street's only lighting. Héctor closes his eyes and opens them again. Around him the crowd begins to vanish; the bodies suddenly disappear, evaporate without leaving the

14

least trace. Only the vendor remains at his stall. Wrinkled and smiling, he takes one of those snow globes out from under the counter.

'For your wife,' he says. And Héctor is about to answer that, no, Ruth detests those glass domes; they've upset her ever since she was a child, like clowns do. Then the flakes clouding the interior fall to the bottom and he sees himself, standing in front of a toy soldier stall, trapped within the glass walls.

'Papa, Papa . . .'

Shit.

The television screen covered in grey snow. His son's voice. The pain in his neck from having fallen asleep in the worst possible position. The dream had been so real on *Reyes* night.

'You were shouting.'

Shit. When your own son wakes you out of a nightmare the moment has come to resign as a father, thought Héctor as he sat up on the sofa, sore and in bad humour.

'I fell asleep here. And what are you doing awake at this time of night?' he counter-attacked.

Guillermo shrugged his shoulders without saying anything. As Ruth would have done. As Ruth had done so many times. In an automatic gesture, Héctor searched for a cigarette and lit it. Cigarette butts were spilling out of the ashtray.

'Don't worry, I won't fall asleep here again. Go to bed. And don't forget we're going out early tomorrow.'

His son nodded. As he watched him walk barefoot towards his room, he thought how hard it was to act as a father without Ruth. Guillermo wasn't yet fifteen but, at times, looking at his face, you would say he was much older. There was a premature seriousness in his features that pained Héctor more than he cared to admit. He took a long drag on his cigarette and, without knowing why, pressed the button on the remote. He couldn't even remember what he'd put on that night. With the first few images, that still black-and-white photo of Jean-Paul Belmondo and Jean Seberg, he recognized it and remembered. *Breathless*. Ruth's favourite film. He didn't feel up to watching it again.

Approximately ten hours earlier, Héctor had been contemplating the white walls of the psychologist's practice, a space he knew well, a tad uncomfortable. As usual, the 'kid' was taking his time before beginning the session and Héctor still hadn't worked out if those minutes of silence served to gauge his state of mind or if the guy was simply a slow starter. In any case, this morning, six months after his first visit, Inspector Salgado wasn't in the mood to wait. He cleared his throat, crossed and uncrossed his legs, then finally leaned forward and said, 'Would you mind if we started?'

'Of course.' And the psychologist raised his eyes from his papers although he added nothing further.

He remained silent, interrogating the inspector with his gaze. He had an absent-minded air that, combined with his youthful features, made you think of one of those child prodigies who solve complex equations at the age of six but at the same time are incapable of kicking a football without falling over. A false impression, Héctor knew. The kid took few shots, certainly; however, when he fired, he was on target. In fact, the therapy sessions, which had begun as a work requirement, had become a routine, weekly at first then fortnightly, that Héctor had followed of his own volition. So that morning he took a deep breath, as he'd learned, before answering.

'Really sorry. The day didn't start off well.' He leaned back and fixed his eyes on a corner of the office. 'And I don't think it will end any better.'

'Difficulties at home?'

'You don't have teenagers, do you?' It was an absurd question, given that his listener would have to have been a father at fifteen to have offspring of Guillermo's age. He remained quiet for a moment to reflect, then, in a tired voice, he went on, 'But it's not that. Guillermo is a good boy. I think the problem is that he was never a problem.'

It was true. And although many fathers would be satisfied by this apparent obedience, Héctor was worried by what he didn't know; what was going on in his son's head was a mystery. He never complained, his marks were normal, never excellent but never bad either, and his seriousness could be an example to madder, more irresponsible kids. However, Héctor noticed – or rather he sensed – that there was something sad behind this absolute normality. Guillermo had always been a happy child and now, in mid-adolescence, he'd become an introverted boy whose life, when he wasn't at school, basically passed by within the four walls of his bedroom. He spoke very little. He didn't have many friends. All in all, thought Héctor, he's not so different to me.

'And you, Inspector? How are you? Still not sleeping?'

Héctor hesitated before admitting it. It was a subject on which they couldn't agree. After months of insomnia, the psychologist had recommended some gentle sleeping pills which Héctor refused to take. Partly because he didn't want to become accustomed to them; partly because it was in the early hours that his mind worked at full capacity and he didn't want to dispense with his most productive hours; partly because sleeping plunged him on to uncertain and not always pleasant ground.

The kid deduced the reasons for his silence.

'You're wearing yourself out uselessly, Héctor. And, without wanting to, you're wearing out the people around you.'

The inspector raised his head. He rarely addressed him so directly. The kid held his gaze without turning a hair.

'You know I'm right. When you started to come to the practice we were dealing with a very different subject. A subject that was put aside after what happened to your ex-wife.' He spoke in a firm voice, without hesitation. 'I understand that the situation is difficult, but becoming obsessed won't get you anywhere.'

'You think I'm obsessed?'

'Aren't you?'

Héctor gave a faint, bitter smile.

'And what do you suggest? That I forget Ruth? That I accept that we'll never know the truth?'

'You don't need to accept it. Just live with it without rebelling against the world every day. Listen to me while I ask you as the police officer you are: how many cases remain unsolved for a time? How many are cleared up years later?'

'You don't understand,' Héctor replied, and took a few seconds to continue speaking. 'Sometimes . . . sometimes I manage to forget it all, for a few hours, while I work or when I go out running, then it comes back. Suddenly. Like a ghost. Expectant. It's not an unpleasant sensation, not accusing or asking, but it's there. And it doesn't go away easily.'

'What is it that's there?' The question had been formulated in the same neutral tone that marked all the young therapist's interjections, although Héctor noticed, or perhaps feared, that he was picking up a particular nuance.

'Relax.' He smiled. 'It's not that sometimes I see dead people. It's just the feeling that . . .' He paused to find the words. 'When you have lived with someone for a long time, there are times that you just know they're at home. You wake up from a siesta and you sense that the other person is there, without needing to see them. You understand? That wasn't happening to me any more. I mean, it never happened during the time I was separated from Ruth. Only after her . . . disappearance.'

There was a pause. The psychologist scribbled something in that notebook to which Héctor had no visual access. At times he thought that those notes formed part of the theatrical ritual of a session: symbols which served only to make the interlocutor – that is, him – feel listened to. He was going to put forward his theory out loud when the other man began to speak; he spoke slowly, amiably, almost carefully.

'You know something, Inspector?' he asked. 'This is the first time you have admitted, even in a roundabout way, that Ruth might be dead.'

'We Argentines are well aware what "disappeared" can mean,' replied Héctor. 'Don't forget that.' He cleared his throat. 'Even so, we have no objective proof that Ruth is dead. But—'

'But you believe it's so, right?'

Héctor looked over his shoulder, as if he were afraid someone might hear. 'That's what fucks me over most.' He had lowered his voice, speaking more to himself. 'You can't even mourn her because you feel like a fucking traitor who threw in the towel too early.' He took a deep breath. 'I beg your pardon. Christmas has never agreed with me. I thought I'd have come further with this, but . . . I had to give in. There's nothing. I've found nothing. Damn it, it's as if someone erased her from a drawing without a trace.'

'I thought the case was no longer in your hands.'

Héctor smiled.

'It's in my head.'

'Do me a favour.' That was always the prelude to the end. 'From now until the next session try to concentrate, at least for a while every day, on what you have. Good or bad, but what your life is made up of; not what's missing.'

It was almost two in the morning, and Héctor knew he wouldn't go back to sleep. He took his cigarette and mobile and left the house to go up to the roof terrace. At least up there he wouldn't wake Guillermo. The therapist was right in three things. One, he should start taking the damn sleeping pills, even if it annoyed him. Two, the case was no longer in his hands. And three, yes, deep down within him there was the conviction that Ruth was dead. Because of him.

It was a nice night. One of those nights that could reconcile you to the world if you let it. The coastline of the city extended before his eyes, and there was something in the bright twinkling lights of the buildings, in that dark but tranquil sea, that managed to chase off the demons Héctor carried within him. Standing there, surrounded by planters with dry plants, Inspector Salgado asked himself, with complete honesty, what he had.

Guillermo. His work as an inspector in Catalonia's police force, the *Mossos*, simultaneously intense and frustrating. A brain which seemed to function correctly and lungs which must be half black by now. Carmen, his neighbour, his landlady; his Barcelona mother, as she said. This roof terrace from which he could see the sea. An annoying therapist who made him think about bullshit at three in the morning. Few friends, but good ones. An immense collection of films. A body capable of running six kilometres three times a week (despite lungs worn out by the damned tobacco). What else did he have? Nightmares. Memories with Ruth. The void without Ruth. Not knowing what had happened to her was a betrayal of everything that mattered to him: his promises from another time, his son, even his work. This rented flat where they had both lived, loved and fought; the flat she had left to begin a new life in which he was only a supporting actor. Even so, she loved him. They continued loving each other, but in another way. He was learning to live with all this when Ruth disappeared, vanished, leaving him alone with the feelings of guilt against which he rebelled every minute.

Enough, he told himself. I'm like the protagonist of a French film: fortysomething, self-pitying. Mediocre. One of those that spends ten minutes looking at the sea from a cliff, plagued by existential questions, only then to fall in love like an idiot with an adolescent ankle. And just after this reflection he remembered the last chat, more

21

accurately an argument, he'd had with his colleague, Sergeant Martina Andreu, just before Christmas. The reason for the dispute was incredibly petty, but neither of the two seemed capable of putting an end to it. Until she looked at him with that insulting frankness and, without a second thought, fired point-blank: 'Héctor, really, how long has it been since you had a fuck?'

Before his pathetic response could reverberate in his head, his mobile rang.

2

Plaça Urquinaona was bathed in the blue light of the patrol cars, to the surprise of the four beggars, pickled with alcohol, who usually used the wooden benches as mattresses and couldn't sleep that night.

Héctor identified himself and descended the metro stairs, feeling apprehensive. Suicides who chose this method to carry out their angel's leap were more numerous than the ones covered in the media, more than were accounted for in the statistics, although not as many as urban legend suggested. Some cited the existence of 'black stations', platforms from which the number of people who decided to end their lives was disproportionately higher than normal. In any case, and to avoid what was known as the 'copycat effect', these deaths were kept from the public. Héctor had always thought, with no proof other than intuition, that these suicides were more the result of a moment of desperation than a plan laid out beforehand. In any case, the police procedure was characterized by prompt action: remove the body as soon as possible and re-establish service, although in this case, given the hour, they had more time; hide the occurrence under the alibi of an incident or breakdown during the time in which the traffic was necessarily suspended. Because of that he thought it strange that Agent Roger Fort, who was on shift that night, had bothered to call him at home in the middle of the night to inform him of what had happened.

The same Roger Fort who at this moment was looking with a hesitant expression at Inspector Salgado as he descended the second flight of steps that led to the platform.

'Inspector. I'm glad to see you. I hope I didn't wake you.'

There was something about this boy, a respectful formality that Héctor appreciated yet distrusted at the same time. In any case, Fort was the most improbable replacement for the young, determined and shameless Leire Castro. Héctor was convinced that the last thing that would have occurred to Agent Castro in these circumstances was to call a superior: without a doubt she would have felt herself qualified to deal with it on her own. That was the only objection Héctor had about her work: Leire was incapable of waiting for others to reach their conclusions; she went ahead and acted of her own accord without asking permission. This was a trait that wasn't always looked on favourably in a job where order and discipline were still considered synonymous with efficiency.

But, much to his regret, Castro was on maternity leave and Superintendent Savall had put this agent, recently arrived from Lleida, on the team. Dark, with a permanent five o'clock shadow which persisted despite shaving, average height and with a rugby player's complexion; his surname, Catalan for 'strong', seemed to fit him perfectly. Like Leire, he was not yet thirty. Both belonged to the new crop of investigative agents filling the *Mossos d'Esquadra* with guys who seemed to Salgado too young. Maybe because at forty-three he sometimes felt like an old man of seventy.

'You didn't wake me. But I'm not sure if I'm happy you called.'

Fort, somewhat disconcerted by this answer, flushed. 'The corpse is already covered and it's being taken away, as ordered . . .'

'Wait.' Salgado hated the official terminology, usually the fallback of incompetents when they don't know what to say. And then he repeated something said to him when he started, a phrase that had gained meaning over the years. 'This isn't a ten o'clock series. "The corpse" is a person.'

Fort nodded and his cheeks became a more intense red.

'Yes, it's a woman. Between thirty and forty. They are looking for her bag.'

'Did she jump on to the tracks with it?'

The agent didn't answer the question and stuck to his script.

'I want you to see the images. The metro CCTV recorded part of what happened.'

The sound of voices proceeding from the platform below made it clear something was happening.

'Who else is down there?'

'Two boys. The patrol guys are with them.'

'Boys?' Salgado summoned up his patience, but his dissatisfaction was evident from his tone. 'Didn't you tell me on the phone that the suicide occurred a little before two? I would've thought you had plenty of time to take a statement from them and send them home.'

'We did. But the boys came back.'

Before Roger Fort had the chance to explain further, the security guard approached them. He was middle-aged, with bags under his eyes and a tired look.

'Agent, are you going to watch the tape now or would you prefer to take it with you?'

In layman's terms, Héctor translated: Are you going to let me finish my damn shift? Agent Fort opened his mouth to say something, but the inspector beat him to it.

'Let's go,' decided Héctor, not looking at his subordinate. 'Then you can explain the thing with the boys, Fort.'

The booth where the images of what happened on the platforms were recorded was small and a thick odour hung in the air, a mixture of sweat and must.

'Here you are,' was all the guard said. 'Though don't expect too much.'

Héctor looked at him once again. Either there were people born to carry out a specific job, or the job moulded those who did it until symbiosis between person and task was achieved. This wan-faced individual with sour breath, slow-moving and a monotonal voice, seemed the perfect candidate to sit there for eight hours, if not more, observing this bit of subterranean life through a low-resolution screen.

The camera focused on the platform from the end at which the train entered, and Salgado, Fort and the guard silently contemplated the arrival of the metro at exactly 01.49. In an instant Héctor remembered his dream: perhaps because of the diffuse, greyish shade of the screen, the individuals waiting on the platform looked like bodies with blurred faces and syncopated movements, like urban zombies. Just when the whistle was announcing the train's departure, a group of kids, dressed in baggy jeans, hoodies and caps, came running on to the platform and, furious on seeing they'd missed that train, they beat against the already closed doors – a reaction as absurd as it was useless. One of them made a telling gesture with his finger to the camera when the metro pulled out, leaving them in the station.

'They had to wait six minutes because––' said the guard, his voice finally expressing something resembling satisfaction.

Agent Fort interrupted him. 'There she is, Inspector.'

And indeed, a woman entered from the other end. There was no way of telling if she was short or tall. Dark-haired, with a black coat and something in her hand. She was so far from the camera that her face was hardly visible. Because of the distance, and because again and again she turned her head back to where she had come on to the platform.

'See, Inspector? She keeps looking behind her. As if someone is following her.'

Héctor didn't respond. His eyes were fixed on the screen. On that woman who, according to the clock showing the countdown to the next metro, had a little more than three minutes of life remaining.

She was keeping away from the tracks, her profile to the camera. Close-up, two of the four kids had sat down, or rather fallen on to the benches. Héctor then made out a girl among them. He hadn't seen her before. Tiny black shorts, very high heels and a white anorak. Beside her, one of the boys tried to grab her waist and, bad tempered, she broke free and said something to him that made the other two erupt into laughter. The kid turned to them, threatening, but both continued making fun of him.

Héctor's eyes were fixed on the woman. She was uncomfortable, that was obvious. At first, she made as if to go towards the kids; however, on hearing the laughter she stopped and clutched her bag tightly. No one else had come down to the platform, but she kept looking stubbornly behind. Maybe it was an attempt to ignore the teenagers, obviously of Latin American origin. Finally she shifted her gaze to what she had in her hand and, thoughtful, took a couple of steps which put her on the yellow line that marked out the safe area, as if she wanted to gain a few seconds by being at the edge of the platform.

'She's looking at her mobile,' Fort pointed out.

And then everything seemed to happen at once. The kids leapt up, taking up the entire image at the time the train entered the station.

'She must have jumped just at that moment,' said the guard, while on the screen the convoy stopped, the doors opened and the platform filled with curious passengers. 'But you can't see it because of those Latinos. In fact, it was the driver of the train who raised the alarm. Poor guy.'

Strange, thought Héctor, he feels more pity for the driver than the suicide. As if she was inconsiderate in her final act.

'Are there no other cameras that capture the image from another angle?' asked Salgado.

The guard shook his head and added, 'There are the

ones monitoring the turnstiles, so that people don't sneak through without paying, but in that time no one came in that way.'

'Okay. We've seen it now,' declared Salgado. And if Fort had known him better he'd have recognized that that dry tone didn't bode well. 'We'll take the tape so this man can close up and go home.'

The guard didn't object.

'For Christ's sake, Fort, tell me you haven't made me come at this time just to show me a tape where you can't see anything.' Fort had been under his command for only a couple of weeks, so the inspector expressed his disgust in the most polite way possible over the short distance separating them from the platform, although speaking quietly didn't manage to conceal his bad mood. He took a breath; he didn't want to be too harsh, and at that hour of the morning it was easy to get carried away. To top it all, the agent had such a contrite expression that Salgado took pity on him. 'It doesn't matter, we'll talk about it later. Since I'm here, let's sort out those boys.'

He hurried down the steps, cutting Fort off mid-sentence.

The boys, just two of them, were sitting on one of the benches, the same one they'd occupied before. Not laughing now, thought Héctor, seeing them totally rigid. The party had ended all of a sudden. As he went towards them, he tried not to see the black plastic bags scattered over the track. He turned to the agent.

'Make sure they're finished, and remove the body immediately.'

The faint station light made the boys look dirty.

Two uniformed agents stood in front of them. They were chatting, seemingly removed from the kids, but without taking their eyes off them. When Salgado approached, they both greeted him and took a step back. The inspector remained standing and fixed his eyes on the adolescents. Dominican, almost certainly. One of them was around eighteen or nineteen; the other, who judging by appearances must be his younger brother, was younger than Guillermo. Thirteen, fourteen tops, Héctor decided.

'Well, boys, it's very late and we all want to finish as soon as possible. I'm Inspector Salgado. Tell me your names, what you saw and explain to me what brought you back,' he added, remembering what Fort had told him. 'Afterwards, we'll all go home to bed, okay?'

'We didn't see anything,' the younger one retorted, looking at his brother with a certain resentment. 'We were out partying and we were going home from Port Olímpic. We changed from the yellow line to the red, but we missed the metro. Only just.'

'Name?' repeated the inspector.

'Jorge Ribera. And that's my brother Nelson.'

'Nelson, you didn't notice the woman either?'

The older boy had very black eyes and his face had a hard, distrusting expression. Impassive.

'No, sir.' He looked ahead, not fixing his eyes on anyone. The tone of his answer sounded hostile.

'But you saw her?'

The little one smiled.

'Nelson only has eyes for his girl. Even though she's mad at him . . .'

Salgado recognized him as the one who'd been pestering

the girl with the white anorak. Nelson gave his brother a withering look. Jorge must have been accustomed to it because he didn't so much as flinch.

'Good. Was there anyone else in the station?' Héctor knew there wasn't, although there was always the possibility that someone had entered the station at the last minute. However, both boys shrugged. It was clear that they'd been entertained by the argument between Nelson and the girl. 'Fine. Then what did you do?'

'They threw us out of the metro, so we ran to catch the night bus. And when we were already at the stop, Nelson made me come back.'

His brother elbowed him to continue and Jorge lowered his head. His self-confidence seemed to have suddenly evaporated.

'Tell him,' ordered Nelson, but Jorge just looked away. 'Or do you want me to tell him?'

The little brother let out a snort.

'Fuck, I saw it on the platform. Before the doors opened. The metro braked suddenly, without coming right into the station, and then I noticed that there was something on the ground. I grabbed it without anyone seeing.'

'What was it?'

'It was a mobile phone, Inspector,' answered Roger Fort, who had joined them after carrying out his orders. 'A pretty new iPhone. This.'

Jorge looked at the bag Fort was holding with a mixture of frustration and longing.

'You made your brother come and bring it back?' It was obvious that it was so, but the question came out without thinking.

'We Riberas don't steal,' answered Nelson, serious. 'Also, there are things it's better not to see.'

The little one rolled his eyes, like someone sick of hearing nonsense. Héctor noticed, and after winking at the elder brother he turned to Jorge with a very severe tone.

'Okay, kid. You and I are going to the station. Agent Fort, bring him.'

'Hey, I haven't done anything! You can't—'

'Theft, tampering with a crime scene. Resisting arrest, which is something I'm adding because you are going to resist for sure. And . . . how old are you? Thirteen? I'm sure the minors' judge won't like a kid your age going out "partying", as you say, in the early hours of the morning at all.'

The kid looked so terrified that Héctor held back.

'If it weren't . . . if it weren't for your brother, who seems a sensible guy, assuring me that he'll take care of you. And you promise me you'll listen to him.'

Jorge nodded, with the same fervour as a young shepherd to whom the Virgin appears. Nelson put his arm around his shoulders and, without his brother seeing, returned the inspector's wink.

'I'll take care of him, sir.'

The station was almost deserted; only Salgado and Fort remained, along with two cleaners, who, after crossing themselves, got to work and rapidly forgot that the station had been the setting for a violent death. The world must keep turning, thought Héctor, unintentionally falling into cliché. None the less, it was almost horrifying that everything could continue in such a normal way. In a few hours the line would re-open, the platform would fill with people. And only scattered pieces would remain of that woman, kept in black plastic bags.

'We've found the bag, Inspector,' said Fort. 'The woman was called Sara Mahler.'

'Was she foreign?'

'Born in Austria, according to her passport. But she lived here, she wasn't a tourist. There's also a clock-in card in her wallet. She worked in a laboratory. "Alemany Cosmetics",' he read.

'The family will have to be contacted, although that can wait until morning. Go back to the station, file the report and start tracking down the relatives. And don't call them until daytime. We'll let them have one more night's sleep.'

Héctor was exhausted. His eyelids were heavy from pure tiredness, and he didn't even have the energy to tell Fort off for making him come. He wanted to go home, lie down and sleep with no nightmares. He would try those damn sleeping pills, even though the word, mixed with what he'd seen there, made him think of a painless death, but death all the same.

'There is something else I want to show you, sir.'

'Do it. I'll give you five minutes.' Then he remembered that in barely a few hours he was going on holiday with his son, and thought the sleeping pills would have to wait for another occasion. 'Not one more.'

Héctor let himself fall on to the bench and took out a cigarette.

'Don't tell anyone I smoked here or I'll plaster you.'

The agent didn't even respond. He handed the mobile to his superior as he said, 'This is the only message. It's strange – the diary is empty and there are no calls.

Therefore, this is what she was reading on the platform, before—'

'Yeah.'

Héctor looked at the screen. It was a message with only two words, written in capitals, with a photo attached.

NEVER FORGET

When he downloaded the photo, Salgado understood why Fort had called him and why that Dominican had dragged his brother by the ear to bring back the damn mobile.

At first he thought they were kites trapped in a tree. Then, after enlarging the photo and seeing the details properly, he realized they weren't. There was a tree all right, with thick, solid branches. But what was hanging from them, the three shapes suspended by ropes, were animals. The rigid bodies of three hanged dogs.

LEIRE

3

New year, new life . . . although at the moment pretty much like the one before, Leire said to herself as she looked at herself side-on in the mirror. This was another of the treacherously unprecedented components of her current existence. They'd brought it up from the shop, because from the first moment she'd wanted it to decorate the hall of the flat she'd just moved into and couldn't yet call home. She kept seeing herself as a whale in it.

But she'd been very lucky. Everyone said so, and she'd ended up shutting up and agreeing. That flat, with its high ceilings, with two spacious bedrooms and sun in the morning was without doubt the best of those she'd visited, and the price, which had supposedly come down a lot in recent times, was in fact the maximum her income would permit. The ad promised 'views of the Sagrada Familia', and strictly speaking it didn't lie. It could be seen from the wooden-framed window that gave access to a diminutive balcony. However, you couldn't spend the day looking at those needles that stuck out among the buildings in front, however nice they were. What the ad didn't say, nor did the woman from the estate agency who showed her the flat mention, was that the pipes were a hundred years old and got blocked; that the bathroom tiles, a shocking orange colour that the woman defined as 'happy seventies', tended to leap into the void because of the damp; and that the radiators were more futuristic ornaments and gave off about the same heat as a Chinese vase. Clearly, she was to console herself about the damp, the cold and the toilet cistern, which sometimes gurgled as if an alien were about to emerge from the wastepipe, by going out on to the balcony and admiring the Sagrada Família. A total luxury if you were Japanese.

In any case, what made the flat feel strange to her wasn't its defects, and of course not its views, rather that for the first time in years it didn't seem wholly hers. One of the two bedrooms had a cradle, a beech wardrobe and a border of yellow ducks running all round the four walls, dividing the two shades of green that her friend María had chosen as the ideal colours for a baby's room. And not only that: in part of her wardrobe, which had always been for her alone, some masculine garments had gathered almost without warning.

Overwhelmed, Leire Castro went towards the balcony, happy to be able to move around the flat without boxes in the way. That was definitely a change. 'The first of many, right?' she said, directing her words to the child currently living within her. Sometimes he answered with sudden movements; at other times he seemed not to take the hint. She tried to imagine the features of this baby, Abel, floating inside her, but she only managed to give him a wrinkled face, like a sleeping gnome. Would he look like her, or Tomás? Well, if he looked like him it wouldn't be too bad, she thought with a smile. 'Although best if the resemblances are just physical, hey kid?

Otherwise, you and I are going to have problems . . .'

Tomás had been a one-night stand that then lengthened to three, and later the odd weekend. No-strings sex. Taboo-free sex. And once, only once, although no one would believe it, sex without a condom. But accurate. Tomás's reaction, after a plate of reheated croquettes that had already acquired mythical status for them both, was that 'I need time to get used to the idea', which in Leire's opinion was usually the prelude to 'This isn't for me.' Nevertheless, Tomás surprised her by returning just a couple of days later to have a 'serious talk'.

And they did, long and drawn-out, weighing up the pros and cons as if it were all a rational subject, and at the same time knowing it wasn't. In the end, however, they had come to a series of agreements. One, they weren't in love, at least not in that idyllic way in which you can't imagine life without the other. Two, they lived in different cities, although separated by barely three hours on the AVE fast train. Three, the baby was part of both of them. So the conclusion, nicer in the wording than in the small print, had been: no, they wouldn't be a couple – at least at the moment – but they would be parents. 'Parents with touching rights,' María called them.

They were satisfied by this resolution and they truly were doing all they could to carry it out. Tomás was spending some weekends at Leire's; he'd taken care of the move and of tasks like putting in sockets; he spoke of Abel with enthusiasm and threatened to make him a member of Real Madrid. They hadn't touched on the subject of money; María had bought them the few things in the baby's room and, with regards to the flat, Leire didn't plan on accepting even a euro from him. Until the birth of the baby no more can be asked of him, she thought. Although deep down she would have liked to have had someone by her side at the antenatal classes, at the scans, when the on-screen sight of what was inside her brought out tears she couldn't understand, or, for example, on Friday nights, when she was too tired to go out but not so tired that she wanted to be alone. Or also during that interminable *Reyes* bank holiday, she thought as she contemplated the Sagrada Família, that unfinished witness to her boredom that she was beginning to hate at times. However, Tomás was in the Sierra – the name of which made Leire think of resistance fighters or bandits – skiing with some friends. It wasn't Tomás's fault that she had nothing to do and that her best friend, María, had gone away for the weekend, although it hardly encouraged her to think of him fondly. Leire's mother, Asturian and not one to mince her words, had summed everything up in some phrases that were becoming prophetic. 'Alone. When the baby is born you'll be alone. If you cry in the night, you'll be alone. And the day he learns to say "Papa" you'll show him a photo. That's if you have one,' she'd predicted before starting to cut a chicken into pieces with unusual fury. And she, though she didn't dare say it aloud, had murmured inwardly something along the lines of: 'I'll worry about that when the time comes.'

Nevertheless, the truth was that she sometimes did feel lonely, not helped by her early maternity leave due to some rogue early contractions she'd had in mid-December. She'd already spent months condemned to office work, but at least she was at the station, she could participate in cases, she had people around her. There was still a month and a half before Abel's birth. Six weeks in which – as she saw it – she would do nothing but get fat, visit her doctor, see other pregnant women and choose baby clothes. She knew by heart all the magazine articles about the best way to bathe, change and stimulate a baby, a distraction already forming a pillar of sage advice that reached half the height of the sofa.

It was as night was falling the next day that, lying on the sofa watching an episode of a detective series that had been shown at least twice before, the feeling of abandonment became so intense that she didn't even have the urge to cry. The unfamiliar flat, the lack of obligations and the absence of contact with others, increased by so many holidays, ended up submerging her little by little in a melancholy state in which laziness and boredom also played a large part. 'Abel, your mama is being very silly,' she said out loud, in order to hear some sound that didn't proceed from the television. She felt like crying, like letting the world know she was still there. And, without meaning to, almost automatically, she thought that if she disappeared, no one would miss her until at least Monday. And that with a bit of luck . . . Her mother called her every day, although certainly, knowing her, she wouldn't raise the alarm until the mountain of unanswered calls became worrying. Tomás might send her a message over the weekend. Or not. And María, certainly, would scream the place down if she couldn't locate her on Monday as soon as she got back. But it was Friday. Like Ruth, her boss's ex-wife, no one would begin to look for her until it was, perhaps, too late. A vague, out-of-character fear overpowered her. You have to stop this, she told herself, and closed her eyes in an attempt to banish so many clouds from her generally clear mind.

And then, when she opened them and saw that nothing would change just by wanting it to, she knew what she was going to do for the remaining six weeks of her pregnancy.

'Leire, you're on maternity leave.' Sergeant Martina Andreu said the sentence, stressing each syllable. 'You're going to have a baby and the doctor has ordered you to rest. Know what "rest" means? I'll tell you: no work.'

Leire bit her lower lip, cursing herself for not having foreseen that the sergeant, the epitome of sense, would stop her project outright. Throughout the weekend she had gone over the idea to find the best way of putting it, but that Monday morning her arguments met the devastating logic of Sergeant Andreu head on.

'Also,' she continued, 'the case isn't ours any more. Superintendent Savall assigned it to Bellver, you know that.'

'Exactly.' She struggled to find the right words, which, given her opinion of Dídac Bellver, wasn't exactly easy. She took a breath. At the end of the day she had nothing to lose. 'Sergeant, I believe not much can be done to resolve this case from the station. You know how it is – emergencies build up and are replaced by others. And missing persons merges runaways and adults who leave without warning with genuine criminal cases. Like me, you're aware that they can't cope. And the subject of Ruth Valldaura is already old news . . . it's been six months since she disappeared.'

This – both were aware – was the worst thing of all.

When it came to disappearances the first hours were critical, and in the case under discussion the alarm had been raised too late. The lack of clues made them think homicide, although Savall had used the absence of a body and the special circumstances surrounding this disappearance to assign the case to Bellver and his team.

Leire had the feeling her words weren't falling on deaf ears. Martina Andreu's expression softened. Just a little, enough that she, who knew her well, could gather new strength.

'On the other hand, we don't lose anything if I spend part of my time on the case. I don't want to do it without your permission,' she lied with the audacity of someone sure that she was right.

What was certain was that she needed information, to see what stage the file had reached, and concrete facts, to know if there was anything new since the case had been officially taken out of Salgado's hands in a stormy conversation with Superintendent Savall, after which everyone had feared that Héctor Salgado would resign from the corps.

'Inspector Salgado did as much as he could, but, let's not kid ourselves, the superintendent was right in one thing: Héctor was, still is, too involved in the case to be objective. And Bellver—'

'Don't go there,' Martina Andreu interrupted her. 'As you've said, Bellver and his people are overburdened with work. Like everyone.'

'Exactly,' insisted Leire. She'd perceived a shift in her superior's tone, so she was careful not to lose ground already conquered. 'It would be six weeks, maybe less. If the baby comes early, it's over. But I believe I can cast a fresh pair of eyes on the case. I didn't know Ruth Valldaura. While we were investigating I always had the impression that, given the victim's identity, everyone took a series of things for granted. And Inspector Salgado couldn't see it either, however much he wanted to.'

'I know.'

Leire smiled. She sensed that she was about to win the game.

'Listen,' Martina went on. 'I don't know what this will come to, or why you're getting me into this mess. However, I know you well enough to understand that you'll do whatever you feel like, with or without my approval. No, Leire, don't lie to me. You came to me because I can facilitate certain things for you, not because you plan to listen to me if I forbid it. At the end of the day, it's your free time and you can use it as you wish.'

'If you say no, I'll abandon the matter. I don't want to get you in any trouble and I promise if I discover anything, I'll inform you directly. You can decide how to proceed with Bellver from there.'

Agent Castro knew she was treading on dangerous ground. The sergeant's ill-will towards Bellver had been public since he snatched the role of inspector from her with merits more personal than professional. But Leire suspected that the most insignificant allusion to the affair would make Martina Andreu dig in her heels.

'Fine. Come and pick me up at seven, at the end of my shift, and you'll have a copy of the file. Oh, and not a word to Inspector Salgado if you come across him.'

It was unlikely, and the sergeant knew it: Savall had summoned him to his office, along with others, to discuss something with a National Police guy, some Calderón.

After only half an hour, it looked as if it would go on for a while.

'Leire, if you want to work during leave, the same rules apply as if you were on duty, so, for your own good, I want to be kept informed. Keep me up to date on every move and every detail. Don't do anything off your own back or I assure you when you return your life here will be very difficult. Is that clear?'

The grateful look that Leire Castro gave her convinced the sergeant for a moment that she wasn't doing anything wrong. As the agent had said herself, they lost nothing by trying and, deep down, Martina was almost sure that the Ruth Valldaura case was doomed never to be resolved. At the same time, and not without a certain professional envy, she was sure that if there was anyone in that station capable of tackling an apparently unsolvable mystery, that person was Agent Castro.

4

So, that same night, file already in hand, Leire did what her mind and body were crying out for. She needed activity, a focus, and the file she had in front of her, although mostly familiar, represented a challenge that, among other things, made her feel alive. And useful. With a discipline she'd learned to appreciate, she read it slowly, as if she were facing it for the first time, convinced that on occasion the most insignificant details could culminate in the answer.

Then, after a good while of intense concentration, she did something that had helped her internalize things since she was small. Sitting at the dining-room table, she wrote down the most relevant details. It was a somewhat tiresome task now that practically nothing was written by hand, but Leire was aware that this forced her to slow down. She didn't follow a precise order, but rather allowed her hand to outline what for her was a first approximation of the facts.

Ruth Valldaura Martorell. 39. Designer/illustrator of considerable success due to a line of home accessories very popular recently. Separated and mother of one son, Guillermo, who lived with her. Disappeared from her home, a loft-type apartment she also used as her studio, located on Llull, on 7 July 2010, although it wasn't reported until two days later. There were no signs of violence in her home and the door hadn't been forced. According to her partner, Carolina Mestre, a suitcase and four garments were missing, which tallied with the last she knew of Ruth, who had declared her intention of going away to spend the weekend at the apartment owned by her parents, which they still own, in the coastal area of Sitges. Her car was found parked close to her home, which led us to believe that probably its owner had never come to take it on the morning of 7 July, when she told her parents, her ex-husband and her new partner that she wouldn't be back until Sunday night. Her messages had been succinct. Seemingly, Ruth wanted to spend a couple of days alone near the beach.

On Sunday night, her son Guillermo, whom she was meant to collect from a friend's house where he was spending a few days' holiday, called his father, Inspector Héctor Salgado, asking about Ruth. This raised the alarm.

The primary investigations focused on the threats uttered against Inspector Salgado's family by Dr Omar, a witch doctor of African origin linked to a woman-trafficking network which had been dismantled around the middle of the previous year. The pimps were detained and although it was suspected that Omar used voodoo to terrify the young Nigerian prostitutes, only one agreed to testify against him. This girl's violent death led Inspector Salgado to turn up at Omar's clinic in an alley near the Post Office and give him a beating which was the source of the threats to Salgado and those around him. Later, the doctor was murdered by his accomplices.

However, according to what Damián Fernández, Omar's lawyer and killer, confessed, before dying Omar carried out a ritual curse against Ruth Valldaura. The aim was, obviously, to revenge himself on Inspector Salgado. This witness affirmed that Omar was certain that Ruth would disappear without leaving the least trace. As it happened in the end.

Leire paused. The objective facts were as simple as that. It made no difference that she didn't believe the quack's claims; the astonishing reality was that, due to the curse or not, Ruth's destiny had been as the bastard Omar had predicted. And although for a time it was thought that the doctor himself had contracted someone to carry out his threat, Leire had never been convinced by this hypothesis. If anything became clear from studying a character as dark as the quack's, it was the faith he had in his own power: despite it appearing like a cock-and-bull story, Omar was sure the ritual curse would work.

For the first time in months, Leire missed having a cigarette, but she resisted. She'd given up smoking at the end of the summer and had no intention of starting again. To calm herself, she went to the kitchen, grabbed a couple of biscuits, also forbidden by the doctor, and returned to the table. It was late, but she could sleep as long as she liked. She took up her pen once again and returned to her task.

Ruth Valldaura was a reserved person, with few friends and no known enemies. The general opinion held that she was a balanced, attractive and friendly woman, with a pronounced tendency to be introspective. She maintained a cordial relationship with her ex-husband, and in her subsequent involvement with Carol Mestre didn't seem to have any problems more serious than the usual tensions of any couple. Ruth had accepted her lesbianism, or bisexuality, openly. She hadn't attempted to hide it from her parents or her son. Her work, although well paid, didn't make her rich, or well known outside her professional circle. She worked alone, although she collaborated with her partner and associate in marketing her designs. In fact, it was in the professional sphere that they fell in love.

The investigations into her disappearance immediately came to a dead end. The street where she lived, located in the old industrial area of Poblenou, not very far from where her ex-husband still lives, was fairly deserted during the summer weekends, and the few neighbours interviewed didn't contribute any significant information.

There are, a priori, two alternatives that, despite being mere supposition, must be taken into account:

1. Dr Omar and his people, including the curse, whatever it means.

2. Someone close to Ruth, however improbable
   it may seem. Her ex-husband, her girlfriend,
   a friend.

Leire inhaled. Something in the last sentence made her
feel like a traitor. She was very fond of Héctor Salgado.
She respected him as a boss, and got on well with him
as a person. And she found him handsome, she thought
with a smile. Abel seemed to protest from her womb, or
perhaps to warn her that it was late and she should just go
to bed. 'I'm going, kid. But you should know if he hadn't
been my boss, if you weren't here, and if everything
were different, mama would have hooked up with that
Argentine.' The baby kicked again and Leire caressed her
belly. Although initially it had seemed strange, now she
loved feeling how he moved. It was irrefutable proof that
he was alive.

Rapidly she wrote one more paragraph.

As always, there is a third option. Persons unknown.
Someone we don't know anything about, someone
who had something against Ruth Valldaura and
turned up at her house that Friday before she left.
Someone Ruth knew and whom she allowed into her
house not suspecting anything strange.

This killer or kidnapper X would have benefited
from the clues pointing to Dr Omar and would have
had time to hide their trail.

To the point, Leire thought before going to bed, that
six months later no one had managed to find them.

50

SARA

5

Sara Mahler. The name came back into Salgado's head during the interminable meeting in one of the rooms at the station. Not the whole time, since the meeting was intense and required concentration, but in flashes, unable to avoid it, his mind went back to that woman who had jumped on to the tracks early on Thursday morning. By her passport photo, which he'd seen again a few hours before, Sara Mahler wasn't pretty. She had a pale complexion, wide nose and very small blue eyes. Central European features betrayed by obviously artificial jet-black hair, which made the pallor of her skin stand out even more.

When the meeting finished it was almost seven in the evening. The inspector hurried towards Fort's desk; he hadn't seen him since the day of the incident. The agent was there with Martina Andreu.

'Do we know any more about Sara Mahler? Have you tracked down the family?'

Fort almost stood to attention before answering.

'Yes, Inspector. It took me all day Friday and part of Saturday to find them, but I got there in the end. Her father arrived this morning from Salzburg.' It took him a few seconds to add, in an almost mysterious tone, 'Honestly, he's a strange one. I haven't been able to communicate with him much because he only speaks German, but all the same it was clear that he wasn't too upset. According to the little I know, they haven't seen each other in years. Sara came to Barcelona in 2004 and, from what I understand, she only went back to her country on one occasion, the following year. And her father has never been to Spain, so he said.'

The agent kept the additional words the interpreter had translated for him to himself. Joseph Mahler, taking advantage of the journey, planned to spend a few days in Mallorca, where he had friends. The fact that someone might consider such a journey as the excuse to take a holiday had left poor Agent Fort speechless. And saddened.

'Okay,' said Salgado. 'And Sara? What else do we know?'

Fort consulted his notes, as if he feared forgetting something.

'Sara Mahler, thirty-four. As I said, she arrived in Barcelona seven years ago, around the middle of the year. She lived on Passatge Xile, near Collblanc market, and shared a flat with another girl. Kristin something . . . I didn't catch the surname. She'd also been away over the *Reyes* bank holiday, so I only spoke to her today.'

Héctor nodded, encouraging Fort to continue.

'According to Kristin, Sara was personal assistant to the managing director of Alemany Cosmetics, a company that develops and markets cosmetic products.'

'Did she give you any motive that might explain Sara's suicide? An unhappy love affair, problems at work?'

Fort shook his head.

'No, sir, but that doesn't mean there wasn't any.' Seeing his boss's perplexed face, he hastened to add, 'I mean that Kristin had been sharing a flat with Sara for barely two months. They weren't friends or anything like it. I asked her if she'd found a note in Sara's bedroom. You know . . .'

'Yes, I know. And?'

'She found it hard to go and look. It seems Sara didn't like anyone going into her room. I told her she wasn't going to know now and then she went. But nothing. No note, or anything resembling one.'

For the first time, Martina Andreu, who had been listening silently, turned to Salgado.

'Is there anything, apart from that macabre message, that might indicate it wasn't a suicide?'

'Quite honestly, no. The most likely thing is that this woman, in a state for whatever reason, threw herself on to the metro tracks of her own will. But I don't like the message and photo. Do we know who sent them, Fort?'

'It'll be tricky, Inspector. It was sent from a free texts website. We're waiting for the IP, but it doesn't usually help much.'

'Then focus on more concrete things,' Héctor advised him. 'Andreu, I know all this will go nowhere, but it can't hurt for Fort to go to see this Kristin something. And Sara's work – you called them too, right? Strange no one has turned up. No boyfriend, no friend . . .' And he added, with his usual half-smile, 'Or girlfriend or friend.'

'Maybe that's why she threw herself on to the tracks,' said the sergeant. 'Because she knew no one was going to miss her much.'

'Not her father, anyway,' Fort said. That man's lack of emotion had unsettled him.

At that moment the telephone on the desk rang and the agent answered. It was a brief conversation.

'Well, speak of the devil.'

'The boyfriend?'

'No, Inspector. Her boss. Sara's boss, I mean.'

'Yeah, I got that.'

'He's at the door and wants to see the inspector in charge of the case.'

Héctor glanced at his watch. He was dying to go out for a cigarette, but his curiosity stayed him.

'Bring him in. What did you say his name was?'

'Sorry, I didn't say.' Fort seemed not to notice the irritated expression that came over his boss's face. 'His name is Víctor Alemany, managing director of Alemany Cosmetics.'

Before Fort could conclude that, given the coincidence of the names, it was a family business, and even worse, say so aloud, Héctor turned and went to his office. At the door, he turned to add, 'Martina, tomorrow we need to talk. About the meeting with Savall. First thing, okay? It's important. Fort, you get to go alone to speak to Sara's flatmate. Have a look at the poor girl's bedroom.'

Víctor Alemany was definitely upset, Héctor said to himself. Or uncomfortable, at least. He had sat down at Héctor's desk just a few minutes before and his face expressed something that could only be defined as bewilderment.

'Inspector Salazar—'

'Salgado.'

56

'Oh yes, I beg your pardon. All this seems terrible . . .' He gave the impression that he was seeking another adjective, but immediately gave up and said again: 'Terrible.'

Héctor observed him. In his line of work he tended to evaluate people quickly and after those few minutes he could say that Víctor Alemany was a decent sort. In his forties, not much older than Salgado, Alemany had an almost Nordic appearance. Blonde, with some grey; he wore a good suit and glasses that looked expensive, hiding a pair of sky-blue eyes. Despite the attire, there wasn't much of the aggressive executive head honcho in him. In fact, as soon as he walked through the door he'd reminded Héctor of Michael York's student character in *Cabaret*. A few years older, of course.

'When did it happen? We didn't hear until this morning, when we realized Sara hadn't come to work . . .'

'Was that unusual? That she didn't come to the office, I mean.'

'I don't think it's ever happened. Actually, I'm sure of it. Sara was never absent. Or even late. On the contrary, she was usually one of the first to arrive.'

'Your company produces . . . ?'

'We're a cosmetics company.' Víctor Alemany smiled. 'All sorts of face and body creams, make-up . . . My grandfather founded it, in the forties, and we're still here.'

'Tough times?'

Alemany shrugged.

'We can't complain. Although I fear the worst is yet to come.'

'What exactly did Sara do?' asked Héctor, directing him back to the subject at hand.

'She was my secretary for five years.'

'And were you satisfied with her?'

'Of course,' the other man answered with what seemed complete honesty. 'There were no complaints with her work. She never made an error.'

Never late, never made mistakes, never absent . . . Salgado thought Sara Mahler did everything to perfection. Even committing suicide.

'Did you know her well?'

'I told you. She was my secretary. If you mean did I know anything of her private life, I'd say no, at least not that she told me. She simply completed her tasks to an excellent standard, but she didn't tell me too much about herself.'

'And the rest of the staff?' asked Salgado. He was proceeding a little blindly, since he was unaware of the size of the company in question and thought it preferable not to ask. He would know soon enough if it were necessary.

'Sara was a reserved woman. I'm not sure she had friends at work.'

And it appears not outside it either, Héctor said to himself. But Víctor Alemany continued, 'I think it was a question of mentality, you know? Sara was Austrian, she had a very strict upbringing. There are still certain cultural differences.'

'Yes.'

There was a pause while they both reflected. Salgado began to consolidate his profile of Sara Mahler: organized, punctual, unsociable, demanding of herself and of others; no important family ties.

'Do you know if she had a boyfriend?' the inspector finally asked.

Alemany seemed to come back to himself.

'I don't know, although honestly I don't think so. I suppose at some moment or other she'd have talked about it.'

Héctor nodded.

'Listen, Inspector Salgado, if there is something we can help with . . . Anything. I know she scarcely had family, so if money is required to repatriate the remains or . . .' The word 'remains' suddenly didn't feel adequate, given the circumstances of the death. 'You understand me. I still can't believe that . . . It could have been an accident, couldn't it? Maybe she got dizzy and fell . . .'

'It's always difficult to accept. Although you are right: there is the possibility of an accidental fall.' He paused, 'Or that someone pushed her deliberately.'

'Who would do such a thing?'

That's the big question, thought Héctor. From the little he knew of Sara Mahler, she seemed to be a woman capable of provoking dislike but not hatred.

'Well, if you need anything else, you know where to find us. By the way, I have to go away tomorrow and won't be back until Friday. Contact the company for anything you need.' Víctor Alemany took out a business card and scribbled a phone number. 'It's my sister Sílvia's direct number. We work together.'

Boss together, Héctor corrected him mentally. That kind of business had always fascinated him: the complexity of familial relations made even more tangled by business matters.

Víctor Alemany was making as if to rise when Héctor stalled him with a suave gesture.

'One moment. Does this photo remind you of anything?'

The image of the strangled dogs made Víctor whiten. He was the sensitive type, no doubt about it.

'What's this?'

'Someone sent it to Sara's mobile, with a message that said: "Never forget".'

Víctor remained uneasy, but chose to say nothing more.

'You're sure you've never seen this before?'

'Yes,' he lied.

It was obvious that Víctor Alemany would tell him nothing else. Héctor knew when people were clamming up, and he also knew when not to persist.

6

While the taxi he'd caught at the station exit advanced as much as the traffic lights on Paral·lel – designed to slow traffic already unmoving at this time of the day – would allow, Víctor Alemany resisted the conversational attempts of the driver, an older man with a desire to talk about the economic crisis and the 'gang of thieves' that made up the government. Víctor, who considered himself progressive and who hadn't the least intention of discussing politics with an old-school taxi driver, resorted to giving a couple of monosyllabic answers and consulting non-existent messages on his phone. The driver took the hint and avenged himself by connecting to his colleagues via the service radio, so the vehicle filled with faltering, harsh, somewhat sinister voices communicating in a code which to the passenger's ear was reminiscent of that used by a gang of bank robbers in a film.

He noticed the vibration of his mobile phone and looked at the screen, despite having few doubts as to who it was. Sílvia. Impatient as ever, incapable of waiting for the customary phone call. Not enough that she'd insisted on his going to the station . . . For an instant he felt like ignoring his sister, but habit, instilled in him from tenderest infancy, forced him to answer. 'Hello. Listen, I'm in a taxi. I'll call you when I get home. Yes, yes, all fine. No, they said nothing about that. Don't worry.'

His own words provoked a feeling akin to remorse in him. 'All fine.' All fine for him, of course. All fine for them. And above all, with regard to Sílvia, all fine for the company. He almost laughed out loud thinking how much his sister had changed. When they were teenagers no one would have predicted that the rebellious Sílvia – the same one who shaved half her head and decorated her bedroom with graffiti and anarchist symbols, the one who ran away from home at eighteen to join a group of squatters, who yelled opinions taken from radical pamphlets – would exchange holey tights for tailored suits, graffiti for framed paintings and leftist slogans for others that could generously be described as practical and, realistically, neo-liberal.

A competent executive, strict mother to a teenage girl and an eleven-year-old boy, Sílvia was the antithesis of what she had been. Víctor remembered his father: the old fox must have been the only one to guess what would happen, since he never took his daughter's defiance seriously. 'Give her enough rope and she'll hang herself,' he said the second time Sílvia left home. 'When she gets tired of it, that will be the time to shoot her down.' And so he did: years later, when the prodigal daughter knocked on his door with two children round her neck and no one at her side, the old man imposed his conditions with a simple 'Put up with it, or go.' The surprising thing was that Sílvia not only accepted his authority, but rather, probably weary of her previous wanderings, her lifestyle took a hundred and eighty degree turn. Or maybe,

Víctor suspected, his sister was more ready to convince herself the old man was right than to admit she'd been forced to give in. Now, forty-five and after many years of voluntary celibacy, she'd started a relationship with an employee of the company. Of course, given that in the new Sílvia there was no place for spontaneity, the wedding was already planned for spring that year. Time enough for Víctor to become accustomed to the idea that César Calvo, in addition to being responsible for logistics and storage for Alemany Cosmetics, was going to become another member of the family. A member with a voice, although not too loud, and whose vote would be merely advisory, thought Víctor. He hoped César was aware of it . . .

In any case, the coldness in his sister never ceased to shock him: the fact that Sara had decided to end her life in such a gruesome way had gone from being a tragedy to an inconvenience in a matter of minutes. Sílvia's face, which he read as if it were his own, had reflected this shift of feeling. Those who didn't know her as well, however, would have sworn that his twin sister's serious expression showed feeling for the death of a person who occupied that uncertain terrain that exists in work relationships: not loved as a friend, of course, but more than a simple acquaintance. In the words of Sílvia herself, who in her role as Director of Human Resources had sent around a communiqué to the whole company, Sara Mahler had been 'an esteemed colleague whom we will all miss'. Obviously, the circular made no mention of the cause of death, although – Víctor was sure – the rumours had already begun to spread by mid-morning. And by this time on a Monday evening, gone half past eight, all of Alemany Cosmetics would know that Sara Mahler, personal assistant to the MD, had committed suicide. And that her body was in an autopsy room, in pieces.

The image made him shiver, made his stomach churn. He wanted to get home, embrace Paula. The journey felt unending; he realized they had been stationary for several minutes. A dozen cars ahead the red light went to green without a single car moving, then jeered at them with amber and, when finally a car managed to cross, returned to its original red without the least trace of pity. The taxi driver let out a string of curses that Víctor decided to ignore: it suited him to isolate himself from the problems of others. And then, with this reflection, Sara Mahler's worried expression one of the last times he spoke to her came into his head. It had been just after the company Christmas dinner.

It's late. Night falls so early that he feels as if it's only six, although the clock on the desk shows it's actually twenty to nine. When he lifts his head from the reps' reports he's looking over, a task he wants to finish before leaving, he notices that Sara has entered the office. She has surely knocked and he hasn't even heard her. Tired, he smiles at her.

'Still here?' He knows his assistant usually stays until he leaves. He has never asked her to: Sara seems to have assumed it to be an inherent obligation of her post.

'Yes . . .' Unlike her usual self, Sara is stammering. Finally she decides, half-heartedly: 'I wanted to talk to you, but it's getting late. Better if I leave it till tomorrow.'

Yes, thinks Víctor. Tomorrow. The chat can be postponed; he wants to put a full stop to the day and go home. What he says, however, is very different.

'No, come in and sit down.' He signals the papers and smiles again, without much enthusiasm. 'This can wait.'

Having her sit on the other side of the desk seems strange to him because Sara usually remains standing. The solemnity of his assistant's gestures worries him a little and for a moment he is assaulted by the vague fear that she might put forward a serious problem to him at this hour. She is uncomfortable, that's obvious: rigid, sitting on the edge of the chair. He changes his glasses and then, when he finally sees her clearly, he notices that her eyes are red.

'Has something happened? Is there a problem?'

Sara looks at him as if what she is going to tell him is vitally important. She remains silent, sad, then finally speaks.

'It's about Gaspar.' She says it quickly but with no force.

An expression of disgust appears on Víctor's face. He doesn't want to talk about Gaspar Ródenas. In fact, he'd prefer never to have heard that name. He changes his tone, adds a hard note to his voice.

'Sara. The Ródenas thing' – he feels incapable of pronouncing his name – 'was a tragedy. We will never understand it. It's something that escapes human understanding. Best thing we can do is forget it.'

Although she nods her head as if she agrees, Víctor regrets having started this conversation. He looks away towards the street: he'd love to enjoy a more elegant view, like Diagonal; in the first moments of success, when the anti-cellulite cream, their star product, broke sales records, he thought of moving the offices to a more lofty location. In any case, although the inhospitable empty streets of the Zona Franca can be seen from this window, he still wants to leave the office, not bring up what to him seems a dark, gruesome subject.

'I know,' says Sara. 'And I've tried. We all try . . . However . . .'

She stops herself; perhaps he still looks lost in thought, suddenly absent. She notices this, of course, and hangs her head.

'You don't want to talk about this, do you?' asks Sara. A touch of disappointment makes her voice quiver.

'Not now, Sara.' He turns to her. 'I understand that it was a shock for everyone. For me too. I trusted him, I promoted him.'

His tone conceals that what he says is not completely true: he'd given his vote to the other candidate. Sílvia and Octavi Pujades, Gaspar's direct manager, had voted for him. And something in Sara's face suggests that she knows it: a gleam in her eyes reveals that she doesn't believe what he is saying. But Víctor lets this impression go and continues speaking, anxious to put an end to the subject.

'It's impossible to know what goes on in people's heads. Or what happens at home, behind closed doors. Ródenas just worked here. What he did, however horrible it seems to us, has nothing to do with us. And we should forget it, for the good of the company. So, in answer to your question, no, I don't want to talk about it.'

In the last few minutes Sara has regained her usual composure. She is offended, thinks Víctor. Nevertheless, it is too late to back down, to ask her what she wanted to tell him. She doesn't give him the option anyway. She murmurs an apology, gets up and walks to the door. She stops a moment before leaving. For an instant, Sara seems resolved to turn around, interrupt him again and let out what she had on her mind when she came in, point blank. She doesn't. Víctor tries not to look directly at her so as not to invite her to unburden herself, but even so he notices that Sara's face doesn't express disappointment, or wounded pride, but sadness.

The taxi braked sharply on Nou de la Rambla, just in front of the address he'd given on getting in. Víctor paid and got out with a brusque goodbye and, although he was dying to see Paula, he stopped in front of the old-fashioned door, 'with character' as she said, and took out his mobile to call Sílvia. There were certain subjects that he didn't wish to discuss at home and another that he didn't wish to discuss with his sister, so to keep it brief he confined himself to giving her a recap of his interview with the inspector.

7

Kristin Herschdorfer loved Barcelona. She said this a number of times, as if her good opinion of the city might ingratiate her with the agent who had come to see her and talk to her about her flatmate, when the reality was that Roger Fort wasn't altogether comfortable in the City of Counts yet. To him it seemed big, full of people and not especially welcoming. This morning, for example, he'd circled several times to park the car near Collblanc market and then had taken a while to find Passatge Xile, the street where Sara Mahler had lived. And yet he understood that for this twenty-four-year-old girl born in Amsterdam the fact that the sun shone in January was already a big point in Barcelona's favour. Kristin was attending a course in Spanish at the university, not very far from her house, with the intention of starting a Masters in renewable energy in September. Like the majority of foreigners, the Dutch girl was slightly bemused by the bilingualism which prevailed in the city.

'But now I have a Catalan boyfriend,' she commented with a smile, and Fort couldn't work out if this was for emotional reasons or the need to learn the language without paying for another course. In any case, he was sure Kristin wouldn't be short of volunteers if the chosen one didn't turn out to be a good teacher.

'Tell me about Sara. I already know you hadn't lived together long . . .'

'Since October. At first I live, *lived*, with two other girls in the city centre, but one was crazy. Totally crazy. And there was too much noise. I couldn't sleep at night. So I looked for another flat. I saw a few and in the end I moved here because it is closer to the university.'

'This is quieter than the city centre, of course. And how was it with Sara?'

Kristin shrugged her shoulders.

'Well . . .' She twisted a long lock of blonde hair and looked away. 'The flat is nice. To be honest, I don't think I can pay for it. On my own, I mean.'

'I was asking about Sara,' the agent said gently.

Kristin seemed reluctant to talk about her flatmate.

'Okay.' She smiled, as if she were going to say something unfair. 'Well, it's not nice to criticize those who aren't here. But . . . Sara was a bit peculiar. How to explain it?'

It was clear that she wasn't finding a way to do it, so Fort decided to be more specific.

'Had she shared a flat before?' He wasn't up to date with the salary of a PA, but the rent on this flat didn't appear to be very high. And, somehow, it seemed strange that such a solitary person, or at least with as few friends, as Sara Mahler would have allowed a stranger into her house.

'No. Well, maybe a while ago. When she arrived in Barcelona.' Kristin kept playing with the blonde lock until she became aware of it and let it go. 'I think that was the problem. I paid what she asked me, but she acted as if she were the landlady and I were a guest. I don't know if you understand.'

Roger Fort had shared a flat while he studied in the academy and was aware that the oldest tenant enjoyed acquired rights they wouldn't give up easily. So he nodded, and Kristin smiled, relieved.

'And do you know why she rented out one of the rooms?'

'She didn't tell me. She said something about becoming afraid to sleep alone in the flat . . .' She lowered her voice before continuing, 'Although then it was as if it annoys, *annoyed*, her to have someone here. I think she'd become used to living alone.'

'Yes. Flat-sharing isn't easy.'

Kristin shook her head as she sighed.

'I'm sick of it. I'm going to look for a studio or something like that, however small it is.'

'Was Sara very . . . fussy?'

'What do you mean?'

Fort tried to explain.

'Demanding . . . I don't know, about housework or noise.'

'Oh yes! She was more like a bored mother. No, not bored . . .'

'Nagging?' he suggested.

'Yes! If I left dirty plates in the kitchen at night, she would leave me a note in the morning: "You should wash these." If I left a sweater on the chair, she would fold it and bring it into my room. With another note.' Kristin blushed. 'I'm not messy. Honestly. In the flat before I was the only one who cleaned. But Sara was . . . excessively?'

'Excessive, I suppose,' said Fort.

Kristin nodded, and began to rant about Sara Mahler without the caution she'd shown at the beginning.

'Look, see that vase? The one on the table. Well, it broke. I broke it, by accident of course, while I was giving it one.'

The phrase made Roger Fort smile, although she didn't notice and went on talking, as if the essence of her flatshare with Sara Mahler was contained in the story of the broken vase.

'It's not very nice, is it? I mean it's cheap. Ugly. Not something to cry over.'

'Sara cried about the broken vase?'

'Almost . . . She looked at me as if I had run over her mother. I told her I would buy her another one. A nicer one. And she answered that I didn't understand. That it wasn't about the money but the affection she has for things. Afterwards she spent the night glueing the pieces back together. You see? You notice if you're close.'

'Did she often get angry?'

'Not get angry. She would make a face. And she was always here,' she added, now being blunt. 'She hardly ever went out. Apart from going to work, of course. She was at home the rest of the time, in her room, in front of the computer. I'd say she was addicted to Facebook. My boyfriend says she was looking for . . . you know, sex, although I don't think so. I don't think she liked sex.'

She elaborated on seeing Agent Fort's surprised face.

'She told me. Not in those words exactly, but she told me. Albert, my boyfriend, stays over sometimes. And one morning, when he left, Sara told me she had heard us. You know . . .' Kristin blushed a little. 'She also asked me to please try not to make noise. But she had a look of disgust on her face. Seriously,' she insisted, as if it was inconceivable to her.

'Didn't she have boyfriends? Or girlfriends?'

Kristin shook her head.

'Not that I know of. Although I didn't hear about much. With one thing and another, I don't have much free time . . .'

'And didn't it surprise you that she didn't come home on Wednesday night? If she rarely went out?'

'Oh, it would surprise me a lot. No.' She corrected herself. 'It would have surprised me a lot. That's right, isn't it? But I wasn't in Barcelona. Albert and I went to a house his parents have in the mountains and we didn't come back until Sunday. And then I heard the message from the police and called.'

Roger Fort cleared his throat.

'You spoke to me.' He paused briefly. 'I don't want to be unpleasant, but do you believe Sara was capable of taking her own life? Did you ever see her sad, truly sad? Depressed?'

Kristin pondered her answer and took a while to respond.

'Well . . .' she said finally. 'I'd think about suicide if I'd been her. Although, of course, then I wouldn't be her exactly.' Seeing the agent's perplexed face, Kristin elaborated. 'I mean Sara was fine. She didn't seem happy, but not sad either. It was as if she was always worried, yes. Sometimes about silly things, like the vase or because the lift wasn't working properly. But I can't imagine her jumping . . .'

And for the first time in the conversation, the young

woman seemed to realize that her flatmate, the woman she had described as fussy, over-the-top, solitary and frigid in one breath had thrown herself on to the tracks of the metro. Kristin reddened and her eyes filled with tears that she made no effort to hold back.

'I'm sorry . . .' she murmured. 'It's strange to be here talking about Sara while she's . . . Excuse me.'

Kristin got up and shot off to the bathroom. From the other side of the door, Agent Fort heard her sob inconsolably, like a little girl. He waited patiently for her to emerge, but seeing that she'd be some time, he rose from his chair and took a walk around the flat.

It was an impersonal space, he decided. Neutral furnishings. A painting that must have been there for years. The sofa, perhaps the newest piece of furniture, was encased in an insipid brown cover, certainly the same one which had hidden the previous sofa. It was clear that Sara hadn't been too worried about décor. Fort moved towards the shelves with the vase; the cracks where it had been broken were visible. Kristin was right, it didn't look expensive. It was a rectangular white ceramic vase, the kind sent with a bouquet of flowers. He was already moving away when something caught his eye. There was something inside. He took it out and saw it was a correspondence slip with the Alemany Cosmetics logo on it. It was signed, and it took Fort a while to decipher the names. Sílvia and . . . one beginning with 'C': César. Yes. Sílvia and César. So the vase, no doubt with a bouquet inside, had been a present from the company, thought Fort as he wandered around the flat towards Sara's room. He was just outside the bedroom when he heard the bathroom door opening.

'I was going to take a look at Sara's room,' he told her without turning his head.

Kristin took a couple of steps, but hesitated before crossing the threshold.

'This is only the second time I've gone in without her being there,' she said by way of an excuse. 'Sara told me very clearly when I arrived.'

Roger nodded. Sara must have been a fairly imposing woman to have her rules still stand even after her death. He had only seen her passport photo, so he went over to the ones pinned on a corkboard, on the wall beside the computer screen, thinking his sister had had an identical one when she was a teenager. He'd never understood the value of a train ticket, a cinema stub, or any of the small objects his sister kept on that kind of juvenile altar. It seemed it might be a female custom because Sara Mahler, at the age of thirty-four, did the same.

He was surprised to see a smiling Sara, not alone. On the contrary, the photos showed a somewhat stout girl, radiant, with very black hair; beside her, in different images, almost all the first-team players for Barça, the manager included.

'Oh yeah,' said Kristin. 'She was passionate about football. I think that's why she rented this flat, because it's close to Camp Nou. She was a real fan of his,' pointing to the image in which Sara appeared with Pep Guardiola.

'Did she often go to the ground?'

'No. Some matches, but not many.'

He observed Sara's face closely. It was clear that suicide didn't form part of her plans, nor was it even a remote thought at that point. Her eyes were shining and her smile lit up her face.

74

'I'm going to go. I'm taking this photo, all right?'

Kristin shrugged her shoulders, doubtful.

Another photograph caught the agent's attention, firstly because there were no footballers with her. A group of men and women, dressed informally, were posing in front of a minibus. He took it down and showed it to Kristin.

'No idea,' she said. 'Work colleagues, I suppose.'

'Sara didn't belong to a hiking group or anything like that?'

She burst out laughing, as if the very idea were ridiculous. He looked at the photo again, peering attentively at Sara; she was smiling enthusiastically in this one too, and the expression of happiness gave her an almost child-like appearance. She was wearing knee-length beige shorts which didn't suit her at all. He took the photo, not asking permission this time.

Roger looked around him. There was little more to see in the room. He opened the wardrobe, with few expectations by now, and found nothing more or less than what it should contain: clothes, carefully hung up or folded. Indeed, Sara had been a more than organized woman: the shelves were arranged by colour and the order was of pinpoint accuracy. Beside the computer there were shelves of paperbacks, the majority in German or English. On the bedside table he saw a novel by an author called Melody Thomas, which Sara was halfway through, judging by the bookmark. She would never know how it ends, thought Fort. He left the room somewhat depressed, with the photos of Sara in his hand.

'And what do I do with her things?' asked Kristin, as

if the thought had just occurred to her that very instant. 'Do I have to put them in boxes?'

The young woman's face was worried and, not for the first time since Thursday night, Agent Fort, who came from a large, relatively united family, felt overwhelmed by a painful sadness to think that Sara Mahler had no one to collect her belongings apart from this flatmate who'd known her for little more than two months and, in any case, would do so out of mere obligation. Neither did he believe that Herr Joseph Mahler would have much interest in his daughter's things.

Kristin was waiting for an answer, so Fort opted for a compromise.

'I suppose that would be best, if you don't mind. When you're done, call me and I'll come to get your flatmate's boxes.'

'Okay.'

'One more thing.' He didn't want to show this girl the photo of the dogs: she was already upset. Nevertheless, he should ask. 'Did Sara ever talk about dogs? Was she frightened of them or anything?'

She looked at him as if he'd gone mad.

'Dogs?' She shook her head. 'No. Not at all. I don't know if she liked them or not, but what has that got to do with her suicide?'

She'd said the word for the first time. It was strange, Fort reflected, how hard it was to say certain things. People spoke freely of sex, for example, and yet the subject of death, above all when it was self-inflicted, continued to be a taboo difficult to overcome.

'I don't know. Probably nothing,' he responded, not giving her any more information.

Seconds afterwards Agent Roger Fort headed towards the door, not knowing if he'd taken anything definite from that chat, apart from two photographs and a feeling of melancholy that seemed to weigh on his chest.

'Excuse me,' Kristin said to the agent when he was already on the landing. 'I said ugly things about Sara before. They weren't lies. But then I remembered when I was sick and she called the doctor and took care of me. She made soup and brought it to me in bed.' She lowered her head, as if she were ashamed. 'It's silly. I just wanted you to know. Sara was strange, but she wasn't a bad person.'

Roger Fort nodded and smiled at her. The door of the lift opened and out came a person that he assumed was Kristin's Catalan boyfriend. Just as young but much less blonde. While descending, Agent Fort studied both photos. And thought the Dutch girl's last sentence was a good epitaph, although it could be applied to a large part of the world's population. He put away the photos before leaving. Sara Mahler's smile, that childlike expression on the face of a woman, had become lodged in some corner of his mind, along with a sense of despondency which suddenly made the Barcelona streets, overflowing with vehicles and passers-by, seem a strange and hostile place.

8

There are pieces of news you are happy to give because you know they'll be well received; other totally disastrous ones you're forced to deliver with a serious expression. And then a third, more ambiguous category exists, which generates a feeling somewhere between satisfaction and nostalgia; at least to me, thought Héctor while he was preparing to explain the 'opportunity' being presented to Martina Andreu.

Martina was intrigued, no doubt. Since the previous afternoon, Salgado's words had been going around in her head, like an annoying sting too small to pull out. To top it all, he'd spent the whole morning with Savall once more and he wasn't free until after lunch.

'Spit it out, Héctor,' she blurted as soon as she sat down opposite him. 'You have me on tenterhooks and I won't put up with it. You know surprises make me nervous.'

He did know. Sometimes Héctor sympathized with the sergeant's husband, whom he barely knew. Having someone at your side who was always right could be annoying at times.

Salgado took a deep breath.

'You saw I was in a meeting with Savall yesterday?'

'Of course I did. Don't play hard to get,' she warned him with a smile.

'Wait. Don't be impatient.' He'd considered the most appropriate words, but at that moment, with her sitting opposite looking at him with her usual frankness, he ditched them completely. 'Well, Calderón was here. You know him, from the National's organized crime unit.'

Martina knew him by sight. They'd worked together on the Nigerian women-trafficking case the year before, although it had been Héctor who'd worked more closely with him.

'I'll sum it up briefly. Now he's involved in various things, although he is focusing on one thing in particular. Eastern mafia. Ukrainians, Georgians, Romanians . . . and Russians.' The emphasis on the last word was clear. 'Until now, the Russians have used Spain as a site of investment, not crime.'

Martina nodded. The news of the supposed *vor v zakonye*, or 'thieves in law', had been current in newspapers and official circles for some time. They were the equivalents of the *capos* of the Italian mafia, residing comfortably and luxuriously in different parts of Europe, especially in the south, and they laundered money thanks to the great bottomless well that had been property investment, in coastal developments in particular.

'Good,' Héctor continued. 'As you also know, property is no longer what it was and, according to Calderón, some of those who up to now focused only on investment are changing their strategy. They are moving their money somewhere else more profitable, and they're beginning to think of Spain as a place of business. You know – drugs, girls, everything . . .

'It seems they're scattering. Previously they all lived together, on the coast generally, with the intention of going unnoticed and being taken for foreign residents seeking a more favourable climate than their own. According to Calderón, the moves began a few months ago. The boss stays in place, but his associates have been dispatched to different points on the peninsula: Valencia, Madrid, Galicia, Tarragona . . .'

'They think they are building a kind of organized network?'

'Exactly. Tough times, Martina, as we all know. And at a time like this, money is well received everywhere without anyone asking too many questions.'

'You mean corruption?'

'Corruption, necessity . . . Poverty, at the end of the day. The best incentive for crime. The poverty of the new rich, especially those who don't want to go back to being poor.' Héctor shrugged. 'I don't know the details. Apparently the thing is just starting, and perhaps for once we have an advantage over them. At least we know their movements, which is something. And the Ministry of the Interior is firmly resolved not to allow their businesses to flourish. Whatever happens.'

Martina Andreu said nothing, but it was clear from her body language that she didn't understand what she had to do with it all.

'Good. This firm resolve translates into funds for a special unit headed up by Calderón. And with colleagues from all the different autonomous forces. I think Savall called it a "built-in unit".' He smiled.

'And?' Martina didn't dare to ask the question directly.

'And they want you in. Well, actually, they want you

to coordinate our part. You'll be in charge of a small group of agents and will report directly to Calderón.'

Martina leaned back in the chair, as if someone had pushed her.

'But . . .' She wasn't diplomatic, she never had been, and she put the question to him straight. 'Wouldn't it be more logical for you to take charge of this? Or some other inspector?'

Salgado raised his eyebrows.

'Well . . . Martina, let's not kid ourselves, you know I'm more or less on the bench at the moment.' With a movement of his head he hushed the sergeant's imminent protest. 'It's how it is. I asked for it, partly.' He lightly hit his chest. 'Mea culpa. Don't worry about it.'

'Of course I'll worry. It's not fair, and—'

'Martina! As the tangos say, life isn't fair. I pity anyone who believes otherwise. I broke Omar's face – that's a fact that, on record, translates as violent tendencies, with no space for explanations. And then' – his voice became more serious – 'there's the matter of Ruth.'

Martina looked away. She'd come to dislike that name and all it implied, although she'd never say so to her boss. She cared about Héctor a lot; she'd seen him so obsessed with finding an answer that when Savall held firm and took him off the case she'd almost felt relieved. It wasn't fair, but as he'd just said, was life ever?

'So now all you have to consider is whether you're interested or not.' They both knew that was stupid. If the superintendent had put her forward, there was little to be considered. 'Martina, this is a good opportunity. You know it is.'

Héctor was aware, or at least guessed, that there was

81

something else. Savall had wanted to rescue Martina Andreu, a woman he cared about personally and professionally, from the camp of exiles. For better and above all for worse, Andreu's name was associated with Salgado's, and the sooner this bond was broken the better it would be for the sergeant's career. Of course, he wasn't going to tell her so. Martina was so loyal she wouldn't hesitate in raising hell if she suspected anything of the sort.

'My situation is complicated,' she clarified. 'You know Rafa is still unemployed, right?'

He nodded. The sergeant's husband was a technical architect and had been one of the first to feel the pinprick in the property bubble. First he went months without being paid and finally had been left with no work, and with few prospects of finding any, the previous September.

'I don't know if this is the best time for me to . . .'

Héctor understood, but his obligation was to bring her round to the contrary.

'Martina, don't scupper it. Don't sacrifice a great opportunity through misguided loyalty. That won't do either of you any good, not him and not you.'

'You can't imagine what it's like to see him at home.' She wasn't given to discussing personal subjects, even with him. 'He's irritable, he gets angry at the kids over stupid things. Sometimes I think I'm not going to put up with it any more. It kills me to see him depressed and at the same time it makes me angry, as if it's partly his fault. As if the solution is that he should accept anything. And then I hate myself . . . Fuck.'

'It's not his fault and you know it. But if you let this opportunity go then you really will have something to blame him for.'

She forced herself to smile.

'So you want to get rid of me, Inspector Salgado.'

'Of course,' he admitted, feigning seriousness. He looked at the roof, as if he were giving thanks to a supreme being. 'All this is a conspiracy I dreamed up to finally be free of your nagging.'

They looked at each other more affectionately than usual. Neither of the two was exactly effusive in their affections; perhaps that was why they had always understood each other so well.

'And if I accept, when does it all start?'

'Savall is waiting for you in his office . . . now. There's a meeting in Madrid the day after tomorrow.'

'Fuck. Is someone at home packing my suitcase without me knowing?'

'I thought of sending Fort, mainly so he'd do something useful . . .'

Héctor's joke hung in the air like an aimless arrow as the door opened and the person in question appeared on the threshold.

'Excuse me,' Roger apologized.

Salgado almost blushed and Martina Andreu took advantage of the moment to rise.

'I'll leave the boss all to you. We'll talk,' she added, turning to Salgado. She winked at him before leaving and murmured, 'Go on making friends.'

Héctor spent the first few minutes trying to figure out if Fort would have heard his unfortunate comment;

he cursed himself for having said it and yet he couldn't help thinking that that boy had the gift of bad timing. So when he suddenly saw in his face that Fort had just asked a question he hadn't heard, he didn't know how to answer and looked at the photo the agent had placed on his desk with unusual intensity.

'So, Fort,' he finally said, in an attempt to summarize, 'you found this photo in Sara Mahler's flat and spoke to her flatmate. Don't rush, describe the interview slowly.'

His subordinate looked at him, flushing.

'I'm sorry,' he said, and Héctor felt even worse than before. 'I suppose I'm in a hurry to get to the end.'

For the next few minutes Roger Fort obediently told him of the impressions gathered in his brief encounter with Kristin Herschdorfer. He explained that, while not definitive, they suggested Sara Mahler was not easy to live with, she led a solitary life and generally didn't seem happy. All ready for happy Christmas to be the final blow, thought Héctor. Her flatmate was away, the house empty. If Sara had felt depressed in those final days, perhaps she had opted to end it all for ever. Suddenly something occurred to him that it seemed no one had acknowledged up to now.

'And why was she in the metro station at that time? Any idea?'

Agent Fort looked uncertain.

'I mean, according to this Kristin, Sara hardly went out . . . And if she was in the habit of staying out all night, she would have told you so. But in the early hours of Thursday Sara was in the metro. She had to be going or coming from somewhere, right?' He answered himself: 'Even if she had decided to throw herself on to the tracks, she didn't have to go to a station so far away. And I doubt if she left home with that idea.'

It was a more than reasonable doubt. Although statistics were an inexact science, few women chose this method to end their lives. Héctor still believed those who did were succumbing to a momentary temptation, that moment of desperation in which the fatal jump felt like the only option.

Roger shook his head, distressed.

'I don't know, sir. I'm sorry, it hadn't occurred to me until now.'

'Well, don't worry. What else did you want to tell me?'

Slowly, Fort continued with his story: the description of the flat, of the bedroom; the photos of the footballers on the corkboard . . . and finally came to the photograph Inspector Salgado had before him.

It showed Sara with seven people: two women and five men of various ages, between thirty and fiftysomething. Sara was at one side of the photo and, although she was smiling, there was a barely perceptible but real distance between her and the rest of the group.

'Are they all work colleagues?'

'Yes, sir. As soon as I saw it, I had the impression that one of the faces was familiar. The guy on the opposite side of the photo. The one wearing glasses.'

'And?'

'If I'm not mistaken, and I don't think I am, that's Gaspar Ródenas.'

Héctor frowned slightly. An excited Roger Fort finally repeated the phrase he'd said at the start of the conversation that the inspector hadn't heard.

'Last September, Gaspar Ródenas killed his wife and

his fourteen-month-old daughter. Then he committed suicide.'

Salgado looked at the photo. He didn't take on domestic violence cases, but the age of the little girl had stayed with him.

'You mean Sara and Gaspar Ródenas worked at the same company? And both have committed suicide?'

'Yes, sir. Bit strange, isn't it?'

Yes, thought Héctor. Very strange. He looked back at the photo: of those eight people, all relatively young, two had died in a violent manner. In the case of one, the suicide took place alongside his family; in the other, all alone. Although everything could have another explanation, if you listened to the experts.

'Remember the knock-on effect?' he asked Fort. 'If you asked me, I'd say I don't really believe in these things, but there's something in it. If Sara was very depressed, her colleague's action might have given her the idea.'

He said it without much conviction. The acts of a parricidal killer could hardly be taken as an example for anyone in their right mind. And up to now, his idea of Sara Mahler was that she was no lunatic.

Héctor checked the time before speaking again. That day he wanted to leave the office on time.

'Fort, make me a copy of the photo before you go. Tomorrow try to establish what Sara was doing in that station. And get information from the domestic violence people, see what they tell you.' His eyes sought the card Víctor Alemany had given him and finally they found it. 'As soon as we gather a little more information, we'll go and pay Alemany Cosmetics a courtesy call.'

86

Roger Fort nodded, although Héctor wasn't sure he'd picked up the sarcasm.

'Oh, and good work, Fort. Keep it up.'

You said it Savall-style, he reproached himself. Last minute and not looking him in the eyes.

9

Although he'd had the keys to Sílvia's apartment for
months – since before the summer, when they announced their engagement – whenever César used them
when she wasn't there he felt like an intruder. He opened
the door slowly and lingered a few seconds before going
in, like someone fearing the attack of a non-existent dog.
Shortly it would be his home as well, he thought, but he
just couldn't shake off the behaviour of a guest entirely.
He was aware of it, and to tell the truth it annoyed him.
He would prefer to move around and feel relaxed as in
his own apartment: leave his jacket thrown any old way
on the chair, kick off his shoes and change his clothes. In
her place, he hung up his coat on the coat stand in the
hall and loosened the knot of his tie a little.

He couldn't hear a sound, and went towards the kitchen
to grab a beer. He knew Sílvia bought them for him. He
opened it and tossed the cap in one of the three small
rubbish bins, not without checking that he'd thrown it
into the right one. Damn recycling. At his apartment
he had a single rubbish bag, as always, but Sílvia was
obsessed with these details. And her children were as
well. Fuck, once he'd felt like an environment-wrecker

just for putting a milk carton where he shouldn't. The clock showed 18.40, which meant Sílvia still wouldn't get home for more than an hour. Pol had indoor soccer training and Emma, the oldest, must be at some friend's house. Good, César felt more comfortable without them there.

Tuesday was the only day Sílvia left work a little before six to attend her weekly yoga class. Only a devastating tornado could have altered this routine, which was then followed by a light dinner at home, a spell of TV on the sofa and a quick fuck in the bedroom. That was why César was there, although that Tuesday he'd arrived earlier than usual. He'd left work early, not because he had anything in particular to do, but because halfway through the afternoon he was sick of the atmosphere, charged with conjecture, pervading the air at the laboratory.

Since the day before, the news of Sara's death had been on everyone's lips: mostly malicious gossip, which pointed to the suicide of the MD's secretary as the only explanation. 'No one falls on to the metro tracks by accident' had been the phrase of the day, with some minor variations. From there, the musings shot off in various directions, with no more foundation than cheap psychology: the sadness of Christmas, isolation of women, rootlessness, lack of sex. Nonsense really, because very few really knew Sara Mahler; if they carried out a popularity contest in the company, she would have come close to last in the rankings, not because people found her disagreeable, but it wouldn't have occurred to them to mention her. Sara went unnoticed: she preferred email to communicating in person, she barely moved from her desk, she attended company dinners and had good manners, but didn't socialize very much. To top it all, at some point a rumour had gone around that she wasn't to be trusted: too close to Víctor Alemany, too reserved for anyone to include her in general gossip and too foreign to understand people going out to smoke during work hours or spending more than five minutes at the coffee machine. And yet César knew they were wrong: Sara had been perfectly capable of keeping a secret . . . At least, he hoped so.

Enough, he told himself. He'd left work so as not to talk about Sara and now he couldn't get her out of his head. And when Sílvia arrived the subject would certainly come up again. He finished the beer and threw the bottle in the glass bin. Then he went to the sitting room, sat down carefully on a sofa still as miraculously white as its first day and switched on the TV. One of those evening contests, presented by an individual trying to muster enthusiasm in the audience, appeared on the screen. One of the competitors was a black kid, who was verbally duelling with a middle-aged woman whose knowledge he indubitably surpassed. With a slight involuntary gesture of disgust, César changed channel and found a documentary about fish. This is better, he thought, letting himself be rocked by a monotonous and serene voice. Maybe it was the beer, maybe it was having spent the whole of the previous night awake, or maybe it was because deep down he didn't much like fish, but what was certain was that he was dead tired. He told himself just one minute, closing his eyes would help him relax, and a few minutes later he was asleep, head tilted and the remote control on his crotch.

*

He woke suddenly, startled, on feeling a rubbing on his flies. The sleep had been so deep that just then he didn't really know where he was, or whether it was day or night. It took him a few seconds to come back completely to the conscious world, to that white sofa, the TV on. And to Emma, in a bathrobe, smiling at him with the remote.

'Good morning,' she said to him, sarcastically. 'You were snoring like a wild animal in the zoo. Poor Mama – you'll have to buy her earplugs.'

He yawned, unable to help it. He had an uncertain air which seemed to amuse her. César realized then that someone, Emma, had just turned off the television.

'I don't think you were watching it,' she declared.

Her hair was wet, and when she left the remote on the coffee table César realized that Sílvia's daughter wasn't wearing anything under the bathrobe. Curled up on a corner of the sofa, she resembled a white angora cat, docile in appearance only.

'What time is it?' asked César. 'Were you here when I arrived?'

'In the shower, I suppose.' She looked at the digital clock beside the TV. 'And it's early. Mama will be a while yet.'

Emma's tone woke him fully. He looked at her out of the corner of his eye. Sixteen years old. 'Like sixteen suns,' her mother would have said. César leaned his hands on his knees and made as if to stand up, but she extended her bare legs and left her feet on the coffee table, forming a ridiculous barrier, easily passable.

'Emma . . . Let me past. I'm going to the bathroom.'

She laughed.

'Only a coward would run away.' She looked down.

'You should certainly throw out those shoes. They're shabby. I'm sure Mama doesn't like them at all. Neither do I.'

César took a few seconds to react. The cheek of the girl left him speechless.

'Fuck, Emma, enough!' The tone of annoyance sounded exaggerated, artificial. She lowered her legs, obedient. But he didn't move. 'Listen. I told you loud and clear a while ago: this isn't funny.'

It was true. He'd repeated it often enough, especially during the previous summer, during the three weeks they spent together in a rented chalet on the Costa Brava. At first it had been nothing more than casual brushing against one another, always when they were alone, without Sílvia and without Pol. In the car, the aisle of the supermarket; on the beach, while the two were swimming . . . Or, with absolute nerve, one evening they stayed together in the swimming pool because Sílvia had gone to the hairdresser in town and Pol was out cycling with his friends. Then he wanted to settle the subject for the first time. A firm 'no', like you yell at a puppy who persists in chewing the cables. She had only smiled, like a perverse Gioconda, and whispered to him, almost at his ear: 'And what will you do if I keep going? Tell Mama?'

It was what he should have done and he knew it. He simply didn't dare. Emma was the perfect daughter: good marks, well mannered, responsible, punctual. Sílvia was so proud of her she wouldn't have believed him. On the other hand, what was he going to say to her? That her adolescent daughter was harassing him? Him, an ordinary guy of forty-six? The mere idea of saying it out loud was ridiculous. And yet, Emma finding him attractive filled him with a stupid pride that often helped him masturbate between Wednesday and Saturday.

'Look, we've already talked about this. Find yourself a boyfriend your own age.' He tried to make light of it, play the whole thing down, although the result was that Emma twisted it, annoyed like a little girl.

'Don't tell me what to do. You're not my father.'

'Of course not,' he replied. 'Do whatever you want, but leave me alone, okay?'

She laughed again.

'If you give me a kiss,' she dared him. 'Just one . . .'

'Don't talk nonsense.'

'Come on . . . on the cheek. A kiss from Papa.'

She was beside him, closer. The bathrobe had loosened a little, enough to outline her young breasts. Emma grabbed his hand and tried to guide it to her skin. Smooth, white, smelling of soap. César closed his fist to resist and grabbed her forcefully. They looked at each other, defiant. Her lips half-open, innocently eager. Seconds passed, but in that heartbeat they understood each other. They guessed that some day the inevitable would happen.

But not then: he managed to extricate himself and she gave a cry of pain.

'You twisted my wrist, you brute.'

'I'm going. Tell your mother I had to leave. And, as you're so brave, you can tell her why.' César spoke without thinking. This time the words worked.

'No! César, don't go . . .'

He strode towards the hall, put on his jacket. Emma shouted at him from the sitting room.

'César, come back! Please . . . I don't want you to go.'

César saw himself as if he were observing himself from a distance and he was only half pleased. He, who had handled himself easily in brothels and bars, was playing at being offended now, playing the role of the dignified, inflexible man, when in reality he was no more than a pathetic guy incapable of handling a young girl. Only a coward would run away, he repeated. Even so, anger overcame him and he already had his hand on the door-knob when Emma ran towards the hall and said hoarsely, 'If you go, I'll do what that Sara at the company did. I'll kill myself. With bleach. And I'll leave a note explaining that it's your fault.'

César didn't know if she was serious. He decided to turn around.

'Emma . . .'

Mistake. He should have left. He knew it although he was incapable of doing it. Her eyes were shining. Perhaps they were tears, of fury or frustration, but they didn't fall. They remained in that blurry look, contained, threatening.

'Your fault and Mama's. Both of you. I'll leave a note that'll sink you into misery for ever.' She became more daring as she watched his face, paler every moment. 'And you'll have to explain the Sara thing as well. The reason she killed herself, if she did kill herself.'

'What are you saying?' His voice was scarcely a whisper.

'I know everything, César. Mama talks to you on the phone thinking I don't hear her.' She laughed; it was a bitter chuckle, unhealthy, inappropriate for her age. And she repeated: 'I always know everything. Don't forget it.' She paused, took a step forward, lowered her head a little. The possible tears had disappeared, engulfed by the sensation of victory. 'Now, are you going to give me that kiss? Just one . . . A kiss from Papa.'

For a moment he didn't know whether to kiss her or slap her across the face. And standing there, motionless and sweaty, he understood with fear that neither did he know which of the two options excited him more.

10

It was an inappropriate night for the month of January. Quiet, peaceful. Deceptively warm. If you were very determined, you could even pick out the odd star that dared let itself be seen through the great veil that covered the city and had already become its only heaven. If we continue contaminating the city, thought Héctor, Christians will have to find another synonym for Paradise, some remote island or something, because no one's going to want to stay in that sky. Maybe they'd get rid of Purgatory, a place he'd always imagined as a dirty ochre colour, to keep the low-rent sinners far away. The authentic ones would still be condemned to Hell. Like suicides.

He'd always found it strange that the Church condemned them irrevocably. There was no justification that might absolve those who killed themselves. There were no good or bad suicides. The same punishment was inflicted on them all, without exception and without taking their previous path into account. Taking one's own life was the ultimate sin. But if we don't even have that, what is left to us? Héctor said to himself as he lit his fourth cigarette since he'd gone up to the roof terrace. Smoking and killing himself little by little, he thought. He approached the railing and exhaled a mouthful of smoke to further cloud the night sky; he hadn't the least doubt that sleep wouldn't come through natural means.

And the night had started on a promising note. For Christmas, in an indirect and completely unsubtle way, he'd bought Guillermo some trainers, a gift his son contemplated with the same interest as if it were a knitting machine. However, the day before, at breakfast, in the turnaround which was clearly the distinct feature of adolescence, the boy had asked him when he would be going running and Héctor had hastened to seal the deal, before his son could change his mind. Tuesday evening, around eight.

And so it was. A reticent Guillermo was waiting for him at home, already changed and ready to go out when he arrived after half past eight. Not paying too much attention to the protests about the delay, Héctor put on shorts and running shoes, fearing in advance that the plan to 'do things together' wasn't as good an idea as he'd thought at the time of buying the present. Damn modern pedagogy which turns us all into imbeciles, he thought just before leaving. Guillermo's bad-tempered face didn't bode well.

And his foreboding turned out to be accurate. The kid was partly to blame, and so was Héctor. As always. He wasn't accustomed to having company while he was running, and being constantly obliged to wait for someone put him on edge. On the other hand, Guillermo seemed embarrassed to be doing exercise with his father, who, moreover, was fitter than he. Certainly one doesn't usually talk much while running, but a tense silence built up between them. Héctor had chosen a short route, a straight line, parallel to the sea. However, his rhythm was faster and, although he limited his pace, he left his son behind every few metres. Finally, when it occurred to him to say, out loud and in a mildly teasing voice, 'Guille, son, speed up a bit,' the boy looked at him as if he had just subjected him to the worst humiliation, and with a sullen expression turned around and ran off in the opposite direction, really running then. Héctor hesitated between following him and continuing his route. In the end, knowing it was better to let time pass and tempers calm, he opted for the second.

When he arrived home, his son had already showered and shut himself in his room. He deduced that he'd also eaten, given that he found plates in the sink, unwashed. Adding another reproach seemed excessive and he pretended not to see them. But when he saw the shoes in their box, on the table, in a gesture that to all appearances was a challenge, he knocked on his son's bedroom door. No answer. He opened it and Guillermo didn't seem perturbed by his entry: the computer was on, of course, and the headphones connected. Héctor had to make a Herculean effort his therapist would have been proud of to refrain from disconnecting all the electronic equipment to make him pay attention.

Then they had a chat which, in hindsight, it would have been better to avoid. The content and form didn't matter; the result had been that Guillermo had invited him to leave the room – 'Would you mind leaving me alone?' – and he'd responded with a typical caveman father phrase, in the Argentine accent that only emerged when he was angry, and that he had never thought he would say. To top it all, when the clichés were in full flow, each of them playing their role, Carmen had called.

The landlady didn't seem to realize she was interrupting a father–son encounter. She was excited, nervous even. A state which, Héctor knew, could be due to only one thing: yes, Carmen's son, Carlos, Charly to everyone, had called her that evening after years of not giving any sign of life. Every stray bullet finds a hole in which to lodge, Héctor reflected. And Charly was a long-range bullet who always ended up causing damage. Nevertheless, a mother is a mother, and although Carmen wasn't foolish and knew what her son was like, the woman was happy, and Héctor spent some time talking to her. Charly was to arrive on Friday to stay for a while. Obviously he had no job, no money and hadn't worked out a concrete plan. No doubt the crisis suited the return of thirty-something prodigal sons.

After Carmen left, restarting the argument with Guillermo seemed absurd, so he ate a little, watched the TV for a while and, finally, he went up to the roof terrace, laptop under his arm. Nothing was as it should be, he thought: not fathers, not sons, not this winter night.

Convinced he wouldn't sleep, he switched on the computer and launched into the search for information. It was a little ridiculous, given that he could obtain all this the following day from Roger Fort, but he wanted to do something and the name Alemany Cosmetics kept reverberating in his head. He didn't feel like reading the history of the company just then, although he did watch a corporate video, skilfully done, on the values that defined the company: youth, freedom and inner beauty . . . 'Inner', an adjective that seemed to be on the increase.

The video included brief interviews with members of the company, and he recognized some from the group photograph among them. Sara, and the other suicide, Gaspar Ródenas, didn't feature in it. Víctor Alemany did, of course, and his sister Sílvia, one of the women in the photo. With the copy of the photo in his hand and a second viewing of the video, he also identified Brais Arjona, brand manager of the Young line, and Amanda Bonet, a beautiful young woman who, according to the subtitles, was responsible for design and packaging for the same line. Three people remained nameless: three men who appeared in the photo but not in the video and must belong to technical departments. No, one of them was there: Manel Caballero, deputy technical director. He was almost unrecognizable, but yes, it was him: the same slightly long-haired boy who had spoken about 'innovation and development' with little ease. Much less, of course, than Brais Arjona, a guy who demonstrated an enviable aplomb. In cinematic jargon, the camera loved him, although not as much as it loved Amanda Bonet. Amanda was certainly one of the most beautiful women Héctor had ever seen, and she spoke slowly, clearly and with no affectation.

He carried out another search. 'Gaspar Ródenas'. Not many links appeared, since the press were usually careful about mentioning surnames. He didn't mind: the following day he'd have the official report. He was going to leave it – it was hardly the time to be reading stories of fathers killing their one-year-old daughters – when an article caught his eye. The title 'A Normal

Family' suggested a note of irony he liked, although the real surprise was the name of the journalist who signed it: Lola Martínez Rueda. Lola. Fuck, Lola . . . After all this time.

He smiled, remembering. Her carefree appearance, her contagious laugh, those hands that were never still. Lola . . . He hadn't thought of her in years. He'd learned to relegate her to a remote space in his mind, bury her under the weight of the decision made. However, at that moment, in that falsely warm early morning, he saw her face as if it were before him and the memory dissolved his bad mood.

11

Cities, like dogs, are never fully asleep. At the most, they doze, relax, gather strength to endure the coming and going of cars and pedestrians who await them the following morning. Their streets breathe a little more freely, occupied only by the reduced number of people who move in the early hours. Nocturnal animals of a different fur, strolling on almost empty pavements or roads, always colder, more silent. There are hours in which any noise, however petty, becomes a roar. A car door being closed becomes an explosion, firm steps provoke echoes, voices seem like sirens.

For years Brais Arjona had belonged to that world of shadows. He was used to going out alone and coming home alone, but that didn't matter to him. What he sought, what he needed, was to fill those hours with anonymous faces and unknown bodies. Unfortunately, even in a city like Barcelona, the night animals always tended to be the same and sometimes, discovering guys he already knew by sight among the fauna, he felt uncomfortable, sickened by this atmosphere of dark corners and solitary individuals. He would pass older men and look away, not to ignore them but so as not to see himself when he was no longer as young, as attractive. As desirable. So, invariably, despite many firm late-night resolutions to cut down on these escapes, to go out only with his friends, to stay at home watching a film, the scent of the night awoke an almost irrepressible urge within him. And, past twelve, when the majority of responsible workers were getting into bed, he would take to the street. Like a wolf. In search of his pack. In search of prey. In search of something to assuage his hunger.

Just as in Madrid, during his first year in Barcelona there were memorable nights and others to be forgotten. But there was something stimulating even in the worst nights. None the less, little by little, they all started to blend into one: the good and bad were blending into a single category, mediocre and grey. The same men, the same dark rooms, the same bars. The same glances that, requiring no words, set in motion the complex yet simple mechanism of sex. And then, when tedium threatened to devour him, or perhaps because of that, David appeared.

David, his husband, who was at that moment asleep hugging the pillow as if it were a lifejacket. David who went to bed at twelve at the latest and awoke at seven, brimming with energy. David, who hunted the wolf and converted him into a friendly little domestic animal. Brais had never had problems accepting his homosexuality, not even back in Galicia twenty years ago, in those rainy lands he'd hated so much and now had begun to yearn for. Probably the lack of a family smoothed the way for him: there was no one to come out to, or at least no one who would care. But had he been one of those who hide their true desires, David's presence would have dissolved the least hint of fear or shame. Because loving someone so much couldn't be bad. For that reason they had married, in a symbolic gesture: to proclaim to the world that they were together, would be together and, with a bit of luck, would grow old together. An old age which still seemed distant. Brais was thirty-seven; his husband had just turned thirty-one. Life stretched before them as a long, happy road. None the less, that night the road appeared to be cut short, to lead to a sheer and dangerous precipice. At least for him.

A night of eternal minutes, a dawn refusing to come. It's almost three when, sick of thinking, Brais gets out of bed, and barefoot, moves towards the laptop he'd left on the dining-room table. He knows he shouldn't look at it, but there is something perverse in that image that he finds addictive.

The photo is attached to an email of two words. 'Never forget.' As if anyone could forget that. Brais closes his eyes for a few seconds, the time it takes for the photo to open. Despite already knowing what it contains, his whole body tenses. Leaning slightly forward, both hands resting on the table, he contemplates the screen and feels the desire to destroy it with a fist. He could do it, but there's no point. The three strangled dogs would still be in his head: their slack jaws, stretched necks, rigid paws.

He remains still, tense for a few more minutes. His body demands action, to react in some physical way to this fixed, unshakeable stimulus. Because of this, still standing, he closes the window with the image and returns to his email. He composes a quick message and sends it to the personal email accounts of the five people involved: Sílvia Alemany, César Calvo, Amanda Bonet, Manel Caballero and, the oldest of all, Octavi Pujades.

Those still alive, he thinks indifferently. Those who can still save themselves.

Then he goes back to bed and embraces his husband in a vague attempt to catch that tranquillity of spirit that bestows a deep, restorative sleep on David, the sleep of the innocent. This is all that matters, thinks Brais, being able to sleep with David by his side for what is left of his life.

For months now day and night have become a kind of continual slumber for Octavi Pujades. He's read somewhere that this was used as a means of coercion for prisoners of war: when the notions of time and space disappeared, the mind lost its footing and tumbled into incoherency. He wants to believe that's not the case with him, that his brain still functions with the same precision, that he analyses and decides using pure logic. For Octavi, financial director of Alemany Cosmetics for over twenty years, two plus two have always equalled four on balance sheets and in life. So it makes him uncomfortable that in other professions, other spheres, people could be so inexact, so mathematically incorrect.

When his wife was diagnosed with the cancer that has her lying prostrate in bed, the doctor affirmed that, unfortunately, Eugènia wouldn't see in the New Year. In his actual words, it would be an achievement if she managed to survive until Christmas. And Octavi Pujades therefore acted according to this prognosis. He spoke to Sílvia and Víctor, appointed an acting replacement – not whom he would have chosen, but the only one possible given the circumstances – and took some months of leave to nurse his wife. Eugènia had asked only one thing of him: to die at home. In the same space they had lived in for eighteen years, since they exchanged the city apartment for this detached house in Torrelles de Llobregat, in an area where there were still birds. He'd made her that promise and taken on the task with the same discipline he applied to his work environment. It would be five months at most, from August until the end of the year, a substantial but not excessive amount of time. He was relatively sure that Gaspar Ródenas, the chosen replacement, would fulfil his role and at the same time keep him informed. Never, in the worst moments of doubt, did it cross his mind that Gaspar would die before Eugènia and in the end he would have to resort to the person who should have been the first choice. Life has a strange way of seeking justice, he thought. At one time they used to say the Lord worked in mysterious ways, which came to more or less the same thing.

This dawn, Octavi enters what was once his bedroom and is now a death chamber with a corpse refusing to die. He finds the strength with which Eugènia clings to this world, to these scant hours of consciousness without pain that make up her life, admirable and surprising at the same time. He'd never have believed that this tiny slim body could harbour such a capacity for resistance, such a desire to face death, huddled in some corner of the room, a vulture ready to drive its claws into its prey.

Eugènia is sleeping. The medication keeps her sedated for the greater part of the day. He knows he is doing everything possible. None the less, however much he tries to force himself, he can't manage to share this bed with her, and this pains him. At the beginning, he moved to his eldest son's room, empty since his marriage. In fact, when Eugènia dies, he will sell this house. It's absurd to keep such a big house, built for a family of at least five. He tells his wife so, despite her not being able to hear him. He does what he has not done in years of marriage: explains his plans to her, taking into account the opinion she would express if she could. The good thing about being married to the same person for so long is that in eighty per cent of cases you know what they will say to you. Or what she would say if she were in control of her faculties.

He talks to her then about their son, who has come to see her that evening while she was dozing; about their daughter, who refuses to visit them because every time she does she breaks down in tears; and about their other daughter, the youngest, the most troubled, who shows up unannounced and leaves without saying goodbye. Octavi trusts his wife's opinion about her. Don't worry, she has always told him; there are people who find their path naturally and others who need to go round and round, step backwards to then suddenly advance. And when the time comes, Mireia will take a jump that leaves us all behind.

Once he has exhausted the subject of the children, Octavi goes on talking. After a few seconds he glances at the ceiling, as if he fears that having heard his confession, this predatory killer will switch victims and take him. As he took Gaspar and has taken Sara, leaving only that foul photograph as a note. And without wanting to, he remembers Gaspar's words when he came to see him, that phrase branded into his mind. 'We don't deserve anything else. We'll all end up like that, Octavi. Dead like dogs.'

The alarm clock, set for a quarter to six, announces the beginning of the day for Manel Caballero. He's always found it hard to get up; as a child he'd have given anything to put off the moment of returning to the real world. He hated classes with the same intensity with which he now hates the research lab where he works, not because of the job itself, but because it forces him to come into contact with people. If he had the choice, he'd work from home or, at most, surrounded by a select few. Intelligent, clean, quiet. The type that don't interfere in the lives of others. That is to say, practically no one.

Just as he does every day, he grabs a clean towel to dry himself and then immediately drops it in the laundry basket. He proceeds to dress himself with the clothes he left out ready the night before, and when he finishes he goes to the kitchen to make breakfast. Just coffee: at that time his stomach can't take anything solid. Before leaving the kitchen, he washes the cup and teaspoon, dries them carefully and puts them where they belong. He returns to the bathroom and brushes his teeth for three minutes exactly. He glances around and although not a single drop of water fell to the floor as he showered, he mops it meticulously. He likes to go knowing he has left the flat unpolluted, the bed made, the kitchen tidy. It gives him the strength to endure the worst part of the day: the journey on public transport to Alemany Cosmetics. Noisy people he has to share space with for almost forty minutes. He would have changed jobs just because of it: he had very seriously considered it, but the current situation doesn't allow for whims. Moreover, his job prospects have become much improved since the summer and he decided months ago that it is worth putting up with minor inconveniences like this. So every day he endures the journey like someone subjecting himself to a terrible ordeal. Isolated from everyone by headphones or a book; standing, because those plastic seats revolt him and because this way he can move if someone stands a little too close. He leaves home early for this reason, because he knows for a fact that the next bus is much fuller. He hasn't been able to breathe on the few occasions he's had to take it.

Today for some inexplicable reason the bus is half empty, so he doesn't have to pretend to read. If someone looked at him, they would never guess that this neat, clean-cut boy, dressed in unstylish but exquisitely ironed clothes, is thinking about his two colleagues who have died in a matter of months. His face reveals no sorrow or surprise. Rather an intense concentration, as if he were trying to solve an equation too complex for his abilities.

Manel doesn't see the email with the photo attached or the one that Brais sent in the middle of the night until he switches on the computer at work. His habit of being the first to arrive gives him a few minutes to evaluate the situation and weigh up the options. It doesn't take him long to decide: with a rapid click he deletes both emails and then empties the bin. His bin is once again clean like his flat. Free from the least hint of dirt.

Amanda Bonet, on the other hand, does look at her email at home, her personal and work accounts. In fact, it's the first thing she does every morning and the last before going to bed. Always in the hope of receiving a special message, one of those emails that fill her with excitement and make the night and waking up better. She's spent months like this, overcome with suppressed emotion, hooked on these messages and passionate weekly encounters. Happier than she's ever been, although perhaps 'happiness' is too simple a word to describe her feelings.

So, this Wednesday, Amanda follows her usual routine and her eyes acquire a special shine on seeing that there are four new messages in her personal account. Not because of the quantity, but because of one in particular. She looks at the senders of the other three: one is from a friend and another from Brais Arjona, and she tells herself she will answer them later, while the third is from an unknown address, with no subject. She deletes it without opening it for fear of a virus and concentrates on the only one that interests her. After the night she's had, plagued by atrocious nightmares she can't fully remember, she needs to communicate with him, and she can do so only through email. A cold medium, perhaps, but in any case better than nothing. She opens the message and smiles at the first line, an affectionate, encircling, protective greeting. She imagines him writing it in the middle of the night, thinking of her from his bed, composing this text while he evokes her in his memory.

She continues reading and, as always, she is succumbing to the effect these words arouse in her. It still astonishes her that he brings about this response from her body with words alone. Sometimes, very rarely, she thinks that these moments satisfy her almost as much as the Sunday-evening encounters. In any case, she knows the reality would have no meaning without this part of the game, in the same way that emails and text

110

messages would lack emotion if there were no moments of skin, touch, rewards and punishments.

She reads the message to the end, savouring every term, every bit of praise, every remonstrance and, above all, every order. He gives her precise instructions on how she should dress, comb her hair, smell. The underwear she has to wear. She sometimes disobeys him – it's an unwritten rule – although never too overtly. She appears to follow his orders to the letter and it arouses her to put on the skirt he has chosen for that day, dab on the perfume he wants to smell, or be aware that her lingerie, difficult for him to see at work, is not the required colour. The fact that they work at the same company adds the charm of disguise to the situation, the risk of illicit romance he accentuates on occasion with controlled daring. What's more, no one has noticed their games . . . No one knows about them, especially now Sara is dead.

She doesn't want to think about Sara. Suddenly she remembers the nightmare that terrified her tonight. The image of Sara running through the long metro tunnel, pursued by a pack of dogs. And her, Amanda, watching the scene like someone watching a horror film, suffering for Sara, trying to warn her that the worst is not behind her, but at the end of that damned tunnel. But it's useless: the woman fleeing without looking back didn't hear her no matter how much she shouted. 'Stop, Sara. No one is going to hurt you. It's not dogs, it's us.' Then she saw herself, with the others, running in vain through the same tunnel to reach Sara. She wasn't sure if they were following her to save her from her terrible fate or to see her die run over by a train.

LEIRE

12

She had been waiting for fifteen minutes and was beginning to get impatient, not because she had so many things to do, but because deep down she was afraid Carolina Mestre wouldn't turn up. She consulted her mobile to see if there was any message apologizing for a delay. Nothing. Dejected, she contemplated the herbal tea she had in front of her, and for something to do she took a small sip and made a disgusted face. The most insipid brew, matching the place.

She glanced around her, more and more convinced that Carol wouldn't come to the meeting. She had phoned her on Tuesday morning and, after a kind of monologue on her part, rehearsed to give the right impression, the other woman had hung up with a terse 'I've nothing to say to you.' Leire had marshalled all her patience and tried again a little later. That time no one answered the phone and she left a long voicemail. Almost a whole day passed with no response from Carol, but when she had already given up, a short, unfriendly text message arrived, asking her to meet in this café, on Wednesday at six. And there she was, in this city centre café with white walls and blackboards announcing things like brunch and blackberry muffins, her only company a languid, blonde waitress who seemed to think of her job as a necessary step before achieving fame, and another customer, a young tourist plundering the wifi connection for the price of a black coffee.

Leire flicked through a free magazine, full of photos and interviews with singers she didn't recognize and who, with few exceptions, looked like they'd been hungry for a good while. Her infusion was getting cold but she couldn't drink it. After the first trimester the nausea had given way to sudden foolish fads about a wide range of foods. At that moment she found the red fruits tea indescribably revolting. She told herself that she would get up and leave when she got to the last page of the magazine, and so she would have had she not received a message on her mobile, not from the person she was awaiting, but from Tomás. Asshole, she thought as soon as she saw his name on the screen. He'd shown no sign of life since New Year's Eve – that is, twelve days before.

How are you? I'm coming to see you this weekend. T.

Annoyed at herself because deep down she felt like seeing him, she was preparing to answer him when she heard someone clearing their throat nearby. She looked up and tried to change her irritated glare to a smile. Though she'd arrived almost twenty-five minutes late, Carol hadn't stood her up.

She'd only seen her once, at the station, just after Ruth's disappearance, and even then she'd been astonished at how beautiful she was. Very dark, even in winter, her whole body silently proclaimed her physical fitness. With an angular face and hair cut very short but stylishly, she couldn't help her expression and gestures having a brusque, almost belligerent air, as if she lived in a constant state of alert. Her dark eyes and long eyelashes expressed wariness, and her tone of voice was less firm than on the phone when, after requesting a Diet Coke from the apathetic waitress, she said, 'Well, go ahead.'

It wasn't a very promising beginning, and Leire was going to lumber her once again with the discussion she'd already had twice by phone when suddenly her patience deserted her. The tea she couldn't drink, the skinny waitress, Tomás's message and the recent arrival's indolent pose formed a kind of internal spring that made her lose her temper.

'Listen, if you don't want to talk to me, you don't have to. Really. This isn't an interview and I'm not here in an official capacity, so there is no obligation on your part.'

Carol raised an eyebrow without saying anything and looked at her intently. Then she shrugged and almost smiled.

'Calm down. Don't get upset, it mustn't be good for—'

'I'm not upset,' Leire lied. 'Or no more than anyone would be having spent half an hour waiting for a person who, to top it all, doesn't even have the decency to apologize when they arrive.'

Carol exhaled and looked away. The other customer in the café watched them, though only out of the corner of his eye. Leire grabbed her bag and made as if to get up.

'No. Don't go. I'm really sorry I'm late.' Carol spoke in a low voice. 'In fact, I arrived before you and saw you go in. I went for a walk, to think a bit . . . And in the end I was late.'

This is better, thought Leire. So she also softened her tone in her reply.

'What do you say we start again?'

'Well, go ahead,' repeated Carol, but this time the sentence was accompanied by a half-smile. And she immediately added, 'You said on the phone you wanted to talk about Ruth.'

'Yes. I know it seems strange. I'm not even sure I understand it, but . . . I have the feeling that this case wasn't dealt with in the best way.' She corrected herself before her listener could come to inappropriate conclusions. 'We were all too involved, Inspector Salgado especially so. And a lot was going on at the time.'

She stopped for a few seconds before finishing her reasoning.

'I'd like to take another look from a cooler perspective. And for that I must know things about her: what she was like, what she did . . . What worried her.'

Carol nodded slowly. Although a hint of uncertainty clouded her gaze, she seemed determined to give Leire a minimal vote of confidence, at least.

'I wish I could tell you what she was . . . is like. I don't want to speak of her in the past tense and I'm not exactly objective on the subject.'

'It doesn't matter, be as subjective as you like.' She understood that Carol wasn't given to confidences, so she decided to help her. 'How long were you together?'

'I don't know if I should tell you . . .' She wasn't looking at her; her eyes were fixed on the magazine cover.

'This is between you and me. I already told you, Inspector Salgado isn't aware of what I'm doing. And I want it to stay that way,' she stressed.

Carol exhaled.

'Héctor . . . God, how I've come to hate that name! Something about that guy, isn't there? There are men like that, who make the world spin around them. No, I know, they never ask for anything. They act as if they are self-sufficient, but at the same time they are screaming for help. Or that's the impression they give you . . .'

Leire took advantage of this road to approach the subject that interested her.

'Is that what Ruth thought?'

'Ruth has spent her whole life understanding Héctor. Not as if she were his mother, but in some reactions she seemed like his . . . I don't know how to say it. His elder sister. She was breaking free of this role little by little, although it took a great effort for her to do it.'

'When did you get together?'

'Officially, six months before she broke up with her husband. In reality the mutual attraction arose when we met each other. At least on my part, and bearing in mind how things developed, I'd say on hers also.'

'You were working together, right?'

'Not exactly. Ruth had spent years focusing on illustration. I don't know if you're aware, but it pays very badly. She'd had an exhibition as well, though not with much success. But I saw some of her work and I proposed using some of her designs in the field of interior design. At first I thought she was going to be offended: some artists shudder at the thought of "commercialization".' She smiled. 'But she threw herself into it with enthusiasm, as if it were an adventure, something that had never occurred to her. And with amazing results.'

Leire knew it. Over the last few days, among other

119

things, she had focused on reviewing Ruth Valldaura's designs. She had started with a home textiles line, but within a couple of years she had increased her collection to a great variety of objects, revealing immense creativity. If you searched for Ruth Valldaura on Google, in an instant a good number of shops, mostly in Spain, France and Italy, where her products were exclusively sold would appear. Not especially expensive shops, but all original, well chosen by the woman in front of her now.

While they were talking, the young customer had decided to leave the virtual world and return to his true occupation, that of a tourist, and the waitress was still standing motionless behind the bar, less beautiful than she believed herself to be. Leire was thirsty, but she was almost afraid to disturb the stillness of that sphinx by reminding her that she was there to do something useful. Luckily, Carol decided she needed something stronger than Diet Coke and Leire took the opportunity to ask for a bottle of water. Carol went to the bar and returned five minutes later with the water, a glass of red wine and an amusing expression of desperation.

'God, I thought she was going to break in half uncorking the bottle,' she said.

Leire laughed and drank half the bottle in one gulp. She was beginning to like Carol.

'I don't know what to do now,' Carol said thoughtfully, after taking a small sip of wine. 'I mean the flat, and the money that keeps coming in. I suppose I should speak to Héctor . . .'

'He's not a bad guy,' replied Leire. 'Really.'

'Ruth used to say that. When I got pissed off – excuse me – she'd always defend him. It's so hard not to be jealous of someone who has been with your partner for so long . . .' She went on before Leire had time to interrupt, eyes fixed on the contents of the glass: 'No, it wasn't that. It was her. You know something? Sometimes Ruth made you feel like you were the centre of the world. When you had a problem, when you were talking to her in the middle of the night, making love . . . But there were times her mind was far away, and then you realized you'd never be the centre of her life. Ruth was much more free than she believed herself to be. And whoever was at her side had to accept that position without hoping for more. Of course I see it now; at the time she drove me crazy. I lived in perpetual fear of losing her and I was striving to keep her.' She drank another sip of wine. 'I suppose she would have ended up leaving me. I never imagined I'd lose her in such a way.'

She hesitated before those last words. Carol didn't look like a person who cried in public, but the pain was imprinted in every gesture.

'What do you think happened?'

'I don't know. One thing is certain: she'd never have gone off for no reason. She was too serious, too responsible. And there's Guillermo also. At first I thought it was something to do with her ex. I know, I know, he's a good guy.' She sighed. 'I'm not saying he'd hurt her, although I admit I did suspect him. But as soon as I saw him, I knew that however much I hated him that man wouldn't be capable of such a thing. When something hurts you, you become more receptive to the pain of others.'

She took a last sip of wine. All that remained in the glass was a deep-red shadow, like a trace of blood.

'It had to be something related to him, anyway. With

121

his work, that man he beat up . . .' She looked Leire in the eyes, with an expression of absolute uncertainty. 'Nothing else occurs to me. If not, who would hurt Ruth?'

'Forgive the question, but are you sure there was no one else?'

'Can anyone be sure of that?' They both smiled. 'Not on my part, I can swear to that. Not even now, six months later. No one can compare to Ruth. Or even come close.'

Carol plunged into her memories for a few moments and Leire could almost feel nostalgia overwhelming the café, its blackboards and empty tables. Even the waitress, once again a pillar of salt, also seemed to evoke a lost love.

'I'd swear Ruth was faithful to me. I believe she'd have told me the truth. The months she deceived her husband were torture for her. I know it's a cliché, but it's the truth.'

'Was there ever a woman before you? Forgive my intrusion. It just seems strange to me that someone could discover their attraction to the same sex at the age of thirty-eight.'

Carol shrugged.

'I'm pretty sure I was the first, if that means anything.'

'You never asked her?'

'It's so obvious that you didn't know her. Ruth only said what she wanted to. And she was capable of leaving you speechless with only a look. Sometimes I used to laugh at her, saying she seemed to have been pulled out of an English TV series. You know, the ones with ladies and gentlemen upstairs and servants downstairs.'

Leire nodded. That aristocratic air could be seen in the photos of Ruth as well. Even in jeans and a T-shirt she was elegant. With her own style. In the bar a gentle music was playing, a sort of *bossa nova* to a jazz rhythm that filled the air with a murmuring, cloying melody.

'I don't know what else I can help you with. And I don't know if I want to continue talking about this,' Carol admitted, with honesty.

'I understand. Just one other thing – was Ruth working on anything new?'

'She always had something in mind. There are various files with sketches and loose drawings. They're still in her house, of course.'

'Would you mind if I had a look?'

She didn't hold out much hope; what she really wanted to see was the house, the place where the trail was lost.

'I have keys. I suppose it won't matter if you see them, although I don't see how it will help.' Carol sighed. 'I definitely have to talk to Héctor about all this. No, not about you,' she clarified. 'I mean what to do about the rent, Ruth's things, the money . . .'

The money. It was the second time Carol had mentioned the subject, and the untrusting police officer in Leire couldn't help noticing it. If she'd learned anything in her years of police experience it was that greed was one of the oldest emotions in the world. And one of the most lethal . . . In this case, however, and leaving aside personal impressions – she couldn't imagine the woman sharing her table killing for money – there was one obvious fact: Ruth was worth much more alive than dead. She was young, with a professional career of many years ahead of her, which would generate benefits Carol would share. Without the creative mind, the commercial half of this partnership wouldn't have anything else to sell. In spite of all this, she made a mental note to ascertain the financial state of the partnership they shared. The danger of any investigation, she knew, was to leave loose ends based on personal impressions or pre-conceived ideas. Anyway, she decided to concentrate for the moment on the possibility of seeing the space where Ruth had lived and worked. She wasn't sure that Carol wouldn't regret the offer if she didn't seize the moment, so she risked asking, 'Are you in a hurry? I was thinking it's not too late and we could go over to Ruth's house now, if it's not inconvenient.'

'Now?' Carol hesitated.

'Suits me.' She didn't want to insist too much, just enough. She perceived that she'd managed to build a climate of trust, of cooperation that evening, which might cool as soon as they separated.

She wasn't mistaken. Carol thought for a moment and then agreed.

'All right. I have the car in the garage and I have the keys. Actually, I still haven't managed to leave them at home.'

Leire didn't say any more. She paid the bill, ignoring Carol's protests, and turned to the door. The sooner they left, the fewer the possibilities for her companion to change her mind. Already at the door, while she was buttoning her coat – a type of shawl that according to her friend María made her look as poor as a Russian singer-songwriter – she looked at the waitress through the glass. In that café, so big and empty, she seemed an insignificant figure. She was still sitting behind the bar and at her shoulder rose a wall of bottles. A green slippery backdrop for that pale creature, with very red lips and plucked eyebrows, leaning her elbows on the white marble.

13

Empty apartments are like actresses in decline, thought Leire. Well kept, always awaiting the arrival of the person who gives them meaning so that they can once again become welcoming, lively spaces, they never manage to shake off a dusty, rancid air, an aspect of assumed neglect that repels rather than attracts. With grand dimensions and high ceilings, Ruth's seemed even more hollow, more abandoned. More melancholy.

It wasn't exactly a loft, more a hybrid between a studio and a conventional apartment. On one side was the sitting room and a breakfast bar that separated it from the kitchen; a prefabricated partition ate up a few metres: this had been Guillermo's room. On the other side, at the end of a long, rather gloomy corridor, it opened up into a square space, equipped to serve as a studio and also supplied with some plasterboard walls, which marked out Ruth's bedroom. In fact, it was like two symmetrical flats, linked by that corridor.

As if she perceived the poor impression the flat was giving, Carol turned on all the lights and somehow managed to enliven that cold space. Standing in the middle of the sitting room, Leire was perfectly capable of imagining Ruth and her son sitting on the brown leather sofa that leaned against a brick wall. She examined the size of the place, the brown beams furrowing the ceilings. A couple of large abstract paintings were a contrast to the sombre sofa, and an immense rug – one of Ruth's designs – brightened the wooden floor, which was crying out for a good polish. There were books piled in the corners, but the overall effect didn't create a feeling of chaos, rather a cosy disorder that emanates from places where people live calmly, relaxed, carelessly happy.

'The studio is at the end of the corridor. If you don't mind, I'd prefer to wait here for you.'

Leire understood. She was sure Ruth and Carol had shared more time in this work area, bedroom and bathroom included, than in the sitting room. From the little she knew of her, she guessed that Ruth valued her privacy; she couldn't imagine her cavorting with her lover, whichever sex, on the sitting-room sofa, beside her son's bedroom.

The studio was what you would expect of an illustrator. Two desks, one supplied with a computer and another, bigger one, resembling the one Leire had used in art classes at school; resting on it were stacks of files, all labelled. Ruth Valldaura was an organized person, no exaggeration. Sensible, thought Leire, not tolerating mess or excessive tidiness. She glanced at the pieces of work on the table, for the most part illustrations for a book of haiku.

The same elegance she displayed in the few photos Leire had seen of her came through in those drawings in simple but expressive strokes. Ruth spoke through her drawings: each one that lay before Leire told a brief story.

126

'Excuse me.' Carol's voice came from the other end. 'Are you going to be much longer?'

The question was the well-mannered translation of 'Can we go please?' and Leire decided to pretend she hadn't heard her for a few minutes. Then she realized that if she wanted to really look at all of it she'd need more time than she had just then. That's the worst of investigating off your own back, she told herself. She moved towards the big files on the ground, not really knowing what she was looking for or what they could contribute. Probably nothing . . . And yet part of Ruth's nature had to be reflected in her work, no doubt about that. Leire began moving the files and looking at the labels. Ruth's more commercial work didn't interest her; she was relying on finding something else, a more personal, more private trove . . . the designs an artist would do for herself, not to order.

Carol was insistent and this time Leire answered her with a vague 'Just a second, I'm almost done.' She was starting to get flustered and considered the possibility of asking for the keys so she could come back another day, when a small file, the kind used to keep receipts, appeared inside a much bigger one. It had no label, so she opened it and took a quick look inside. Leire had never had many scruples: she checked that it would fit in the enormous bag she was carrying, put it in and went back to Carol. She was so ready to go she didn't even pay attention.

They turned off the lights and went out to the landing. The door closed with a resigned whine, the assumed sadness of one who knew their best days were behind them.

Carol insisted on seeing her home and Leire barely protested, though what she was carrying in her bag made her feel like an ungrateful thief. They spoke little during the journey – there wasn't much to say – and when they arrived it was obvious the driver wanted to be gone as soon as possible.

'By the way,' Carol said before wishing her goodbye, 'I don't know what was going on with your phone when I arrived, but murderous desires won't make you feel better.'

Taken aback, Leire took a few seconds to react. She had completely forgotten Tomás's text.

'Well,' she said looking at her belly, 'it wouldn't be good to leave this baby fatherless so soon.'

Carol smiled and said nothing. From the pavement, Leire watched her leave and then headed towards her building. She went up in the lift, alone, thinking that for once it would be nice if someone were waiting for her at home. Perhaps the conversation with Carol was to blame: the love of others always provokes envy. And if there was one thing she didn't doubt, it was that this woman had lived a true love story with Ruth. Requited or not, it didn't matter. Carol had loved Ruth, and so had Héctor. To be honest, she wasn't sure anyone had ever loved her that way, and an enormous desire to know the object of these passions overcame her: to ask her what was her secret, her potion, her spell that managed to bewitch men and women so. And then she became firmly convinced, with no proof to support it, that the people who possess this charm unknowingly live in danger, because there's always someone who loves them from afar, or loves them too much. Or simply can't bear loving them that way.

Sitting on the sofa, Leire opened the file with the intimate feeling of committing a reprehensible act, all the more so because she certainly wouldn't gain anything useful from it other than satisfying her ever-growing curiosity about Ruth. Although maybe everyone would be equally interesting if their lives were examined under a microscope: details enrich even the most anodyne of existences.

Inside the file were drawings, receipts, exhibition catalogues, magazine clippings on various subjects, old photographs, piled up with no order or coordination. Leire looked through them all with the patience of a collector. Although those who knew her would confirm she was a woman of action, if there was one facet of her work that characterized Agent Castro it was her obsession with not leaving a single fact, a single link, without close examination. So, tired but not sleepy – by the end of the day her feet were so swollen she barely recognized them – she slowly sorted the photos from the drawings, the receipts from the scraps of paper with a phone number or address scribbled on them. A little later she had several distinct piles, and to eliminate them she began flicking through the pile of receipts and catalogues, which, as expected, contributed little information. That Ruth liked art and photography and design exhibitions she knew already. She moved on to the photos, because there were only a few. Computers have taken the place of photo albums, she said to herself, thinking of the ones her mother had at home. And instantly she remembered her mother had called her that afternoon, and made a mental note to get in touch with her first thing in the morning. If she didn't, the scolding might be epic.

There were some strange photos, she supposed taken by Ruth herself. A shadow on the floor, a drain, a cloudy sky. Of course there were a few of her with Carol, very few; and some even older, of Ruth and Guillermo and Ruth and Héctor. Leire paused a moment to observe her boss, younger but with the same sad-dog expression. Even when he was smiling. Beside him, Ruth was splendid, in one photo in particular; he looked at her from the corner of his eye, as if incredulous that this woman was at his side through anything other than luck. On the other hand, she was looking at the camera with the intensity of someone who is happy. There were one or two other photos of that same day, which had to have been five years before, because Guillermo didn't look more than eight or nine. A serious kid, resembling his father in his expression and his mother in his appearance.

Leire went through the family photos and noticed that, leaving those aside, only one much older picture remained. Two little girls in gymnastic leotards; the outfits and combed hair made them appear almost identical, yet looking closely Leire recognized one of them as Ruth, with a friend or classmate beside her. Luckily, the date was written on the back: Barcelona, 1984. Ruth would have been thirteen then.

The pile of drawings was next, some simple outlines and some more elaborate. One caught her eye because the girl who appeared in it was so like the girl with Ruth in the photo. Once again, Leire admired Ruth Valldaura's talent: some simple lines created a serious face, completely recognizable as such. In the drawing the little girl was somewhat older and dressed in a type of cloak. She was standing beside a cliff, looking down. Ruth had drawn her as if she were in front of her, as if she were suspended in the air or at the bottom of the precipice, observing her from below. Something in this drawing was disturbing, the tragic air enveloping the figure. There was something written underneath – Ruth's handwriting no doubt, but it took Leire some time to work out what it said.

Love creates eternal debts.

The phrase remained in her head as she attacked the final pile of paper: addresses and phone numbers, press clippings and such-like. She didn't expect to find anything, so when she saw the street name written on a scrap of paper she paid no attention to it. A few seconds later, however, her heart beat faster on recognizing on one of the scraps the address and phone number of Dr Omar's clinic.

14

The next morning, after a balanced, healthy breakfast, nothing like the doughnuts she used to eat a few months before, Leire emerged on to the street. It was cool, just as the meteorologists, who had spent a few days forecasting the arrival of real winter, had warned. Although she had left in plenty of time, once on the street she decided to treat herself to a taxi to her destination. It wasn't a visit she wanted to make at all, but she thought it necessary and, in contrast to what she'd expected, there had been no objection. Montserrat Martorell, Ruth's mother, was expecting her at twelve. She had only requested, in a tone that had little in the way of entreaty and much of warning, that Leire be punctual: her husband was in the habit of going out at that time every day and apparently 'it was better that he not be present as he gets too upset.' No wonder.

The taxi driver left her in Plaça Sarrià, very close to the pedestrianized street where Ruth Valldaura had grown up, an area that couldn't be more different from where she had ended up living. Despite the plaza itself looking quite ugly, the area was certainly pleasant, especially this street, which retained a village air, as if it were the main street of another, smaller, more select city, nothing to do with the rest of Barcelona.

Montserrat Martorell, Señora Valldaura, was as imposing as her name suggested, thought Leire, when the woman in question received her in the sitting room, which was the size of Leire's entire flat.

'It's too cold to sit on the patio,' she said, as if it were an indisputable truth.

The woman before her, mature but in no way old, looked her up and down. In ten seconds – Leire was sure – this woman had formed an opinion of her. Only her eyes had revealed slight disapproval when resting on her bulging belly, as if she thought it improper that a woman in her condition should go to strangers' houses. However, the expression lasted barely a second; then she smiled and adopted the role of hostess to perfection. She offered her coffee, tea or a cold drink, which Leire declined with extraordinary friendliness.

'Well then, go ahead.'

The phrase was more or less identical to the one that initiated the conversation with Carol, but on this occasion Leire answered with an elaborate explanation, the same she would have given to the headmistress in the school she'd attended if she'd had to explain not having her homework done. Señora Martorell listened to her attentively, neither interrupting nor making her task any easier. It was impossible to know what was going on behind those piercing grey eyes, too cold to be beautiful. Leire finished her soliloquy and awaited the verdict, but instead she received a question.

'And my son-in-law knows nothing about this?'

The fact that she still referred to Inspector Salgado

as her 'son-in-law', though not with excessive affection, didn't go unnoticed.

'It may seem strange, but no, he doesn't know. We thought it best.' She used the plural that always disguises controversial decisions.

'I beg your pardon,' Señora Martorell said after a silence that betrayed her doubts, 'I must admit that the way things are done nowadays astonishes me. My daughter's husband is a police officer and yet you are in charge of investigating her disappearance.'

Leire was sure that there were other things in this world which astonished her more, so she merely pointed out: 'Her ex-husband.'

Clearly not many people corrected Señora Martorell.

'Technically they hadn't started divorce proceedings. Didn't you know?'

'No.'

'Well, that's how it is.'

'You do know that your daughter was in a relationship with—'

'Of course,' she replied, not allowing her to finish the sentence. 'Ruth informed me of that.'

'Did you think it wrong?'

She hadn't meant to be so direct, but there was something in that woman that made beating around the bush impossible. Though Montserrat Martorell might be a woman of the old school, Leire guessed she preferred frankness to being handled with kid gloves.

'What does it matter what I thought? Listen, you don't know this yet: there comes a time when children go their own way. For better or worse, but they do it. And your role, like mine, will be to keep quiet and accept it. Sometimes it's difficult, and you have to bite your tongue on more than one occasion. Like everything, you learn in the end.' She stopped a moment to take a breath. 'Anyway, in answer to your question, I say no, I didn't think it wrong. Are you surprised?'

Leire's face must have looked puzzled, because Señora Martorell smiled.

'You young people, you think you invented everything. There have always been women and men who love those of their own sex. It's not a new thing for this century, believe me. What is new is that they do it openly; however, the deed is the same, isn't it?'

'Yes. But you must have been surprised. Just like that, all of a sudden . . . It would surprise my mother, for example,' she admitted sincerely. 'I don't mean she'd disapprove, but she'd certainly be surprised.'

'When your child is born you'll see how few of the things they do surprise you.' Her tone was so haughty that Leire became irritated in spite of herself. 'In any case, you haven't come to find out what I thought about my daughter sleeping with another woman, correct?'

Leire blushed, and hated herself for not being able to help it.

'No. I came because I feel I need to know Ruth better to find out what happened to her. And the relationship with family usually reveals a lot about people.'

'I suppose that's true,' admitted Montserrat Martorell. 'I should tell you that my relationship with my daughter was good. She didn't devote her life to us because I educated her that way: to be independent, to succeed, to find her own path. And I did it well.'

'And your husband?'

The woman made a vague gesture with her hand, as if that were a trifling detail.

'Husbands aren't much use when it comes to raising little girls. At least at first. They only know how to spoil them.'

Leire looked at the woman in front of her. Her seeming impassivity astonished her and she had the impression that it might be hiding a terrible evil temper.

'What do you think happened to her?'

'I think what happened is that you didn't do your job properly. Because, if you'd done a thorough investigation, we wouldn't be talking about this now. I think that my son-in-law, or my ex-son-in-law if you prefer, has been inept both in keeping his wife and in investigating her disappearance. And I think you should be ashamed of showing up at my home, half a year later, to ask me a heap of questions from which it can only be assumed you haven't the least idea of what happened to Ruth. Would you like to know what else I think? I think my daughter should never have lived alone in that *barrio*, I think this city is full of criminals doing as they please. No, it didn't matter to me that Ruth was sleeping with another woman. Or left her husband – he deserved it. What matters to me, what drives me crazy is that . . . is that to this day I don't know if I have a dead daughter or not. I don't know if I should weep or retain some hope. I don't know if—' She stopped herself, upset, and gave the impression of forcing herself to calm down. 'If you have nothing more to say, I'd like you to leave. My husband should be about to return.'

The answer had been so sharp that, even sitting down, Leire leaned backwards.

Leire stood up as quickly as her enormous belly allowed. Señora Martorell's telling-off was by far the worst she'd had in years. Perhaps it was due to wounded pride, or maybe it was about finding a dignified exit to this visit, but when she was already on her feet, she asked: 'You said before that no mother is too surprised by what a child does, and I assume by that you meant you knew Ruth well. Was there any other girl in her life? I'm talking about years ago, when Ruth was very young and still lived here.' She asked thinking of the little girl in the photo, the figure on the cliff, though with little hope of getting an answer.

Señora Martorell fixed her eyes on her, as if all of a sudden that pregnant young woman had finally said something sensible.

'Of course there was. Her name was Patricia, Patricia Alzina. She was in Ruth's rhythmic gymnastics class. And her best friend.'

'And what happened?'

Montserrat Martorell looked away, half-closed her eyes and answered in a neutral voice, less indifferent than she would have liked.

'Patricia died aged eighteen in a car accident. She was returning from Sitges after spending a few days at home. She was an inexperienced driver and lost control of the car. She came off the motorway in the Garraf mountains.'

GASPAR

15

With a brusque swipe, César turned off the car radio. On this part of the motorway, dotted with bends, there was constant interference and the half sentences put him on edge. Moreover, neither was he in the mood to be interested in a sports panel in which the commentators dissected the line-ups and analysed the shots with the same caustic tone the panellists on a gossip programme would use.

He needed silence. An absolute silence that would allow him to think about everything that was happening. About Sara, about Gaspar, the strangled dogs and, in another area, about Emma and the risk that spoiled brat posed to his relationship with Sílvia. Too many problems, he said to himself, as he moved into second to approach the next bend on the secondary road which led to the small town of Torrelles de Llobregat, where Octavi Pujades lived. All for him, thought César. He'd never understood people who complicated their lives by going to live far away from the city just to have a house with no neighbours, to enjoy this absurd peace which would end up destroying their nerves. He hadn't even arrived and already felt daunted by the return journey on this motorway through the forest. A forest hidden then by darkness, but which he guessed to be dense, threatening.

The headlights of another vehicle moving in the opposite direction warned him with a couple of flashes that he had his lights on full beam. He hadn't even noticed and changed them immediately. From then on he moved more slowly: he could see only a few metres ahead and this made him uneasy. He was a careful, cautious man and he'd learned the best way to go through life without unpleasant surprises was to take things calmly and prevent problems. See them coming. For this reason he was going to speak to Octavi behind Sílvia's back. There were few people César could trust, but the finance director was one of them. Because of his age, his knowledge, even his life experience, he considered his opinion worth taking into account. He trusted him much more than show-off Arjona, for example, among other reasons because deep down he'd never trusted those who deviate from the norm and also make a big deal about it. He wasn't a bad guy – each to their own in the bedroom – yet this fact traced an invisible line that, along with Brais Arjona's arrogant self-sufficiency, made him insecure. As if he were a vulgar individual, an anodyne, limited forty-something. And best not to speak of the others: Amanda was a child and the guy from the lab couldn't be any weirder. There was Sílvia, of course, and he'd spoken in full and at length about it all with her, to the point of exhaustion, but César had the impression that to clarify his ideas he needed to chat with an older, responsible man. Someone solid.

Suddenly a small animal crossed the motorway and

César swerved out of pure instinct. Damned forest, he thought. Damned shadows. Damned dead dogs.

He is too tired for the road. He has reached the steepest stretch and just at that moment the sky suddenly darkens. It's a cloud so sudden, so dense, that the day is extinguished before his eyes, as if in the presence of an eclipse or the effects of a biblical curse. Then, little by little, the sun recoups its strength to assert itself in the struggle and once again show its power. It is then, alone in the middle of the field extending as far as his eyes can see, that he realizes the wooden shed, the same one drawn on the stupid map they gave them in the house before leaving, is five hundred metres away. Beside a solitary tree, with a sturdy trunk and branches. César is puffing, tired, and notices his mouth filling with a bitter saliva, more like a Sunday hangover than a Saturday morning in the country. Fucking nature, he grumbles almost out loud. Fucking *team-building*. As if he hadn't spent years organizing human resources for the warehouse. As if these instructors would teach him anything he didn't already know.

He looks behind: his colleagues will take at least ten minutes to arrive, so he can stop there, as a mark of respect for the group and to take a rest. He's run too much, he thinks as he waits, satisfied by being the first to arrive. For once this weekend he's beaten Brais Arjona. It seems competitiveness is one of the few attributes that don't weaken after the age of forty.

Four and four, those were the directions the instructor gave them this morning. A quick draw. Eight numbered scraps of paper put into a bag: he, Gaspar, Manel and

143

Sara had taken out even numbers; Brais, Amanda, Sílvia and Octavi the odds. Each member of the team had been given various envelopes with clues marking two different routes with the same final objective. A real wonder of imagination on the part of the organizers, a cabinet of recruitment and development personnel earning money on every one of those envelopes as if the secret formula of Coca-Cola were hidden inside them. Well, here he is: a plain extends before his eyes and straight ahead, silhouetted against some dry, earthy mountains, is the damned cabin. Or the shed, or whatever the hell those four badly assembled logs are, where according to clue number seven, which Sara read aloud, the 'loot' is to be found.

A loot his team will reach, if all goes well, before Brais's. He doesn't understand why it pisses him off so much that the brand manager is shining on these away days, which really aren't important. But it does piss him off, a lot, that the previous day Brais Arjona turned out to be the fastest, most mentally agile . . . in short, the cleverest. Even beating Octavi and Sílvia in solving problems of logic – a diabolical form of entertainment dreamed up by those repugnant instructors. Then, what he'd been led to believe was a canoe trip, a purely fun, calm activity, had become a race when Brais, rowing with Amanda, had insisted on challenging him and Sílvia. She'd accepted, not thinking anything of it and, as expected, they'd lost spectacularly. In fact, halfway through their canoe had started to move in circles instead of in a straight line, and when they finally righted it and got to the opposite bank they'd had to endure Arjona's wolfish smile and Sílvia's own comment: 'I know who I need to go with in the next test.' Well fine, luck has decided she's on Brais's team, but that doesn't mean victory.

He hears footsteps and turns to the top of the trail. It's Gaspar, the finance-department guy, who, like him earlier, is climbing laboriously up the slope. César doesn't know him very well – that's one of the criteria the company considers when choosing people for these away days – but in the day and a half they've spent together he's been getting on well with him. The worst that could be said of him is that he's a little dull. Bland. He extends his hand to him to help him cover the last bit of the track.

'Hard going, isn't it?' he says, smiling. 'I hope they give us a good lunch.'

Gaspar nods, breathing easily, and squints in the dazzling sun. The cloud has moved and is now above the shed, tingeing the depths of the scenery a stormy grey-blue. It's a beautiful sight: a furious sky about to unleash repressed rage over a simple cabin. On the right, defining that sort of country picture postcard, is the tree. Immense, unshakeable. Stormproof. Gaspar Ródenas, who has binoculars he has brought from home hanging around his neck, brings them to his eyes to enjoy the view.

'What a cloud. Have you seen it? Fuck, all of a sudden it's gone dark. Now it seems to be moving away. I think we should go to the hut and see what's there before—'

César stops. Gaspar is not listening to him, but has let out an exclamation of extreme surprise. He takes the binoculars away from his eyes and blinks. Then, without saying anything, he puts them to his eyes once again and adjusts the image, as if he is seeing something shocking.

And then, before he can ask him what the matter is,

César hears voices to his left and sees that Arjona and his group are moving diagonally towards the hut. Sílvia turns to him and waves, and César, not really knowing why, feeling like a schoolboy, starts running in the same direction. Brais, for his part, sets out on the race, followed closely by Amanda.

César wants to stop. He knows he'll lose – they are closer and faster – and that his humiliation will be greater for having tried when there was no chance, but he can't help it. The only thing that could make him more ridiculous would be to trip and fall flat on his face. And suddenly he notices his right foot is tangled in something sticking up from the ground, a treacherous root just there to fuck him over, and his whole body is propelled forward. Having foreseen it, however, helps him to cushion the fall with both hands, which just then affords some small comfort to his ego, more battered than his poor knees.

He stays still on the ground for a few moments, and hears Gaspar's voice, more upset than normal, saying to him: 'César . . . César, are you all right?'

It takes him a little while to answer. He is ashamed to raise his head from the ground and face Sílvia's smiling or, even worse, compassionate expression, but when he does he meets neither. In fact, no one is looking at him. The other four, and Gaspar too, appear hypnotized by something in the tree. When he looks towards it he understands why.

Dogs are hanging from its branches. Three, as far as he can see. Ropes have been put around their necks and they move, suspended like ornaments from a profane fir tree.

'Was finding the house difficult? Sometimes at night it can be hard to navigate these towns if you don't know them well.'

Octavi Pujades received him dressed in a blue track-suit, which he wore with the same grace as his office suit.

'Well, just a little,' answered César, who had spent twenty long minutes going in circles on a road of de-tached houses all alike until he found the one he was looking for. He felt obliged to add, 'Octavi, I'm sorry to turn up here like this.'

'Don't be silly. You haven't shown up without warn-ing, and, anyway, I'm happy you're here. I feel very dis-connected from everything these days.'

César nodded.

'How is she?' he asked, still standing in the hallway.

Octavi Pujades shrugged his shoulders.

'I don't know what to tell you. In June the doctor gave her no more than six months to live and here we are almost halfway through January and still the same. I suppose it could happen any time . . . But go through, sit down.'

The sitting room was a big, comfortable space, with no obvious luxuries but well furnished with colonial-style pieces. César was grateful the fire was lit, as the temperature had started to drop. There, although they were only a few kilometres from Barcelona, it was much colder.

'Would you like something to drink? I'd offer you a whisky, but then you have to drive.'

César thought of the bends in the road and shook his head.

'I have alcohol-free beer for visitors,' suggested Octavi, smiling. 'Sit down, I'll bring you one.'

César watched him go towards the kitchen and thought it would be better for death to take his wife before he was consumed by the job of taking care of her. He found him older, bags under his eyes. Octavi Pujades wasn't yet sixty, but the last half-year had aged him ten years, César told himself. If he compared him to the man who had participated in that damned team-building weekend, which had taken place in March of the previous year, the whole of him seemed to have shrunk. He was thinner and the weight loss was noticeable above all in his face: his cheeks sharp as corners and his eyes sunken, black as stubbed-out cigarette butts.

'Here, do you want a glass?'

'No need. Thanks.'

'Cheers.'

They drank and contemplated the fire for a few seconds. Octavi put the beer on a wooden side-table and took out a cigarette.

'You don't smoke any more, do you?'

César was going to shake his head; but he changed his mind. He'd given up smoking when it became serious with Sílvia, who profoundly detested the smell of tobacco. At that time he believed that whatever happened with his relationship, giving up wouldn't do him any harm. 'I only smoke the odd time,' he said, also taking a cigarette.

'All this stuff about health and tobacco is nonsense,' affirmed Octavi. 'Eugènia has never tried a cigarette in her life. Anyway, you have to die of something.'

The last sentence wasn't especially reassuring and César, who'd just taken his first drag in almost eleven months, had a sudden attack of nausea. How could he have liked something that tasted so bad? And yet at the same time the flavour was like meeting up with an old friend, one you've known so long you'd forgive them anything. The second drag felt better. He took another gulp of beer before resolving to speak.

'You know why I've come. Sílvia is very anxious. Well, I suppose we all are . . .' The cigarette felt strange in his hand and he left it in the ashtray. A fine column of smoke rose between them.

'No wonder. The Sara thing was a terrible blow. Killing yourself in such a . . . bloody way.' He shook his head as if he couldn't believe it.

'Yes, although it's not just that.' César chose his words carefully. He didn't want to be alarmist. 'When the Gaspar thing happened . . . Well, I thought it would all end there. But now there are two: two deaths in little over four months, two people who were there that weekend. And then there's the photos.'

Octavi continued smoking slowly. The brightness of the fire was reflected on his tired expression when he spoke.

'Did you really think Gaspar would be the end of it?'

César took a breath and looked away.

'He came to see me, did you know that?' Octavi commented. 'At the end of August, when he had only a couple of days of holiday left.'

'And what did he want?'

'I thought he wanted to talk about work, of course. He was going to replace me officially until . . . until this whole thing with Eugènia is over. And we all know that my early retirement is coming, so in a couple of

149

years Gaspar would have been the financial director of Alemany Cosmetics. That weighed on him a little . . .'

'And I suppose having to deal with Martí Clavé weighed on him too,' César suggested.

The other man shrugged.

'Clearly Martí expected to be chosen. He's older, he's been with the company longer . . . He was my natural replacement.'

Neither of them made any further comment. Octavi leaned towards the ashtray to put out his cigarette and César noticed his hand was shaking a little.

'But it wasn't just that . . . I mean he didn't just come to talk about work. He was . . . How can I put this? Upset.'

'And remorseful as well, no?'

Octavi sighed slowly, as if there were still smoke in his mouth.

'I calmed him down as much as I could. I also assured him he was prepared for the job. That he deserved it . . . I don't know if I convinced him, although he gave me the impression that he left a little calmer. Then, barely a week later, I heard about what he'd done. I suppose he was weaker than we thought.' He paused and asked again: 'Did you really think the Gaspar tragedy would be the end?'

'Maybe I was kidding myself.' César slowly shook his head. 'What I never thought for a moment was that it would affect the others so badly. Sara, for example.'

'We agree on that. And maybe – I only say maybe – it will end here.' Octavi Pujades leaned forward and lowered his voice. 'César, the worst thing we can do is panic. Up to now, yes, there have been two suicides. A

150

young man who lost his head and killed his family, and a sad secretary who was fed up of being alone. That's what I think, and what everyone will think. Both of them working for the same company is simply a coincidence. At least neither of them revealed anything.'

'That's what Sílvia says. But what about the photo?'

'That's another matter. Only one of us could have taken that photo. That is, you, Sílvia, Amanda, Brais, Manel or I, of course. Do you remember who was carrying a camera that day?'

'Not me. Sílvia, I think. And Sara too. I'd say almost everyone. Also you can take photos like that on mobiles.'

Octavi nodded.

'Of course. I hadn't thought of that. I show my age in these things . . . The photo. And that command: "Never forget."'

'Have you forgotten?' asked César. 'Because I haven't. For a few months, yes. Not that I totally forgot, of course, but . . . it faded. Like those confessions that come out when you're drunk. With time, they lose importance, and, in the end, they're forgotten.'

Octavi smiled and took another cigarette.

'I'm not sure that's a good example, César.'

'I suppose not . . . Though it doesn't matter. It's not what I came to discuss with you. We have to work out a plan.'

'Sílvia told me on the phone you're meeting tomorrow, just as Arjona proposed in his email. I don't think I can attend, but I'll agree with whatever the majority decides.'

'That's why I came to see you. Sílvia is in favour of continuing as we are, and the truth is I couldn't care less about what the others think. Even Arjona, not because he's an idiot, but because I don't trust him an inch. I really want to know what you think.' He said it sincerely, almost begging.

Octavi Pujades slowly exhaled smoke. César seemed to hear a groan proceeding from the depths of the house.

'It's half past eight. In a moment I'll have to give her morphine. It's all I can do for her: alleviate the suffering.' His tone changed and he looked César in the eyes. 'I don't know if I have a very clear-cut opinion on what should be done. What I do know is panicking won't help at all. That must be made clear. And, César . . . if I were you, I'd trust no one. No one,' he repeated.

16

'Speak to his mother,' his landlady Carmen had said that same morning as they had breakfast together. Héctor Salgado trusted this woman's instinct more than all the police reports written up by conscientious experts. 'Think about it – she was his mother, but she was also a grandmother. She had to know if her son was capable of something so horrible.'

Héctor disagreed. He was certain that maternal affection could cause a kind of permanent blindness to filial defects. That it wasn't the case with Carmen, who recognized that her Carlos was a layabout who out of sheer laziness didn't get into deeper trouble, didn't mean that the same applied in general terms. Even so, there was reason in her argument: Gaspar Ródenas's mother was grandmother to Alba, whom officially he had smothered with a pillow while she slept the same night he shot his wife dead. All before shooting himself.

The police reports left little doubt about how the events had unfolded, although they contributed few certainties as to why. That's if a thing like that could be explained in a rational manner, something Inspector Salgado tended not to believe. The how, the sequence of events which led to the killing of the family, seemed clear. Halfway through the month of July, Gaspar Ródenas bought a pistol. Héctor's colleagues in the domestic violence unit had followed this lead with relative ease to the seller, a small-time thief who dabbled in gun-running from time to time. There was no proof of whether Gaspar informed his wife or not. All Susana Cuevas's family lived in Valencia, and although they had spent some of the holidays together, the daughter visiting from Barcelona hadn't mentioned it. This isn't the States, thought Héctor. Here people don't usually have pistols at home to protect themselves, much less a young couple with a little girl, living in an apartment in Clot, where the chances of this weapon being useful were nil.

So it was more logical to assume that Gaspar hid the purchase of the pistol from his wife. According to the report, her family had thrown little light on the case. They were so devastated by the tragedy they could barely speak. They simply said that Susana was very happy with her daughter, Gaspar had been promoted recently and to all appearances at least they were getting on well. It was clear that the family's attention had focused on the little girl, whom they saw very seldom. 'He must have gone mad,' Susana's elder sister, who had been with them in Valencia, had said. 'Su told me he was a bit stressed about the new job. But it was just a comment and she said herself it was "a question of time" and he'd get used to it.'

No one kills their family just because of a problem with stress at work, Héctor said to himself. He was sure about that. In any case, continuing the chain of events, on the evening of 4 September Gaspar Ródenas had arrived home around 7.45. A neighbour passed him on the stairs and, as usual, they greeted one another. The building where Gaspar and his family lived was made up of only six flats, two doors on three storeys; the Ródenas lived on the first floor. A lady in her eighties, rather hard of hearing, lived on the same floor and the flat above, until then occupied by a family of 'darkies' according to the same neighbour, had been empty since they returned to their own country. The other neighbours were on holiday. The man who had passed him that night from the right-hand flat, second floor, thought he'd heard noises in the middle of the night but hadn't for a moment suspected they were shots.

The person who found them was Gaspar's sister, María del Mar Ródenas, who went to see her niece on Saturday at noon, just as they'd arranged. 'Gaspar wasn't answering his phone, but as I'd promised them I would come, I went anyway. I thought they were busy with the little one . . . And, well, the fact is Susana never picked up when we called. But when I arrived and they didn't answer the bell or their mobiles it did seem strange. To be honest, I was a bit annoyed. I work almost every Saturday, at the Hipercor in Cornellà, and Gaspar knew I was looking forward to having lunch with the little one on the one Saturday I was free each month.' María del Mar returned home, it must be assumed pretty pissed off, given that it was at least a forty-five-minute journey by metro from L'Hospitalet, where she was still living with her parents, to Clot. She kept calling all afternoon and finally, seeing that her brother was still not responding to her messages, she took the set of keys Gaspar had left at her house and returned to the flat. 'I'd never done that, gone in when they weren't there. And I was sure Susana wouldn't like it, but I didn't care. Something wasn't right . . . I just wanted to reassure myself that nothing had happened.'

It will take that poor girl a long time to forget what she saw, thought Héctor. It pained him to have to remind her of it, yet there was no other way. If he wanted to understand Gaspar Ródenas, know what he was like, work out what had led him to commit such an atrocious act, he had to speak to his family. He'd thought of doing it the day before, but Savall had once again brought him into a meeting with Andreu and Calderón all afternoon. So he'd finally arranged a meeting with María del Mar at five precisely, in a café close to the town hall of the area where she lived. She wasn't Gaspar's mother; nevertheless, for the moment she'd have to do.

It was a big noisy place, and the clientele at that hour, made up largely of business people of the area, gathered around the bar. Or, with the anti-tobacco law having recently come into force, in the street, smoking while retaining the flavour of coffee in their mouths.

Héctor had gone alone, leaving Fort two tasks: to establish what Sara Mahler was doing at Urquinaona metro at that time and, while he was at it, to gather information about Alemany Cosmetics. He'd planned to approach the company the following day, Friday, to see Sílvia Alemany and, if possible, the other colleagues who appeared in the photo. In some way, that image of eight people in hiking gear was connected to that other disagreeable one Sara Mahler had received on her mobile. Two pieces which could form part of the same puzzle or not, thought Héctor. And the analogy made him think of Superintendent Savall – a huge fan of jigsaw puzzles – with whom he'd have to discuss the case sooner or later. Tomorrow, he thought. Before or after going to the cosmetics lab.

María del Mar was waiting for him at the door. They entered the bar and looked for an empty table at the back. Luckily for them, there was more than one, and they chose one in the corner which ensured them at least some privacy.

Héctor waited until the waitress had served them their drinks and spent a few minutes breaking the ice. María del Mar – 'Please call me Mar' – had studied education and for a few months had been a cashier in some big department stores in the area. She'd been unemployed since November. According to what she told him, so was her fiancé. He was named Iván and had worked in construction until the previous year; all he'd been able to find since then were 'a couple of odd jobs with his cousin'. Minor work, pay that was a thousand euro if he was lucky . . . At twenty-seven, both were still living at the homes of their respective parents, since, just as they were preparing to rent a flat, Iván was out on the street.

'I don't know if we'll get to marry one day,' Mar said sadly. 'But you haven't come to hear my troubles, Inspector. Is there something new in the case of my brother?' She asked nervously, as if within her she was nursing the suspicion that Gaspar Ródenas was still hiding sins yet to be uncovered.

Héctor decided to be as honest as possible; the last thing he wanted was to raise hopes in a case officially closed.

'In all honesty, no.' He chose not to mention Sara's death. 'I'm just trying to find out a bit more about your

157

brother. To close the case with a better explanation than "fit of temporary insanity", if possible . . .'

It was a fairly implausible explanation, but Mar seemed trusting by nature, so she said nothing and waited for the inspector to continue speaking.

'There were a few years between you and Gaspar—'

'Ten.'

'I suppose you wouldn't know his friends . . .'

'Well, I knew the ones from the *barrio*, but Gaspar left them aside as soon as he started going out with Susana.' She smiled faintly. 'She and I didn't get on very well.'

Héctor had guessed something of the sort on reading Mar's statement, and he told himself that a good way of getting to know Gaspar's personality through his sister was by delving into these differences and the relationship between the couple.

'How long were they together?'

'I don't know . . . five or six years. Wait . . .' She did a mental tally. 'Yes, five years. They married the year I finished studying; they'd only been going out a few months.' She smiled. 'They decided quickly.'

'And they got on well?'

'Yes, she organized things and he went along with it. It's one way of getting on well, I suppose.'

'Was Susana a bossy woman?'

'More than bossy, she was one of those who sulked when things weren't done her way. So Gaspar tried not to contradict her. In the end, he'd convinced himself that the only correct way to do everything was exactly as Susana said.'

'And you didn't get on with her?'

She looked around her. It was a fleeting, almost invisible move.

'It's horrible to speak ill of the dead. And even more so in this case . . . The truth is, no: I didn't get on with Susana. I didn't care that she bossed my brother around, that was her business, but the way she treated my parents made me really angry. Especially after Alba was born.'

'Did you see the little one often?'

'Often?' Mar shook her head. 'My mother almost had to request an audience to see her granddaughter. It was never the right time. I feel awful saying that . . .'

Héctor knew. It was a common reaction; but in an investigation there was no room for consideration towards those no longer here. On the contrary, their secrets had to be brought to light, their faults unravelled, their mistakes aired. The victims had lost their lives and with them the right to privacy.

'What do you think happened?' asked Héctor.

'I don't know. When I went in . . .' She trembled and lowered her eyes, as if she had that scene before her once again. 'When I went in I thought it was the work of a thief. You know, one of those gangs of Romanians that rob flats.'

She looked on the verge of tears so Héctor asked if she wanted to stop for a minute. She shook her head. She had lovely dark hair and a tense expression, but it was precisely that expression which rendered her neutral features, too correct to be beautiful, attractive. Mar Ródenas, like her brother, belonged to that immense group of people neither handsome nor ugly. They lack intensity, Ruth always used to say about that type of person. However, in circumstances like these, repressed emotion gave them strength and something resembling beauty.

'I knew you were coming to talk about this, Inspector,' she added, looking at him. 'You know something? My home is like a cemetery and my parents dead people walking. My parents . . . God, graffiti appeared on the door of my father's workshop a week ago. "Killer. Son of a bitch" it said. As if he was the killer! My father, poor man, who never even raised his voice to us . . .'

Héctor's expression darkened. Yes, this was another consequence in these cases: incomprehension, indiscriminate insults.

'Don't they realize we've lost a son, a brother? A grandchild?'

Mar couldn't hold back any more and burst out crying. The sobbing wasn't restorative, but bitter. Furious.

Héctor suddenly felt bad. He hated this part of his job, torturing souls even without wanting to.

'We'll leave it at that,' he murmured.

'I'm fine. I'm fine.' Mar grabbed a paper napkin and dabbed at her face. 'Where were we? Oh yes. What I saw.' She cleared her throat before continuing. 'My brother was in the dining room, with his head on the table. The pistol was on the floor, beside him. I thought he was alone because I couldn't hear the little one. It's ridiculous, but that's what I thought. I went running towards Alba's bedroom, and passing the bathroom I saw the door was open: Susana was lying on the floor, on her back, with a bloodstain on her nightdress. And then I knew Alba had to be at home as well.'

She was speaking as though in a trance.

'Alba was in the cradle, in the bedroom next door.

160

She hadn't been sleeping alone for long. For a moment I sighed with relief seeing that there was no blood. She's asleep, I thought. Whatever had happened, she's asleep and doesn't know anything. I took a step towards the cradle and tripped over something. A pillow. And then I realized she wasn't sleeping. That you couldn't hear anything in that room. That she too . . .'

She closed her eyes and was unable to go on. Her hands were shaking. Héctor thought she looked even younger than she was.

'Just one more thing,' he said in a low voice. 'Do these photos mean anything to you?'

He took the two photos from the inside pocket of his jacket and put the one of the work group in which Gaspar appeared on the table. Mar looked at it. Her face altered a little on seeing her brother, but she shook her head.

'I think he came to the funeral home,' she said, pointing at the older man, the one Héctor hadn't yet identified. 'He was my brother's boss but I don't know his name. He was with a woman, although I don't remember her very well.'

Before showing her the photo of the dogs, Héctor asked: 'Did they find a note in your brother's house? Or anything like one, by any chance?'

'There was nothing . . . The police already asked me. They took his computer and everything . . . Then they returned it to us. My father threw everything away.' Then she looked at the photo and repressed a cry of disgust. 'What is this? What does it have to do with my brother's death? It's horrible.'

'I know. Don't worry, it's nothing. It's a loose end I haven't managed to explain,' said Héctor. He didn't want to give away any more information and felt even worse because of it, so he ended the conversation there.

They went out into the street and Héctor inhaled deeply, as if he'd emerged from an airless well. He remained in the doorway for a few minutes, smoking, as he watched Mar walk away. At the corner a boy was waiting for her and without saying a word put his arm around her shoulders, as if wishing to console her. At least she isn't totally alone, thought Héctor, throwing the cigarette on the ground, something he detested but which seemed the only solution when obliged to smoke in the street.

If he'd remembered the address correctly, the garage owned by Gaspar Ródenas's father should be in one of those streets in the centre. Héctor found it without difficulty and spent a few minutes standing at the door, looking inside. He didn't know if it was worth going in and speaking to the owner, and he was almost on the verge of leaving when a man came out of the garage and lit a cigarette. He was a man of about sixty, and, judging by his appearance and his hands, he'd been working for more than forty. Not really knowing why, Héctor approached him and asked for a light. Smoking is an unhealthy ice-breaker, he said to himself, remembering he'd just stubbed out a cigarette less than ten minutes before.

'Are you Señor Ródenas?' he asked as he returned the lighter.

The man pointed to the garage sign, but did so with a glance of distrust.

'Excuse my bothering you,' continued Héctor. 'I'm Inspector Salgado, and—'

'What do you want?' The question sounded almost hostile.

'Maybe it's not a good time, but I'd like to talk to you about your son.'

Señor Ródenas smoked in silence. Héctor was going to add something else when the other man spoke without looking at him.

'Do you have children, Inspector?'

'One.'

'Then you'll understand. I raised mine to know the difference between good and bad. So I can't believe Gaspar did this. I'll never believe it. I don't know what happened, but I know it didn't happen as they say it did.'

He threw the butt into the street and turned around. From inside he pulled down the shutter without another word. On the metal some traces of the graffiti could still be made out, a reddish shadow, accusatory and unjust.

17

Sílvia Alemany looked in the car's rearview mirror before turning the engine on. God, if the face was the mirror to the soul both were in need of a professional make-up artist. In the end that's what we do, she thought, as she manoeuvred out of the company car park. Falsify souls. She could make a list of their products: rejuvenating creams, nourishing creams, anti-oxidant creams . . . Whichever: their effect on the face was at best circumstantial; the inner face, the one that really mattered, aged with no remedy. It would crack, it would dry up and there was no balm or salve that could prevent it. Because of that, wrinkles reappeared, because of that, businesses like theirs went on being necessary. At heart they were like Dorian Gray's picture: they relegated old age, evil and decay to that internal secret face, maintaining the visible one relatively young, beautiful and pure. But the picture was there, crouching within you, ready to betray you when you least expected it.

Her car merged into the many vehicles entering Barcelona at that time of the evening. An army of obedient, industrious beings retiring for a few hours, who would the following day make the opposite journey. As tired and bored in the mornings as by night: the epsilon men of 2011 who'd found happiness in buying on hire purchase. She smiled ironically at the thought that she at least had the pleasure of being something resembling an alpha woman for a few hours. A kind of queen consort, necessary and appreciated and slightly feared.

The queue of cars stopped and Sílvia was taking advantage of it to put on some music when her mobile rang.

'Hello?'

The hands-free disorientated her: she always had the feeling the other person couldn't hear her.

'Mama?'

'Hello, sweetheart. I'm in the car.'

'Are you coming home for dinner?'

'I don't know. There is food at home, isn't there?'

'Yes of course. But Pol says he's starving and he fancies pizza. If you're not coming, we could order one.'

The car behind beeped the horn, impatient. Sílvia realized the traffic had moved a few metres forward.

'I'm moving, I'm moving . . .'

'What?'

'No, not you, Emma. I'm in a traffic jam.'

'Well, can we?'

Sílvia hesitated.

'No.'

'But Mama—'

'I said no. Emma, there is chicken in the fridge. And pasta salad I made yesterday. If I'm not back in an hour, make dinner for yourself and your brother, sweetheart.'

For a moment there was silence. Then she heard Emma's voice: docile and polite.

'All right. I already told him you wouldn't say yes. Don't worry about the time. I'll take care of it.'

'Thank you, angel. Listen, I'll see you at home; you know I don't like talking while I'm driving. A kiss, and tell Pol not to argue.'

'A kiss, Mama. See you tonight.'

Sílvia blew an imaginary kiss to her daughter. If only everyone was like Emma, she thought proudly as she turned on the car radio. She was sure dinner would be made and the kitchen tidied when she arrived. She had raised her well – not an easy thing nowadays. Few girls of sixteen were so responsible, so trustworthy. If in the end she went abroad to study Second Baccalaureate, she would miss her a lot. Emma still hadn't decided but she couldn't take too much longer. And this wasn't the only thing Sílva had to attend to. The wedding, for instance. However simple the ceremony would be, there were a number of things to be done . . . She took a breath. She was in no mood to think about celebrations just then. She had even considered the possibility of postponing it, but she didn't know how César would take it. And despite rarely admitting it, the truth was she wanted to marry him. Have someone in the co-pilot's seat, empty for years. He wasn't the love of her life. Thank God, she'd beaten that, as if it were the measles, and been immunized for ever. She found something else in César: respect, company now the children were beginning to fly the nest . . . She was sure he was a good man, someone she could trust who, at least, loved her as much as she did him.

You've become a cynic, she thought. Cynicism wasn't good for the soul, but it was necessary for survival. Sílvia had had to swallow many things when she returned to face her father. Yes, the old man had helped her: he supported her while she finished her degree, left half-finished when she scarpered. He'd given her a role in the company, although he'd made sure her brother, the good twin, would be the true heir. Old hypocrite: lots of moral lessons only to end up dying of a heart attack in a Cuban prostitute's bed. Fortunately, Víctor was easy to manipulate, and she'd acquired large reserves of cynicism over the years so that she didn't say aloud that her brother's mediocrity would have sunk the company if not for her, steering from the shadows, avoiding unnecessary expenses and crazy risks. Luckily Víctor, deeply infatuated with that idiot Paula, had stopped being involved in company affairs, leaving them in her hands more and more.

He's getting a good deal, Sílvia told herself, but in exchange she'd gained something else that was better compensation than money: exercising power. An addiction she wasn't planning to give up.

That very afternoon, for example. She was leaving when Saúl, her second in command, told her Alfred Santos wanted to see her. The lab's technical director was a friendly guy, with an easygoing manner, one of those men who caused few headaches. Because of that she'd received him immediately. If there was anyone who deserved attention it was Santos; he certainly wouldn't disturb her over trivialities.

It really wasn't trivial. An indignant Santos, more angry than she'd ever seen him, spent a long half-hour setting out the faults, conflicts and problems that Manel Caballero was generating in the laboratory. So many, and in Santos's opinion, so serious, that he'd decided to fire him. In fact, he would have done it some time before had it not been that the lab assistant's attitude and words hinted that if necessary he could turn to higher powers than his direct boss and thereby make him look ridiculous in front of the whole department. Sílvia had had to muster all her diplomacy to keep the idiot Caballero in his post. After a good spell of excuses and reasoning that seemed to be lifted from the cowardly business person's manual, Santos had looked her in the eyes and blurted out: 'You're not going to fire him, are you? He's right: I have no say.' And for once in her life, Sílvia Alemany hadn't known what to say. 'I don't know what the fuck is going on around here lately, but I don't like it. Suicides, assholes who think they're the king of everything and managers who seem incapable of managing sensibly.'

To hell with it, she thought as she accelerated to cross an orange light only to have to stop ten metres on. She had to speak to Manel Caballero and she'd do it that very day, as soon as the meeting in César's house ended. They'd all be there: Amanda, Brais and the asshole, as Alfred Santos had called him. Octavi couldn't attend, as she'd imagined, but generally he was on her side. And of course, Sara and Gaspar wouldn't be there. Sara and Gaspar. Gaspar . . .

She'd never have believed that it would be Gaspar Ródenas who would have a crisis of conscience. She'd have expected it of Amanda, for example. She was so young, so innocent, and at the same time belonged to that group of creative people who in her opinion dealt with the general business of life in a very impractical way; the perfect combination to suffer remorse or apply mottoes that appear in calendars beside photos of sunrises. But no: Amanda hadn't shown the least sign of worry, perhaps because the only thing young and innocent about her was her appearance. That almost virginal, unpolluted, luminous beauty . . . Like Dorian Gray, Amanda seemed immune to the evils of the world.

No, it had been Gaspar who had stood in her office after the summer, weighed down by a feeling of guilt from which he couldn't free himself. Gaspar, the pragmatic, honest and upright accountant; the father of a family with most to lose. Sílvia had turned to her powers of persuasion, all her ability to convince. She even resorted to a veiled threat in a clear demonstration of that cynicism now part of her character and, subsequently, almost without blinking, went from reprimand to praise: 'You're very important, we count on you, don't let us down, I rely on you so much . . .'

'We're a team, Gaspar. I understand, believe me. But you gave us your word – we made a pact. I'm sure that you are a person for whom giving their word means something, isn't that right? At the moment we've all behaved like gentlemen. And I find it difficult, no, I find it painful, to think that someone as honourable as you wants to go back on his word, retract what he promised his colleagues and consequently lose everything he's gained in the name of . . . of what, Gaspar? Of what exactly? Do you really think it's worth it?'

A brilliant, twisted argument as false as a Christmas wreath. Appealing to solidarity from a position of authority, distorting concepts like honesty and responsibility, and placing the other person in a position in which, freely, by their own will, they decided to do as she asked, not to obtain any benefit from it but because they felt it was how it should be. In the company, as in life, friendliness generated deeper debts than imposition. Sílvia knew it and used it, especially with weak or insecure people. This couldn't be applied to Brais Arjona, for instance, although neither was it necessary. Brais understood that they were all in the same boat and he either paddled in the same direction or sank with them. It seemed with Gaspar she hadn't found the right carrot, and the result, that family tragedy, was something she preferred not to think about.

She saw a tight space in which to park and, as the rules demanded, she signalled her stopping and began the manoeuvre. She was about to get out of the vehicle when her phone rang again. Number withheld. She answered out of habit, although she was sure it was one of those promotional calls from some communications company.

18

Héctor caught the metro at L'Hospitalet station to go towards Plaça Espanya, the same line Sara Mahler had chosen to end her life. Standing as the train moved through the tunnel, he focused on observing the passengers. At that time the majority were workers or students returning home after the working day. Buried in freesheets or concentrating on their mobile phones, the carriage emanated fatigue, the disillusion of monotony. A girl was shouting into her mobile: she was shamelessly arguing with someone and no one seemed to pay any attention. We are in an ever more autistic world, thought Héctor. He was brought out of his musings by the entrance of an older lady into the carriage, weighed down by a heavy trolley she could barely drag. There was no free seat and for a few minutes the lady leaned on the trolley, tottering, until a young man sitting to his right saw her and signalled to her to take his seat. The passengers in front of the old lady blatantly turned their heads.

The young man remained standing, near Héctor, and greeted him timidly. The inspector suddenly remembered: this boy was Nelson, or Jorge – he couldn't remember which – the older brother who had come back to the platform to return Sara Mahler's mobile on *Reyes* night. Héctor loved this provincial facet of Barcelona, a city that wasn't as big as it liked to believe.

'How are you?' asked Héctor.

The boy shrugged his shoulders.

'Life is hard,' he said by way of an answer. He looked at Héctor as if he was surprised to see him here, in a metro carriage. 'Have you found out anything else about that woman? The one who jumped on to the tracks . . .'

'Not much,' replied Héctor.

'Well, I'm getting off at the next station. Don't worry, my brother won't be getting into trouble again.'

'I'm sure he won't.' Héctor smiled. 'But don't let him out of your sight just in case.'

The doors opened and Nelson, or Jorge, nodded and got down on to the platform.

As soon as he arrived at the police station, Héctor knew Agent Fort had news for him. He hoped that playing poker wasn't included among his subordinate's hobbies, because he'd never manage to hide a good hand.

'I've been going through Sara Mahler's bank transactions,' he told him, faithful to his habit of explaining the whole process through to its conclusion. 'Generally they're pretty routine, direct debits and little else. A standing order to the Hera Women's Association caught my eye. I have to investigate it. However, between October and December, Sara withdrew some significant sums of money. Here are the details.'

It was true: two hundred euro one day, one hundred on another occasion, two hundred and fifty just before Christmas. In itself it wasn't anything strange, but judging by previous bank statements Sara was one of those who preferred to carry very little cash, and took out twenty or thirty euro a few times a week.

'There's more: she spent five hundred euro in a jeweller's on 22 December and another hundred on an underwear set.'

At first sight, it was clear that in the last few months Sara had spent more than three times her usual amount. Lingerie, jewellery . . .

'What do you think?' asked Héctor.

'I'd say there was a boyfriend or friend around . . . which would explain why Sara was in Urquinaona station at that time of the night. Maybe she'd met him . . .'

And maybe he'd stood her up, thought Héctor.

'Any idea of where she'd gone that night?'

Glum, Fort shook his head.

'No, and I don't know how we can find out, to be honest. We've asked in all the surrounding restaurants and bars and no one remembers having seen Sara. We haven't found her on the CCTV cameras in the area either. Unless this boyfriend turns up and tells us . . .'

'Strange that her flatmate didn't notice anything.'

Fort smiled thinking about Kristin. That girl was too busy to interest herself too much in Sara's life. He was going to say so when the telephone on the desk rang. He answered the call then looked at the inspector.

'I think you can ask her yourself.'

In the corridor, accompanied by a friendly officer in uniform carrying a box, Kristin Herschdorfer appeared, carrying another cardboard box, smaller but equally heavy.

'Hello,' she greeted them, somewhat nervous on finding herself in a police station. 'I've brought Sara's things.'

Fort blushed a little.

'There was no need for you to come. I offered to pick them up from your house myself.'

Kristin raised an eyebrow, as if that wasn't what she had understood.

'Well, it doesn't matter. My friend brought me to the door in the car.'

'Is this everything?' asked Héctor.

Two boxes couldn't really contain all of Sara Mahler's belongings.

'Oh, no. Just what was in her bedroom. The clothes are still there. I don't know what to do with them. And some of the furniture must be hers, of course. I think you'll have to speak to the owner of the flat. I'm moving out at the end of the month.'

Héctor nodded.

'By the way, but did Sara tell you anything about a new friend? Did she tell you she had met anyone special lately?'

Kristin shook her head. Her eyes lit up with genuine curiosity. 'Did she have a boyfriend?'

'Possibly,' was all Héctor said. In fact, he wasn't really sure of anything.

'If so, she must have met him on the internet. He never came to the house, at least when I was there.'

'Did you spend much time at home?'

'No,' said Kristin. 'My friend didn't like Sara much. He said she used to . . . spy on us.'

'One other thing: did Sara ever mention the Hera Association?'

Kristin's face made it clear this meant nothing to her.

'Okay,' said Héctor. 'Thanks very much, Señorita . . .'

'Herschdorfer,' she said, smiling. 'I know it's a tricky name. Oh, another thing. Not sure this is important, but the other day, when you left, I remembered Sara did have a visitor one day. A girl from work.'

Héctor took the group photo from his pocket. 'Is she one of these?'

Kristin studied the photo for a moment.

'Yes, this one. She was really very beautiful.'

Amanda Bonet, Héctor said to himself.

'If they worked together it's natural they should be friends,' added Fort.

Kristin looked at the agent and shrugged.

'Actually I only saw her once. When I first moved in, that's why I'd forgotten.' She sighed, as if she wished to erase Sara and everything about her from her mind. 'My friend is waiting for me outside.'

'I'll see you out,' offered Fort.

She rewarded him with a radiant smile.

'That's nice, thanks. By the way, do you speak Catalan too?'

Héctor didn't understand why the question made Roger Fort go red to the roots of his hair. He saw them walking away and couldn't help smiling, but his expression froze on seeing Dídac Bellver appear and pass Fort and the Dutch girl, almost running into them. He marched towards Héctor with the force of a locomotive and, judging by his face, in a seriously bad mood.

Ten minutes later, shut away in his office, Héctor was still at a loss to understand his colleague's rage.

175

'You have no right to interfere in my work,' Bellver repeated for the nth time, pointing his index finger a few centimetres closer to his colleague than necessary.

'Look,' replied Héctor. He was leaning on his desk, and fast losing his patience, 'I swear I have no idea what you're talking about, so it might be worth explaining it better.'

'Come on, Salgado, don't give me that. This air of innocence might work on others, but not on me.'

Héctor began counting backwards, from ten to zero, a basic technique for remaining calm; but, when he got to five, he was sick of counting.

'No fucking air of innocence, Bellver. Do me a favour and tell me what this is about, or get out of my office.'

'Yeah right, you don't fool me.' He inhaled and dropped the bomb, like a gob of spit. 'Maybe it wasn't you who asked Sergeant Andreu to take out your wife's file from my archives?'

Héctor was so taken aback that for once he had no answer.

'You don't expect me to believe Andreu did it off her own bat? Come on, Salgado, I wasn't born yesterday.'

'I swear I don't know anything about this,' Héctor repeated very slowly.

Bellver's face was disbelieving.

'What the hell are you looking for, Salgado? If you want to know something about the case, come and ask me. Don't send your henchmen to do the dirty work.'

'I don't give a damn whether you believe me or not, I'm telling you for the third and last time: I have nothing to do with this.'

'Well, you should.' Bellver's sentences were running

into each other. 'You should give a damn, Salgado, because you're not always going to be as lucky, you know that? Anyone else would have been given the boot. I don't know why they keep you here.'

'Maybe because I solve cases?'

It took Inspector Bellver a few seconds to react.

'What are you implying?'

Héctor knew he'd pay dearly for what he was going to say, but he'd wanted to say it for a while.

'I'm implying that if people are judged by results, your department's score wouldn't be so great. I'm implying, though you might not like it, I haven't the slightest need to swipe Ruth's file to see your progress, because I bet you anything there isn't any. And I'm also implying that you'd better not break my balls if you want me to stop implying and—'

'And what? You'll split my head open like you did the black's?'

They were so close to one another that they could feel each other's breath. Héctor started the countdown again, determined not to lose his temper completely. For his part, Dídac Bellver must have decided likewise because he retreated to the door. Palm on the knob, he said, 'This isn't over, Salgado. I swear. I'm starting to think maybe you have more to hide in this case than I supposed.'

'Get out of my office.'

Bellver wasn't finished yet.

'At first I assumed it was just the disappearance of a grown woman who was emotionally unstable—'

Héctor leapt up as if the desk had propelled him forward.

'Ruth wasn't emotionally unstable. Don't you dare say that again.'

Bellver laughed. Fucking hyena, thought Héctor.

'Well, call it what you will. But it must fuck you up, right? Your wife leaving you for another lady.'

He would have hit him. Carried on till he'd wiped that smile off his face, had it not been for Roger Fort opening the door and giving them a serious look. It was as if a blast of cold air capable of putting out the fire had entered with him.

Bellver murmured something under his breath, and Salgado nodded. Agent Fort stood aside a little so Inspector Dídac Bellver could leave.

'Thank you,' Salgado said to Fort. This time he did look him in the eyes.

19

'Now what are we going to do?' asked César.

During the entire meeting he'd sensed that Sílvia was anxious to be alone with him, to tell him something, but he'd never imagined that the matter would be so serious.

She didn't answer. She seemed absorbed in contemplating the rug, a cheap IKEA thing with a coffee stain in one corner.

'Sílvia,' he repeated, taking a step towards the woman who usually had an answer for everything, 'are you listening to me? I don't understand why you waited until they'd left to tell me. It affects them as well. It affects all of us.'

She turned towards him and for a second César didn't know if the look of disdain on her face was directed at the dirty rug, the flat in general or exclusively at him.

'Don't be stupid. Don't you realize that one of them is behind all this?'

They, that is Brais, Amanda and Manel, had arrived two and a half hours before, as agreed. Brais Arjona was the first to knock at the door but, luckily for César, Amanda appeared shortly afterwards. Manel was second last and,

179

submerged in an uncomfortable silence, they all focused on waiting for Sílvia for fifteen long minutes, an eternity that César would have broken with a cigarette if he'd had one. As far as he knew, none of those present smoked, so he swallowed the pang with gulps of beer. At least Brais joined him; Manel and Amanda had refused his offer with a visitor's forced friendliness, and he had no other sort of drink in a fridge that was never full any more. When Sílvia finally arrived, surprisingly late, César exhaled deeply, as if he'd been holding his breath the whole time or was expelling the smoke from an imaginary cigarette.

'Sorry,' she said, in a tone César didn't wholly believe, 'this area is terrible. I couldn't find a parking space.'

All five were seated around a central table: three on the sofa, with Brais in the middle, Sílvia in the adjacent armchair and César on one of the chairs he'd brought from the dining-room table. No one said anything, out of inertia or nerves; it was Brais who opened fire with the desperate question that a little later, in an almost empty sitting room, César would also ask.

'What are we going to do?'

César sought Sílvia's complicity with his eyes, but seeing she wasn't game he decided to speak up. Their position was clear: they'd spoken about it to the point of exhaustion over the last two days.

'We're here to decide between us all, aren't we?' And after a few seconds, 'By the way, I went to see Octavi the other day. He couldn't come, but he'll go along with what the majority agrees.'

'How is his wife?' asked Amanda.

It was an absurd question, because they all knew how

Octavi Pujades's wife really was. And because they hadn't come together there to exchange small-talk.

César was going to answer that all was going as expected when Manel Caballero interrupted him, turning to Sílvia.

'Excuse me, are you feeling all right?' He was the only one who spoke so formally to her at this level, perhaps because he was a bit younger, perhaps because in his day-to-day work in the lab he scarcely had anything to do with her.

They all looked at Sílvia Alemany, who was indeed very pale, as if something were making her ill.

'I'm fine, thank you,' she said, the colour returning to her face as she spoke. 'And I'd feel a lot better if I didn't have to defend you to your boss every minute. Don't look at me with that face, Manel, you know what I'm talking about. In a situation as delicate as this, the last thing we want is for someone to stand out, don't you think?'

César hid a smile. That was the real Sílvia: the woman who took the initiative, undaunted. Who expressed herself firmly and with conviction.

'Brais has asked a question and I want to answer him with another,' she continued, now in charge of the situation. 'What options do you think we have?'

She waited a few seconds for everyone to process the question. 'That night we came to an agreement, which some at least, and I include myself here, have strictly adhered to. It seems necessary to remind you that up to now no one knows anything of what happened up there. The police closed Gaspar's case and I am sure they will do the same with Sara's if we don't lose our nerve.'

'But . . .' Amanda interjected, 'what happened to them? Why did they die?'

The directness of the question left them all speechless. Amanda had spoken softly, as she usually did, and César felt obliged to give her an answer.

'I know Gaspar Ródenas was very depressed but I was still shocked he would do such a thing. With Sara . . . Maybe it was an accident or maybe she fainted at the worst moment.'

'Come on, César, let's not beat around the bush,' Brais replied. 'As far as I know, you haven't bugged this room, have you? Then let's speak candidly.' He paused. 'Up there we made a pact, as Sílvia pointed out. And Gaspar Ródenas immediately regretted it; we all saw that and tried to convince him to keep his word. Am I right?'

'That's right,' conceded Sílvia.

'With Sara, I think it's a different story. At least I never saw the slightest sign of depression or remorse in her, although I must admit she wasn't an easy woman to read.'

'I totally agree,' said Amanda, almost without thinking, and everyone turned to her. 'I mean she was very reserved, an odd one . . . It was impossible to know what was going through her head.'

It was fairly obvious that the explanation didn't reveal all Amanda had wanted to say, but she didn't elaborate. Unconsciously she pushed up the sleeves of the jacket she was wearing then rolled them down again.

Brais, who was beside her, decided it wasn't the right moment to insist.

'That said, there is the possibility that, like Gaspar, Sara couldn't handle the pressure. Or it was simply the straw that broke the camel's back. She never seemed a happy woman to me.'

César looked at Sílvia: they had planned to steer the conversation, yet Brais was calling the shots and in a manner that, at least up to that point, matched their own intentions. She nodded almost imperceptibly.

'I don't wish to be cold, but what is worrying me, the reason I proposed we meet today, isn't really Gaspar or Sara, but those damned photos. Who the fuck is sending them? And what are they playing at? Because it has to be one of us.'

Brais threw a direct glance at Manel, perhaps with intent or perhaps just because he was sitting beside him. In any case, the lab analyst reacted, offended.

'Hey, if you're implying I spend my time sending those things you're wrong.' He was blushing and his voice was a little sharper than normal. 'I got the email as well. I believe the only person here who knew nothing about this until I mentioned it was Amanda.'

'I delete half the emails in my inbox without opening them,' she replied forcefully. 'But if I were sending a photo like that I'd have made sure to send it to myself as well. I'm not so stupid, you know.'

'Hey, hey, let's not get upset here,' César intervened. 'Before we start accusing each other, there's something you haven't considered, Brais.' He obviously took great pleasure in pointing out something the other man had overlooked. 'Clearly only one of us could have taken that photo, God knows why. Perhaps they showed it to someone, or shared it with a friend . . . That wouldn't be so unusual: what we saw was a huge shock.'

They all denied having taken it.

'It didn't even occur to me to take a photo and I haven't told anyone about it,' Amanda explained. 'Maybe Sara did it . . . You saw how upset she was about the animals.'

Brais finally spoke up in his characteristically decisive voice.

'Be that as it may, these messages show that someone wants to remind us what happened. And we all know that the dogs are just a symbol. My question is: why? What the hell do they want?'

No one had an answer, or seemed to have, so Sílvia plunged in once again, although she had to wait a moment while a mobile rang – Amanda's – who hung up without answering.

'Let's be logical, Brais. We don't know why, so the practical thing is to drop it and decide what it is we're going to do. Look, I'm sure it won't be long before the *Mossos* turn up at the lab, even if it's just a routine visit. After all, two people linked to the labs have died within five months. They have no reason to suspect anything else, but they'll come to see us because of Sara. They did when the Gaspar thing happened—'

'What Sílvia means,' César interjected, 'is that we must act normally. Really Sara's suicide has nothing to do with us.'

'And if they ask about the photos?' Manel enquired. 'We don't know if she received one as well. Mine arrived some days after her death; maybe the person sending them sent one to her before. And another to Gaspar.'

'Like a kind of death sentence?' César wanted to sound sarcastic, but didn't quite manage it.

'Well, I'm certainly not thinking of jumping out the

window, or shooting myself,' declared Brais, 'so they can keep sending photos to me for ever.'

'If they ask about the photos we tell them the truth,' said Sílvia. 'We have nothing to hide. We found those poor greyhounds, or bloodhounds or whatever they were, hanging from a tree and we did more for them than most people would have. And if, as you say, there is a moron who photographed it and is using it now to play a joke on us, I don't think it's very important.'

As she said it, it seemed as though she meant someone to take it personally; however, no one considers themselves a moron, thought César.

'We haven't considered Octavi,' Amanda said. 'Maybe, with all that's happening to his wife—'

'Octavi would never betray us, Amanda!' Sílvia cut her off. 'I'd like to be as sure of everyone as I am of him.'

Amanda coloured, an unconscious act that somehow made her even more beautiful. Even Brais, not sensitive to female beauty, had the urge to protect her.

'Are you accusing me of something?' she murmured.

'I'm just saying that, if this comes to light, some of us have more to lose than others. But I want to remind you of something: we all share the responsibility; the pact was unanimous.'

The terminology almost made César laugh. Pact, responsibility, unanimous.

'Let's not move away from the point,' he said when Sílvia cast him a withering look. 'Are we all agreed on what we're going to do?'

Although César didn't like the expression, the group renewed the pact.

*

185

'Don't be stupid. Don't you realize that one of them is behind this?'

Sílvia's question hung in the air, stinging like an insult.

'It doesn't have to be that way,' replied César, although it was obviously a fairly reasonable explanation.

'Oh no? Then how did they know what we did?' She wasn't annoyed at him, but she needed to blow off some tension.

'Are you sure it was a man on the phone?'

'I'm not sure. The voice sounded strange, as if they were chewing something. What are you thinking?'

'Manel came late, a little before you.'

She exhaled, somewhere between beaten and furious.

'I don't care who it is. I don't plan on giving in.'

'Then he'll go to the police. He has proof, he told you so! He sent us the photo!'

Sílvia took her time before answering.

'I don't think he'll do it,' she said finally. 'At least for the moment. Going to the police would end all his hopes . . .'

'And then?'

'He told me that if I don't deliver the money, someone else will die on Monday.'

César looked at her, incredulous. Could this be the woman he planned to marry in a few months?

'That changes everything, Sílvia, don't you realize? For the love of God, we have to go to the police and—'

She grabbed his arm.

'Don't even think about it.' She spoke very slowly and with every syllable she squeezed more tightly. 'We'll do nothing at all. Understand? Nothing.'

20

The 09.10 AVE left Atocha station on time, filled for the most part by businessmen and women, who, laptops in hand, took advantage of those three hours to work, or at least to look at the screen with intense concentration. Stuffed into their combat uniforms, they threw bombs in the shape of incendiary emails or studied the best plan of attack. Or at least so Víctor Alemany saw them that Friday morning. He was in an especially good mood. Exultant, almost. Although in his outward appearance he wasn't so very different from those other soldiers, inside he knew his war was about to end, settled with a victory as profitable as it was glorious.

It had been an intense week, the culmination of other sporadic meetings which had begun months before. However much Octavi advised prudence, the whole negotiation had been so long, so irritatingly unending, that by the end of the summer he was on the verge of resolving it by accepting the offer without further delay. And what Víctor wanted above all was to start again, with Paula and without baggage. Without a family business glued to him, a parasitic Siamese twin, for as long as he could remember. For years he'd believed that this had to be the centre of his existence: directing the company, moving it forward, making it grow. Something which, contrary to general opinion, he had done. And what for? So his life could change only outwardly: a bigger car, more expensive suits, some absurd journey to a seemingly exotic destination. Boring, indeed, his reality had been until he met Paula. He smiled to think that it was precisely thanks to the company and their new campaigns that he'd ended up meeting Paula de la Fe. He didn't even recognize her face, since he watched little television and very few soaps. Maybe because of that he treated her more naturally, maybe because of that she noticed him. Or maybe not. It didn't matter. The result was that he and Paula were together, that boredom was a thing of the past and, little by little, he'd begun really to live, rather than breathing, eating, sleeping and even fucking mechanically.

At forty-something, Víctor Alemany had fallen in love as only frustrated forty-somethings and ugly adolescents do: wholeheartedly. He wanted to travel with her, spend the day with her, and had he been a monarch of the feudal era he would have laid his kingdom at her feet. Now and again he was seized by a fear of going too far, of throwing away everything that had been his life until then, that this euphoria overwhelming him in the mornings until it almost made him explode was the prelude to a freefall. In these moments he thought of his father, dead in the bed of a young whore not because he was overindulging, as Sílvia said, but because his body wasn't accustomed to enjoying itself. The heart also rusts, thought Víctor, but he had reacted in time. And once this organ started up, there was no enemy fire that could stop it.

The decision to sell Alemany Cosmetics sprouted from a conversation with Paula, when for the first time in his life he confessed how bored he was. And being younger, she gave him an answer that glowed with clarity: 'It's your company, Víctor. You're not obliged to work there. You can choose.' Choose – a word not much used in the Alemany house and always in a negative sense. His sister, for example, had 'chosen badly' years back and had suffered the consequences. He, though, whom his father often rebuked for his indecision, had carried off the prize.

Clearly the moment had come to choose, or at least to consider the possibility of doing so . . . He'd sought advice from Octavi Pujades, of course, and he'd tried to repress this desire for a change that threatened to overwhelm him at a time when the economic situation made good offers and hasty decisions suspect. Prudence, moderation, *sense*, reasoned arguments which lost their grounds when Octavi's poor wife was diagnosed with cancer, condemning her to an early death. From that day on, Octavi Pujades could do no more than give him information on their basic proposals, although he still made him keep the negotiation absolutely secret and be cautious in his dealings with those seemingly heaven-sent investors weighed down with cash. Taking advantage of Octavi's leave, they'd been able to meet numerous times with the future buyers unbeknownst to everyone, especially Sílvia – not that she had the authority to prevent a sale, but the pressure from his sister would have been an added burden to the whole affair. Only the ill-fated Sara could have suspected that her boss and the finance director were up to something, but Víctor was sure of his secretary's loyalty.

Now, thought Víctor, he couldn't postpone speaking to Sílvia any longer. He'd been on the verge of coming clean with her at Christmas, and it was more from laziness than fear that he hadn't, because they'd almost closed the deal. But Octavi had advised him to wait until January, until this last meeting he'd just had, and Víctor came to the conclusion that there was no harm in that, in pretending a little longer, even if it made him feel bad. Like the company dinner, his final act, that pantomime he'd played out like a consummate actor.

And it was in thinking about that event that his memory – that fickle, treacherous faculty – decided to capture the thread going around in his head since the inspector with an Argentine accent had shown him that horrible photo, and linked it to another memory with the force of a punch.

'Every woman wants to feel beautiful.'

The voice of Víctor Alemany, managing director of the laboratories that bear his name, easily dominates the room, despite the statement sounding pompous, out of touch with these times to some ears. However, those present keep their disapproval to ironic expressions, immediately hidden beneath a mask of polite attention; all that can be heard is the odd throat being cleared, the sound of a spoon scraping a dessert plate. Almost a hundred people, in one of the lab rooms effectively converted into a dining room for a night, prepare to listen to the speech, or pretend to, at least. It's part of the tradition: every year there is a company Christmas dinner, every year the director speaks for a few minutes, every year they applaud respectfully at the end. Then the party, if it can be called that, goes on without further interruptions. So it might be said that the majority of faces observing Víctor Alemany show some interest, the same with which they would listen to the father of the bride who insists on toasting the happy couple. No one expects him to say anything interesting or original, but you have to smile and nod.

On this night, however, after the initial six words, the lights go down little by little until the room is dark and a reproduction of a painting is projected on the wall behind Señor Alemany. A woman with white skin and long blonde hair – so long she partly covers her nudity with it – balances on a large shell floating on a calm sea. To her left, suspended in the air, a pair of winged gods embracing each other – they could be angels, although everyone knows they are sexless – blow her blonde tresses with their breath and, on the other side, a woman dressed in white holds a pink cloak, ready to envelop the recent arrival, as if her beauty is too extreme for mere mortals. Everyone recognizes this image, although there are those who'd have problems getting the exact name of the painting or artist. In any case, it's not an art-history exam, and another image is immediately superimposed on the previous one. It's a detail of the same woman, the face of the same golden-haired Venus. Her honey-coloured eyes have a lost look; the complexion, although slightly pink-cheeked, is of an unblemished alabaster; the mouth, remains closed, unsmiling. The woman is a stranger to her surroundings. Young, timelessly beautiful.

'The canon of beauty has changed over the centuries.'

Víctor Alemany pronounces his second sentence of the night, an obvious remark which at least is not politically incorrect. It heralds a series of beautiful female faces projected onto the wall with backing music. They follow no chronological order. The serene bust of Nefertiti alternates with the sensual, wild face of an adolescent Brigitte Bardot, and a calm Renaissance madonna gives way to the face, almost Machiavellian in its attractiveness, of Snow White's stepmother. No one knows who made the selection, but the first impression is that whoever is responsible has a marked preference for blondes. It's almost a relief when suddenly Grace Jones's shining ebony face appears and most of those present recognize her as the grave voice of the soundtrack. Shortly afterwards the projection finishes and for an instant those present hesitate over whether they should applaud or not. Someone begins, timidly, and others follow. The attempt at applause is halted by Víctor Alemany, who, though acknowledging the gesture with a nod, raises his right hand, like a political leader who knows the best is yet to come.

'For years, we have focused on offering women the chance to feel beautiful, the illusion of recovering lost youth. And, more importantly, at a reasonable cost. Our brand has been synonymous with quality and a good price, and it's these two basic concepts that have carried us for more than six decades.'

He then begins the classic discourse, the one everyone was expecting at the beginning. The one that covers the birth of the company. He goes over the past year: it has been a turbulent period, of restructuring, of change. At the table closest to Víctor Alemany, two people look at each other. Amanda Bonet and Brais Arjona are aware that they've been part of these changes:

new faces in a company with a history of more than half a century.

The MD continues: difficult years are approaching, no one will be left untouched, but he's sure they are prepared for the new challenges. The company has made risky decisions, yes, although with a particular vision in mind. The new line of products is already in the market. AC/Young. Those most involved in Young know what is coming. The ad was filmed just before the summer, so the models are lightly tanned. Alfred Santos is the first to come on screen to present the line: soft creams for young skin, an area of the market Alemany Cosmetics hasn't specifically targeted up to now. Skin that doesn't need a firming cream, but one that gives it radiance. Also, as Víctor Alemany is well aware, their public objective goes further, because many women between thirty and thirty-five still feel young. So Brais Arjona chose Paula de la Fe, who had achieved a certain notoriety playing the role of a teacher involved with a student in a soap opera, as model for the photos of the whole line. Paula is twenty-nine, although in the series she has just finished her degree and has a youthful appearance. What neither Brais nor anyone from the team could imagine was that their boss and Paula would begin a relationship which contributed an unexpected and, in Sílvia's opinion, frivolous celebrity to the brand. Víctor would have liked Paula to be with him tonight, but in the end Sílvia's opinion prevailed – 'This is a company dinner' – and he's decided not to argue with his sister.

The report continues with Amanda, who could well be the model for the campaign, speaking about the packaging design, moving away from the classic pot that evokes mumsy creams. After her, Brais Arjona, brand manager for the Y line, explains the marketing concepts: youth, innovation, freedom. All mixed together in the campaign presented by a Paula de la Fe who's just woken up, obliged to go to work after a night of partying, the ravages of which are rapidly diminished by a light coat of After Hours, the star product of the range. While she applies the product, a tired but happy Paula with bags under her eyes hums the chorus of a Supergrass song; finally, when the mirror reflects a perfect image, the song is turned up to full volume.

At the end of the presentation a friendly and almost sincere applause can be heard. Víctor abandons the role of orator and, before returning to the table, to his sister, to the others, he decides to go to his office for a moment and leave his notes there. He walks quickly; speaking in public has always made him nervous.

Before entering his office he sees a light in Sílvia's and moves closer to the door. It is ajar. Víctor is astonished when, pushing it open, he encounters Sara.

'Sara! What are you doing here?'

Sara Mahler, always so efficient, seems embarrassed. And awkward, because, as she stammers that she suddenly remembered that Sílvia had asked her for some papers, the file she was holding falls from her hand. Her boss, friendly, makes as if to help her, although she ducks and scrambles to pick up the contents. But something catches Víctor's eye, although at that time he attaches no importance to it.

A photo in the country, a mountainous landscape. Víctor barely has time to distinguish the image of a tree, seen from a distance, and even less to notice something hanging from its branches, before Sara, efficient once again, puts it into the file and leaves the office with a simple 'Come, Víctor. The host shouldn't absent himself from the party.'

21

In little more than twelve hours the rumour about the argument between Salgado and Bellver had spread throughout the station; and, in barely another hour, it would reach the high-ups. Héctor had appeared at his place of work at eight in the morning and en route to his office he'd already noticed the odd sideways look, an interrupted conversation. He was sure that he'd have to bring up the subject with the super at some point, but he had another hour of peace before that chat could take place. Enough time to look over the Ródenas and Mahler files for the last time before going to Alemany Cosmetics, although he harboured few hopes that this visit would give him anything useful. The autopsy on Sara Mahler, routine given the circumstances, didn't contribute any information that would suggest that the victim hadn't jumped on to the tracks of her own will. That of Ródenas, along with those of his wife and daughter, was if possible even more conclusive. And yet, the suicides of two people from the same company, who to all appearances led lives as normal as most people's, kept alerting the instinct that Héctor had learned to trust over the years.

He studied the photo of the group once more, trying to read those unmoving faces, immortalized for posterity in an unflattering portrait. He focused especially on Gaspar and Sara. She was smiling, confidently obeying the instructions of whoever was holding the camera. Gaspar Ródenas was concentrating on looking ahead, as if he had in front of him a balance sheet that wouldn't tally: the furrowed brow, the tense body. An expression rather similar to that in the photo taken at the beach that appeared in Lola's article. Maybe it was the face he put on in photos, Héctor said to himself, leaving both on the desk. He trusted his instinct, yes, but he knew it was sometimes very easy to be swayed by false impressions.

If he'd spent another two minutes thinking, he wouldn't have done it. Especially because half eight in the morning was no time to call anyone. And even less so someone he hadn't seen in more than seven years. In fact, he rang partly because he didn't think that Lola would still have the same number after so much time and partly because he'd wanted to do so since the first time he saw her name on the byline of that article. When the sleepy voice of someone recently awakened picked up, he didn't know what to say.

'Yes?'

'Lola?'

'Says who?'

'Lola. Did I wake you?'

There was a pause, a silence during which Héctor imagined her in bed, with the cloudy look of interrupted sleep.

'Héctor?' The voice sounded completely awake now.

197

'The very same.'

'Fuck. I'm going to sue my horoscope. It promised me a peaceful week, with no surprises.'

He smiled.

'It's Friday. It was almost right.' Silences on the phone are as bad as on the radio, thought Héctor. Static nervousness. 'How are things?'

Lola's laugh suggested more sarcasm than humour.

'I don't believe it.' She laughed again. 'So many years of silence and you call me at half eight on a January Friday to ask me how I am? This is like an episode of *Sex and the City*, although without sex. And in Carabanchel.'

He was about to respond when she cut him off.

'Héctor, forgive me, but I think I need a shower and a coffee before talking to you.'

'No cigarette?'

'I don't smoke any more.'

'Listen, have breakfast and I'll call you later. I'm on a case you wrote about a few months ago and I'd like your input.' He was hoping she would ask what case he meant. 'Gaspar Ródenas. The guy who—'

'Who killed his wife and daughter and then shot himself. I remember.'

'Could I take a look at your notes?'

'I suppose it's important if you're asking me like this.'

'I'll leave you in peace to wake up. Lola,' he said, 'it's good to talk to you.'

He didn't know if she'd heard him or not, because the line was cut immediately, but a goofy smile must have been on his face long enough to be seen by Superintendent Savall, who summoned him to his office five minutes later.

'Are you in an especially good mood, Héctor?' he said by way of a greeting.

'Well, Superintendent, they say skulls smile too. And they don't exactly have many reasons to be happy.'

Lluís Savall looked at him without fully understanding his answer.

'Never mind skulls, Héctor, sit down. Tell me what the hell happened with Bellver yesterday.' His tone didn't bode well.

There was something about that woman he found repellent, although he wouldn't have been able to say exactly what it was. Up to now, Sílvia Alemany had been as friendly as she was efficient and had answered his questions without hesitation. And yet Héctor Salgado couldn't shake the irritating feeling that he was attending a forced performance. Something he'd become used to after so many years of service, given that generally he believed everyone lied to a greater or lesser degree. Self-deception, or deception of those around you, was as natural as breathing; very few people would tolerate a crude, honest judgment on themselves or their loved ones. But even taking that into account, Sílvia Alemany's acting revealed an academic edge, somewhere between feigned and condescending, that was starting to grate.

He had been at Alemany Cosmetics for half an hour. He'd been accompanied by Agent Fort, whom he immediately sent to take a look around the lab with deliberately ambiguous instructions though a definite aim: sound out the atmosphere, take the pulse of this organization dedicated to beauty products. The agent's detailed report noted it had been founded in the forties and had kept going, with no great ups or downs, throughout its history. Only in the last decade had they become competitive, thanks to the development and marketing of AC/Slim, a cream that had caused a furore among ladies and gentlemen with a few extra kilos. From then on, Alemany Cosmetics had widened its products and ambition, moving from a low-profile brand sold in supermarkets to the high pantheon of artificial beauty. At the end of last year they'd launched a line aimed at younger women, Young, which Héctor had never heard of, but according to the advertising campaign was a great investment within the company.

Sílvia Alemany was neither adolescent nor beautiful, and was naturally thin, without needing additional help. She looked like her brother, Héctor thought, though she lacked charm. If at the time he had silently compared Víctor to Michael York, his sister vaguely reminded him of Tilda Swinton, an actress he admired despite the fact her roles usually unsettled him. He was aware that his bad mood was largely due to the chat with Savall a little earlier, but a significant portion was also caused by this polite and highly reasonable woman sitting on the other side of the desk.

The office wasn't at all ostentatious, which had surprised him. Rather sparse of detail, with an austerity that had little to do with what he'd imagined of a company dedicated to aesthetics, the space was deceptive. No doubt about it, Sílvia Alemany wasn't a straightforward woman.

'To tell you the truth, I don't know how we can help you, Inspector. We're still in shock over Sara's death. In fact, we know very little about the private lives of our employees. I never would have suspected that Sara was so . . . unhappy.'

'She wasn't a woman with many friends, correct?'

Sílvia shrugged her shoulders, as if giving to understand that this was none of her business.

'I haven't the faintest idea whether she had friends or not. Personally, I believe Sara wasn't one who struck up friendships with her work colleagues; however, that doesn't mean she didn't have them elsewhere.'

Of course. No one could argue with that.

'And Gaspar Ródenas?'

Sílvia took a deep breath.

'Inspector Salgado, I've already spoken to your colleagues about Gaspar,' she replied, in a voice half tired, half willing. 'I don't see what he has to do with Sara's death.'

'Neither do I, as yet,' said Héctor. He took out the group photo from the file. 'But it seems at the very least strange that two of the people in this image have died, don't you think?'

She didn't even look at the photo.

'I wouldn't qualify it as strange, Inspector. Sad, perhaps.'

'When was the photograph taken?'

'Last year, in March or April, I'm not exactly sure. And I don't know what—'

Héctor interrupted her.

'Was it a company outing?'

'It was a few days of "team-building", as they say in English. I don't know how to translate it . . .' The condescending tone emerged once more.

'I know what it is, thank you. I see you attended as well.'

She smiled.

'Having a management role doesn't mean being outside the team, Inspector. On the contrary. We usually organize various days like that throughout the year with different employees.'

'Can you give me the names of the others?'

Sílvia looked at the photo, as if she couldn't precisely remember who had participated.

'The dark-haired man, with very short hair, is Brais Arjona, brand manager of the Young line; beside him is Amanda Bonet, in charge of design—'

'Of the same line?'

'Yes, but not exclusively. I don't know if you're aware that Alemany Cosmetics has experienced huge growth in the last few years. Our packaging was old-fashioned and when we hired Brais Arjona, he insisted on modernizing the packaging of the product. It was he who proposed Amanda. And, of course, she has handled the design of the new line directly.'

'I understand. And the others?'

'Apart from me, there is César Calvo, manager of storage and distribution.' In the photo, César had his arm around her shoulders, so in a cold voice she added, 'And my fiancé. We're getting married in a few months.' Not leaving room for any comments, she went on: 'Manel Caballero, the youngest, is part of the R & D – Research and Development – department.'

Héctor couldn't decide if Sílvia Alemany was explaining obvious concepts to him out of friendliness or with the intention of irritating him. Whatever the reason, it irritated him. If she noticed the inspector's furrowed brow, she paid no attention to it.

'Octavi Pujades, the eldest, has been our finance director for years; he was already director in my father's final years. And the other two, as you know, are Gaspar Ródenas and Sara Mahler.'

'If I remember correctly, Gaspar belonged to the same department as Señor Pujades, isn't that right? Is it normal for two people from the same department to attend these away days?'

She smiled.

'It depends. On occasion they are organized by department, to unite the group. Other times, like this, it's about bringing people from different divisions together. So the answer is no, it's not normal in this case.'

'How are the participants chosen?'

'Well,' Sílvia was maintaining that friendly smile, 'it's not a lottery. Brais and Amanda had had months of intense collaboration, with the contact that always entails, and I thought it would be good for them to work together in a different atmosphere. At the same time, it seemed convenient for them to establish a more personal relationship with the managers of other areas: César, Octavi and me. Sometimes creative personalities like theirs tend to forget they form part of a broader whole, that there are other employees who take care of more concrete areas. The group is also balanced by age, so Manel Caballero from R & D, and another person from Sales who couldn't come in the end. Gaspar Ródenas was on the same level, so although he was also from finance, we decided to include him.'

'And Sara Mahler?'

'I'm afraid that the administrative personnel sometimes feel a little excluded. We needed another woman to make it up, and Saúl and I thought of Sara.'

'Saúl . . . ?'

'Saúl Duque. It's he who takes care of organizing the details of these activities. My second-in-command. I hate the word assistant – it's somewhat servile, don't you think? You saw him as you came in – his desk is just in front of the door to my office.'

Sílvia had relaxed. Clearly speaking about the ins and outs of the company was a pleasure for her.

'And were they good? I mean the away days.'

'Neither good nor bad. Between you and me, Inspector, I'm coming to the conclusion that this kind of thing has more of a motivational effect than anything else. The people feel valued, which is positive in itself.'

Héctor nodded.

'But in this case the away days served another purpose. At least for Gaspar Ródenas, right?'

Sílvia was on her guard once again.

'You mean because afterwards he was chosen to carry out Octavi's duties during his leave of absence? Well, I wouldn't say that happened as a result of those days. A couple of names were considered, and Gaspar's was one of them.'

She was lying. And when she was lying her voice took on a slight note of disdain.

'And what tipped the balance in favour of Ródenas?'

'It was Octavi Pujades who preferred him, and my brother and I agreed, of course. At the end of the day, it wasn't a definitive promotion. It wasn't so very important, Inspector. Just a few months of extra responsibility.'

Héctor smiled inwardly; he was sure that the other name considered on that shortlist hadn't seen it that way. However, he decided to move on to another subject.

'And was it by any chance during those days that this other photo was taken?' he asked as he placed it on the table.

'Let's see . . .' Sílvia Alemany picked up the print and looked at it without too much interest, although with a serious expression. 'Where did you get this, Inspector?'

He decided not to lie.

'Sara Mahler received it in a text message shortly before . . . she committed suicide.' The pause was intentional and the other person noticed. 'Have you seen it before?'

'I don't understand why anyone would send her something like this. It seems in very bad taste.'

'It's not a nice image, of course,' Héctor agreed. 'Nevertheless, you've seen it before, haven't you?'

'Inspector, I don't know what exactly you're insinuating, but I can assure you I've never seen this photograph before. And it's not something easy to forget. What's more, the idea of photographing a scene like this is macabre.'

Héctor waited. He was about to rephrase his question when she got ahead of him.

'I hadn't seen the photograph, but yes, we saw that tree. And those poor animals hanging there. Some hunters do it, you know? When the animals are old, they've lost their sense of smell or they're just sick, they hang them. It's barbarous.'

'Of course. It must have affected you all.'

Sílvia nodded with a shudder that this time was genuine.

'One of the tests consisted of a trail game. Two teams were formed and we set out on a hunt. The objective was to get to a cabin relatively far from the house we were staying in. That tree was beside it.'

'I see.'

'In fact we arrived almost at the same time. The two teams, I mean. There was even a final race between César and Brais to see who could reach the end first.' She said it scornfully, as if she were speaking of two little boys chasing after a ball.

'Do you remember anyone taking a photo?'

Sílvia shook her head, as if the mere idea was an aberration.

'Why would someone do something like that? It's horrible.'

'I don't know, but someone did. And sent it to Sara for some reason.'

Sílvia's acting was so convincing that Salgado started to doubt his reading of the situation.

'I can't help you with that, Inspector. But believe me when I tell you that we were all very upset. Maybe you think it's silly, but in the flesh it was very shocking.' She took a breath and added, 'So much so we decided to bury them.'

'Bury them?'

She smiled.

'In hindsight it sounds ridiculous, I know. At that time we felt we couldn't leave them there. Out in the open, hanging by the neck. The house where we were staying was far from the town and I wasn't sure anyone would have come quickly just for some dogs.'

'Violence against animals is a crime,' Héctor clarified. 'Someone would have come, you can be sure of that.'

'I suppose you're right. It didn't occur to us. That was

mid-morning and in the afternoon, when we'd finished the activities, we decided to go back and bury them. I think we'd been infected by the idea of group spirit and shared tasks.'

She said it with a hint of irony that didn't escape Héctor.

'So you went back, took them down and buried them there.'

'Yes.' She shrugged. 'I find it hard to believe that after we took so much trouble, one of those present had the bad taste to take a photo and then send it to Sara.'

'Do you get any pressure from environmental groups?' asked Héctor. 'For using animals and—'

'Our products are a hundred per cent natural, Inspector. We don't experiment on animals. There is always some radical group who tar us with the same brush as other labs, but in fact it hasn't happened for a while.'

Héctor was thoughtful for a moment. Sílvia Alemany's explanation was reasonable, although she still hadn't given an answer to the question. Who had taken the photo? And, above all, why had they sent it to Sara Mahler, especially just before she died on the tracks of the metro?

'We're entering the realm of hypothesis, Señora Alemany. If you had to bet on one of them, who would you say took that photo?'

'This isn't fair, Inspector.' Seeing he was looking at her inquisitively, she continued, 'What I'm going to say may seem an attempt to deflect the matter, but to be honest I think the only one of us capable of something like that was Gaspar Ródenas. No, not in the sense you're thinking. Gaspar belonged to various associations for the defence of animals and it may be that he wanted a picture of the tree to report what had happened.'

Héctor nodded. It was probable, although there was no mention of environmental activism or animal rights in Ródenas's file.

'It will seem strange to you that I know that about Gaspar Ródenas, but when the tragedy occurred I went through his work file. You must understand, it was a complete shock when someone we saw every day suddenly became a murderer-suicide. So I went over the psychometric tests and reports done on him in the years he worked here. It was mentioned in one of them and that's why I remember it.'

'Was there anything in those tests which could have predicted what he did?'

Sílvia Alemany shook her head.

'If we managed to see that with such a simple test, you would be out of a job, don't you think?'

There was little more to say and Héctor accepted Sílvia Alemany's offer of visiting the factory accompanied by Saúl Duque.

'I would show you around myself, Inspector, but I have a meeting in less than ten minutes.'

'Your brother still hasn't arrived? He told me he was going away.'

Seeing it was already a quarter past eleven, she continued: 'He must be about to arrive, although maybe he went home to drop off his suitcase first. Did you want to see him?'

'No, there's no need.'

'If you want anything else, you know where to find us.' She'd stood up, an unequivocal sign that the meeting

208

was at an end. 'Inspector, I trust you will be discreet with the workers. There have been enough unpleasant comments after the deaths of Gaspar and Sara . . .'

'Don't worry,' said Héctor, 'I'll try not to spread panic.'

'I'm sure you will.'

It was false praise; the satisfaction revealed by Sílvia Alemany's voice was too obvious for Héctor not to perceive it. And without really knowing why, this pissed him off even more. What neither he nor Sílvia herself knew was that air of confident superiority was to be shattered some two hours later, when Víctor arrived at the company and, behind closed doors, held a confidential conversation with his sister that would erase every trace of her good mood.

22

As he ran along a dark, solitary maritime promenade Héctor hoped that the tension in his body would evaporate through sweat and fatigue, but the cool night air was making it rather difficult. An invisible sea, present only in the form of an agitated, almost furious murmur, didn't help much either. So he speeded up, seeking the relief that only muscle exhaustion can bring, when the brain dilutes worries to concentrate on withstanding the race. But for the moment there was no way of achieving this and the day's images, unpleasant for the most part, kept floating back into his mind, rebellious and disorganized like starving piranhas.

The scolding from Savall, which he'd tried to fight off with expert irony, had been no surprise. Only the delivery had taken him aback. The superintendent had listened to him, of course, and had agreed that Bellver could be, putting it bluntly, a first-class idiot, but at the same time he'd refused to believe that Héctor knew nothing about the removal of Ruth's file from the missing persons archives. And he'd adopted a tone somewhere between solemn and offended to make it clear he 'felt deeply disappointed'. After all he'd done for him, after having supported him when he put his foot in it and taken advantage of the force, Savall had made it clear that he expected, if not thanks, then at least a little loyalty. And honesty.

There's nothing worse than the truth which seems to be a lie, thought Héctor. However much he argued, the super had been unwavering, and he'd also accused him of using Sergeant Andreu to carry out 'what you don't have the balls to do yourself'. Héctor, who'd called Martina Andreu twice since the night before without getting an answer, reiterated his ignorance, although he was hurt that Savall didn't believe him. At least this will be cleared up soon, he thought as he started to notice the heat of the exertion: Martina will be back on Monday from Madrid and everyone will have the chance to talk. In fact, he also found it strange that the sergeant had done something which in other circumstances wouldn't be that important. In these, however, Ruth on one side and Bellver on the other, she must have realized that the result could be catastrophic. The superintendent's final words, expressed in that tone of paternal anger that Héctor hated above all other things, left no room for doubt: 'You're making too many enemies, Héctor. And you can't permit yourself that luxury. Not now. And the time will come when even I can't defend you.'

If the gossip had pointed out the possibility that he'd smash Dídac Bellver's face in, the superintendent had reason to worry. It had been a long time since he experienced that blind fury, the physical need to hit someone, and only Agent Fort's appearance had stopped that from happening. Bellver's face, when he made conjectures about Ruth's emotional instability and Héctor's

211

humiliation on being left for another woman, was crying out for a punch that would dislocate the jaw with a dry, painful crack. As he ran, Héctor guessed that that was exactly what Bellver wanted: to make him lose his temper, to demonstrate once again that Salgado was a crazy, violent Argentine, capable of assaulting not only a suspect but a colleague as well.

I managed to control myself, thought Héctor, although he knew it wasn't altogether down to his own merit. On Monday it'll all be cleared up, and this gave him the strength to accelerate even more on an almost deserted promenade, beside waves that seemed to become more furious as he calmed down. It was going to rain; the sky was swarming with dirty clouds and in the distance he sensed an isolated bolt of lightning. The most intelligent thing would have been to turn around, but Héctor was determined to reach the goal he'd set himself before leaving home, the chimneys of the old Sant Adrià power station, and he hadn't the least intention of giving up the little he was able to control himself, through his own efforts. The only aim of the day that didn't depend on other people's will, on people like Sílvia Alemany telling him the truth.

In short, he thought, the visit to the labs had been as fruitless as he'd feared and, as they discussed during the journey back, Agent Fort's enquiries hadn't thrown up any exceptional revelations. The employees seemed appropriately shaken by the news of two consecutive deaths, but didn't make any connection between them. The comments, according to Fort, indicated that Sara Mahler was a strange woman, 'no man by her side' – something that sounded to Salgado like the most antiquated machismo – and that Christmas was sad for those who were alone. With that he did agree, he said to himself as he noticed the first drops of rain. The subject of Gaspar Ródenas was already a remote event for the majority of the workers; they'd spoken about it ad nauseam when it happened and had little more to add.

The only significant information had been the confirmation of his suspicions regarding the promotion of Ródenas. According to what Agent Fort had been told while chatting to the people at the coffee machine, Martí Clavé, the other candidate, had taken it more to heart than Sílvia Alemany had admitted. 'It seems they almost came to blows,' Fort confessed, not looking at him, probably uncomfortable at a situation similar to the one he'd witnessed in his boss's office the previous afternoon. 'This Clavé confronted Ródenas during his first days in the job and didn't hide that he felt it an unfair promotion.'

They said that Gaspar hadn't reacted to the outburst; he'd stayed quiet. They also said that when he heard the news of his death, of the murder of his whole family, Martí Clavé, taciturn and remorseful, had gone a number of days without speaking to anyone.

All this was logical: promotions, undeserved or not, people who felt under-valued; it happened everywhere, all the time, and didn't merit much comment. Even in times of crisis, it was unthinkable that someone would kill a whole family to get a promotion. On the contrary, maybe in another era Martí Clavé, offended, would have left the company, but as things were his protest had been only vocal, not active. And, in any case, none of it was at all related to Sara Mahler, the hanged dogs or the feeling that Sílvia Alemany and the other participants in the away days had lied to him with insulting nerve.

The rain was now a reality and Héctor knew he'd end up soaked, but he kept going. Too much accumulated frustration for him to give up now. A dissatisfaction that had grown during the walk around the factory with Saúl Duque, who was a pleasant guy and chatty enough to have some information wheedled out of him, although in the end what he revealed wasn't much use: he was happy working there, under Sílvia Alemany, a hard but fair boss; the economic crisis wasn't affecting them too badly, although it was feared the situation would get worse, given that the green shoots announced by the government didn't seem to be flowering; there was a good atmosphere, despite these sudden tragic deaths. In that, at least, Saúl had been adamant: 'Gaspar was on edge, but I never thought he'd lose his head that way. I'm sure that there must have been something else, some marriage problem we don't know about.' With regard to Sara, Saúl hadn't been able to conceal a certain dislike, a reaction the poor girl seemed to arouse in most people. 'But that doesn't mean anything, Inspector. And I never thought she was depressed, just that she didn't fit in.'

The guided tour was as uninteresting as he'd expected. With Saúl Duque at his side, he met Brais Arjona and Amanda Bonet, who confirmed the version given by Sílvia Alemany. Héctor didn't even bother to speak to the others: he was sure Manel Caballero and César Calvo would have said the same in different words. Perhaps the only point he scored was when he casually asked Amanda if she was good friends with Sara Mahler. The girl had blushed, a reaction which could be shyness with the police, but which Héctor felt was a little excessive, and she just said that she'd gone to her house one evening for coffee. All very reasonable, all stinkingly normal. He and Fort had returned to the station more despondent than when they left. Just one more loose end to cover: Sara's supposed boyfriend, if he existed, something Héctor was beginning to doubt . . .

Héctor turned around when a bolt of lightning showed he'd reached his goal. The hardest bit was still to come: the way back, retracing his steps. And thinking about the way home took him directly to the image of Lola, whom he still hadn't called back. Later he would, but at that moment he just ran, drawing strength from weakness to flee from the rain, flee from memories. To flee from Ruth's wounded face when he confessed what had been going on. And, above all, flee from the bitter moment he decided to leave Lola for ever.

23

It was after five in the morning on Sunday when César returned to cold sheets, to an accusatory hollow, to the bed where Sílvia was sleeping alone without even realizing.

It had been a leaden, rainy Sunday, as grey as a Berlin winter, matching Sílvia's mood; she had barely said two words all day. César had never been too good with sick people and he preferred to be left alone when he wasn't well. So when Sílvia rejected his attempts at conversation, claiming she was coming down with the flu, he gave her a kiss on her singularly icy brow and advised her to go to bed. It was no wonder she was getting sick, bearing in mind the tension of the last few days. Faithful to his role and with nothing better to do, he'd stayed at Sílvia's the whole evening, snoozing in front of the TV, trying little by little to appropriate this space which would also be his in a few months. They were alone: Pol had gone to a friend's house, and it appeared Emma was also studying with a friend. César never asked about them and was happy to have the sitting room to himself. In the middle of the afternoon Sílvia got up, although it was obvious she didn't feel any better. On the contrary, the long nap had left her dazed, with a severe headache. Not for a moment did César suspect that the upset caused by the conversation with Víctor was hidden behind these symptoms.

Sílvia had decided to go to bed because she had the feeling she was losing control of her world and needed to take refuge in the intimate personal space that was her room, her bed. Clinging to her pillow and closing her eyes to forget, even for a few hours, that her life was going to change despite everything. She felt betrayed, sold by Víctor, and more so by Octavi Pujades, who had collaborated with her brother's plans and hidden them from her with the determination of Judas in a suit and tie. She could have confided in César, and if she hadn't it was above all out of shame: she didn't want to be the conned woman, the loser that the truly powerful ignore without the least decency. Of course she'd keep her job, if she wanted it. Víctor had made an effort to show her that she meant something to him, but they both knew the truth: the duties Sílvia carried out in the company went beyond her job description and her power came as much from her efficiency as from her surname. No amount of money in the world could make up for that.

Any other time she would have fought with her brother, battled to protect her own interests, hurled real and imaginary insults in his face. But on Friday, after the inspector's visit, she was feeling so pleased with herself that Víctor's news left her speechless. Mute and empty as a dried-up skull. And twenty-four hours later, lying in her bed, all she felt was a bitter taste in her mouth. Even the threat received by telephone two days before had lost

217

its force. It was absurd, she knew; that evening nothing seemed important.

They had dinner together, she and César, not hungry and with no desire to talk, and only Emma's arrival lifted the atmosphere a little. For once, Sílvia let herself be fussed over and agreed to drink the hot infusion her daughter prepared especially for her. She drank it in bed, Emma by her side, happy for once that the roles were reversed and it was her daughter who put her hand on her forehead, said she had a temperature and gave her a goodnight kiss. She'd spent half the day in bed and was afraid she wouldn't sleep, but in fact shortly after Emma left her room and turned out the light, Sílvia fell into a calm, restorative sleep, just what her exhausted mind was demanding.

César stayed a little longer in front of the TV, not watching it. He would have gone home to his house if it hadn't started raining again, if he hadn't become drowsy on the sofa. Or if Emma had come down to keep him company, which didn't happen. He decided to go to bed when it wasn't even twelve. Sílvia had been asleep for at least two hours and he lay down beside her, against her body without disturbing her. He gave her a suggestive kiss on the nape of her neck and, seeing that she was in a deep sleep, he opted to turn over and move a few centimetres away from her, although he knew it was pointless. He was too restless to sleep and couldn't be bothered to masturbate, so he closed his eyes in the hope that sleep would resolve both. But sleep didn't come, and the heavy rain falling on the city was keeping him awake. César wasn't imaginative or susceptible to the elements;

however, there were too many worries going round in his head that impeded his rest: he *was* scared of the threats, he *was* starting to believe that there was something behind the deaths of Gaspar and Sara.

Did they deserve to die? No more than he did, or Sílvia, or any of the others. Perhaps the terms were ridiculous, but for once they expressed the facts: that spring night they had all collaborated, to a greater or lesser extent. It didn't really matter who struck the first blow, who suggested the subsequent plan, who was most frightened or most sure of themselves. If what had happened to Gaspar and Sara was the work of fate, with the same justice it could also attack the rest of them. A thunderclap endorsed this conclusion.

Despite being in bed for only forty-five minutes, he felt like he'd been there for hours. He needed a cigarette and this time he had a pack in his jacket, bought on the sly like a schoolboy. He would have to smoke by the kitchen window if he wanted to conceal the smell of tobacco. So he went down, in pyjamas and barefoot, because he never remembered to buy slippers for his second home. On tiptoe, so as not to wake anyone, he found his jacket on the coat rack and took out the pack and lighter. Then he went to the kitchen and opened the window a crack. Outside it was still raining. Drops that by the light of a nearby streetlamp seemed a thick veil, a liquid curtain. He lit the cigarette and took a first brief drag, to get used to the flavour.

He didn't hear her come in. He only heard the fridge door and turned around. It was dark, but the fridge bulb gave enough light for him to recognize Emma. He went on smoking, not saying anything, wanting her to leave and at the same time stay. She said nothing, just came nearer. She took the cigarette from his fingers and took a long drag before throwing it out of the window. She exhaled the smoke slowly and then embraced him as would a child frightened by the storm.

'I don't like little girls,' said César, realizing that his voice was hoarse. 'If you want me to treat you as a woman, act like one.'

César couldn't see her face but he didn't need to. The kiss she then gave him was enough to know what she wanted. What they both wanted. After that young, inexperienced kiss he knew nothing now could halt the inevitable. Emma said only one thing, in his ear.

'Please don't hurt me.'

And then it was he who kissed her with a mixture of passion and tenderness, before grabbing her hand and taking her to her bed. He longed with all his strength to possess the body she was offering him. And not just that: he wanted to do it well. To be, even just for a night, the best lover in the world.

When he went back to his room it was after five in the morning. Sílvia was sleeping. The storm had abated and the fridge door was still open.

César lay down, exhausted, and closed his eyes, but the apprehension about what he'd just done and the memory of the threat Sílvia had ignored kept him hopelessly awake.

24

Sunday dawns with a hungover, lifeless sky, even more cloudy than the day before. Lying in bed, Amanda turns over, seized with that absurd happiness which makes you lazy on a day off when nothing, or almost nothing, forces you to get up.

Unlike most people, she has liked storms since she was a little girl. She finds the sort of battle that develops in the sky stimulating, and the feeling of being protected, under cover, safe from thunderclaps and lightning bolts, fills her with an almost childish glee. What's more, the rain was the perfect excuse not to have to go out with her friends on that route which has made Saturdays a monotonous round: dinner at La Flauta, a first drink somewhere nearby, then another in the Universal before going into the Luz de Gas.

The variations are so minimal and end in places so similar, that she sometimes doesn't remember exactly which bar she went to the Saturday before. To top it all, Amanda doesn't drink – she dislikes the taste of alcohol – and the pests that surround her to buy her a drink and feel her up in exchange are repulsive. She continues to go out with her old friends, although every time it's more of a battle. For a large part of Saturday night her mind is elsewhere, thinking about Sunday, about what he'll do to her, the feelings that will explode in her body. Her friends find it strange that she doesn't have a boyfriend, or even sporadic hook-ups, although she has confessed to one close pal the existence of this friend-with-benefits, someone from work about whom she doesn't want to give more details. This seemed to calm them all, given that it would be unthinkable that such a beautiful girl doesn't have sexual relations regularly.

It is almost eleven when Amanda finally decides to get up and turn on her computer, a reflex gesture. While she waits for it to boot up, she always feels the vague fear that he might let her down. That some Sunday the message with the instructions to follow won't come. In fact, it has happened once, an unexpected punishment she found much more unbearable than any other of the many he is capable of imagining and executing. But this Sunday she knows it won't be like that; he told her so on the phone on Friday, around nine at night, as he usually does. He calls her every Friday, not caring where she is. She must answer – it's part of the deal. So that night, during that horrible weekend with Brais and the others, she had to move away from the house to take the call.

'Touch yourself, caress your breasts under your clothes. Turn yourself on thinking I'm here, watching you, ready to whip you if you don't please me. I want to hear you moan.'

She doesn't want to think about it. Not this Sunday; she has agonized enough over it. She can't tell anyone about it. She had bad enough luck with Sara . . .

It was careless, an unforgivable error. After that

222

weekend, the eight had exchanged personal emails in case they needed to get in touch. They hadn't used them much, to be honest, and she always respected the order: eliminate all traces as soon as you've read it. But Gaspar's death affected them all, especially Sara, who started to write to her from time to time. Sara was so alone, she needed someone to talk to, albeit so cold a comfort as an email. So one day when she wrote a message to Saúl Duque, her lover, one of those breathtaking texts full of intimate details, the name of the addressee was automatically filled when she wrote the first letters without Amanda realizing. And the damned message landed in Sara's inbox, not Saúl's.

Amanda could have whipped herself when she realized the error, but it was already too late. She could only rely on Sara's discretion. And she showed herself to be discreet, although especially interested, with a curiosity she never would have suspected in her. They were in her house and Amanda tried to explain how she felt. But, how? She could only tell her details, games that sounded ridiculous or disturbing when expressed aloud, judging by Sara's reaction.

How to explain that finally, after years of unconscious searching, she has found the man who makes her most intimate fantasies a reality. Someone she finds attractive and with whom, of this she is certain, she can play without fear. Although Saúl can be and is hard, he never goes too far, always seems to know when to stop the pain and console with caresses. Moreover, it's not just about sex: Amanda feels guarded, protected. She couldn't explain to anyone why the feeling of belonging to someone, obeying him, fills her in this way. Sometimes she is scared at the thought of losing him, not because she loves him, at least not in a conventional sense, but because she knows it will be difficult to enjoy similar stimulation again. No doubt this will end up happening, and both are aware of it. But for the moment it's better not to think about it.

As she makes coffee, Amanda reads the email and frowns. There are games she likes more than others and the one Saúl has ordered for this evening is nowhere near one of her favourites. However, she doesn't protest; she answers in the required submissive tone and arranges everything for later.

Brais leaves the house around five because he thinks that if he spends another minute inside, he will punch the walls apart. He's been inside for a day and a half. Too much time idling for someone like him. He needs to let off steam and the gym is as good an option as any other. He also needs to escape the worried face of David, who asked him at midday, seriously, what the hell is happening to him. Luckily, Brais was able to blame his restlessness on work without lying too much, but David isn't stupid and, although he pretended to accept the excuse, he doesn't fully believe it. He tried to be sociable during lunch, tried watching a couple of episodes of *Mad Men* that his husband had downloaded, a regular pastime on winter Sunday evenings, but he was eaten up with nerves and couldn't sit still on the sofa. Finally, David suggested going to the gym for a bit to 'see if you calm down'.

It's almost night, although on such a grey day you'd scarcely notice. Brais leaves the lights of the theatres beginning to be lit on Paral·lel, and walks towards the centre. He starts to walk rapidly, with the sportsbag on his shoulder, but when he gets to the Sant Antoni market he changes his mind. It's not there he wants to go. There's something he has to do to calm his mind once and for all, and it isn't running on a treadmill until he's out of breath. Problems aren't resolved by fleeing but by confronting them. And right now his problem has a name: Manel Caballero.

Night has fallen when Octavi Pujades watches his son's car moving down the road. They all leave, he thinks unresentfully. Night and illness combined are frightening. Not far from his house a dog howls, as if he can chase away evil spirits with his barks. Octavi enters the house and closes the door. The silence inside hits him again and he switches on the television, just to hear a voice. Eugènia is sleeping upstairs, if you can call it that. More like slowly dying, being consumed until she can no longer open her eyes. In recent days she has worsened, the deterioration is evident, and he can barely stand to watch. Pain and fatigue are another dangerous combination: sometimes one overwhelms the other and gives him the strength to continue struggling, but there are moments, like this one, in which fatigue prevails and what he wants, with all his heart, is for it all to be over.

Desiring the death of someone he loves is terrible, and Octavi is aware of that. But he can't deny the facts. This house which embraced them when they were in love is little by little turning into a tomb. Her tomb.

Sitting on the sofa, before the fire, he tries to get these dark thoughts out of his mind. He's been expecting Sílvia to call him all day long, but she hasn't. The time will come, no doubt. He spoke to Víctor yesterday. Víctor –

so excited, so childish in his approach . . . Or maybe not; maybe people like him and Eugènia are the ones who have lived in error, tied to work, routines and obligations. And what for, in the end? To end up dying when they are just about to enjoy a little freedom earned through years of work. He can't fault Víctor Alemany wanting to buy his freedom back if he has the means to do so.

The dog's howls sound closer, more urgent, and Octavi goes to the window and pulls back the curtains. As he expected, he sees nothing. He stands there, attentive to those ever more hysterical howls. Someone must be prowling around, he thinks anxiously, before going up to Eugènia's room to see how she is. To see if she's still alive or if death has finally won.

'I want you to wait for me asleep. For you to be my sleeping beauty. This will be your punishment: only I will enjoy your body tonight.'

And Amanda obeys, knowing what he expects of her. She has changed the sheets, as she always does, and put on some new white ones. Also white is the nightgown he demands for this game. White are the pills she must take so that when he arrives he will find her deep in sleep and enjoy her unconscious body as he pleases.

She takes them sitting on her bed, with a glass of water. From previous occasions she knows the necessary quantity. He will be annoyed if she wakes midway through the game. It happened the first time and he was so upset Amanda decided not to fail him again. She lies down and lets herself be caressed by sleep; she imagines what he will do while she's asleep . . . She sees him naked, handcuffing her still arms, treating her body as the beautiful piece of flesh it is. She is about to lose consciousness when she hears the door of her bedroom opening. It's not her fault if the pills haven't fully taken effect yet; her eyes are closed, her body is heavy and, although she feels as if she is sleeping, she feels hands grabbing her shoulders and sitting her up.

Amanda knows she should be asleep. So she doesn't resist when she notices the hands opening her mouth and starting to give her pills, and then water, and more pills. With the little strength left to her she manages to swallow, and the last thing she thinks is that Saúl will be happy and will stay the night. So she can see him when the game is over, when she regains consciousness. When she awakens . . .

LEIRE

25

'You were asleep and I didn't want to wake you. I have to go. See you soon. Kisses. T. And look after the Gremlin.'

The note was on the nightstand when Leire returned to the world after an unusually long Sunday siesta. She'd gone to lie down around half past three, convinced that she wouldn't sleep more than thirty minutes, but having read the note and looked at her watch she realized it was almost six; taking into account that it was the time the AVE departed, Tomás had left some time ago. Too dazed to react quickly, she remained seated on the bed, feet on the floor, debating whether to go back to sleep or restart the day halfway through the evening. In the end she opted for the latter, above all because, although it seemed strange, she was hungry again. The Gremlin, as Tomás called him, provoked a voracious appetite in her at unexpected moments. Or, more accurately, at almost every moment. A little later, after wolfing down a couple of cheese sandwiches and eating a bit of fruit, she felt more alert, as if instead of an afternoon snack she'd breakfasted and had the whole day ahead of her. That only five hours remained of the day didn't worry her too much; she was beginning to get used to the anarchy of not having schedules and doing what she liked. 'Take advantage of it now. When the little one is born he'll be the one calling the shots,' her mother had said to her. It seemed curious to Leire that no one referred to him as Abel, a name decided months before: to her mother he was 'the little one'; 'the Gremlin' to Tomás; and 'the baby' to her friend María. On the other hand, she thought of him with his name, maybe to get used to the idea that very soon someone so named would occupy a space outside her body; someone who would be a sleepyhead or a crybaby, or both, someone with their own body and personality.

That weekend Leire and Tomás had again discussed the subject of how things would be once Abel abandoned his shelter and launched himself into the world. In fact, it was Tomás who had brought the subject up, suddenly and in a casual voice, as if it were all overwhelmingly obvious.

'I'll have to start looking for an apartment here,' he'd said just before bed the night before. 'I can't be a squatting father for ever.'

'You're going to move to Barcelona?' she asked him, not sure she'd heard right.

'It's the most practical thing, don't you think? I'll have to keep on travelling a lot – you know what my work is like – but as I have to rent a place, it's only logical for it to be in the same city as my son.'

It was the first time he had expressed himself in those words and Leire felt overcome with an absurd feeling of gratitude, which she struggled against, similar to one she'd experienced on Friday night when he arrived. Although she wasn't completely sure of her feelings towards Tomás, Leire had looked at herself in the hall mirror just before he appeared and saw herself as huge, like a Botero model. The idea that all pregnant women are beautiful had never sat well with her, so she almost burst into tears when, just in the door, he dropped his suitcase, practically leapt on her and, resting his hands on her breasts, murmured something like, 'You'll let me, won't you? I spent the whole journey wanting to do it. They're glorious.'

Then he focused on caressing and licking them, as if she were a porn queen and he her most devoted and aroused admirer.

'Well, what do you think? Will you be able to stand living less than ten kilometres from me?' he asked, eyes smiling. 'I promise not to raid your fridge.'

Leire nodded, vaguely conscious that logically it made more sense for Tomás to move in with her and Abel instead of looking for his own apartment. But if he was expecting her to suggest that, he had the sense not to mention it. And of course she didn't. The offer, or rather the absence of one, hovered over them both all Sunday morning like a UFO, and after lunch acquired such solidity in the air that Leire went to bed for a while to ignore it.

She dressed as if she were going out, though leaning out on the balcony she was struck by doubt. The weather had been terrible all weekend and, although it wasn't raining just then, the cold air stung her cheeks. Bad-tempered because of this indecision which seemed to cover even the most trivial aspects of her life, an insecurity new to her, it suddenly occurred to her that Ruth Valldaura would have known what to do. It was an absurd, inappropriate thought, but one of which she was absolutely convinced. Ruth, who had decided to go and live with Héctor Salgado when she was little more than twenty, who had had a child at twenty-five, who at thirty-eight had separated to begin a different emotional life, taking that child with her, didn't give the impression of being an indecisive person. Maybe therein lay her charm, looking at the photos again: the apparent tranquillity was hiding an iron will, the capacity to exchange a well-trodden road for another less certain, without rejecting those left behind. As far as she knew, Ruth had managed to maintain good relationships with her parents, her ex-husband, her son. People little given to praise, like Martina Andreu and Superintendent Savall himself, had been affected when the news of her disappearance broke six months ago. And not only because of the esteem they felt for Héctor, but because of her. Because of Ruth. And even when Carol had mentioned she thought she'd end up leaving her, she'd done so sadly, not with hatred. 'Love creates eternal debts.'

You were brave, Ruth Valldaura, she said to the photo. What else did you do of your own accord? Why had you written down the doctor's address? That, at least, she might soon know. The good thing about her position, an officer on leave, was that she still had friends in various places, and simultaneously had a lot of free time. So, after finding the scrap of paper with Omar's address, she'd pulled some strings. It hadn't taken too much to get an acquaintance at the Brians 2 prison to allow her special permission to interrogate Damián Fernández – the lawyer who had killed Omar and had already spent a

234

few months inside waiting for the case to come to court – in private. The following day, Monday afternoon at four, she could speak to him.

However, she hadn't found out much about the girl in the photo, who, according to Ruth's mother, had been more than a friend to her daughter. Patricia Alzina had died in a traffic accident in August 1991, at the age of nineteen. Just as Montserrat Martorell had said, the car Patricia was driving had gone over a cliff in the Garraf mountains and the accident was attributed to the driver's inexperience and the relative difficulty of the road, riddled with bends. What Leire still didn't understand is why Patricia, a novice driver, had chosen that road instead of using the motorway which went through the mountain in a straight line. Any new driver would have done so in spite of the toll. But Ruth's mother had refused to give any further explanations and Leire didn't feel like tracking down the family of the dead young woman. At the end of the day, the accident had happened twenty years ago . . . And Leire didn't believe in ghostly girls lying in wait for their childhood friends at the bends in the road. Not even on nights like this, she thought, looking towards the street, when the wind seemed capable of breathing life into the dead. You're becoming macabre, Leire, she told herself. And Abel, who seemed to read her mind from inside her, indicated with a kick or two that he fancied a bit of movement. Without really knowing where she was going, she put on the Russian singer-songwriter coat and went out into the street.

It was the first weekend of sales and this had inspired people, despite the cold that had invaded the city with accumulated spite, as if it had been circling for months

235

and at last was ravaging pedestrians as they returned to their homes. An audible wind, one of those that evokes nervous branches and whirlwinds of dry leaves, assaulted the streets and mercilessly whipped those who dared to occupy pavements. Leire had barely taken a few steps when she considered turning around, but seeing the green light of a taxi that stopped at the traffic lights she changed her mind. Suddenly it occurred to her – and although the night didn't invite adventure, the desire to carry out her plan against all logic defied the elements almost without intending to.

After saying Ruth's address aloud, she asked herself why the hell she'd thought to go to a house so charmless. A closed house. Maybe it was the drone of the wind combined with the glacial atmosphere that pushed her towards that temporarily abandoned place. Or maybe it was that, with no reasonable explanation, she needed to see one of the scenes of the case that had plagued her for the last two days. Like someone visiting a secret tomb where no flowers could be left. 'You have a crazy mama,' she said to Abel in a quiet voice. 'But I promise we'll go straight home.'

The taxi left her in front of the building. The street was as deserted that night as it might have been the previous summer, the weekend Ruth disappeared. Leire walked to the corner and saw only a couple walking a dog. During the month of July, with the city even emptier, someone strong could have killed Ruth and put her corpse in a car in the middle of the night with little risk of being seen. But you already knew that, she reproached herself. What the hell was she doing there, then, other than wasting money on taxis? She raised her eyes to the large window of Ruth's flat, visible from the street. And was surprised to see a light inside.

She rang the bell without thinking, believing it would be Carol, and only a second after doing so the horrible possibility occurred to her that it might be Héctor who was there. If he answers I'm running away, she told herself, although she knew that, at the moment, running wasn't a possibility. She was surprised to hear a young masculine voice. She didn't recognize it, although it couldn't be anyone other than Guillermo.

'Hello,' said Leire. 'I . . . I'm a friend of—'

She didn't have to finish her sentence. A metallic hum permitted her entry into the hall.

The boy was waiting for her upstairs, the door ajar.

'Are you looking for my mother?' he said without crossing the threshold. He looked at her with a mixture of curiosity and suspicion, which didn't lessen on seeing that she was pregnant.

'You must be Guillermo. My name is Leire, Leire Castro. Maybe you've heard your father mention me?'

He nodded, but remained beside the door, blocking her way.

'Mind if I come in?'

Although she didn't really know what she was going to say, it was clear that she'd been presented with a golden opportunity to talk about Ruth with the one person around her to whom she wouldn't have had easy access. And she didn't intend to waste it.

The boy took his own sweet time thinking about it; then he shrugged and turned around, letting her through. Leire followed him and for the second time that week entered that space of large dimensions and very high ceilings. Ruth's tomb, she thought with a shiver.

The television was on and from the corner of her eye she saw a blonde in bed on the screen, but immediately realized it wasn't what it seemed. She didn't remember ever seeing porn in black and white.

Guillermo fell on to the sofa and she sought a chair: she preferred a less soft seat.

'You work with my father, don't you?' he asked.

Leire smiled.

'Well, really he is my superior. But now I'm on leave. Because of . . .' She pointed to her belly. As she feared the next question, 'What are you doing here?', would be difficult to answer without seeming a lunatic, she decided to ask it, albeit in the friendliest tone she could muster. 'And what are you doing here?'

For a moment she thought he was going to reply with, 'What are you doing here?' However, he didn't.

'It was my home. Now I come sometimes.'

'Of course.' Guillermo wasn't hostile or curious about her, so Leire decided to be honest. Teenagers can't bear being lied to, she thought. 'Look, I know it must seem strange my appearing like this. You know . . . you know we're still looking for your mother.'

Guillermo tensed and looked away from Leire to focus his attention on the screen.

'Are you watching a film?' She had to turn towards the television to be able to see it.

'It's *Breathless*.'

'Is it good? I haven't seen it . . .'

He shrugged again. When he spoke it was without emotion.

'It was Mama's favourite film.'

238

And then, perhaps because Abel was changing her, perhaps because the weekend had been strange and this Sunday evening even more unexpected, Leire felt something akin to compassion for this boy seeking refuge in what had been his mother's house. An immense, silent place with echoes of Ruth everywhere.

Guillermo had to be fourteen, but he wasn't very tall and was still more of a child than a teenager. She stared at him shamelessly, looking for resemblances, and came to the conclusion that there was much more of Ruth than Héctor, at least physically. His expression, however, was serious. Yes, that was the word. Not sad, not excited, just serious. One that belonged on an older person. The scarce light in the room, coming from a footlamp, was sketching a still shadow on the wall.

'Listen, I know that I've turned up here out of the blue and I understand you mightn't feel like talking to me. It's not as if you know me.' She tried to give her sentences a casual tone. 'But I want you to know we're doing everything we can to find out what happened to your mother.'

'I know they took my father off the case,' he said. He was succinct, concise.

'Against his will, I can assure you,' replied Leire. 'So I'm taking advantage of my leave to investigate a little off my own bat. He doesn't know, so if you don't mind not telling him . . . Or he'll crucify me.'

It was the first time Guillermo had smiled, though he made no comment.

'What's it about? I mean the film. Is it good?'

He shook his head, as if it pained him to admit it.

'It's pretty boring. He's a thief being chased by police and he asks his girlfriend to go on the run with him. She

239

loves him, although she betrays him in the end. She gives him away and they kill him.'

He said it as if it were incomprehensible. It probably would be for a kid of his age.

'I don't know why she does it,' he continued. 'Mama told me it was because she loved him too much and because sometimes that's scary. But I didn't understand that explanation either.'

No, thought Leire tenderly, you didn't understand. She felt a shiver and realized the house was freezing. She suddenly had the strongest urge to take that boy out of there as soon as possible.

'Aren't you cold?' she asked him.

'A little.'

'Want to . . . go and get something to eat?'

He looked at her, vaguely surprised.

'My treat,' said Leire. 'I'm sure you know a pizzeria around here. If you feel like it, of course . . .'

Guillermo nodded. He switched off the television with the remote and rose from the sofa.

'I can't be back too late,' he said, smiling. 'Or Papa will crucify me.'

They went to a nearby pizzeria as empty as the loft they'd just left. Leire entered thinking she wouldn't eat very much and ended up ordering two portions of pizza, the same as Guillermo. They chatted a little about everything – Carol, school and even Héctor as a father, but in the end, while they were waiting for the bill, the conversation went back to where it began.

'We'll find out what happened to her, Guillermo.'

He lowered his head and murmured, 'At first everyone

240

said, "We'll find your mother." Everyone – Papa, Carmen, even my tutor at school. They don't say that any more.'

'Well, if we find out what happened to her, perhaps—'

'You think she's dead.' He said it in a quiet voice, and had it not been for the look on his face Leire would have thought he didn't understand the full extent of what he'd said. 'Everyone thinks so. Papa most of all.'

She swallowed. She searched for something to say; every phrase seemed ridiculous.

'That's why I go to her house sometimes. To think about her without Papa noticing. Some day they'll close it and we'll take away her sketches and things . . . but while they're still here I can think she might come back some day.' He looked at her with an expression she'd never seen on a boy so young. 'No, I'm not stupid. I think she's dead too, but, sometimes, deceiving yourself for a while isn't bad, is it?'

'Of course it isn't. We all do it,' murmured Leire.

'The worst is when I go home and see Papa isn't sleeping, hardly eats. He just smokes, non stop. And I'm scared something will happen to him too.'

'Your father is much stronger than you think. Nothing's going to happen to him.'

He shook his head.

'Mama always said that Papa is only strong on the outside. And she knew him very well.'

The waiter brought them the bill, and when he left Leire was on the verge of taking Guillermo's hand. It was a spontaneous gesture that would have surprised her more than the boy and she managed to hold back. The maternal instinct appeared to be growing within her of its own will.

'Listen, I can't promise you that I'll find your mother alive. But I'll do everything possible to find out what happened to her. And when we know the truth, your father will be able to relax. I promise you.' She sensed Guillermo was looking at her sceptically, so she continued. 'Another thing: I'm going to give you my address and number, and if you want to talk about Ruth, about your mother sometime, phone me or come to see me. Okay?'

He saved her number in his mobile and they both went out into the street. Though it wasn't even ten o'clock, it was getting colder. Leire stopped a taxi and offered to drop Guillermo close to home.

'But please remember not to say anything to your father,' she repeated.

He smiled and accepted the deal.

Neither of them noticed the car following them.

26

Prisons, like hospitals, give off an unmistakable, characteristic smell. However much they try to remove any external connotations of prison by giving them an appearance closer to that of a big school, as soon as you cross the threshold, the yards, the bars, and even the offices that the prisoners rarely enter whisper of exclusion, of confinement. Of punishment.

This was the case even though Brians 2 was relatively new and the philosophy advocating rehabilitation had been applied emphatically in all its details. Planned to ease the human burden on hundred-year-old prisons like the Modelo in Barcelona, this new building, situated on the Martorell motorway, had been proudly inaugurated in the first decade of the twenty-first century. In January 2011, just a few years later, the Modelo was not significantly less full, nor was Brians 2 still managing to conceal its true purpose in spite of the fact that a quick glimpse would have shocked prison wardens of an earlier era. Its real nature dominated the architecture, as if infecting it from its nucleus. Absurd to fool oneself, thought Leire, whose opinions in this respect were not politically correct: those interned had committed a crime and therefore were condemned, for months or years, to live apart from society. Whether they took advantage of this time to re-educate themselves or not ended up being, like everything, the result of combining each personality with their circumstances. Some achieved it, others came out worse than they went in. That was life.

While she waited for her contact among the wardens to come to the visiting room with the prisoner, Leire felt the classic tingle of the investigator who believes they are about to discover something important. It was a familiar sensation and never wholly unfounded. Despite the fact that Inspector Salgado had rigorously interrogated Damián Fernández, who had been witness to the alleged 'curse' Dr Omar had carried out against Ruth, there was always the possibility of finding out something new. And for her, that was a shot of adrenaline. She heard the door open and turned around.

The months of imprisonment had made their mark on Damián Fernández, and, seeing him, Leire wondered how this man had been capable of doing away with Dr Omar, that old fox who in all likelihood had faced more threatening adversaries in his life. Perhaps that was his secret: that bland face, that normal appearance. Fernández's appearance had just one quality – that is, if going unnoticed is something to brag about. The only thing that drew attention to him was a bluish bruise on his right cheek.

'I suppose you don't remember me, Damián,' Leire began, thinking this was probably the case. 'My name is Leire Castro.'

'Yes. I remember you; you're Inspector Salgado's colleague, aren't you?'

They'd only seen each other a couple of times, at the station. Leire suspected once again that a gifted brain lurked within this guy, so she decided to proceed cautiously.

'I suppose you've come to see me because of the disappearance of your boss's ex-wife.'

'You're very astute.'

'Why else would you come?' he asked, shrugging his shoulders. 'All the visits I get are about that. The inspector himself, on various occasions, and even his superior . . . At the start they were more frequent. It's been a while now since anyone came to see me. I think little by little they're becoming convinced that I have nothing to say. Only what Omar told me.'

'And what was that, exactly?'

Damián seemed bored, sick of having to tell the same story again and again.

'I don't remember his exact words now. The general sense was that he was planning to strike a harsh blow against Salgado. "He will suffer the worst of sentences", or something like that. Omar never spoke clearly: he liked ambiguity.'

'And you didn't feel curious? Weren't you interested in his plans for revenge?'

'Omar wasn't a man you could ask questions, Agent Castro. And he liked to be enigmatic. He only added that he'd investigated him thoroughly, and then he began to say his old phrases, about the origin of evil, destiny, chance . . . His usual litany.'

'He didn't tell you if Ruth, Salgado's ex-wife, had come to see him?'

He seemed surprised at that.

'No. He had a photo of her, but he never said anything like that. And I don't think so. Why would she go?'

That was the question. Why? thought Leire. The only possible answer was that Ruth felt herself responsible for what Héctor had done and wanted to help him, although that meant venturing into the lion's den.

'Maybe to ask him to stop his efforts to destroy the inspector.'

Damián laughed.

'If she did, she was naive. Omar was determined to finish Salgado. Deep down the inspector should be grateful that the old guy is no longer in this world.'

'I doubt Inspector Salgado would agree,' replied Leire, while she wondered how to proceed. If Damián Fernández couldn't confirm whether Ruth had gone to see Omar, she'd have to find out some other way. And there was only one way. 'Damián, what happened to the tapes? You know the ones I mean: the ones Omar recorded in his clinic of all his visitors.'

'I have nothing to say about those tapes,' said Damián.

'Not even in exchange for my help?'

'Your help?'

'Let's not kid ourselves, Damián,' Leire pointed to the bruise, 'jail's not going too well for you. And I've friends among the wardens here. Good friends, you know. Are you sure a kind of special deal wouldn't suit you? You're looking at a long time behind bars.'

'I know those promises, Agent. They're forgotten so quickly . . .'

Leire decided to play her last card.

'Look, Damián, to be honest with you I don't think eliminating Omar from the world was such a terrible deed. But obstructing the investigation into Ruth Valldaura's disappearance does seem so to me. So I'm going to propose a deal.'

'You're more intelligent than the others. At least you don't threaten me.'

'I'm not investigating Dr Omar's death. All that interests me is finding out if Ruth went to see him or not. If you tell me where you put those tapes – and we both know you hid them somewhere – I promise you I'll make sure your life in prison is different. Better. And if in the end I manage to find Ruth thanks to your help, I'm sure Salgado and even the superintendent will be more than willing to intercede for you. Not to free you of your sentence, of course, but it could be shorter . . . and more comfortable. If not, you'll continue having it just as bad in here.' She was about to say she could arrange for his stint to be worse than it was, but she didn't.

'And what would I have to do?'

'Tell me where the tapes are.'

He lowered his voice. 'I only have some of them, the ones from the last few months. Since the day Inspector Salgado attacked Omar.'

'Where?'

'In a storage facility in the city, along with other stuff. I didn't want to keep them at home.'

Leire was surprised. How could they have overlooked this?

'Did you rent it in your name?'

He smiled.

'I'm not that stupid, Agent. I rented it in the name of Héctor Salgado.'

'Will you give me the address and key?'

'Promise not to forget me?'

Leire vowed to be true to her word.

'I'll do what I can to improve your life here, Damián. I swear.'

And he believed her.

27

Under normal circumstances, Leire would have gone to the storage locker that same Monday afternoon, but the prospect of crossing the entire city to get there persuaded her otherwise. Also, when she got off the train in Plaça Espanya, she was tired. The station was nearby and for a moment she was tempted to go in and speak to Sergeant Andreu. She decided to wait; it would be more sensible to do so when she had opened the locker than to raise false hopes beforehand.

In front of her, in the Arenas bullring, the grand opening of which as a shopping centre was planned for a few months' time, they were testing the lights. After years of work, those lights reminded her of her elder brother's Exin Castillos toy sets. Although Leire deeply detested the so-called 'national party', converting that space into another mountain of shops seemed almost disrespectful to the poor animals who had died in the arena. But the word 'shop' had given her an idea: she'd drop into a video store she'd seen near her house and rent or, failing that, buy the film Guillermo had been watching at his mother's house.

She finally arrived home after seven, truly exhausted,

determined not to go out again until the next day. She had an appointment with the doctor at ten a.m. and wanted him to find her well rested. Abel seemed tired too and she had to wait a good while for him to move. She smiled when at last he did. 'So you're there, kid? Today Mama did a little too much, but I promise now we're going to stay at home in peace, watching TV.' She called María, who accompanied her to her medical appointments as often as she could, and arranged a time for the following morning. We haven't seen each other in days, she thought, which must mean there is a new boyfriend in her life. After the African adventure, María had come back without her NGO boyfriend, ranting about him but happy to have spent the summer doing something different. Strange, Leire thought. Pregnancy had changed her perspective on life, and her friend's exploits, which she used to find amusing, were starting to bore her. You're acting like an old woman, she warned herself. And you're going to be a mother, not a grandmother.

She had to agree with Guillermo with regard to *Breathless*. Apart from starring Jean-Paul Belmondo, with whom she'd run away without thinking twice, the pace was so slow that Leire fell asleep on the sofa half an hour into the film and awoke at the end when a heartbroken Jean Seberg, hatefully slim, informed on her lover and watched him die from a bullet wound. 'She loved him too much,' Ruth had said. 'Sometimes that's scary.' She was so tired that even thinking hurt and she went to bed feeling that, had she been more alert, she'd have understood Ruth and her preference for this film of doomed love a little better.

*

The following morning, true to her word, María picked her up and accompanied her to Sant Joan de Déu, the hospital where she would give birth to Abel in a few weeks, all being well. According to the doctor, everything was going wonderfully, although he insisted severely that she should rest. There was still the risk of premature labour: Abel might decide to be born before his due date, he warned her. On the other hand, he congratulated her on her weight, which she couldn't believe and attributed to her walks and to having been restrained with food, and he made her an appointment for the following week. 'Not long now,' he encouraged her. 'And rest. I know it's boring, but soon it'll be over.'

They emerged on to the street and headed towards the car park where they'd left the car.

'So,' María said, 'I'll take you home, eh?'

Leire hesitated; she knew her friend would tell her off if she asked her to take her to the storage locker Fernández had rented on the outskirts of Poblenou, Héctor's *barrio*, instead of obeying the doctor. But, on the other hand, someone taking her there by car and then home was difficult to resist.

'You mind taking me somewhere?'

'Don't tell me you want to go shopping?'

'I have to pick something up.' She didn't want to seem mysterious, though neither did she feel like explaining further. ' Call it . . . a craving.'

María gave in, unwillingly, nudged as much by the wish to please her friend as by her curiosity. In exchange, Leire brought her up to date on what Tomás had said before leaving.

'Holy shit! So he's planning to come and live here?'

251

said María when she heard. 'He'll be a model papa in the end. And how do you feel about it?'

'I suppose it'll be good to have him closer when Abel is born. Above all, for the little one.'

Her friend smiled.

'Why is it so hard for you to admit you're excited?' But seeing Leire's serious face, she added, 'Okay, I'm shutting up, Miss Daisy. I'll drive, no more questions.'

But she couldn't keep her mouth shut when they arrived at the address Leire had given her. They found themselves in front of a new building: an invention to alleviate the fact that the city's apartments, at least the affordable ones, were so much smaller than people needed.

'Coming here is a craving? Eating strawberries is a craving!' María blurted out.

'Wait for me. It'll only take a moment.'

And, by one of life's flukes, it did. Leire opened the door of storage room 12, which in fact was practically empty. It didn't take long to find a sportsbag, full of video tapes, and return to the car.

'See, grouchy? Done!' she said as she got in.

'What do you have there?'

Leire unzipped it and pulled a tape partly out.

'Porn,' she told her. 'I have to do something at home, don't I?'

'Well, it must be vintage porn, sweetheart,' she replied. 'Don't tell me you still have a video player at home?'

She didn't have a video player at home, but it occurred to her to ask in the same shop where she'd rented the film the day before, and she emerged with one for a reasonable price. She spent a few minutes installing it and then started to go through the tapes. Although there weren't many, Leire felt a good spell of dark-image, fixed-camera, silent cinema was ahead of her. Before inserting one at random she examined them thoroughly: the tapes had only a number identifying them, and Leire told herself that, had Ruth gone to see Omar, he would have marked the tape recording that visit in a special way. It was logical to think so, even with no proof of it, and when she saw that one of the tapes had an asterisk beside the number she decided to begin with that. If she wasn't right, she hadn't lost anything.

The camera had to be situated in a corner of the room, because Leire could see Dr Omar's desk, with him in profile, and the person who would enter and take a seat across from him. For twenty minutes she watched the fixed image of that desk and the people sitting opposite the doctor, and couldn't help wondering how they could trust someone so sinister. As she'd imagined, there was no sound on the tapes, so setting aside the disagreeable feeling of seeing that old man, the contents were rather boring. But suddenly, when she was starting to think the asterisk meant nothing, she straightened up in her chair, open-mouthed. For the first time in her life, Leire saw Ruth Valldaura alive and moving.

Her heart rate accelerated. So she *had* gone . . . 'Love creates eternal debts.' And Ruth had loved Héctor Salgado, so it was likely that she would go to see Omar with the intention of helping her ex-husband, accused of having severely beaten the black witch doctor. She cursed the lack of sound with all her heart, moved closer to the screen and focused on their faces. Ruth, half worried, half surprised, scornful at one point; he indifferent, almost sarcastic and, at the end, extremely serious. Then Ruth rose and left quickly, as if wishing to flee from that room she'd entered of her own will.

She watched the recording again and again, not getting much more from it, until her eyes hurt from fixing them on the screen. Frustrated by not managing to understand what they were saying, she was preparing to switch it off when the intercom buzzed. Leire pressed pause on the remote and went to the door.

'Yes?'

'Leire Castro?'

'Yes. Who is it?'

Leire noticed that the television screen was being reflected in the hall mirror, where Dr Omar's image was frozen. Wrinkles from evil, not just old age, she thought. The profile of a black vulture.

'You don't know me, but I think we should talk.'

A middle-aged man's voice.

'Who are you?' she repeated.

'My name is Andrés Moreno, but my name won't mean anything to you. I have reason to believe we're both interested in the same person.'

'Listen, I don't know—'

'I can give you information about Ruth Valldaura.'

'What?'

The old man seemed to be smiling; one hand raised, a hand with fingers delicate as wire that looked as if they could cut you with a caress.

'You heard. I think there's something you should know about her. Let me in, please.'

254

Leire felt a sudden fear and refused. She didn't plan on letting a stranger into her home and told him so.

'As you wish,' the man replied. 'We'll do something else. I'll give you my number: call me tomorrow and we'll arrange a meeting in a public place. Does that seem better?'

Somehow the voice resembled the reflection of the face on the screen, although that was absurd. He didn't have the accent of an old Nigerian, and neither was it a voice from beyond the grave. Leire noticed that her knees were shaking and she forced herself to calm down.

'All right,' she said, jotting the number down.

'Please call me.'

In the mirror, Dr Omar was still ecstatic. Immortalized. Threatening as a serpent ready to spit his venom.

AMANDA

"AMANDA"

28

Seated on one of the chairs in Terminal 1 of the airport, Héctor contemplated a small screen announcing that the flight from Madrid was delayed by forty minutes. Seven years and forty minutes, he mentally corrected. It was the first time in his life he'd welcomed a delay of that kind, and, as he watched the terminal shops closing, he thought he needed a little silence, albeit in a public place with black tiles that gave off an almost insulting shine. He hadn't slept in over forty hours and he closed his eyes just for an instant, to rest them from the light. He didn't stir from the terminal because he didn't want to smoke any more – he'd fought tiredness with nicotine and felt the weight of too much tobacco combined with little food and accumulated fatigue. He looked at his watch. 22.35.

The previous night, that same hour, a cold Sunday of grey, sluggish skies was coming to an end. Guillermo had just arrived and immediately shut himself in his room, saying he'd already eaten, without further explanation. And he, watching Marilyn languishing in *The Misfits*, that Western played out by actors who would die shortly afterwards, chose to let it go. The film hadn't yet finished when he received the call from Agent Fort from the station, informing him – in a voice not quite concealing a newbie's hint of excitement – that Saúl Duque, Sílvia Alemany's assistant, had just contacted the *Mossos* to confess that he had killed Amanda Bonet.

White death. That was his first thought on entering the bedroom where Amanda lay and Fort had already arrived with Forensics and the court representative. Walls painted ivory white, a bed with immaculate sheets and a young blonde whose pale features would never again recover the flush of the living. The presence of a corpse always disturbed him; it affected everyone, say what they might. However, Amanda's body exuded a serenity he'd rarely felt at the scene of a sudden death. Her lips seemed to be smiling, as if she'd experienced a sweet vision before leaving this world and slipped towards the beyond, or towards nothingness, her conscience calm and full of hope. Martyrs must die like that, Héctor said to himself, though he doubted Amanda Bonet could qualify as such.

'She took an entire bottle of sleeping pills,' Fort told him.

'She took them?' asked Héctor. Roger Fort's voice had brought him back to reality, moving him away from tragic fantasies. 'I understood on the phone that Saúl Duque had said he was to blame.'

On coming into the flat, Héctor had seen Saúl sitting on the sofa, so tense he seemed about to split into two, guarded by a judicial agent.

Fort breathed in and exhaled slowly before answering.

'It's fairly complicated, sir,' he finally said. 'I think it'd be better for him to explain it to you directly.'

Héctor nodded. He looked over the room, trying to

pick out some jarring detail, something that would drive from his mind the notion that they were faced with a third suicide, the continuation of the macabre series that had started with Gaspar Ródenas in September the year before. Everything appeared in order: an antique-style cast-iron bed, bars painted white, matching the nightstands. Two black cords, coiled like snakes on the nightstand nearest Héctor, broke the harmony.

'And these?' he asked Fort.

'Cords,' he said, somewhat uncomfortable. 'They would use them to play. She and Saúl Duque . . .'

'That explains the marks on the wrists,' said the forensic officer, who had remained silent until then, examining the body. 'Look.'

Héctor came closer. Indeed, reddish marks could be seen on both.

'She died only a few hours ago, right?' Héctor asked him.

'Yes. She's been dead no more than four hours.' It was a quarter past eleven at night. 'I'm almost finished; we'll take her as soon as the judge authorizes it.' He looked towards the corpse with a slight unease not typical of someone who'd spent years dealing with them. 'She looks happy, like she's enjoying a magnificent dream.'

'And the sleeping pills?'

'Here you are.' He'd kept the box in a pre-sealed bag. 'Amobarbital. Very common. She had to have taken a good quantity to die that way. She didn't even try to bring them back up. Sometimes they do, and as their strength fails they drown in their own vomit. She simply went to sleep; her brain was deprived of oxygen and she died. That's why she looks so . . . peaceful.'

'Let's go and talk to Duque,' Héctor decided. 'I think he'll have things to tell us and that way we let the forensics get on with their work.'

Saúl Duque was still seated. He was immobile, leaning slightly forward, hands gripping the edge of the sofa as if he were facing a precipice and scared of falling into the abyss. He was dressed head to toe in black and Héctor had the feeling he'd chosen this outfit knowing full well a funeral awaited him. Or perhaps as a contrast to the white prevailing in the whole flat.

'Would you mind leaving us alone?' Héctor asked the officer guarding him. And turning to Duque, he added: 'Saúl . . . Saúl, are you all right?'

He laid his hand softly on his shoulder and then, feeling the touch and hearing that friendly voice, the man collapsed. The tension keeping him upright evaporated and his body slumped, exhausted. He covered his face with his hands and Héctor wouldn't have been able to say if he was sobbing out of sorrow, fear or remorse. Perhaps all three.

It took him a few minutes to calm down enough to be able to speak.

'I . . . I'm sorry,' he murmured. 'I'm better now. I didn't expect to see you again, Inspector,' he said in an attempt to restore normality in such abnormal circumstances.

'Neither did I, Saúl. I believe you have already spoken to Agent Fort, but I need you to tell me what happened here tonight.'

Duque gave Roger Fort a quizzical look, but he didn't take it personally.

'Have they told you anything about the relationship between Amanda and me?'

Héctor thought he detected some shame in that young man's voice. He was going to assure him that no one, except those participating, should meddle in erotic games between adults, when Fort answered, 'Better if you explain it to the inspector yourself.'

He took a deep breath and looked Salgado in the eye. Any trace of shame had vanished. 'Amanda and I had a dominant-submissive relationship.'

'Do you mean a sado-masochistic relationship?'

'Well, yes . . . call it what you want. I'm not going to fuss about technicalities.'

'Explain to me what it consisted of.'

Saúl gestured indifferently and made a face that at any other time could have been an ironic smile. Just then, thought Héctor, it expressed more nervousness than anything else.

'It was just a game . . . It's . . . it's very difficult to explain it to those not involved in the scene. If I tell you I was her master, I controlled her, I told her how she must dress, what she must eat for dinner, you'll think we were a pair of nutters.'

'Not at all.' He said it in a tone which must have sounded convincing because Duque continued.

'I don't know why I like it, and Amanda, for her part, didn't know either. We simply enjoyed ourselves with it. With the phone calls and emails. With the cords, with the spanking.'

'When did it begin?'

'A little while after Amanda started working at Alemany Cosmetics. You must be wondering how we came to discover how much we complemented each other.' He smiled. 'I suppose we were both looking for

263

it and sounded each other out on the subject, casually, a couple of times. The second time we met I chanced hinting at it, half joking, and saw that the idea attracted her as much as me.'

'Did you see each other often?'

'Every Sunday and a day here and there, by surprise. But not many: you can't abuse it too much or the spell is broken.'

Héctor nodded.

'Did she give you keys to her house?'

'No, only to the front door. She'd leave the other one under the doormat just before I arrived. It formed part of the set. So I'd come in as if it were my house and she would already be waiting for me . . . Well, waiting for me in her role.'

'I understand. And today?'

Duque took another deep breath. At that moment his appearance portrayed weakness rather than the ability to dominate.

'The one today was a special game,' he finally confessed, blushing. 'She had to wait for me asleep. Completely asleep,' he stressed.

'And you would have sexual relations without her knowing. That was the game?' asked Héctor sarcastically.

'I knew you wouldn't understand. When you say it that way I sound sick and she . . .' He interlaced his fingers and fixed his gaze on the inspector in a desperate attempt to appeal to his empathy. 'Our relationship was more about the presentation than the sex, strictly speaking. She would offer me her body in exchange for nothing other than for me to enjoy it. The maximum proof of submission, of obedience . . .'

Héctor took a few seconds to react.

'Fine,' he said in a neutral voice. 'So she had to wait for you asleep, which I suppose meant she took the sleeping pills a while before you were to arrive. Am I right?'

'Yes. I suppose she . . . she took more than the usual amount—'

'Wait a second, we'll get to the dosage.' The inspector's furrowed brow indicated deep concentration. 'What I meant before is that she had to leave the key outside a good while before your arrival.'

'Ye— I hadn't thought about it. Of course. Before the pills took effect.'

'And what time did you come?'

'Later than expected. Some friends came round and I didn't get away from them until half past eight, so I didn't get here until after half nine. I didn't look at the time. The key was where it always was, so I came in and went straight to her room.'

For an instant, Héctor and Fort feared that this confession might be more than they could take without being unprofessional.

'What you're thinking didn't happen,' said Saúl Duque. 'She was beautiful, just as I had asked of her. White sheets and white nightgown. Sleeping for me. I was admiring her for a few minutes and began to get aroused. She was so beautiful. She looked so defenceless, lying there on the bed . . . I took the cords from the drawer of the nightstand and when I tied her wrists I realized they were inert. I tried to bring her round, I shook her, I kissed her . . . I was like a madman. I don't know how much time passed before I finally called the police.'

'You called the station at 22.34,' Fort interjected.

Héctor meditated for a few seconds.

'Saúl . . . What I'm going to ask you now might surprise you, but have you realized that three people from the company have died in strange circumstances in only a few months? Three people,' he went on in a quiet but firm voice, 'of the eight that were part of a single group.'

Saúl looked at him, uncomprehending. Then, little by little, his expression reacted to this revelation.

'Gaspar. Sara. And now – Amanda. What are you trying to say?'

'I don't know. That's what we're trying to find out. Saúl, did Amanda tell you about anything that happened that weekend? Anything strange, unusual? Anything relating to the dogs they found strangled, perhaps?'

He shook his head and Héctor felt overwhelmed with exasperation. For a moment he'd believed maybe this man would know, that he'd have the answer, even if unconsciously.

'Well, the only thing that happened – that happened to Amanda – was the fright she got on the Friday night, when I called her. But it didn't have anything to do with the dogs . . .' He seemed confused.

'Tell me.'

'I called her every Friday night, around nine. She had to be free to answer. Obviously I knew she was with everyone in the house, but I called her anyway and ordered her to go outside. She obeyed me, as always.'

'What else?'

'We started to play. I told her to move away from the house, I rebuked her, I asked her to . . .' He stopped himself, suddenly embarrassed once again.

266

'Go on,' ordered Héctor.

'You don't know the house, right? It's an old *masía* in Empordà, converted into an activity centre now. It was run as luxury rural accommodation as well. It's away from the town and surrounded by woods, although you can reach it by motorway with no problems. Amanda had taken the lantern and, so as not to be surprised by any of the others, moved down the access path to go a little way into the trees. She said she didn't like it, it was dark; I insisted, so she did as she was told. In that and in touching herself. I wanted her to get aroused, touch her breasts in the open air . . . I wanted to hear her moan and she started to. And then I heard a scream and the call was cut off.'

'Amanda screaming?'

'She called me a few minutes later, very upset. It seemed she thought she saw a man watching her in the darkness. Seeing how she was touching herself. The man did nothing, didn't follow her or anything like that; anyway, Amanda was frightened and ran back to the path.'

'Is that all?'

'Yes. But that was on the Friday. They found those poor animals the following day.'

'And they buried them, everyone has told us so,' confirmed Héctor, annoyed. 'Are you sure nothing else happened?'

'Not then, later on – but it was to do with that weekend. After the summer, Amanda said we should be more careful because she suspected Sara Mahler had found out about us. Sara was strange, you know? You never knew what she was thinking.'

Héctor nodded. Her Dutch flatmate had also made

some comment of the sort. The image of Sara, this unattractive and solitary woman, listening to the secrets of those enjoying a more intense sex life, caused him a moment's unease.

'Do you know if Amanda confirmed her suspicions or was it just conjecture?'

Saúl Duque shook his head, although before he could add anything further the court secretary, who had appeared mid-conversation and gone towards the room where Amanda had died, ordered the removal of the body. Saúl stood up, as if he wished to pay his respects to that body, covered with a white sheet, being transported on a stretcher towards the door by a retinue of strangers.

Héctor observed the boy's face and was surprised by the expression of sorrow that appeared. Unmistakable and difficult to fake. And he thought Saúl Duque might have some unusual sexual preferences, enjoy exercising mild power over a victim who offered herself to the game with the same desires, get turned on by whipping her or humiliating her . . . However, at the same time he was sure that this man had felt something for Amanda that not many would call love, but went further than mere pleasure.

'I'm sorry, Señor Duque, you'll have to accompany me to the station,' Héctor told him, partly because he couldn't be discounted as a suspect and partly because, for a moment, he feared Saúl Duque would do something terrible if they left him alone that night. Enough suicides, he thought. Real or fake. Enough deaths. 'Fort, do a thorough search of the house. The bedroom above all. Prints, you know, anything . . .' And without Duque hearing he added, 'Treat this as if it were a homicide. Three suicides is too many. Call it instinct or stubbornness, but I don't buy it.'

Without the shops and bars that disguised its function as a simple crossroads, the terminal was becoming a silent, calm space. If the seat were more comfortable, he could almost call it cosy. Some travellers were advancing along the moving walkways, effortlessly hastening away from him in the direction of their boarding gates, like automata in a silent film. The sight calmed him after a long stressful day. A Monday that seemed never-ending.

'Three suicides is too many.' Héctor repeated the sentence in front of Sílvia Alemany, who, standing in her office, had the decency to look upset.

At eight a.m., after spending the night at the station guarding Saúl Duque, he'd managed to locate a solicitor friend of his, who went through the necessary processes to send the young man home. Héctor drank a quick coffee, not hungry for breakfast, and assuaged the feeling of nausea with two cigarettes. A brief conversation with Fort, who'd already returned from the alleged suicide's apartment, had thrown some light and further shadows on the case. If any doubt remained about the relationship linking Amanda to Saúl, the accessories found in her flat had dispelled it completely. One of her wardrobes could have been part of a sex shop, judging by the abundance of toys: a whip, various riding crops, a fine bamboo cane, a number of leather paddles of various sizes and thicknesses, cords, handcuffs, vibrators of differing sizes, Chinese balls, lingerie and other costumes . . . Each to their own, but Amanda and Saúl certainly hadn't been bored. The unanswered questions came from a different angle. Amanda's death could be the suicide of a young woman whose sex life seemed to indicate some internal conflict. It could also be a homicide, because it was difficult to believe that someone like Amanda wouldn't know that an entire bottle of sleeping pills would put her to sleep for ever. This hypothesis was what led him, for the moment, to Saúl Duque.

Héctor decided he would be the one to bring the news of Amanda Bonet's death to the company where she worked. He wanted to see Sílvia Alemany's face when she found out and wanted to take advantage of the shock to catch her with her guard down. To get information out of her once and for all. But Sílvia was a tough nut to crack, as she was showing.

'I can't believe it, Inspector.' She brought her hands to her face and seemed to sway a little. 'Let me sit down. Amanda . . . But when? Where?'

'Last night, at home. Forensics estimate that she died between eight and nine. They found an empty bottle of sleeping pills beside her.'

Héctor spoke as coldly as possible. If he wanted to break the will of the woman before him he couldn't pussyfoot around. And to tell the truth, he didn't feel like being polite.

'Do you want to tell me where you were at that time?'

'At home. I was ill all weekend. But, Inspector . . . you don't think that I . . . ? Come on, that's ridiculous.'

She flushed, more out of fear than because she felt offended, Héctor was sure.

'Right now I'm not thinking, Señora Alemany. I'm just trying to tie up loose ends. And the loose ends bring me to Gaspar Ródenas, Sara Mahler and Amanda Bonet. Three healthy young people, no apparent problems, whose only common link is their work here and this photo. You can say whatever you like; you won't convince me you're not hiding something from me. Not this time.'

Cards on the table, the declaration of war spelled out.

'You think we're hiding something from you?'

'I was only speaking of you, but I see you move quickly from the first person to the plural.' Héctor had the satisfaction of seeing her grow pale. 'Does this "we" refer to the others? César Calvo, Brais Arjona, Octavi Pujades and Manel Caballero? Or only some of them?'

'Inspector, you're in my office so I request you don't raise your voice to me.'

'And you're before a police inspector, and I request you stop lying to me.'

'The truth has to be discovered to prove a lie, Inspector Salgado. Until then, lies don't exist.'

He smiled. He quite liked having a worthy adversary.

'Do you have a meetings room here? Then call the others and tell them to come immediately.'

'I repeat, I will not take orders from you. I'm a solicitor, Inspector, and, although I don't practise as such, I will not permit you to treat me or my employees as mere criminals.'

'Get rid of the "mere". Certainly not that. Whether criminals or not remains to be seen.' He paused briefly and softened his tone a little. 'Listen, it would be much more intelligent on your part to cooperate. The way you're behaving, it's easy to come to the conclusion that you all have something to do with the deaths of your colleagues.'

Sílvia was still pale. Maybe it was true she'd been sick all weekend. In any case, she didn't seem very well.

'I repeat: can you do me the favour of gathering the others in the room? I think it's better to bring them together there than go and interview them in front of the whole company, don't you agree?'

She didn't answer. She lifted the receiver to let them know.

The room was between the offices of the Alemany siblings and Héctor noticed Víctor's was still empty. Bosses never turn up before ten, he told himself, thinking of Savall.

He asked them to sit down, but Sílvia Alemany remained standing beside him, as he explained his reasonings point by point. Octavi Pujades wasn't there, of course, and Héctor would have to send Fort to interview him at his home if he couldn't go himself. The faces of the three men expressed different emotions, though one stood out among the rest: surprise on Brais Arjona and Manel Caballero, the latter almost on the verge of panic; on the other hand, César Calvo seemed to have accepted Amanda's death with more composure.

'So that's how things stand, gentlemen. Of the eight people who spent that weekend of team-building together,' he said, looking at Sílvia out of the corner of his eye, 'three have died in suspicious circumstances. On 5 September, Gaspar Ródenas shot himself after killing his wife and child; exactly four months later, in the early hours of 6 January, Sara Mahler jumped on to the tracks of the metro. And last night, scarcely ten days later, Amanda Bonet allegedly took a whole bottle of sleeping pills. Three suicides. No apparent motive. No notes explaining their reasons. No warnings or previous attempts. And now I ask you: are you sure you have nothing to tell me?'

Manel Caballero's hands were shaking. He was the only one showing anything other than concern. However, it was not he who spoke, but Brais Arjona.

'I understand all this is strange, Inspector. I must admit it's beginning to worry me too. But I don't know how we can help you. At least I don't know how I can.'

'Where were you last night, between eight and half past nine?'

'At home, with David. Well, I don't know what time I got back.' He turned to Manel Caballero, who looked at him with the same fear with which he watched the inspector. 'What time did we say goodnight? Must have been around eight, right?'

Héctor almost smiled. So that's what it was about now: shared alibis. He didn't wait for Caballero to answer but turned to César Calvo, his voice heavy with sarcasm.

'And I suppose you were with your fiancée, right? All very convenient.'

'Even if it seems like a lie to you, that's correct.'

'I was in bed,' interrupted Sílvia. 'I've already told you I didn't feel well. I don't know what time César left, but my daughter could tell you. And spare us the sarcasm, Inspector. We're doing all we can to cooperate.'

Héctor hated her just then. He took a deep breath and remained calm. The only thing he'd got from the conversation with Saúl Duque was Amanda's fleeting encounter with someone in the wood. Best not to mention it, he thought. Hold on to that card until you know where to place it, Salgado.

273

'If you wish to speak to Octavi Pujades, my assistant will give you his number. You are aware that Señor Pujades has taken a leave of absence, due to his wife's illness.'

Héctor smiled. Here, at least, he could score a point.

'When you speak of your assistant, are you referring to Saúl Duque?'

'Yes.'

'I thought you didn't like the term.' He stopped smiling and put on a worried expression. 'I'm afraid Señor Duque won't be coming to work for a few days. He's very upset, disturbed frankly, after finding his partner dead in her bed.'

The ceiling of the room could have caved in and no one would have even screamed. The expression on every face in the room was a mixture of shock and fear in which Héctor took pleasure. Sadism is contagious, he said inwardly.

'Perhaps you didn't know that Saúl and Amanda were in a relationship?' He didn't want to go into detail – there was no need. 'Well, life is full of surprises for everyone, don't you think? Surprises and secrets. But it's only a matter of time: little by little the truth rises to the surface . . . That's what my work consists of. Bringing the truth to light, exposing it for everyone to see. And I assure you, I enjoy it.'

The forty minutes had already been sixty and felt like two hundred. Héctor was no longer capable of thought; his brain was beginning to run down, wanting to disconnect. And then, when fatigue was about to send his consciousness to hell, the doors began to vomit people out. Stressed travellers with bags under their eyes, looking at the clock, wishing to end a day already longer than expected.

There she was. He saw her walk towards him and smiled although it was difficult to keep his eyes open.

Lola.

Seven years and many minutes later.

29

No doubt about it, the best remedy for insomnia wasn't the tablets the therapist had recommended, but skipping a night altogether, tiring the body until it was exhausted and went out like a mobile with a dead battery. Although Héctor hadn't slept more than six hours, he awoke more refreshed than he'd felt for some time. Alert enough to face the case at hand: this mystery of suicides and strangled dogs.

So that Tuesday morning, as he had breakfast with Guillermo – an hour in which his son's silence was a blessing – Héctor contemplated with satisfaction a page of the paper he'd gone down to buy even before filling the cafetiere. There it was, the article agreed with Lola by telephone, which she'd written with the scant information he'd emailed her the previous afternoon. Héctor smiled at the headline: 'Young, free and . . . dead. Strange wave of suicides among the workers of a single company'. Lola had been careful: she hadn't referred to Alemany Cosmetics at any point, but the slogan was unmistakable. The photos of Gaspar, Sara and Amanda completed a text that implied more than it explained.

That was the deal, or perhaps, if he were honest with

himself, the bait to lure her to the city: he was giving her information on a case that seemed to be becoming far-reaching; she was writing for a national newspaper. And between us, Héctor was thinking, we put Alemany Cosmetics in the eye of the hurricane, to see if the current of air clarifies their thinking or makes them more loquacious. He was sure that the concepts of their new campaign wouldn't mesh well with a text talking about three dead employees.

He must have smiled while he was thinking, because his son looked at him, curious. It wasn't a very edifying example for an adolescent, and so as not to explain he chose to say, 'Guille, I'm going to be slightly crazy with a case over the next few days. You saw what happened on Sunday: they called me in the middle of the night and I didn't get back until very late last night.' He blurted out the question all of a sudden. 'You're all right, aren't you? It's just I know living here isn't the same as living with Mama . . .'

His son shrugged.

'I don't know what that means.' Héctor poured himself a second cup of coffee and was tempted to leave it there, but something impeded him. 'Yes, yes I do. I suppose this isn't ideal for a boy your age, and I know I should pay you more attention, although honestly you don't help much either. No, it's not a criticism, not completely. It's just that we're alike and that complicates things. Before—'

'Before Mama was here. But now she's not.'

'Exactly. Now she's not. But I am . . . though not very much and maybe not very well. I'm here and you can count on me. Always.'

277

It was one of those phrases that, said out loud, seemed lifted from an American family film, one of those where fathers and sons tell one another all the time how much they love each other; but nothing better occurred to Héctor. Maybe because some of us had to learn to be a father through cinema, he thought somewhat bitterly.

Guillermo nodded and poured more cereal into his bowl of milk. Héctor took a gulp of coffee. The teaspoons hit the dishes. The kitchen tap was dripping. If we had a clock the ticking would sound like fucking bullets, Salgado thought.

Héctor cleared his throat and rose in search of a cigarette. His son put his bowl in the sink then went for his backpack. Before leaving he stuck his head around the kitchen door.

'Papa,' he said, looking at the floor.

'What?'

'I just wanted you to know I'm here too. And you can count on me.' He smiled. 'Almost always. Running, you're on your own.'

Héctor smiled and threw a tea towel at him, which Guillermo threw back even harder.

'Go or you'll be late. Guille!' he shouted after him. 'If some days I'm not here by dinnertime, go to Carmen's, okay? I'll speak to her. I don't want you eating a sandwich every night.'

'Okay. That way I see Charly.'

He'd forgotten. That was why they hadn't seen her all weekend: she had the prodigal son at home. Héctor was going to say something else but Guillermo was already gone. He drank the second coffee with a second cigarette, unable to rid himself of a strange nagging feeling, although shortly afterwards the memory of Lola and the short journey to her hotel forced it out.

As he drove, Héctor had realized the years had stolen away something so essential: complicity. It was also clear that they were both tired, as well as a little unsure how to treat one another. En route to the hotel, they exchanged vague remarks about flights and delays, but finally, when they reached their destination, he asked her, 'How's life?' Lola looked at him, gave him that characteristic smile and said, 'I'd need more than seven minutes to cover seven years, Héctor. I'm tired. We'll talk.'

The offices of CCDC, the Corporate Continuous Development Centre, were located on Diagonal, not far from Plaça Francesc Macià, and had an even more American air than the conversation in the kitchen. On a bright summer day there would be a fantastic view from the window, but on that mid-January Tuesday dirty raindrops were blotting the glass and blurring the background. After getting the information thanks to Saúl Duque, Héctor had called the day before, mid-afternoon, to arrange a meeting with the instructors in charge of the Alemany Cosmetics group. And here they were before him: an older, heavier, greyer man who answered to the name of Señor Ricart, and a young but completely bald man. When they had granted him a meeting the article hadn't yet been published, but both seemed to be up to date with the situation. And in all likelihood Sílvia Alemany will have called them this morning, thought Héctor. To warn them.

'On the phone I didn't really understand how we can

help you, Inspector,' the younger man began. The other, his boss no doubt, watched and stayed quiet.

'To be honest, neither do I,' Salgado admitted. 'According to my notes, a while back you took over Alemany Cosmetics' training days. In March last year, you organized a weekend away for a group of eight. Sílvia Alemany, César Calvo, Brais Arjona, Octavi Pujades, Manel Caballero, Gaspar Ródenas, Sara Mahler and Amanda Bonet. As you already know' – he waited for them to nod, but neither did – 'three of these people have died in the last few months in . . . let's say strange circumstances. Too much of a coincidence, don't you think? So I'd be grateful if you could give me all the information you have about those away days.'

The two men exchanged a quick glance and for the first time the elder of the two spoke.

'I shouldn't think that'll be a problem, Inspector. Although to be honest I don't think there's much to tell.'

He put on his reading glasses and looked over some papers lying on the table.

'I remember now.' He took them off and continued. 'It was an interesting group from our point of view, Inspector.'

'Oh yes?'

He was quiet for a moment, unsure of how to approach the subject. 'Do you know anything about group theory?'

'A little, though I'm sure you can expand my knowledge with an enlightening summary,' said Salgado, smiling.

'I'll try, Inspector. Joan,' said Señor Ricart, turning to his assistant, 'I don't think there's any need for us both to be here. If Inspector Salgado wishes to speak to you, he can do so afterwards.'

Joan seemed surprised but caught the most direct hint Salgado had heard for a while and left.

'This way we'll be more relaxed. I have to be so politically correct in front of my employees. First of all, Inspector, I should tell you that I don't think what I'm going to say will give you any relevant information . . .'

'Let me be the judge of that.'

'I'll try to be clear, at least. Let's see, I've already said it was an interesting group from our point of view and I'll explain why. In a group of eight we usually identify one leader, two at most. However, in this one we counted three, and that's unusual.

'There was of course the official leader, Sílvia Alemany, and the one who we call the leader by experience, Octavi Pujades. But immediately another very strong one emerged who relegated the first two to second place.'

'Brais Arjona?' Héctor ventured.

'Ten points, Inspector. Yes: the natural leader through ability, not responsibility, age or experience. Señor Arjona fulfilled all the requisites for that role: young, strong, intelligent. Very involved and decisive.'

'What do you mean by that?'

'I mean he inspired confidence when it was time to work, although he didn't try to win the others over socially.'

'The others?'

'Amanda, Gaspar, César . . . Mere followers, of one type or another. I did pick up on some tension between Brais Arjona, the natural leader, and one of Sílvia Alemany's unconditional followers, César Calvo.'

Intrigued, Héctor nodded.

'Was there an argument?'

'Not in the sense you mean. Simple disagreements between them when facing common tasks. Note when I speak of tension I'm referring to concrete, finite moments: a tendency to compete, align themselves in different groups, put forward opposing viewpoints to resolve something. For the first two days. On the third, the Sunday, the situation had changed.'

'In what sense?'

Señor Ricart smiled.

'I see you appreciate what I say. Normally people listen to our explanations sceptically, but I tell you, group theory is a fascinating subject . . . The majority of the time our days follow a very similar pattern: tests, tasks are planned . . . call it what you will. Nevertheless, sometimes an element outside them and us alters the dynamic of the group much more than planned.'

'And this element appeared in this case?' Héctor guessed the answer but he didn't want to get ahead of himself.

'Yes!' The instructor's expression revealed a satisfaction akin to that of a football fan whose team has just won the league. 'During one of our tests the group stumbled upon a . . . disturbing external element.'

'The strangled dogs?' prompted Héctor.

'Bravo. Yes. It was an unpleasant experience, of course, and shocking enough for the group to carry out an activity of their own, according to what I found out afterwards. They found them mid-morning on Saturday and although they returned to the house to complete the planned task, afterwards they decided to go and bury

282

them. Neither Joan nor I was there then; usually they are left alone on Saturday afternoon to interact without intermediaries: this is also part of the programme. So the group met, voted and acted as one. A great achievement bearing in mind that only a day before they couldn't agree on sharing bedrooms.'

'Did they argue over bedrooms?'

'There are always disagreements, Inspector. In this case, I remember very well, one member felt uncomfortable having to share a room. Wait . . .' He glanced at his notes. 'Yes, Manel Caballero. He asked if it were possible to sleep alone, which isn't the point of away days. In any case, and although the observations come from only one weekend, I'd say Manel was the classic disruptive participant. He never protested overtly, but took advantage of any opportunity to call the whole group's task into question. A most obnoxious young man, to be frank; an uncomfortable element, not at all inclined to cooperate. One who thinks the whole world is against him.'

'And who did he share with in the end?'

'That I don't remember,' he answered. 'Although more than likely he shared with the youngest two men. The house is big and there were empty rooms but, as I say, it shows scant spirit of cooperation to ask for a private room. They were days of teamwork, not a weekend's holiday.'

Héctor was processing this information with the nagging feeling that there was an essential piece missing in this jigsaw.

'I did say I didn't think it would be of much help to you,' added the man, a sage reader of the expressions of others.

'In an investigation everything is useful,' replied Héctor.

'You're the expert, not me. I can only say that they left as a much more cohesive group than they arrived. Not that this then continues in their workplace.'

'No?'

'Not at all. Although something of it can last, of course. In some groups a positive energy, of common purpose, is generated, but it's not a permanent feeling. When conflict puts it to the test, it deteriorates.'

'In that case, what purpose do they serve? The away days, I mean.'

'I'll deny ever saying this, Inspector,' the man said. 'Very little and a lot. I'll explain it quickly: employers have learned that conflict is costly on many levels. One way of avoiding it is by making their employees feel well treated, comfortable, appreciated. Before, categories were clear and members of the different classes fought among themselves. Now a kind of harmony floats between everyone, a harmony that interests some and makes others happy. A harmony that lasts only while there are benefits . . . We're already seeing it.'

Héctor was beginning to get lost and didn't want to forget the point of his visit.

'One more thing, do you remember if Amanda Bonet complained of having seen someone on Friday night? Someone prowling around the house, I mean.'

'No . . . At least I don't remember her saying anything like that, although it's not unusual. The house is a bit isolated and city people tend to feel somewhat afraid, especially at night.'

'Where is it, exactly?'

The man took a photograph from a drawer. As Duque had said, it was a typical Empordà country house.

'It's within the Garrigàs municipal area, but it's outside the town.'

'Do the instructors go back and forth every day?'

'No, that would be exhausting. It's about ten kilometres from Figueres, and the weekends we have to work at the house we stay there.'

'Right. And does someone take care of maintenance, food . . . ?'

'Yes and no. The participants take charge of the house for the time they're there: that is to say, they cook or eat out except when the activity requires catering. We do have a couple who live relatively nearby – about one and a half kilometres away – contracted for cleaning and maintenance once the house is vacated.'

Héctor nodded. He didn't have much more to ask, but he couldn't help putting one last question.

'Did you notice anything in particular about the members of that group? Nothing you'd have to swear to before a jury – just any subjective impression. It won't leave this room,' he assured him.

'No. That's the truth – I've been thinking about it since you rang yesterday and even more since I saw the news in the paper.' He shook his head, with a touch of regret. 'The final day, the Sunday, they were tired, but that's normal. They were interacting much more positively, as I told you, but that's not strange either. Sometimes the opposite happens and they leave more confrontational. Groups are unpredictable, Inspector. Mostly because they're made up of people, or rather, individuals. Different individuals obliged to work together. They wouldn't have chosen each other as friends, and they're not linked by family ties; they share only a space, responsibilities, goals.'

'Like at work.'

'Exactly. Permit me a comparison to the animal world. Do you know the most sought-after quality in a pack of dogs for hunters?'

'Sense of smell?' ventured Héctor.

'More than a sense of smell.' He paused somewhat theatrically, before announcing in a didactic tone: 'Cohesion. While the hunt lasts, the dogs must prove that they can work together to achieve a common goal. However . . .'

'What?'

'When the hunt ends, give them something to eat and watch how they fight among themselves for the best morsel.'

30

Although on this occasion he had company, the road to Octavi Pujades's house did not feel any the shorter. Eyes fixed on the bends of the road, drenched by the morning rain, César drove in silence, not saying a word to his companion. Brais, for his part, didn't seem to want to talk much either. An atmosphere of doubt permeated the car, unasked questions in a confined space consuming the oxygen. Brais must have noticed it, because he instinctively opened the window a little.

'Do you mind?'

César shook his head. He'd accelerated and had to brake sharply before taking the next bend.

'Sorry,' he said to Brais, in a tone expressing little regret.

His companion shrugged.

'It wouldn't be bad if we had an accident,' he replied. 'Some might say it was poetic justice.'

In César's opinion, such a comment didn't merit a response.

'Don't you think so?' Brais insisted. 'Don't you think it would be a good way of ending all this?'

'Fuck, Brais. Don't come at me with these ideas, all right?'

Arjona smiled.

'I'd love to know if you dislike me so much because I'm gay or because I beat you in the canoe race.'

César snorted.

'I don't like you because you say that sort of thing.'

'I'll give you that.'

Brais laughed and the guffaw, even though brief and slightly bitter, eased the tension a little.

'Seriously, César, don't you ever have regrets? About what we did? I'm just curious and no one's listening.'

'What does it matter? What's the point of regretting the past?' He shook his head. 'I've learned that regrets are best swallowed. Or spat out. Anything but letting them live.'

'What's done is done, right?'

'Something like that.' They were almost there and César wanted to take the opportunity to ask the same question. 'You?'

Brais took a little longer to answer. And when he did, it wasn't exactly what the other man was expecting.

'I'm scared David will hear about it. I'm scared of losing him if he finds out.' He looked at César with an honesty that would have broken down any barrier. 'You at least have someone to talk to about it. The others can't talk about it, or at least I can't. And I don't know if I have more regret about what we did or about hiding it.' He gave a faint, ironic smile. 'And at the same time I know I can't do anything but keep lying to him because I know him and I'm sure telling him the truth would mean the end, and I can't handle that. Not yet.'

The house came into view over the hill. This time,

César had found it without a problem. He parked the car and for the first time in the whole journey he turned to Brais with a worried expression and honesty in his voice.

'I don't really know what we're doing here . . .'

'Sílvia insisted we come.'

'Yeah.'

So it was, and what César couldn't explain was Sílvia's change of heart regarding Octavi Pujades. A few days before she'd reacted like a fiend when Amanda insinuated that she suspected him. It was true they didn't know where Octavi had been on Sunday evening. Nevertheless, just as he'd lied about what time he left Sílvia's, when by mid-afternoon he couldn't take it any more and had to leave, Brais could have made up his alibi.

'By the way, why did you meet up with Manel?'

'Want to know the truth?' Brais lowered his voice. 'I went to see him for the same reason we're here now. To find out if he'd betrayed us, if it was he who was sending that damned photo.' He continued without the other man insisting. 'And if it was him, to make sure he stopped.'

They got out of the car in silence, and César was walking towards the house rapidly, cursing the cold, when Brais added, 'Earlier I talked about regrets. Know what I've found out? They're limited, and they fade. And something else: if they are confronted by fear, better that they lose. It's called survival.'

Similar notions were going round and round in Sílvia's mind, fear and survival, as she contemplated the newspaper page where, in broad strokes, the company's image was being destroyed. The article didn't name names, but the headline 'Young, free and . . . dead', was a poisoned dart aimed at the heart of Alemany Cosmetics.

She'd spent the morning answering some emails and ignoring others, in an attempt to minimize the effects of the catastrophe. A company even indirectly causing the suicides of its employees – three in only five months, to be exact – became a kind of living toxin. Moreover, if the name of said company was linked to concepts like beauty, well-being and health, the irony reached surrealist proportions.

At five in the afternoon, a little before César and Arjona left for Octavi's house, Sílvia decided to log out of her email, switch off the computer and focus. Something that it seemed was going to be impossible, because scarcely ten minutes later her brother entered the office, very differently to the morning when he'd burst in brandishing that very newspaper as if she and all the people in the company were a bunch of disobedient kids and he a justly furious boss.

'How is it going?' he asked her.

'I suppose it could be worse . . . at least nobody is talking about the products as such, just the company in abstract.'

He nodded.

'Yes. People demand our products for their name, not the cosmetics lab.'

'Is that what you told your buyers?' She couldn't help being sarcastic.

Víctor sighed.

'Something like that. Sílvia . . . this has to stop as soon as possible.'

'What do you want me to do? Offer a bonus to everyone

who promises not to throw themselves off their balcony?'

He sat down on the other side of the desk.

'Don't change the subject, Sílvia. Is there anything I should know about that weekend?'

'That you should know?' She shook her head, perhaps out of tiredness, perhaps out of pure disdain. 'All there is to know, and you should be clear on this without needing to ask me, is that I would never do anything that could put our company in danger. Never. It's you who seems not to feel the least regard for it and is ready to sell it to the highest bidder.'

'You're just like Papa,' he replied, and the scar left by sad truths could be heard in his voice. 'The company is a thing, Sílvia. You can love it, but it's never going to love you back. Being satisfied with that is pathetic.'

'Yeah. I'm sure Paula returns your affection with interest.'

'Leave Paula out of this – she has nothing to do with it.'

'Oh no?' Sílvia was going to make an unpleasant comment, but she bit her tongue. 'I'll tell you something, Víctor: the company is not a thing. It's alive, with people, projects, ideas . . . and of course you get back what you put into it. More than with people.'

Víctor looked at her as if he wished to understand her, as if for an instant he could get inside her body and mind, feel and think as she felt. As children it was like that, more or less: there was a strong bond between them, something that felt unbreakable then. Now, the distance between them was so great he didn't have the spirit to cross it.

'I don't know when you started confusing life with

291

work . . . This is a business, nothing more. Difficult times are coming, we both know that. It's much wiser to sell now at a good price than hold out until the storm comes. And it will come, I assure you.'

'It'll come, yes. But don't try to deceive me, Víctor. You're not selling out of prudence, or fear of the future; you're doing it out of boredom, a late attack of immaturity . . . The desire to do what you didn't have the balls to do at eighteen. I assure you, youth's not catching, Víctor. However much you sleep with it. Not catching, and you can't live twice.'

The conversation had come to the cliff-edge, that place where stances were so irreconcilable that to continue talking would only cause injury. Víctor knew it, so he rose and went to the door. Before leaving, he turned to his sister.

'At least I've taken care of you, so you could keep your role and responsibilities. When you left, you didn't even look back. Not thinking for a second about how things would be for me . . .'

She was about to answer, to claim in her defence that she was only seventeen, that he could have done the same, that it wasn't her fault that he'd opted for obedience and that she regretted – yes, she'd always regretted it – leaving him in a hostile home, at the mercy of a cold, demanding father, but, once more, pride won out.

'Well, you got your reward, didn't you? Papa left you practically everything.'

'Exactly. And because of that I'm the one who gets to decide, not you.'

The office door closed behind him and Sílvia was alone, paper spread, and for a moment she thought perhaps none of it was worth it. If the words she said aloud insisted on betraying her true feelings, maybe it was better to shut up for ever. Forfeit the match. Sleep.

'Well, well, more visitors.' Octavi Pujades's tone was unmistakably scathing. 'Poor Eugènia will think she's already died with so many people wandering through the house.'

He didn't invite them into the sitting room, or to sit down, or to have an alcohol-free beer. He came out on the porch despite the evening cold. And it was he who spoke first.

'This morning some Agent Fort was here. A very friendly young man, asking me questions about Amanda. By the way, I know what happened because Víctor rang me yesterday afternoon, but I find it curious that none of you bothered to tell me.'

Both César and Brais felt like schoolboys being suddenly reprimanded by a strict tutor. 'It's not important. I thought you'd forgotten me. Now I see you haven't.'

'I'm sorry, Octavi,' said César. 'I was sure Sílvia would have told you.'

Octavi smiled, and in doing so his expression became even sharper, more tense, as if the skin of his cheeks was going to tear.

'César, César . . . I'm afraid I'm no longer the object of Sílvia's devotion. Now that I think about it, I suppose she sent you. She doesn't trust me any more, does she?'

Brais took a step forward; not too much but enough to bridge the gap that separates a chat from a threat.

'Enough of the sarcasm, Octavi. I haven't come here to waste my time.'

293

'And why have you come? To beat me up? Kill me, perhaps?'

The two were so close, and the difference between the contenders so evident, that César stepped in between them.

'Hey, enough. Octavi, no one distrusts you—'

'Tell that to this thug. You like intimidating people, do you, Brais? Does it make you feel like more of a man?'

'Octavi, please!'

The only light on the outside of the house, a cast-iron lantern hanging on a corner, illuminated the three faces. Three faces covered by masks ranging from confusion to suppressed rage, fear to indifference.

In the distance a couple of dogs howled, as if all these emotions reached them on the night air.

'Get out of here,' Octavi finally ordered. 'Tell Sílvia she can relax: for the moment I have no intention of speaking to the *Mossos* and telling them the truth. If I'd wanted to, I'd have used this morning to do it.' He looked again at Brais, defiant, and César took a step back on seeing him take a small pistol from his anorak pocket. 'Relax, I'm not going to shoot. Just so you know I'm protected.'

Brais didn't move an inch. He held the older man's gaze and then, with a sudden movement, he forcefully bent back Octavi's wrist. The weapon fell to the floor and César kicked it away.

'Having a gun's not enough to protect you, Octavi. You have to have the balls to use it as well,' Brais warned him.

The dogs stopped barking.

31

Héctor emerged from one of the station bathrooms just as Inspector Bellver was entering. Luck makes our paths cross like in a bad western, thought Salgado, although in this case we'd have already fought a duel in the town square in the blazing sun. But Barcelona wasn't the Wild West and the duels were settled behind closed doors, with more sophisticated weapons. Anyway, thought Héctor, a part of that philosophy still holds good: with types like Bellver, it's best not to turn your back on them.

He was going to his desk when he bumped into another, much nicer person.

'Martina . . .'

He hadn't seen Sergeant Andreu since the week before. He'd hoped to speak to her on Monday, but all his plans had fallen apart with Amanda Bonet's death. She smiled faintly by way of a greeting, but her expression immediately changed, becoming very serious.

'Come with me. We have to clear up this mess.'

Héctor didn't have time to ask her how she'd heard about everything. It wasn't hard to figure out: at some point on Monday afternoon or that same Tuesday morning, someone, probably Fort, would have told her. In any case, not really knowing what to expect, Héctor followed her.

Martina Andreu knocked sharply at the superintendent's door and, without waiting for an answer, opened it and went in.

'Andreu – back already?' Savall had never bothered to hide his liking for Sergeant Andreu. 'Everything all right with Calderón and his lot?'

She snorted, as if Calderón, his lot and the whole Russian mafia didn't matter at all just then.

'All right for now.' Martina Andreu adopted a formal tone, different to her usual one behind closed doors after so many years' working together. 'Superintendent, I wish to tell you now and in the presence of Inspector Salgado that I took Ruth Valldaura's file from Bellver's archives myself. Without Héctor or anyone knowing.'

Savall looked at her intently. No one could have said if he doubted her word, but the sergeant's fervour brooked no argument.

'And might one know why you did so?'

Martina hesitated for a moment, time enough for both Salgado and Savall to guess that what she would say next wouldn't exactly be the truth and nothing but. She realized this, and before blurting out the excuse she'd thought up she just said, 'No.'

From the mouth of any other of his subordinates, this refusal would have unleashed all the superintendent's fury. But from Martina Andreu, it left him speechless.

'I will apologize to Bellver if you think it necessary.'

Savall gestured indifferently with his hand, as if linking the words 'apology' and 'Bellver' was absurd.

'Leave it. It would just make things worse. I'll speak

to him.' Then he turned to Héctor, who had observed the scene in silence. 'Anyhow, best if you don't have too much contact with Bellver and his team for a few days. Avoid possible encounters, okay?'

He addressed them both, but no doubt it was directed at Salgado.

'That takes two, Superintendent.'

'I know.' Savall sighed. 'Well, we'll leave it there for now. Héctor, how's the cosmetics lab case going?'

'If you're going to talk about that, I'll leave you to it,' said the sergeant.

'Ask Fort to come here, please,' Salgado ordered. 'He went to interview Pujades this morning and I still haven't had a chance to speak to him, though I'm almost certain he hasn't got anything out of him.'

'I'll send him to you straightaway. But treat him well, okay? Take it easy on him or I'll take revenge.'

She smiled, and the camaraderie that had always reigned between them previously suddenly returned.

'We'll talk later, Andreu,' said Savall. 'You need to tell me how you got on over there.'

A good while later, Savall and Salgado were still discussing the suicides case under the attentive gaze of Agent Fort, too timid to intervene if not asked a direct question.

'Let's see,' said the superintendent in an attempt to recap, 'up to now, were it not that these people have the same place of work, we'd have three cases of suicide, or even one – and I'm referring to Amanda Bonet – which could be classed as accidental death.'

Salgado shook his head.

'She took a lot of sleeping pills, Superintendent. And

according to her lover, it wasn't the first time they enjoyed those "games", as he calls them.'

'All right then, three suicides.'

'Three suicides but five victims,' Salgado pointed out. 'Ródenas's wife and daughter – don't forget them.'

'How could you forget them?' Savall was quiet for a moment, putting his thoughts in order. 'Let's start at the beginning. Gaspar Ródenas. Recently promoted, worried about said promotion, though with no other known issues.'

'True. His case was included in crimes of domestic violence, but there were never reports made by his wife or the least suggestion of ill-treatment in the family environment.'

'Nevertheless, Ródenas did buy a pistol, didn't he?'

'He did. But that weapon could have been to kill his family then commit suicide, or to protect himself and those around him,' Héctor pointed out.

Savall nodded.

'It's a possibility. However, in that case we're dealing with a ruthless killer. A killer who didn't hesitate in killing a little girl only months old so that the crime scene would appear like an extreme case of domestic violence. Do you really believe you have someone like that among the suspects?'

He recalled the faces of the Alemany Cosmetics employees: Sílvia, César Calvo, Brais Arjona, Manel Caballero . . .

'I don't know. Honestly I couldn't say,' concluded Salgado. 'What was Octavi Pujades like, Fort? I know his statement just confirmed the version of the others, but, on a personal level, what impression did you get from him?'

Fort flushed a little and considered his answer before speaking.

'I'd say he's much more affected by the situation at home than he thinks.' He shivered. 'Practically alone, caring for his wife in her final days . . . He seems to be under enormous stress, although I couldn't say more with any certainty.'

'Fine,' Savall intervened, 'we'll leave Ródenas aside for a moment. Sara Mahler threw herself on the metro tracks on *Reyes* night.'

Héctor made an irritated gesture.

'We still don't know where she was coming from or going to at that time. She didn't usually go out at night.'

Fort felt obliged to add: 'We've tracked the movements of her bank account. Sara Mahler withdrew money from an ATM at 21.35, but she did so alone, near her home. The ATM images show as much.'

Poor Sara, thought Salgado. Her final hours were recorded on different cameras: those at the bank, the metro station . . .

'Sara Mahler's death occurred four months after that of Ródenas and his family,' Héctor pointed out. 'So if Ródenas was killed, whoever did it felt safe until then.'

'True. On the other hand, Amanda Bonet—'

'Died a few days after Sara Mahler.'

Superintendent Savall's appearance expressed a mixture of irritation and fatigue.

'And the others say nothing?'

'That's the worst of all. They seem upset,' said Héctor, musing as he spoke, 'shocked, even. Whatever they're hiding, the fear of it being discovered is greater than what they feel about the deaths of their colleagues.'

299

'And you're sure they're hiding something?' asked the superintendent.

'Yes.' Salgado's reply was unequivocal. 'It's intuition: something happened that weekend, something grave enough for them to hide it, keep quiet . . . And for some of them to be dying for it.'

'One more thing in relation to Amanda Bonet,' said Savall. 'Did anyone know a key could be found underneath the doormat? Anyone apart from her lover, this Saúl . . .'

'Saúl Duque. According to him, Amanda suspected that Sara Mahler knew about their relationship. If that's true, Sara could have told someone.'

'Who?'

'Víctor Alemany, for example. She was his secretary, and throughout the company they say Sara was very loyal to her boss.'

'Were they lovers?' said Savall, half smiling.

'I don't think so,' Salgado answered firmly. 'What's more, Víctor wasn't with them that weekend—'

'True,' Fort interjected, daring to do so spontaneously for the first time, 'but if Sara told him everything, perhaps she explained what happened in that house as well.'

'Good point,' said Héctor. 'Even so, we continue as we are and keep going until we establish the root of all this.'

'Exactly.' Savall was starting to show signs of impatience, gestures Héctor recognized easily. 'What are your plans, Héctor?'

'Tomorrow I'm going to Garrigàs, to the house where they spent those days, to see if I can find anything.' Héctor turned to Fort and added, 'On the other hand, dismissing the possibility of identifying the person responsible for the message, we have to keep investigating what Sara Mahler did on the night of her death.'

'Sir, it still seems strange that there is no data on her mobile. It's on the factory settings, but she hadn't bought it that day.'

'Get on those two matters. There are too many loose ends in Sara's death.'

Roger Fort nodded and, sensing that this order implied leaving the office, he went out rapidly.

'Héctor,' said Savall when they were alone, 'I'm not against using the press on this occasion. But be careful. It could cause us problems.'

'I know, but I think this time we needn't worry.'

'Fine, I trust you.' Savall seemed to consider the meeting finished; however, as the inspector was preparing to leave, he added, 'I'm glad to see you back on form, Salgado.'

Already at the door, Héctor stopped. The superintendent went on in a tone grave yet tinted with something akin to affection. 'I'm aware that you felt bad about my taking you off Ruth's case. Believe me, I'm sorry, but I had no choice. I couldn't allow one of my best men to become obsessed in that way.' He waited for a reply from Salgado, then seeing there was none forthcoming, went on: 'Sometimes you have to turn a page, however hard it is. Doing it was very difficult for me. You know I've always supported you, even at the worst times, and both my wife and I care a lot about you both . . . You and Ruth.'

Hearing her name then, Héctor realized he hadn't thought about her for hours, maybe days. He knew it was absurd, but he couldn't help a strange feeling:

he'd promised not to forget her. He didn't know what answer to give the superintendent. He left without saying anything and walked towards Fort's desk. Speaking to the agent with her back to him, he made out a feminine figure who from a distance he confused with Lola. Then the woman turned and he saw it was Mar Ródenas.

32

Mar seemed so out of place in the station that Héctor
decided to talk to her somewhere else. He invited her for
a coffee in a nearby bar. He also needed to smoke and
could have a fag en route.

Once inside, two coffees in front of them, hers decaf,
Mar Ródenas took from her bag the newspaper in which
the article about her brother had appeared. I should have
seen this coming, thought Héctor. Despite the article
speaking of suicides, the coincidence of three in a few
months had to arouse unease in their loved ones, and Mar
Ródenas's appearance faithfully reflected that emotion.

'What does this mean, Inspector?' she asked, straight
to the point though in a faint voice.

'I wish I could tell you,' he replied, 'but at this time we
know little more than what's in the article.'

'But . . . but the text seems to imply that . . .'

Hope, thought Héctor. That was what was in that
glance. The hope that what she'd accepted until then as
a fact was actually an illusion. The hope that her brother
wasn't a parricide, but a victim in the end. Salgado didn't
want to raise her hopes and yet neither could he deny the
truth.

'The case has been re-opened. That's all I can tell you.'

He considered that for Mar, that was enough. It was at least an open door, a road towards a reality different to the painful one with which it was her lot to live.

'Do you have siblings, Inspector?'

'Yes.' He didn't elaborate: he was certain that an elder brother who chose to look away when your father gave you a beating wasn't the example Mar was hoping for.

'Gaspar was a few years older than me.' She smiled. 'Sometimes he was worse than my parents: he didn't let me out of his sight.'

Héctor prepared to listen to her. It was clear this girl needed to talk about her brother, that boy who protected her in school and bickered with her at home; the boy who in her mind had little to do with the man who'd died from a bullet in that domestic tragedy. Mar continued talking for a while, ever more animated, as if for the first time in months she could enjoy these memories, spoiled by Gaspar's sad end. And, without meaning to, Héctor also ended up relating anecdotes from his childhood in Buenos Aires.

'I'm sorry,' said Mar. 'I'm sure you have better things to do than exchange family stories.'

'Don't worry.' He looked at his watch. 'Although I must be going now.'

'Of course.'

She protested mildly when he paid for the two coffees, but the inspector took no heed. They walked in the same direction, he towards the station and she the metro.

'Inspector,' Mar said to him, 'I know my opinion isn't very objective when I tell you Gaspar was essentially a good person. He was incapable of anything so horrible.'

'When it's about people, no opinion can be objective,' he said, affectionately. 'Mar, let me ask you something.' He'd just remembered; it wasn't an important detail, but it couldn't hurt to clear it up. 'Did Gaspar belong to an animal rights group or anything like that? You know, environmental groups . . .'

Mar seemed taken aback.

'Not that I know of. Although maybe . . . Are you asking for any reason in particular?'

Salgado shook his head.

'Someone told us so, but it's not important. Don't worry about it.'

When he returned to his office, Fort had already left and he couldn't see Martina Andreu at her desk either, so Héctor thought of calling Lola and suggesting she come with him to the house in Garrigàs the next day. Although it wasn't following procedure, he was sure she'd like to, and he trusted her discretion. He had to leave the suggestion recorded in her voicemail, since Lola didn't pick up the call. However, shortly afterwards he received a text with a succinct: 'OK. See you tomorrow.'

The brevity of the answer caused him a momentary pang of sadness. He kept his eyes fixed on the screen of the phone, annoyed with himself and these dregs of melancholy which seemed to seek any motive to overflow. No, he corrected himself, not any old motive.

He was going to leave the phone on the desk, like someone banishing the messenger who brings unwelcome news, when he remembered that he had his fortnightly session with his therapist the following day. He picked up the discarded phone and looked for the number among his contacts to cancel the visit, when suddenly it occurred to him that the kid might be able to help, not him, but in the case. He called, hoping he might still be at the practice and could spare him a few minutes. And this time, fickle law of averages, he got the answer he was seeking.

Not having him opposite seemed strange, which was logical: it was the first time he'd spoken to him on the phone. He didn't know if he did sessions by telephone– or even better, on Skype, in this century where the virtual was gaining on an ever less tangible reality. Not one for preambles, Héctor got straight to the point.

'You want to talk to me about suicide, Inspector?'

'Yes, but not mine, don't worry. This isn't a subterfuge to reveal my hidden desires.'

On the other end of the line he could hear a suppressed chuckle.

'It never would have occurred to me to think you had the profile of a suicide, Inspector.'

'No, I suppose my aggression tends to erupt outwards rather than inwards. Now seriously, is there such a thing as a suicide profile?'

'Calling it a profile would be too strong. There are characteristics of personality that, combined with the right circumstances, could increase the risk of someone taking that step.'

'I'll be honest with you.' He regretted it as soon as he said it, since the expression made out that he hadn't been so at other times. 'I'm investigating the possible suicides of three people whose only thing in common was working in the same company.'

If the psychologist had heard about the case, he gave no sign of it.

'And you wish to ask me if there is a possibility that it may be the work environment which is causing the suicides?'

It wasn't exactly what he wanted to ask, but Héctor decided to let him speak. Then he would clarify what he wanted to know.

'It's a very complex subject, Inspector. And it's difficult to talk about it without citing theories or explaining experiments using terminology unintelligible to most people.'

'Try. I've become an expert after six months of therapy.'

There was a moment of silence.

'Well, before anything else let me tell you that suicide is considered a sin here, or an unnatural act, although this idea isn't the norm everywhere. In other cultures it is a dignified exit: remember the philosophers of ancient Greece or, later on, the Japanese and their hara-kiri. It is Christianity which believes that life does not belong to us but to God, and that He is the only one capable of giving or taking it.

'To answer your question, this organization, be it company or group, which aids or indirectly causes suicide would have to confront the individual resistance of its members, owing to the survival instinct and some socio-cultural norms that condemn the suicide. There have been cases of mass suicide in sects where the leader has great influence over the members. But in a modern company this would be unthinkable: workers have social lives, families.'

'But there have been cases—'

'Yes, of course. In the context of great stress, changing conditions, extreme work insecurity, worker anxiety increases. The employee suicides of which I've read clearly express that the cause of the act they are going to commit is at work.'

'A kind of posthumous accusation?'

'Exactly. I'll simplify it so as not to go on too much. Think that the suicide commits this act maybe because he honestly believes he doesn't want to live any more, or because he's trying to place his death on someone's conscience. In the first case, it's a cool-headed decision, reasonable from the subject's point of view: a terminally ill person who doesn't wish to be a burden to their loved ones. In the second, the aim is somewhat more perverse: imagine an adolescent who's been left by his girlfriend; he kills himself and wants the whole world to know that she is to blame, so he leaves a note accusing her more or less overtly. Understand?'

'Of course. And if there's no note? None at all?'

'That's more unusual. People tend to explain themselves, to justify what they're about to do . . . To exonerate some of blame and accuse others. Unless it's a moment of desperation, a heated decision so passionate that, if the attempt fails, the suicide never repeats the act.'

'Does the lack of a note indicate a sudden decision?'

'In general terms, yes, Inspector, but in our world to generalize is to lie.'

Héctor nodded silently. Neither Gaspar, Sara nor Amanda had left a note. Maybe because they wanted to hide the cause from the world; or maybe because someone had decided for them.

'One more thing, Doctor,' he sometimes called him that, though he knew he wasn't one, 'perhaps the subjects don't want to accuse anyone specific.'

308

'If the suicide leaves nothing written down, the guilt is even more diffuse: everyone around them might take it personally, whether it's for not having foreseen it or for fear of having indirectly caused it.'

'So it's even worse. More . . . inconsiderate.'

The psychologist laughed.

'Unlike in your world, there are no good guys and bad guys here, Inspector.' His voice became serious. 'What you call considerate suicides would be those that minimize the guilt for those around them and attribute the blame to themselves in an obvious way. The sick person who decides to end their life and leaves that in writing, for example. Or—'

'Or?'

'Those who camouflage their suicide by means of an accident. They die by choice, but don't want the people they love to feel guilty, so they crash the car. Their suicide is unproven and their loved ones can grieve without feeling remorse. That would be a good suicide, to use your terminology.'

The conversation was depressing him even more and Héctor had the urgent desire to hang up, go home, go running, anywhere he could breathe in life and not death.

'One more thing.' Héctor suddenly remembered the women's association that appeared in Sara Mahler's bank transactions. 'Have you heard of the Hera Association, by any chance?'

'Yes, colleagues have given talks there. Why do you ask?'

'It came up in the course of an investigation. Can you tell me more about it?'

'It's an association run by women for women, specializing in victims of sexual abuse and assault.'

Suddenly, all the unconnected information about Sara's personal life began to make sense.

'Thank you very much. I won't take up any more of your time.'

'Take care. And I hope to see you next week, Héctor. You have to tell me if you've done the task I set you.'

Héctor assured him it would never occur to him to disobey. A while later, perhaps to drive darker voices from his head, as he was considering the positive things in his life he wondered whether or not he could count on Lola.

33

The motorway stretched out before them. A straight, solid, well-delineated space capable of providing a secure setting for a turbulent journey, shaken by a tide of uncertainties. Even the sky helped emphasize this insecurity with some dense clouds, slow as a funeral cortège, although from time to time they were distracted and allowed a tenuous ray of sunlight to slip through. Inside the car, Héctor and Lola had discussed the article and its consequences, they'd expressed their doubts about what they were going to find and in the end had lapsed into an elevator silence, polite and slightly challenging. One of those pauses that can be tolerated for only a limited time and in a static environment, with no pot-holes to prick consciences.

Héctor made as if to take out a cigarette, but stopped himself.

'Smoke if you like,' she said. 'I'm still in the phase when the smell of smoke is pleasant.'

'You sure?' He lit the cigarette with the car lighter and lowered the window halfway. He blew the smoke out. 'When did you give up?'

'Twenty days ago.' She smiled. 'I know. The typical New Year's resolution.'

'I should give up too.' This sentence, just after taking a generous drag on his fag, seemed faintly ridiculous.

'To tell the truth I've tried a few times with no success, but now I'm taking it seriously. At first I was smoking roll-ups. It's supposed to be relaxing but it made me anxious. In the end, rather than put up with substitutes, better to give it up completely.'

The ray of sun was buried once again behind a slow but implacable cloud. Not much longer, thought Héctor.

A quarter of an hour later, they turned off on to the mud track that led to the house. The friendly road on which they'd been travelling became a narrow, treacherous trail, full of stones and holes. Lola clung to the door handle as the car stumbled along, nervous, faster than the terrain permitted.

A woman in her forties was waiting for them at the door of the house, smaller than it looked in the pictures. It was clear the people from the development centre had let her know ahead of time.

Héctor had left the car at the entrance, to one side of the road, although he was almost certain he could have parked in the middle of the road without inconveniencing anyone for a good while. Though the trail didn't end at the house, from that point it became even rougher. He and Lola walked towards the woman, who raised a hand in greeting. It was cold: the sun had already given up in that uneven battle. For the umpteenth time that day, Héctor asked himself what they could possibly discover in this house, ten months after the Alemany Cosmetics group had been there. Lola, however, seemed in good spirits, even if it were simply being out of the car at last and able to walk.

The woman received them with a smile that wasn't free from distrust.

'Good afternoon.' She had a pronounced Catalan accent, like the majority of the region's inhabitants. 'Come in, come in. They told me you were coming, although I was expecting you later. I'm Dolors Vinyals. My husband Joan and I have a little house nearby and we take care of this one when they ask us to, as you already know.'

Héctor introduced himself and Lola, not specifying that she didn't belong to the forces of law and order. Señora Vinyals didn't ask and they went inside.

It was just as the photos had shown: a classic *masía*, with mismatched furniture that somehow managed to create a harmonious whole. The fireplace, unlit, provided the indispensable decorative country touch to a room usually heated by radiators. That day they weren't switched on, which had to mean no group was expected. It was chilly and none of the three removed their jackets.

'If you'd like to see the rooms . . .' said the woman, doubtfully.

'Not just now,' answered Héctor. 'We really wanted to speak to you.'

Dolors Vinyals didn't invite them to sit, though in all probability this was due to the fact that she wasn't in her own home. Neither Héctor nor Lola felt like it; they'd spent hours in the car and it wouldn't hurt to stretch their legs a little, so they remained standing in the middle of that long, narrow dining room.

'I don't know what Señor Ricart has told you . . .' Héctor began.

313

'He told me to give you all the information you need,' she replied, very proper.

'Do you remember this group? They came in March last year and were here for three days,' he said, showing her the photo.

The woman looked at the photograph with interest, and for a moment seemed not to recognize them.

'Maybe it would help if I told you that an unpleasant incident occurred during their stay: they found some dogs strangled.'

The information was enough for Señora Vinyals to nod her head.

'Ah, yes! I didn't remember their faces, to be honest. But that, yes. I don't understand how anyone could do something like that to those poor animals. People from elsewhere, certainly.'

Héctor smiled inwardly. Baddies always came from elsewhere: another country, another region, even from the neighbouring town.

'Not a regular occurrence, I suppose.'

'Of course not!' The decent woman was indignant. 'I'd never seen anything like that, if I'm honest. Well, in fact I didn't see it, although they told me about it on the Saturday afternoon.'

Héctor had listened to the tale of the discovery of the dogs too many times.

'And did they tell you they were planning to go and bury them?' he immediately asked to settle the subject.

'No. I told them I would call the *Mossos* and they thought that a good idea. I suppose they decided afterwards, because mid-afternoon they called me to tell me so. We weren't here; we went to Figueres for the afternoon, with the boys. It's so isolated here and sometimes we go to the city.'

Sílvia Alemany had already told him about the dogs. The group had the afternoon free and set themselves the task of burying those poor creatures.

Answering a question not yet formulated, the woman turned to the window and pointed out a kind of shed attached to the house.

'That's where they picked up the hoes and spades . . . By the way, they must have taken a spade as a memento. Or they lost it.'

'Are you sure there was one missing?'

'That's what Joan said. He was complaining because he had to work in the garden with another smaller one. I told him they must have left it behind when they went to bury the dogs . . . Anyway, now I remember, they were a rather strange group.'

Dolors turned back towards them.

'Don't misunderstand me. Everyone has their quirks, and at the end of the day they come here in their spare time and think this is a hotel.'

'Don't you take care of the food and cleaning?'

'Not while they're here. Joan and I drop by, in case they need anything. Nothing else. And when they leave we clean the house.'

'And why do you say they were strange?' asked Lola.

The woman sighed.

'Well, there was one who asked for a room on his own. I tell you, some think they're at a hotel . . .'

'Was that all?' Lola insisted.

'Well . . . I don't think it matters if I tell you. It seems one of the women was scared one night. She went out to

315

take a walk, alone, and according to her she saw someone. A . . . an immigrant.'

Dolors was about to use another word, but in the end
she decided on the official term.

'Arab? Coloured?'

'Yes, dear, an African. Back then there were more –
they were working in the fields. Now you see them much
less.'

'But he didn't attack her?'

Señora Vinyals gestured disparagingly with her hand.

'Bah, she must have seen a shadow or something!
You'd ask what was she doing taking a walk in the middle of the night. The next day she asked me if there'd
been robberies around here.' She laughed. 'As if no one's
ever robbed in Barcelona!'

Héctor smiled.

'Was she scared?'

'A little – but she gave me the impression she thought
it was our fault. Like she was annoyed.'

Héctor was straightening out the facts. Saúl Duque's
call to Amanda was on Friday. Saturday midday they'd
discovered the dogs. In the afternoon they went to bury
them and they went home on Sunday. If something else
had happened, something they weren't telling, it had to
have been on Saturday night.

'How long do you think it took them to bury the dogs?'

The woman didn't respond straightaway.

'Well, there were a few men, although I don't think
they were very used to digging. They must have been
gone all afternoon.'

Héctor nodded.

'Where did they bury them?'

Dolors went back to the window.

'See: the road you came by continues up to link with the motorway. The *alzina surera* . . . How do you say that in Spanish?'

'Cork tree,' said Héctor.

'So this, the cork tree where those poor beasts were hanged, is about two kilometres away, beside an old shed. Of course in the morning they'd gone on foot; it was part of these games they do.' The woman said it in the same tone she'd have spoken of a sandcastle at the beach. 'In the evening they went in the van. The one you see in the photo.'

It was a large van, almost a minibus, with room for eight people. If they'd decided burying the dogs was the responsibility of the whole group, the most logical thing would be that they all go together, despite neither Amanda Bonet, nor Sílvia, nor Manel having a tool in their hands. Dolors Vinyals seemed to read his mind because she added, 'They all worked together. The women too. Although they were the most tired: they were still complaining the following day. They were pulling faces.'

They must have felt proud, thought Héctor: at the end of the day they'd spent their free afternoon doing something unpleasant just because they thought it right. Surely they'd returned tired but happy.

Lola had said little, but suddenly she turned to Señora Vinyals.

'Dolors – may I call you Dolors? I just realized that we have the same name.'

'Of course, dear. Lola, Dolors, Lolita – it's not a name people have these days. There's no twenty-year-old girls named so, at least around here.'

317

'It's true,' agreed Lola, smiling. 'Less and less. Before, when you said they were strange, were you just referring to them complaining more than others?'

'Oh no. Not only that. That had gone out of my head. It was because of the bikes.'

'Bicycles?' asked Lola.

Héctor let them talk without interrupting.

'The boys, our sons, woke us on Sunday morning saying the bikes had been stolen. Such a row . . . They were good bikes, and expensive too. They cost us a fortune and they were new. Joan and I thought we would have to buy them new ones, but when I came to say goodbye to the group, the bikes were here.'

'They'd taken them? Without permission?' Lola's voice sounded surprised.

'Not exactly without permission. When they arrived we showed them where we lived, in case they needed anything, and told them that if they wanted to use them to go for a ride they were welcome to. Some do, but they tell us they're taking them, of course.'

'Did they explain at all?'

'A young dark-haired man, very good-looking, told me that he and another guy had decided to go for a ride first thing Sunday morning and they didn't want to wake us. He apologized, poor boy, and at the end of the day it didn't really matter, although I couldn't help telling him he'd given the boys a good fright. They could have at least left a note. But I tell you, give them an inch and they'll take a mile. That's how it goes, isn't it?'

'Were the bikes in good condition?' enquired Héctor, who didn't want the conversation to lapse into clichés and sayings.

'As always. It's not as if my boys polish them after using them, believe me.'

She had little more to add. Héctor and Lola looked over the house in five minutes and, after thanking Señora Vinyals, they went to get the car. Before leaving, Héctor wanted to see the cork tree. Even without dogs. And more than anything he wanted to straighten out his thoughts and find a logical solution to the whole business.

34

For the first time in his life, César was happy to barge into Sílvia's flat in her absence. It wasn't the day he usually came, but he'd come back very tired from seeing Octavi the night before and went straight to his own house. He needed to think, analyse everything.

César entered and shut the door firmly. Without knowing, he sensed Emma was there, so he headed for her bedroom with a concrete aim. He hadn't seen her since the previous Sunday, that uncomfortable day, plagued by silences and the memory of what had happened in the early hours. César hadn't completely lied when he told Brais he preferred to spit out remorse rather than let it take root within him, like a weed; however, he was aware that the situation had become very delicate. He wasn't especially skilful at dealing with people, but he had to find a way of ensuring Emma's silence.

The girl's bedroom door was open. Sitting in front of the computer, Emma seemed absorbed in what she had up on screen – maybe a chat with some friend. He knocked on the door, suddenly nervous. She saw him reflected on the screen and turned, slowly, with a slightly annoyed expression on her face.

'Here already? It's not Tuesday . . .'

César didn't really know what that meant; the teenager's tone rattled him. It was as if nothing had happened.

'Emma, can we talk?'

She smiled inwardly, closed the chat window and turned her chair around, legs slightly apart.

'Of course. Whatever you say.' She smiled. 'After all, you'll be like a father in a few months.'

César detested this perverse child manner. He'd come planning to treat her like a woman and found this shameless version of Lolita.

'Emma, stop playing around. This is serious.'

'Whoa, what have I done now?'

She brought her legs together and crossed her arms. 'Okay, tell me – I'm busy, you know? And you should be at work at this time. Mama is going to put you on a warning if you keep leaving the warehouse so early.'

César was unable to work out if she chose her words deliberately to humiliate him, or if they simply occurred to her spontaneously. In any case, she managed to offend him, above all with the stress she'd put on words like 'warning' and 'warehouse'. At the same time he realized she was provoking him, challenging him to a game he didn't want to play. Not any more. Not that day or ever.

'I won't bother you for long. I don't want you to say it's my fault you haven't finished your homework.'

His attempt at being ironic clashed with the evident truth that she, at sixteen, was still at the age of having homework. Emma, however, was generous enough to make no comment, although her expression beat any contemptuous reply she could give him.

321

'I want to talk about what you said the other day. About Sara Mahler.'

César had the satisfaction, indeed, of seeing her confused. He didn't only want to speak of that, of course, although since the day before, since the conversation with Brais in the car, something he'd said had been going around in his mind: 'At least you can talk about it with Sílvia.'

Emma rose from the chair, as if she were bored of the subject, and turned to the door.

'Do you really want to talk about this Sara?' she asked, smiling, as she made as if to caress his cheek.

'Yes.' And in a move he instantly regretted, he grabbed her wrist. Not hurting her, just so the caress remained in the air. 'Emma, you have to tell me what the hell you heard. Don't lie to me. It's very important.'

'Let go.'

He paid no attention. On the contrary, he pressed a little harder.

'Answer me, Emma!'

'"Answer, Emma." "Shut up, Emma." You're the same as Mama. Why not "*Sit*, Emma"? Do you think I'm your pet?'

César then grabbed her by both arms and pushed her against the wall.

'Fuck, answer!'

Looking away, so as not to give him what he wanted, she answered: 'Sara. Loyal Sara. We can trust her. Sara is trustworthy . . .'

His blood turned cold as he recognized sentences he and Sílvia had used in the intimacy of the bedroom.

'You can hear everything, César. From Pol's room you

322

can hear everything and he doesn't mind swapping with me for a night.' She laughed. 'You can even hear your pathetic attempts at fucking.'

He pushed her backwards again. Her head ricocheted off the white wall.

'You brute!'

César realized he'd hurt her. The impact had resonated through the empty apartment and, to his dismay, Emma's eyes filled with tears.

'I'm sorry,' he murmured. 'Emma, this is more serious than you think . . . Please, tell me what you heard.'

'You hurt me.'

'I didn't mean to.'

'And what did you mean?'

They were dangerously close once again and the scent of Emma was an addiction he found hard to resist. Just one kiss, one more. The last, he promised himself.

Their tongues caressed, licked each other; their lips collided at the same time César's hands fell on her breasts. She separated their lips, just for an instant, to catch her breath. To moan, because she already knew these gasps aroused him.

He quelled the moan with another more voracious, furious kiss, and they both closed their eyes. Tongues seeking one another, hands burning. They forgot what they'd been discussing, where they were, who they were. They were just breathing, kissing, touching, smelling.

Not for a moment noticing that they weren't alone.

Sílvia had come in a few minutes before, preoccupied by the threatening phone call she'd received after lunch. The same voice, the same financial demands. And while they spoke, Sílvia couldn't get the image of Amanda, dead in a white bed, out of her mind. As soon as the phone call ended, she felt nauseated; she went to the company bathroom and vomited up her breakfast as well as lunch, then felt too sick to stay at work. In fact, she felt so ill that for a moment, finding that scene, she thought it was a product of her fever. It wasn't. No dream was so real. It was César and Emma, in flesh and blood. About to fuck, kissing each other as no one had kissed her in years. So involved in the act that they hadn't even seen or heard her, until Sílvia, unable to react any other way, started laughing. And it was that bitter, unnatural laugh that made the lovers stop. They remained in an embrace but immobile, refusing to open their eyes; keeping them closed a little longer, not to have to see. It was enough to hear that laugh, that rain of rusty nails that pinned them to the wall as if they were an erotic photo, a poster in bad taste that would shortly be taken down, torn in two and thrown in the bin.

35

The journey back to Barcelona was more relaxed. It was influenced by the fact that they'd stopped to have a late lunch in a motorway restaurant, and that Señora Vinyals's tale opened up a whole series of possibilities, although few certainties. When they got back into the car it was already after five, and Héctor accelerated a little. He wanted to get back to the station in time to see Fort and find out first hand if there was any news. Curiously, the animated conversation they'd kept up over lunch died as soon as he took the wheel. Lola was looking out of the window and he watched her from the corner of his eye. She'd cut her hair, but other than that she'd changed very little in those seven years. She'd always been attractive, although her style was in such contrast to Ruth's that it begged the question how the same man could fall in love with two such different women.

'You're the same.' His thought had been expressed aloud without him even noticing.

'Don't believe it,' she replied, not looking away from the window. 'Just seems so.'

'How are you? Now we have more than seven minutes to talk . . . Tell me, how are things?'

'I suppose they could be worse. And better too. In short, I've no complaints. And you?'

He lit a cigarette before answering; this time he didn't ask permission to do so.

'Let's just say I've been better and been worse as well,' he finally answered.

'I heard about Ruth. I'm sorry, truly.'

The mention of that name was a spell of silence, but this time it was Lola who broke it.

'I came to Barcelona to interview her. Shortly after you separated.'

Héctor was surprised.

'I didn't know you did those kinds of articles.'

'Welcome to the profile of the new journalist,' she said sarcastically. 'Or more accurately, as it states on my card: "Content Provider". Watch out – any day you'll stop being an inspector and become an "Order Provider" or something.' There was a trace of bitterness in her voice that she didn't bother to conceal. 'Everything has changed so much. And I fear there's worse to come. Don't you see it?' For the first time in a while, she turned towards him. 'We've been living in a kind of limbo, Héctor, but this limbo won't be the waiting room for heaven—'

'Have you become religious?' he joked.

'No! I don't think my DNA would permit it; I must be immune to spirituality. Even the incense in shops that sell candles and buddhas makes me feel sick. No, I'm talking about a real hell: poverty, extremism, fear . . . Perhaps getting older is making me a pessimist, but nothing has any meaning in this country any more: not the left, only so in name; not the right that calls itself moderate; not the banks that get more benefits than businesses.' She smiled. 'Not the employers who send their employees to spend a few days in the country as if they are their children, as if they really matter. Too much fun, Héctor, too many lies we all believed because they were pleasant. Because they said what we wanted to hear.'

Lola was quiet for a moment or two and then took up the initial subject again.

'Like I said, I met Ruth. She was a charming woman. Throughout the whole interview I kept wondering if she knew about us or not and I left without coming to a conclusion.'

'She knew,' said Héctor. 'I told her. When—'

'When you left me. Say it. It's been seven years, I'm not going to start crying.'

They were approaching Barcelona. The traffic became heavier and the feeling of intimacy was evaporating.

'We couldn't go on as we were. It was becoming too . . . intense. If it's any consolation, Ruth ended up leaving me.'

'It's no consolation.' Lola's voice was so serious, so sad, that Héctor took his eyes off the motorway to turn towards her. 'You know why? Not because I'm a saint, exactly. While preparing for the interview with Ruth I heard you had separated, she had another partner, and I knew you and I could never be together again without me feeling like an obligatory substitute. A replacement forced by events.'

Héctor took his hand off the wheel and sought hers. He couldn't help it. Lola didn't take hers away.

'Héctor – I left Barcelona, I got over us little by little; I forced myself to stop envying Ruth, to forget you.'

He wanted to kiss her. Park the car on some corner

and embrace her. Go to her hotel and undress her slowly. Caress her until those seven years apart were erased. She looked him in the eyes and understood.

It came out softly, but firmly. 'No nostalgic fucks, Héctor. They're hideously depressing. There was a time when I wouldn't have been able to refuse. But now I can. And you know why? Because there is only one truth and I don't want to deceive myself. You had a choice and you made it. I lost and Ruth won. The match ended there.'

Had it been Martina or even Leire, they would have noticed that the boss was in a foul mood just from seeing him come in. But, logically, Roger Fort lacked feminine intuition and didn't have a huge dose of the masculine equivalent either, so he waylaid Inspector Salgado as soon as he passed his desk.

'Inspector, can we talk?'

Héctor turned to the agent with a look that would have been frustrating for anyone not so excited. Fort, thought Héctor, has the principal quality of superheroes and madmen: he is impervious to disappointment.

'Of course,' he answered. 'Talk to me.'

'I've finally tracked down a waitress who saw Sara Mahler having dinner with someone on *Reyes* in a restaurant near the metro station where she died. We hadn't spoken to her before because she was on holiday. She remembers her, her and her companion, because they seemed a curious pair: one blonde, one dark.'

'Blonde? A woman?'

'Yes, sir. The waitress doesn't remember much more – it was *Reyes* and there were a lot of people. Just that she

328

was young and blonde.' Fort dared to add, 'It might have been Amanda Bonet.'

Damn, thought Héctor. He'd hoped that Sara's mysterious companion would contribute some information to this puzzle.

'Another thing, sir,' Fort continued. 'Señor Víctor Alemany has called a number of times asking for you. He was pretty angry. He wanted to speak to the superintendent—'

'He can go to hell!' Héctor exclaimed. Fort had to force himself not to take a step back. 'They can all go to hell. They think they can give us the runaround then scare us with phone calls. It's run out.'

'Run out?'

'My patience has run out, Fort.' The shine in Salgado's eyes was definitely one of rage and not just exasperation. 'I'm going to destroy this group. Tomorrow you and I are going to Alemany Cosmetics and we'll make a few arrests. Just to question them. Right there, in front of their colleagues, so everyone hears about it.'

Fort remembered the stories that went around the station about Salgado, but he thought it was within his rights to ask: 'Who are we going to arrest, sir?'

'The strongest and the weakest, Fort. The lady who acts like a queen and Manel Caballero. And I swear I'll get the truth out of them even if I have to question them non-stop for twenty-four hours.'

LEIRE

36

I shouldn't have agreed to this meeting, thought Leire when the taxi left her just at the entrance to Los Jardines de la Maternidad in the area of Les Corts. She'd had a bad night and slept fitfully, overwhelmed by unsettling dreams in which Ruth and Dr Omar appeared, talking in low voices. In the end, sick of nightmares, she'd risen around seven, a little queasy. She ate breakfast with no appetite and a while later, despite having promised herself she wouldn't, she picked up her mobile and called the number that the stranger had given her the night before.

And here she was, in these gardens which might be beautiful in summer but in the month of January had the gloomy air of a decaying mansion. It was eleven o'clock, although it could have been six in the evening judging by the sky. An insidious cold, with no wind or rain, was ravaging a city little accustomed to extreme temperatures. Nervous, not knowing why, she waited at the gates of the park; she supposed the man who had to see her would recognize her, because she hadn't the least idea of his appearance.

Standing by the railings, she wondered why this person had chosen this particular place. 'Better somewhere in the open air,' he'd told her. 'That way we can speak more freely.' She agreed: as a general rule open spaces didn't bother her, but just then, off-colour despite the huge overcoat she was wearing, she wished she'd suggested any café where she could at least sit down to wait.

She didn't have to wait long. At five past eleven, a man in his thirties turned the corner and moved directly and unhesitatingly towards her.

'Agent Castro,' he said, extending his hand. 'I'm Andrés Moreno.'

She put out her hand and felt relieved. There was nothing sinister about this guy; on the contrary, his medium stature and friendly face, almost too friendly to be attractive, seemed to dispel any trace of distrust. He was carrying a rucksack slung on his shoulder, which repeatedly slipped down the sleeve of his brown leather jacket.

'Apologies for calling at your house last night,' he said to her, 'but I leave tomorrow and didn't want to go without seeing you. Shall we walk?'

She nodded, although as soon as they went through the gate she sought out a bench. She found one and went towards it. There were few people in the gardens, and the old buildings, bathed in that winter light, had an almost ghostly air.

'Mind if we sit?' she asked, in the same informal manner. 'I weigh too much to move a lot.'

Smiling, he nodded. Opposite the bench there was a statue of white stone: a young mother with a child in her lap. Although the buildings now fulfilled other needs, years back this group of pavilions had been a hospital where mothers gave birth. Leire caressed her bump as she sat down. Abel seemed to be sleeping; as lazy as the day, she thought. He certainly took after his father.

'Well,' said Leire. 'I'm intrigued.'

Andrés Moreno smiled.

'I suppose so. And the fact is, now I have you here I don't really know where to begin.'

'You told me you had something to tell me about Ruth Valldaura. I think that would be a good place to start.'

He placed the rucksack on the bench between them, opened it and was going to take something out, but thought better of it and stopped. Instead, he asked a question that took Leire completely aback.

'Have you heard of the stolen babies?'

'What?' She recovered from her surprise immediately. 'Of course, who hasn't?'

It had been some time since the news, the scandal, had circulated in newspapers and on television programmes. Babies separated from their mothers at birth, believed dead by their real parents and given in shady adoptions to families who believed they were taking in unwanted children. What had begun as a consequence of the war, involving mothers on the losing side who according to the morality of the time were unworthy of the name, had evolved into a plot, a business maintained for many more years: cases of children born in the sixties and seventies now desperately seeking their biological parents; biological parents who until recently were convinced they had lost a child and suddenly discovered the grave was empty; adoptive parents horrified to discover that they had unknowingly been part of an immoral criminal scheme. The subject was spine-chilling and its ramifications implicated midwives, nuns and doctors, although in the

335

majority of cases the law could do very little. The statute of limitations of the crimes added to the difficulty of irrefutably proving they had been committed.

While Leire thought about it all, the snippets of information heard and discussed, Andrés Moreno took some papers and photos from his backpack.

'I'm a journalist and I've spent months delving into this subject. As you already know about it, I won't go into detail. I'll just say that there are many cases to be discovered, to be brought to light. But the names of some implicated doctors come up again and again, as do the names of an uncharitable religious woman, to call her by another name.'

Leire nodded, although she didn't know what all this had to do with her and Ruth Valldaura.

'As you'll see, there are few traces of these illegal adoptions. The method varied. Some biological mothers gave birth in hospitals and were told after the birth that their babies had died. They even had the body of one—Forgive me.' He stopped, seeing that Leire was becoming pale.

'No, it's all right,' she lied.

'Fuck, now I think about it, it's not very appropriate to speak to you about this. I'm sorry.'

'Don't worry. You've started now. Go on.'

He took a deep breath.

'There were other sorts of cases. Single mothers who sought refuge in religious institutions where the same method, or worse, was followed. They simply informed them they didn't deserve to be mothers, that their babies would be better off in the arms of a family as God orders. If they objected they were threatened: sometimes with

336

taking the other children they already had . . . In any case, the babies were handed over practically at birth and the adoptive parents registered them as their own. What is clear is that money was involved.'

'Yes,' said Leire. 'From what I know, in the form of donations, wasn't it?'

'In the case of religious institutions, of course. And that's what I'm getting at.'

Andrés Moreno opened the backpack and took out a red file, so old it looked as if it were about to fall to pieces.

'This was one of the refuges for single mothers at that time.'

He showed her a black-and-white photo. Some young nuns posing in front of a house and large gardens. Everyone was smiling for the camera.

'It was the Hogar de la Concepción in Tarragona and it was run by a nun whose name has come to light in more than one file. Sr Amparo. This one.'

There was little to mark her out from the others: the uniforms served their purpose and gave them all the same appearance, docile grey doves.

'I say "was" because it no longer exists. Neither does Sr Amparo, at least in this world. She died four years ago. The Hogar closed at the end of the eighties and its archives must have gone to another institution, or were destroyed. It seems there were few nuns left, but one of them managed to take away some documents with her.'

'What for?'

'Well, let's say she'd seen certain things there and wanted to keep proof.' Moreno lowered his head and added, 'I can't tell you anything else about her. That was the condition she placed on giving me the information. This information.'

He took out further papers from the file: no doubt they were photocopies of other older ones, which weren't very legible. Leire took them and studied them carefully.

'They are donations. You can see that the quantities varied, but all of them are very high. We're talking about millions in the seventies, when six hundred was a lot for normal people. Look at this one in particular.'

According to what was written there, on 13 October 1971, one Ernesto Valldaura Recasens had donated ten million pesetas to the Hogar de la Concepción.

'What are you telling me?' she asked, although her furrowed brow indicated that she'd already guessed.

'It's obviously not proof of anything. Anyone can donate money to whomever they please. But I started investigating – not him, but all the names that appear here. Although there aren't many, they were difficult to track down. I was lucky with Ernesto Valldaura. This is his daughter's birth certificate.' He showed it to her. 'Ruth Valldaura Martorell, born 13 October 1971.'

Leire looked at both papers with something akin to vertigo.

'This means . . . ?'

He shrugged.

'It's not proof of anything. At least not legal proof. As I said, Señor Valldaura had all the right in the world to make donations as generous as he wished and to the centre he pleased. But it's a meaningful coincidence, don't you think?'

'What else did the nun tell you? The one who gave you all this . . .'

'Not much. That there were mothers who came back to the Hogar demanding their children, there were many "difficult" labours, and that Sr Amparo ruled the place with an iron fist and coffers always full.'

'When . . . when did you receive these documents?'

'At the end of last year.'

Ruth had already disappeared by then, thought Leire.

'When I finally tracked down the Valldauras and the birth certificate I did a quick search for their daughter's name. And I found out what had happened to her, some months later.'

'Did you go to see them?'

'The Valldauras didn't want to see me. I suppose they thought I was one more journalist interested in their daughter's case, and in fact I didn't insist too much. What were they going to tell me? Talking to them about the donation and the suspicions this could arouse seemed out of place when they had to face the disappearance of that daughter. So I focused on investigating Ruth Valldaura, although to tell the truth I haven't achieved much. My only lead over the last few days has been you,' he said, smiling. 'I admit that I've been following you to see if you were also interested in her.'

'But—'

'I no longer have any resources, or time. I thought I might discover something . . . I even considered the possibility that Ruth's birth and end might be linked somehow, however improbable it seems. I also thought about approaching Ruth Valldaura's ex-husband, but hearing about his "violent tendencies" I backed off.'

She smiled. Poor Héctor, some sentences pursue the accused for life. They are the worst – a trail of rumours that refuse to fade and against which the accused can't fight.

'I'm not from Barcelona,' Andrés Moreno continued, 'and now I can't stay here any longer. The rent has to be paid and I have nothing to publish. Also . . .'

'Yes?'

'To be honest with you, I don't know if I want to keep going with this. It's a dirty business, marked by a cruelty that I sometimes find unbearable. I'm getting married in the spring, I want to start a family . . .'

Andrés Moreno blushed. The sentence hung in the air, but Leire understood what he meant perfectly.

'A favour,' she said.

'You want the documents? I've brought you copies. Use them as you see fit, but – be careful. It's a matter that will reach the courts some day, although at the moment it's buried under tons of bureaucracy. And there are many people who want it to remain so. Lots of those implicated have died or retired, lots of the babies are now adults who don't know the truth. There are many others, of course, seeking justice, embarking on a struggle against oblivion, but I fear that time will dishearten them, keep them quiet, make them disappear . . .'

Like Ruth, thought Leire. Her outrage and indignation had overtaken all feeling of nausea or fatigue. Like Ruth.

Montserrat Martorell opened the door of her house to her that same day, a little before two. Leire had gone to see her on impulse, and on this occasion the sombre expression of Ruth's mother made little impression on her.

'Here again, Señorita Castro?'

340

She wasn't in the mood to beat around the bush, so she put the photocopied document under her nose, barely giving her time to see it. 'I think we need to talk.'

Señora Martorell directed her to the same little sitting room she'd received her in the last time, but she didn't bother to pretend she was welcome. She must have seen she was tired, or upset, because she invited her to sit and Leire accepted.

'Explain this to me,' said Leire. 'Please,' she added.

Ruth's mother put on some small glasses that hung around her neck on a delicate chain and glanced at the paper. Then she took off her glasses and focused her attention on her unexpected visitor. Leire stared once again into Señora Martorell's grey eyes, intense despite her age.

'I don't know what you want me to explain. My husband made a donation to this place almost forty years ago. He had a stronger faith then. Time, and life, cure that.'

Leire observed her, unable to decide if this woman was aware of what this document could mean. She decided to get to the point.

'Did you adopt Ruth?'

Señora Martorell folded the sheet of paper and spoke slowly in a voice trying to be cold, but not quite managing it.

'Señorita Castro—'

'Agent Castro, if you don't mind!'

'Don't raise your voice to me. I've been very patient with you, but now you're going too far. Let me remind you that you are investigating my daughter's disappearance, not her birth. And I doubt that, thirty-nine years apart, there is any link between the two events.'

341

Leire was going to answer, but just then Abel decided to enter the conversation and did so in a painful way, almost as if he were protesting.

'Are you feeling all right?'

'Yes.' She took a deep breath. 'I think so. This time he moved more forcefully . . .'

'Why don't you do yourself a favour? Go home, have your baby. Honestly, I tell you this as a mother: nothing is more important. When he is born, everything that seems important now will simply fade away. You'll think only about caring for him, feeding him. Protecting him.'

'I know,' said Leire. Her voice was trembling. 'I'll take care of him, feed him, protect him – but I won't lie to him. I won't invent a romantic story about his father, or the relationship I have with him. Maybe we won't be the perfect family, but we won't pretend to be. My son will know the truth.'

'The truth!' Montserrat Martorell made a gesture of annoyance. 'Young people have an obsession with it that's almost naive. Do you think the world could work on the basis of truth? I'll tell you something, Agent Castro: honesty is an overrated concept these days. And there are others which lamentably have lost their force, like loyalty, obedience. Respect for rules that have functioned, for better or worse, for years. No, Agent Castro, it's not the truth that sustains the world. Think about it.'

'I think the world to which you're referring no longer exists,' Leire replied, almost sadly.

'No?' she asked with an ironic smile. 'Look around you. Do you think the people on the street, normal people, know the whole truth? There are things to which normal people, like you or I, cannot have access. That's how it is, how it's always been, however much people now think they have a right to know. If you take it on another, smaller scale, you'll see that it also applies in refuges, in families . . . When you have your son you'll realize that the truth isn't important if it is at odds with other values like security, protection. And like it or not, you'll have to decide for him. For that you're his mother: to plot a safe path for him and avoid him suffering.'

Leire began to feel queasy again, but that woman's last words made her think of something else.

'Is that what you did with Patricia? Move her away from the road you had planned for Ruth?'

Señora Martorell held her gaze, not blinking.

'I just told her to leave my daughter alone. She was smothering her. We mothers always notice these things. I spoke to Ruth, I put a little pressure on her and in the end she told me everything. She was so frightened, so confused . . . She didn't know her own feelings, inclinations. My duty was to protect her.'

'Protect her from Patricia?' She couldn't help the note of sarcasm in her voice.

'Protect her from something she wasn't yet ready to face. And of which she wasn't even fully aware.' She paused before adding, 'It takes courage to be different in this life, Señorita Castro. My only aim was to avoid Ruth suffering. So, before Patricia left, I had a chat with her, alone.'

Leire imagined this woman, imposing in old age; she must have been intimidating as an offended mother. And Patricia would have felt betrayed, even ashamed in those years. She could almost see her after facing Señora Martorell, driving home alone . . .

'Didn't you feel bad afterwards?' It was hard to believe, it seemed impossible, that this woman in front of her felt not a trace of remorse. 'When did you hear about the accident?'

Montserrat Martorell straightened up and answered in a frozen, emphatic voice: 'My feelings are absolutely none of your business, Agent Castro.'

No, they're not, thought Leire. She almost preferred not to know.

'You're right. I have no right to ask you that, but I have the right to tell you something. Maybe you already know or maybe not, but at least from now on you can't hide behind ignorance.'

And Leire told her about the stolen babies, the Hogar de la Concepción and Sr Amparo; she spoke about the possibility that Ruth's mother hadn't handed over her daughter voluntarily, that they would have deceived her by saying she was dead or taken her from her arms. That her husband's donation was payment in exchange for a newborn.

Señora Martorell listened attentively, not interrupting her. When she finished her account, Leire was very tired and wanted to leave. Her flat with suicidal tiles and blocked pipes suddenly seemed like the best home in the world.

'You are very pale,' Señora Martorell told her. 'I think I'll call a taxi to take you home. And . . . believe me, Agent Castro, because I say it for your good and that of your child: stop raking over a past that, even if it were true, won't help us find Ruth. Focus on the future. Best for you and for everyone.'

Leire would have liked to answer that justice consisted

of that, but she didn't have the strength to do it. She simply looked at her, trying to communicate her incomprehension of this manner of seeing things. The woman didn't appear to take it personally. Apathetic, Leire rose, took the piece of paper where Ruth's father's donation was recorded and went to the door without saying anything else. She would wait for the taxi outside.

She longed to get home, shut herself inside and forget about this world. Perhaps it wasn't deliberately cruel, but it was certainly deeply inhuman.

37

The clock on the nightstand indicated that it was only six a.m. and Leire turned over in bed. She had no reason to be awake so early. She closed her eyes and tried to get to sleep, as if it were something she could force by will. When she finally gave up and stopped lying in bed, a quarter of an hour had passed. Enough time to know it was better to get up although it was still almost night.

She went from the bed to the sofa, strangely without appetite for breakfast, and for a while she awaited movement from Abel. It finally happened and she breathed easily. She'd become accustomed to noticing it and when she didn't she was overcome by a horrible fear.

Facing her, on the table, were the photos of Ruth, her file and the tape with the recording of Dr Omar's clinic. She didn't feel up to watching it again and suddenly she realized that she was beginning to feel unable to continue with the case. It was upsetting her too much, invading her consciousness, making her uneasy. This can't go on, she told herself. And slowly, assuming that for the first time she was giving up on a case before exhausting all the possibilities, she collected everything into the same envelope Martina Andreu had given her. After a moment's hesitation, she left the donation document out. She'd give it to Inspector Salgado, who could do as he wished with it.

She had decided: she would give everything back to Sergeant Andreu, telling her she was too tired to continue investigating. She would speak to Héctor Salgado and communicate all the details clouding his ex-wife's birth. And then she'd concentrate on waiting for Abel to be born, with no shocks or distressing conversations like the one she'd had with Ruth's mother.

But memory played by its own rules, and Ruth's face, just as it appeared in the photo, kept reappearing. Ruth, perhaps adopted without knowing it. Manipulated by her mother until she had the courage to decide for herself. How would Ruth have felt when she heard about Patricia's fatal accident? Like the character in *Breathless*, she'd been frightened by her own feelings and, in a way, had betrayed her friend to her mother. For Señora Martorell it had all ended there, but not for her daughter.

Ruth had kept the photo of Patricia, she'd written that love generates eternal debts. Even to those you no longer love. Through this misplaced sense of responsibility Ruth had gone to Dr Omar to intercede for her ex-husband. Yes, she was sure. What had that perverse old guy said to her? Nothing very serious, because Ruth had changed very little after that visit, about which she'd told no one. Héctor had spoken to Leire about the last time he saw his ex-wife, when she accompanied him to the airport to pick up his missing suitcase. She seemed fine, same as always . . . Then she disappeared.

I can't do it any more, Leire said to herself. She was sure that if Ruth had some way of seeing what was happening

347

in the world, she wouldn't feel betrayed by this pregnant agent. On the contrary, she'd understand perfectly.

Halfway through the afternoon she left the station, bag now empty, seized by a mixture of feelings that went from relief to guilt, passing through a range of different emotions. Inspector Salgado was busy questioning a whole group of witnesses of a case and she couldn't see him. It didn't really matter – what she had to tell him could wait.

Martina Andreu had understood completely and taken charge of everything. 'It's better this way,' she'd added. 'You don't know the trouble stirred up because of the file.' And she must have looked bad, because her words were the same as Señora Martorell. 'Relax, Leire.' And yes, for once she planned to listen: she just wanted to return to her flat, lie on the sofa and do nothing for what was left of her pregnancy. She tried to drive the image of Ruth from her mind without managing it completely, but determined to do it.

Because of that, when she met Guillermo at the door of the building where she lived she was tempted to tell him not to come up, that she didn't feel well. But she didn't: the boy seemed so nervous and she was so tired that she had no choice but to invite him in.

38

'Sorry for turning up like this,' he said, already inside her house. 'I called but you didn't answer.'

He took out his mobile to show her and left it on the table.

'It's no problem, don't worry.' She let herself collapse on the sofa. The room was spinning.

'Are you feeling all right? You're very pale.'

'A little bit queasy, that's all. It'll pass when I've rested for a while. If you'd like something to drink, you can grab it yourself from the fridge.'

Guillermo declined the invitation, but offered to bring her something if she wanted.

'Yes, can you bring me a glass of water, please?'

He obeyed and returned immediately. He held out the glass as he sat down beside her.

'You said I could talk to you about Mama.'

Yes, she had said so, thought Leire, although just then it was the last thing she felt like doing. She took a sip of water and prepared to listen. He was sitting at her side. He was worried, no doubt about that. Even nauseated, she could see.

'I suppose I should tell Papa,' he said, 'but he's been very busy for the last few days and I thought I could talk to you first.'

'Of course.' The water felt good. 'Tell me, has something happened?'

He nodded.

'Do you know Carmen? The landlady of the building where we live?'

Leire knew of her and was aware that she maintained a close relationship with Héctor and his family, one that went beyond what usually existed between a landlady and her tenants.

'Carmen has a son,' he continued. 'His name is Charly, but he doesn't live with her. They've not seen each other for years.'

She remembered hearing something about this Charly from Inspector Salgado and of course it wasn't exactly praise.

'Well, Charly has come home to his mother.'

'I'd say he's not a good influence for you . . .' ventured Leire. 'Do you know him well?'

'Actually, I don't remember him from before he left, but . . .'

'But what?' Curiosity was overcoming her nausea.

It took him a while to speak, as if he were betraying a confidence.

'But I know Mama let him sleep at home, in the loft a few times.'

Leire sat up.

'What?'

'Papa wouldn't have liked it at all and Mama asked me not to tell him. According to her, Charly wasn't so bad and, anyway, she said she was doing it for Carmen. A mothers' thing. It was only three or four nights after we moved there – he never stayed long. I'd forgotten, but now, seeing him again, I thought it might be important, mightn't it?'

'Maybe. You did the right thing in telling me.'

'Do you think he could have done something to her? I wasn't at home that whole week. I went to Calafell, to a friend's house . . .'

He looked so upset that Leire hastened to console him.

'I don't know, Guillermo, but I don't think so.' She didn't know why, but she doubted such a complex case could suddenly be solved by the reappearance of a small-time crook. 'They would have found his fingerprints – he must have a record. Also, your mother didn't usually make mistakes, did she? Maybe Charly isn't such a bad guy.'

A grateful smile appeared on Guillermo's face.

'In any case, you have to tell your father.' Remembering she had things to tell Inspector Salgado, she added, 'I have things to tell him too.'

'Really?'

Leire left the glass on the table. She didn't want to discuss it with this boy. And as she couldn't find Ruth, she told herself the least she could do for her was give her son something for dinner.

Not only did Guillermo accept her invitation, he offered to make dinner, which to Leire's surprise turned out rather good. She forced herself to be cheerful and try to eat the pasta the boy had boiled while making a tomato sauce seasoned with black pepper and a little mince he found in the fridge. She couldn't eat much; the nausea kept coming in waves.

He was clearing the plates from the table when a sudden, violent, stabbing pain left her breathless, and pale as new linen. It was only a few seconds and then the feeling disappeared, but a cold sweat and the constant vertigo remained.

'Are you all right?'

Leire was about to answer when the pain returned. No, no, you can't be born yet, she thought.

'I think . . .' It hurt so much she almost couldn't speak. 'I think we need to call the doctor.'

HÉCTOR

39

The arrest of Manel Caballero occurred at half past nine in the morning on Thursday, 20 January. An offended and frightened Manel, protesting vehemently, was approached at his place of work by Roger Fort and another agent, in front of his astonished colleagues: he had to accompany them to the station for questioning. They handcuffed him without the least compassion. Simultaneously, Héctor Salgado was doing the same with Sílvia Alemany, who, to the inspector's surprise, left her office with her head held high and without saying a single word.

The two were put in separate police cars and transferred to the station. They saw each other then, at the door, though they didn't have a chance to talk. He, handcuffed and almost pushed towards the building's interior; she walking with dignity with the inspector at her side. Two very different interrogation rooms awaited them.

Frightened is nothing, thought Héctor as soon as he entered one of them, ready to get everything he could out of that slippery young man. Since the previous afternoon, when he got back from the house in Garrigàs, he had been setting the pieces of this puzzle in order: the dogs, the bicycles, the spade, the shift in attitude of the participants, Amanda's shock the night before. And although he didn't know for certain how things had happened, he did have at least a vague idea of what could have happened. An idea he didn't like at all.

He sat down opposite Caballero in silence and left a file on the table. He was going to open it when the other man belligerently spat out, 'May I know what this is about? Why the hell have you brought me here?'

'I was just going to explain, don't you worry.'

'You can't treat people like this! You don't fool me, I know my rights—'

'You've seen too many TV series, Manel,' Héctor replied with a condescending smile. 'In any case, since you're so up to speed with your rights, I'm going to recap mine. You're a suspect in a multiple homicide case and you're here to be questioned.'

Manel's expression showed the hit, and Héctor continued, 'I can't force you to talk, although I promise you it wouldn't bother me to do so. On the other hand, I can hold you for seventy-two hours for you to reflect and decide to cooperate.'

'Handcuffing and mistreating me up to now isn't the best way of asking me to cooperate, Inspector! At least tell me what you're talking about, because if you think I killed Amanda and Sara, you're completely mad.'

Héctor smiled again.

'Madmen sometimes guess the truth. Or so they say – haven't you ever heard that?' His tone changed as he added, 'I don't want to talk about Sara, or Amanda. Or

356

even Gaspar. I want us to talk about what happened at the house in Garrigàs.'

He managed to rattle him, though just for a moment. Manel mustered all his strength and replied, 'I have nothing to say about that.'

'Sure? Nothing to tell me about some stolen bicycles? A missing spade?'

Manel flushed, but managed to stay calm and feign a fairly convincing incredulous tone.

'I think you don't know anything, Inspector. You only guess things. So hold me as long as you wish. I'll wait for my solicitor.'

'Of course. No problem.' Héctor rested both hands on the table, rose and leaned towards an astonished Manel. When he spoke it was in a quiet, firm voice. 'But you won't wait here.'

'What do you mean?' stammered Manel.

The inspector didn't answer. He left the room slowly, and shortly afterwards came back in accompanied by two agents. Without a word, they lifted Manel Caballero from the chair.

'What's this? Where the fuck are you taking me?'

'As I said, I have seventy-two hours to get you to co-operate.' He looked at his watch. 'But you're not going to spend them here. You'll be in one of the cells. I need this room to talk with someone more important than you. It wouldn't be wise on my part to send Señora Alemany to a cell, would it? I could get into real trouble.'

The look of rage Manel cast him was the first of his victories. The agents carried him away, oblivious to his shouts of protest, to one of the small station cells, already occupied by a couple of junkies.

'No! No! You can't do this to me . . .'

Héctor slowly exhaled. Manel's screams faded. It was only a matter of time, he was sure. Anyone who wanted to sleep alone wouldn't last too long in those cells.

'How's it going?' Roger Fort asked from the door.

'It will be fine,' answered Héctor. 'Any news?'

'Víctor Alemany called. Not me, Superintendent Savall. From what I understand he's coming here with his solicitor. Well, more accurately, with Señor Pujades. Inspector, I know you're in a hurry, but there's something I'd like to show you. It'll only take a moment. Come with me.'

Fort walked ahead of him and they went towards a room equipped with a screen. On it Héctor saw the frozen image of that damned metro platform.

'I was wondering how someone could have entered after Sara without being caught on the turnstile cameras. And suddenly it occurred to me that there was only one possibility: that they arrived on the metro going in the opposite direction and crossed from one platform to the other, like someone getting off at the wrong station.'

Héctor looked at him and nodded.

'Of course – as simple as that.'

'They didn't come down on to the platform, of course. They must have stayed on the stairs. Sara Mahler didn't move much, so, supposing someone pushed her, they could have waited there, sitting on a step, and emerged only when they saw the train was about to arrive.'

Yes, thought Héctor. A risky, almost suicidal act, but possible. The camera hadn't captured that moment.

'But Sara must have seen them get out. She did pass those steps,' he responded.

'Yeah, I thought that too. But she looked worried. If she'd seen a guy sitting on the steps she wouldn't have looked twice. She'd have thought they were drunk. Maybe . . .'

'Good work, Fort. I mean it. Have you requested the tapes from the other platform?'

'They've gone for them, sir. I'll look at them as soon as they arrive.'

'I leave it in your hands,' said Salgado, smiling. 'I'm going to talk to Sílvia Alemany before her troops arrive. Make sure no one interrupts me while I'm with her. Not the superintendent, not Alemany, not the Pope of Rome, is that clear?

'And another thing. If Manel decides to cooperate, lock him in one of the rooms and call the other two. César Calvo and Brais Arjona. I want them all nearby.'

This time I'm playing at home, thought Héctor when he found himself in the presence of Sílvia Alemany, who still had the bearing and composure given by intelligence united with a kind of class. She appeared indifferent, sitting in the interview room where they had brought her on arrival, but she couldn't help a sidelong glance on seeing the inspector enter.

'Do you wish to talk about the dead dogs again, Inspector?' she asked. 'If I'd known it was going to cause so many explanations, I'd never have agreed to carry it out.'

'You know something, Señora Alemany? I think that's the first honest thing you've said to me since we met.'

'I'm also getting tired of your veiled insinuations, Inspector. If you have something to charge me with, do it. And if not, let me go. I have a lot of work to do.'

'Making sure the others don't talk? I'm afraid it's too late. Manel doesn't have your mettle, that's obvious. It was all the same to him as long as he felt safe. But when he found himself caught between a rock and a hard place—'

'Don't deceive me, Inspector Salgado. When he sees himself between a rock and a hard place, Manel chooses the hard place. Never the rock.'

Héctor laughed.

'You're right. The good thing about proverbs is that they're symbolic, so you never really know what the rock or the hard place mean. I assure you poor Manel Caballero faced a very sharp, treacherous rock.'

She grew pale.

'Why don't you tell me your version of what happened? You're tired, you must be – is such a burden really worth it?'

Sílvia hesitated. He could see the doubt clouding her eyes and the temptation to talk begin to grow within her. But pride got the better of her.

'I'm sure my brother must be on his way here. And not alone. So, Inspector, I think soon I'll be able to leave this room and relax.'

'Oh yes? When you lie down will you forget Gaspar's face? Or Sara's? Amanda's? Three dead people, Sílvia, not counting Gaspar's poor wife and child. You're a mother.'

'One of the subjects that annoys me nowadays is the general opinion that being a mother makes you a better person, Inspector. There are good and bad mothers. Good and bad daughters.'

Héctor didn't know what she was talking about, but

it was clear he'd just hit a nerve in the woman in front of him.

'And don't try to put the blame on me for what Gaspar did to his family. I have enough trying to understand my own.'

Finally he'd made an impression on Sílvia Alemany. The bitter tone couldn't be ignored. And Héctor understood the moment had come to bet, albeit cautiously, so that she didn't guess how low the cards in his hand were.

'Returning the bicycles was a mistake, Sílvia. A silly mistake. Not like you.'

She seemed absorbed in thoughts that had nothing to do with that, and everything to do with her family.

'The bicycles were intact. There were no si—' Sílvia went quiet, but it was already too late and Héctor finished her sentence for her.

'There were no signs of the accident, were there?'

'What accident?' she asked in a voice much less sure.

'The accident that happened when you were returning from burying the dogs.' The bluff was working, Héctor could feel it. 'I think you came back in a good mood, self-satisfied, from the completed task. I don't think you expected destiny to play a dirty trick on you. And to tell the truth, I honestly think the first act of this farce was a genuine accident. Am I right?'

Sílvia Alemany no longer had the courage to continue denying it. She closed her eyes, inhaled very slowly and began talking.

40

The eight of them contemplate their work with the satisfaction that comes from having done something real, with their hands, based on real physical effort and sweat. A feeling to which they are in fact unaccustomed because their jobs have little to do with that.

'Done,' says Brais with a sigh, as he rubs his hand. He is the one who has dug the most and he knows that the following day he'll have blisters all over his hands from the hoe, but the physical effort seems healthy. Invigorating.

The only trace of those mercilessly sacrificed animals is the newly turned earth a hundred metres from the tree. Without them, the branches of the cork tree revert to being inoffensive, vulgar. Dusk bathes the landscape in a comforting, placid light.

'Are we going now, or do you expect us to say a prayer?' asks César. He's the only one who appears immune to the general feeling of well-being. In fact, he agreed to dirty his hands only reluctantly, when he saw the vote was lost anyway. Only Manel had objected to the idea and César didn't like to associate with losers.

Octavi smiles and Sílvia looks sideways at her fiancé. César shuts up.

'Why don't we get going?' Manel intervenes. 'It's almost night.'

'Why don't we wait a moment?' suggests Sara. 'There aren't many opportunities to enjoy a sunset like this one.'

César is tired and wants to go back to the house, but once again the others seem in agreement. And in fact, all of them, him included, watch the sunset on the mountains, partly because it is beautiful, and partly because they're too tired to move or argue. The sun descends behind the peaks, slowly, effortlessly, quenching its orange-coloured shine and leaving the world in shadow.

'Well, that's it,' says Brais quietly. 'It's been a long day.'

They walk towards the van, fatigued but happy. The task and the twilight have satisfied them. A euphoric, contagious peace overwhelms them.

'I'll drive,' says Sílvia, and César, who had driven them there, throws her the keys. 'I like driving at night.'

They make themselves comfortable in the van, which has two rows of three seats as well as the driver and passenger seats: Sílvia driving and Octavi beside her; the others are arranged on the two rows behind. She puts on some music before starting the engine and they all seem to feel as young and free as the song proclaims.

'I love it,' says Sílvia. 'Now my brother can't hear us, I think it's the best of the campaign.'

There is a general laugh: it's unusual to hear the Alemanys criticizing each other, although there's been a rumour going round that their relationship isn't the best at the moment.

Sílvia turns the key and the van begins to move. They feel happy and not at all tired.

'Hey!' César protests after a corner which throws them all to one side. 'Careful. The damned spade is sticking into my ribs.'

'César, don't be a spoilsport. We're nearly there. Put the song on again, Octavi. It cheers me up.'

And Sílvia accelerates, because all of a sudden she feels like she did when she was young and rebellious, and she hasn't experienced a feeling like this in years. She accelerates, not taking into account that visibility isn't good, and neither is the road. She accelerates because she doesn't think she's going to encounter any obstacle to brake for on this lonely road.

They're almost there; the lights can be made out in what would otherwise be a black field. Those sitting behind don't even see what happens. They just hear Octavi's sudden warning, an abrupt swerve and a dull thud. The van stops at the side of the road, opposite the gate of the track leading to the house.

'What was that?' asks Amanda.

No one answers. Octavi gets out of the vehicle and approaches a shape on the ground. Except it's not a shape, or an animal. The overturned bicycle beside him confirms it. César tries to follow him, but the spade, leaning against the seat, is blocking his way, so with an impatient gesture he tosses it outside to be able to get out. More agile, Brais gets there before him once again. And the three men look at the Arab boy, the wound bleeding from his temple, covering Octavi's hand with blood when he tries to sit him up.

'Don't touch him!' exclaims Brais, but it's clear from Octavi's face that it no longer matters.

'Shit . . . fuck.' César scuffs the ground and for once his protests seem justified.

'It was the wing mirror,' says Brais, pointing at the van's mirror.

They look at each other, not knowing what to do and César returns to the vehicle, head down. He walks slowly and approaches the driver's side. Sílvia lowers the window and looks at him and knows by the expression on his face that something serious has happened. She sighs and covers her face with her hands.

Amanda and Manel have already got out of the vehicle, but they're not moving, as if there, stuck to the van, they might be safe. Gaspar and Sara do the same, she with her mobile in her hand.

'We have to call an ambulance. Or the police. I don't know.'

'Don't call anyone. Wait a moment,' César orders and continues speaking to Sílvia in a low voice.

The world seems to have stopped on that section of dark, gloomy road. They no longer feel young and free, but anxious and frightened. The silence of the fields, pervaded by unknown murmurings, is unsettling.

'I don't want to see him,' says Manel. 'I can't bear blood.'

He takes the path towards the house, at top speed, fleeing it all.

'Yes,' says César. 'Go into the house. Go on, Gaspar, go with Sara and Amanda. And don't call anyone. We'll take care of this ourselves.'

They understand that he wants to be alone with Sílvia, who is still inside the vehicle, and Octavi. Maybe even with Brais.

Gaspar picks up the spade from the ground, the one César threw from the van, and starts to walk. Sara and Amanda go after him; they move a little out of their way so as not to pass close to the body, although Amanda can't help a quick glance.

And then, once again, the unexpected happens. They hear a shout from the patio of the house, and a cry of alarm that can only be coming from Manel. Sara and Amanda stop, frightened, and Gaspar, with the spade in his hand, runs towards those shadows thrashing on the ground. The next thing that is heard is an intense, metallic thud.

The crunch of a skull as it cracks.

'What happened then?' asked Héctor, shocked despite himself.

Sílvia Alemany had adopted a neutral tone during the whole tale, a voice that appeared not to be part of the story, not that of one of the protagonists.

'What do you think?' she asked, sounding once again like the woman Héctor knew from these past few days. 'They were two Moors, certainly a pair of petty thieves. A couple of illegal immigrants no one would miss.'

'Did you convince everyone not to report it?'

'More or less. It wasn't difficult, believe me. Gaspar was in shock and Octavi convinced him that it wasn't worth ending up in jail, away from his daughter, for a thief with no family or future. Sara showed herself to be loyal to the company, to me, as did César. Manel accepted it because he knew he could get something in exchange. And Amanda . . . Honestly, Inspector, I don't know what Amanda Bonet thought.'

About her personal life, Héctor said to himself. He was certain it had been an obsession for Amanda: the intensity of her devotion to Saúl indicated as much.

'And Brais?'

'He was the hardest to persuade. I've never known why he gave in. I think he did it for Gaspar. Brais is an orphan, you know? I'm not sure – he's not a predictable man. But a man of his word.'

'So you decided to hide it,' Héctor concluded. 'And it worked out, or at least it all seemed forgotten until—'

'Until the Gaspar thing happened. He was very strange in the months prior to the summer, so much so I was afraid he would tell all. So when Octavi informed me of his leave of absence, we decided a promotion would be good for him. Get him more on our side. But it wasn't like that: he felt even worse . . . I don't know if he received a photo of the dogs before he died.'

'The photo?' Héctor sat up, suddenly alert. 'Did you all get it?'

'I think so, but later on. In fact, not long ago. After Sara's death.'

Héctor's mind was working non-stop, linking facts, asking questions and answering them in the only way that seemed possible. The cruelty towards Gaspar's family, Sara's meal before dying, the photos . . . When he spoke, his voice was serious and accusatory.

'You did with those men the same as you'd done with the dogs. Got rid of their bodies, erased them from sight. Eliminated them so the countryside could go back to normal. But men aren't dogs, Sílvia.'

'Some are worse. Beasts with a treacherous bite.'

Héctor smiled ironically.

'That opinion of others seems exquisitely cynical coming from you, Sílvia.' He raised his voice to add, 'Tell me, what did you do with their bodies?'

Sílvia looked him in the eyes. She no longer had the strength for the challenge, but she retained one primary instinct: that of survival.

'That, Inspector, is the one thing I don't plan on telling you.'

41

Héctor left Sílvia in the interview room and went out into the corridor. After that quiet confession, the noise of the station felt almost like a racket, as if he were coming to the surface after diving in dark and treacherous waters. A surface clear only in appearance, he thought. He still didn't know how Gaspar had died. Sara. Amanda. A voice startled him.

'Inspector. I've done as you asked. They're all in room 2.'

'And Manel?'

Roger Fort spread his hands in a gesture that could be either apologetic or mocking. 'He passed out in the cell, Inspector. We had to take him out of there to bring him round but he was completely gone. We've sent him to hospital.'

Héctor nodded. The weak would always be weak, and in fact he felt better for having made one of the others fall. It's cleaner, he thought, although he certainly knew this was an adjective he could rarely apply to his work. It was two in the afternoon of what promised to be an extremely long day.

*

Judging by their postures, thought Héctor on entering, one would say they form three gangs: Víctor Alemany and Octavi Pujades were sitting very close; Brais and César occupied two chairs with space between them and away from the other two. None of them was speaking when Salgado came into the room.

'I hope you have a good explanation for all this, Inspector.'

'You must be Octavi Pujades,' said Héctor.

'Indeed, and I don't know if you're aware that my wife may be dying at this very moment while I'm here supporting Víctor.'

Despite his elderly appearance, this man retained the air of authority typical of those who have exercised it for a long time.

'I would have made you come regardless.'

'What are you talking about?' Víctor Alemany rose from his seat. 'This . . . this is persecution of my company. I've spoken to your superiors and I assure you they will take measures.'

Héctor smiled.

'Señor Alemany, before you go on, I suggest you listen. It will save you looking ridiculous.'

'I will not consent—'

'Be quiet, Víctor,' Octavi ordered.

'Listen to your friend, Señor Alemany. Allow me to speak.'

And Héctor spoke. He told them, in a shorter form, yet not omitting any important detail, almost all Sílvia had told him. He had the satisfaction of no one daring to interrupt and when he finished the silence was as dense as the unpleasant truth. Víctor Alemany had listened and remained dumbstruck, and if Héctor had any doubt that he was on the margins of that secret, at that moment he knew it was indeed so.

'And now we know what happened up there, have you anything to add, gentlemen?'

There was no answer. Héctor was sure that in some previous conversation they'd decided what the plan would be if it came to light.

'There's nothing you want to tell me?'

It was César who responded. 'I don't know what you're talking about.'

Denial. That was the plan. Because in the end it would be their word against that of the person who had only half betrayed them. Because, if no one revealed where the bodies were, it would be very difficult to charge them formally, however much Héctor wanted to see them all inside.

'Fine. Stay quiet, but I assure you I'll find out what you did with the bodies. And then you'll be charged with murder. All of you.' He looked at Brais Arjona. 'Even those who weren't driving and didn't hit anyone.'

There was no way of working out what Brais was thinking; his face was the epitome of concentration. He snorted, disheartened.

'Better keep quiet, Brais.' Octavi Pujades turned to Arjona, his voice rough. 'Or we'll have things to say as well.' He went on, unable to hold back. 'You threatened Gaspar, he told me. He was scared of you!'

'Old age is making you senile, Pujades.' Brais made a gesture of irritation. 'We've not trusted one another for months. Or perhaps you don't remember that César and I came to see you on Sílvia's orders? Gaspar was hysterical, we all saw it. Don't blame me for what he did. I didn't try to convince him any more than you or Sílvia . . . Then it was still worth it. Now it doesn't matter.'

'Clearly it was in everyone's interest that Gaspar didn't blab.' Héctor looked at each one in turn. 'You made another pact, didn't you? To eliminate anyone showing signs of remorse?'

'And you think we killed him and his whole family?' asked Octavi in a clearly sarcastic tone. 'We're not members of a criminal gang, Inspector.'

'No. You're not. But that night you crossed a dangerous line, Señor Pujades. There's no going back. I don't know how you convinced each other that covering up two violent deaths could go unpunished, but I'm sure you've had few moments of peace since then.'

Brais Arjona rose from his chair and put on his jacket. He seemed extraordinarily calm when he spoke.

'You're right, Inspector. And now, if you don't want anything else, I'm leaving. I have things to do.'

Héctor wanted to keep them in but he couldn't: he'd hoped that discovering what had happened months before in that house far from the city might bring an almost instantaneous solution to the mystery of the alleged suicides. It could be that one of the men before him had been assigned the role of executive arm to protect the others, in the same way that they could all be victims of revenge; just then there was no way of knowing.

He watched them leave, one by one, encased in their wool blazers and well-cut overcoats. Kings and henchmen of a grey army. Subjects without a queen, who was still locked up after betraying them. Enough nonsense, Salgado, he told himself. There are no princes or kings here, just normal men. Albeit with a good bit more money than most . . .

And suddenly, as if they were no longer people but dominoes, able to fall in sequence with the lightest touch, Héctor stood up, left Señor Alemany and almost ran up the corridor towards the room where Sílvia remained. The queen about to be overthrown.

He burst in so forcefully she jumped.

'Answer me a question. When do you have to deliver the money they've asked for in exchange for keeping quiet?'

Sílvia moved her head and pressed her lips together. Much was riding on this answer and she knew it. But she also knew that the enemy wouldn't cease in his pursuit.

'Come on, answer. I can extend the twenty-four hours. You've lost. You've all lost.'

'Friday, tomorrow,' she finally answered. 'Before five.'

'Don't tell anyone. And do exactly what I tell you.'

Héctor didn't see Fort at his desk and decided to go outside and smoke a cigarette. His lungs were craving nicotine and his brain fresh air. It's already night, he said to himself. The day was over and he hadn't even seen daylight.

When he went back in, Fort was waiting for him at the door of his office.

'Inspector,' said the agent, suddenly animated on seeing him, 'I thought you'd left and there's something I wanted to tell you.'

'Something to do with the case?'

'No, sir—'

'Then it can wait until tomorrow,' Salgado resolved.

373

'The thing is, sir, it can't.'

'Okay, tell me.'

There was already too much noise in Héctor's brain to concentrate on something that didn't bear close relation to what had occupied him in the last few hours. So he didn't manage to pay attention until, among the murmur, he made out two words that together set off every alarm: his son's name and the word hospital.

'What did you say?' he asked.

'Your son Guillermo called, Inspector,' repeated Fort. 'He's in Sant Joan de Déu, at the hospital. But don't be alarmed, it's not him. He went there with Agent Castro. She's in labour.'

From then on Roger Fort could brag that he was one of the few who'd seen Inspector Salgado completely floored by something.

42

Newborn babies have the virtue of arousing tenderness in adults, thought Héctor, and fear in kids. Or at least that's what he guessed looking at Guillermo, who was contemplating the tiny creature in a kind of waterless fish tank with a look that fused fear and apprehension.

Although perhaps the fear isn't due to the newborn, Héctor said to himself, but to all Guillermo had had to tell him on his arrival and which he still hadn't processed completely. Little by little, while they waited for news from the doctor attending Leire, Héctor heard about how and why she and his son had met at Ruth's house, and also the Charly story. Damned Charly . . . Héctor didn't know whether to get angry or not, or with whom, but slowly other pieces fell into place: the theft of Ruth's file, the refusal of Sergeant Andreu to explain further . . .

'Are you angry?' Guillermo asked him.

Héctor thought so. Or at least he would have been if he didn't also feel happy about this child, born weak but healthy. And because he was worried about Leire, lying in bed with her friend María at her side. Her family would arrive the following day and Héctor didn't want to ask about the little one's father. He was satisfied by knowing that neither Leire nor the baby was in danger.

'We'll talk about it all another time, okay?' he told Guillermo, putting an arm around his shoulders. 'It's better if we go home now. There's nothing else to do here.'

They spent a few more minutes gazing at the newborn baby, at Abel, who was going to spend his first night in a world that, at the beginning, was already mistreating him a little. He could only hope that it would treat this child a little more gently from now on.

The woman looks at the world through lost eyes, of pale blue. Eyes that no longer seem capable of seeing the present as it is, lost in the mists of a past that insist on pervading that bedroom, furnished with sturdy pieces of wood aged by the years. The half-lowered blinds block the light from outside. Héctor doesn't dare raise them: clearly the old woman prefers shadows to the sun's dazzling rays. Perhaps she feels better enveloped in this friendly darkness. Brightness has become an enemy: in the sunlight everything acquires defined, yet remote and unknown contours.

Héctor approaches the corner where the woman is sitting, facing the balcony, and she finally seems to notice his presence. For a moment the cloud blotting her mind disperses a little, enough to notice someone is there: someone whose features are familiar, although it's been a long time since she had them before her.

'Hello,' he whispers, coming a little closer. And he raises his hand to caress that cheek, which, despite time and illness, is still surprisingly smooth, but the embrace hangs in the air, halted by the sudden panic attack that overwhelms the old woman. Her eyes fill with tears in an instant, although Héctor barely has time to see them, because the woman covers her face with her arm, as if she wants to defend herself against a presumed aggressor. 'Don't hit me. Please. Don't hit me any more.'

Héctor takes a step back and looks at himself in the mirror on the wall, a mirror as old as the furniture, with a gilded frame. And then he understands what is frightening his mother. She doesn't see him, her son Héctor, and yet she recognizes his face. The face of that bastard husband who hit her for years in secret, in that very bedroom.

The worst thing is that he also sees him in that mirror: in his own reflection, in his face, identical to what he remembers of his father when he was the age he is now.

The worst thing, thought Héctor, still awake on the terrace in the early hours, is that this isn't a customary nightmare, but a real and painful memory. The last trip to Buenos Aires while his mother was still alive, seven years before. It was the trip that marked the end of his relationship with Lola and the beginning of a new stage in his marriage to Ruth. There were many ways of hurting a wife, of doling out invisible blows. Of making her suffer.

And that was something he couldn't permit himself.

377

43

'Are you sure they'll come for the money today?' Lola asked. She'd come to the station because she didn't want to leave before seeing the outcome of the case. Héctor knew she had to return to Madrid that same night to cover an event taking place on Saturday in the capital. If the weather permitted, that is: they kept announcing the possibility that, however strange it seemed, snow might fall on Barcelona in the next few hours.

It was five o'clock on Friday afternoon.

'Let's just say I don't think they'll be able to resist the temptation to come. They've done a lot of things for this money, apart from sending photos, and they must really want to get their hands on it. They won't wait.'

Lola gestured as if to agree, although she wasn't totally convinced.

'In any case, we'll know soon enough. Sílvia Alemany has already carried out the instructions and left the bag in the locker. Fort is around there, keeping watch. If someone goes to take it out, he'll see them.'

And, unconsciously, his glance rested once again on the telephone, still insultingly mute.

'I still don't understand how you worked out that they were blackmailing Sílvia.'

He smiled.

'Let's just say it was a sudden inspiration. Pieces were falling into place, but something was missing. Someone had the opportunity and the motive. The motive to report the whole thing, at least to expose it publicly. But they hadn't done that, so I had to look for something else. And in the end it occurred to me that money is usually a very reasonable incentive to do terrible things.'

'I don't know if I follow,' she said.

'There was something worrying me throughout the investigation. I could understand how one of the others might have killed Gaspar, Sara and Amanda, but why be so cruel to Ródenas's wife? And the little one. Octavi Pujades said so as well.'

'Well, someone *was* cruel to them.'

Salgado tried not to think about the terrible incident that must have occurred that night. 'And another thing: of the three victims, Gaspar Ródenas clearly fulfilled the requirements of a possible suicide.'

'He couldn't bear the weight of guilt . . .'

'That on the one hand; the acquisition of a weapon on the other. I don't know if he was planning what he was going to do when he got hold of the pistol or if it occurred to him then, but he certainly used it. Against himself and his family. His case was filed as such, and for four months nothing else happened.'

Lola nodded.

'And then we come to Sara. Another key to this whole affair. So alone on the one hand, and so loyal on the other. At heart, so vulnerable to anyone who might come close and show her affection. When I found out that the photo arrived after her death I guessed this had to mean something. Gaspar had committed suicide four months before and everything had continued as normal for them. The only possible explanation was that during those four months someone had become close to Sara to obtain information—'

Then the phone rang and Héctor picked it up on the first ring. It was a brief conversation of short tense sentences; when he hung up, he leaned back in his chair and exhaled a long sigh.

'They're on their way,' he said. 'Fort has just arrested Mar Ródenas as she was taking the money from the supermarket locker where Sílvia Alemany put it. Her fiancé was waiting for her in the car and tried to run, but they caught him shortly afterwards.'

'You were right,' Lola congratulated him.

But Héctor didn't seem satisfied. 'I didn't believe that Gaspar would have committed suicide without saying why he was doing it. And Mar was the only person who could have found a note that could have put her even partially in the picture of what had happened in Garrigàs. That gave her the opportunity. The desire for revenge against the others was a good motive. And economic necessity, or greed, made her modify her plans. As sometimes happens, she and her fiancé had beginners' luck. The luck of perverse consequences.'

Mar Ródenas was much more serious that evening than the other times Héctor had seen her. Despite everything, he couldn't help a strange feeling on seeing her hand-cuffed, sitting in the same room where Manel Caballero had been. Not compassion exactly, but a kind of sadness. At heart he was sure this young woman in front of him would never have taken that step, but when greed is aligned with revenge the results could be horrible.

'Hello, Mar,' he said.

She didn't answer.

'To tell the truth, I never expected to see you in these circumstances until yesterday.'

'No?' Her voice was hard, bitter. 'We all make mistakes, Inspector.'

'You're right. Mine was trusting appearances. Yours was thinking you could get justice on your own and in passing make the most of it.' Héctor looked hard at her and continued, 'Although in your defence I will say there's something I can understand. The scene you found at your brother's house must have been devastating for you. Seeing that Gaspar had killed his wife, his daughter and then shot himself would be enough for anyone to lose their mind. And reading the note he wrote must have been a traumatic experience. Then, on the computer, among other things, you found the photo of the dogs.'

She remained silent, expectant, but he didn't give her much of a break.

'I want to think that at first you kept that note with good intentions. Without it, your parents could always believe their son hadn't committed that atrocious crime. You kept it and began to become obsessed. Especially because it didn't tell you everything, right? I don't yet know what it said, but I imagine it referred to a killing carried out in the Garrigàs house, after returning from burying those dogs in the photo and with the complicity of the others, not giving more details than their names.

381

If he'd described it in detail, you wouldn't have had to approach Sara Mahler. You met her at Gaspar's funeral, didn't you?'

She looked away, but couldn't help a fleeting nod.

'Poor Sara . . .' said Héctor. 'She was reserved, discreet and at the same time in much need of affection. And you presented yourself to her as what you then were: a girl whose brother had died tragically; an unemployed young woman and, with the way things are, with no very promising future. You told her you'd found Gaspar's note and hidden it to avoid causing further pain to your family. Sara, with a father who didn't love her, was touched and confided in you.'

Mar was still locked in sullen silence and Héctor went on.

'Sara gave you presents and spent money on dinners and other things because she grew to care for you and because, like everyone, she needed someone to talk to. Not only about that, but also about herself and the company, even Amanda and her sexual habits. What's more, if the subject of Garrigàs came up, she didn't feel she was betraying any-one: you'd convinced her you were going to keep a secret of which you already knew something, not for them, but for your parents, and little by little you wheedled the rest of the information out of her. At the end of the day, she must have thought you had a certain right to know. There was only one thing, a detail she refused to reveal despite your insinuations: what they had done with the bodies.'

The inspector paused. There were many things he didn't know, that he had to guess; information to obtain from this girl who right now seemed ready to remain silent for ever.

'What happened, Mar? Did you try to convince her to help you in this blackmail?' He'd been talking to Víctor Alemany that very morning, and the company director had related his strange encounter with Sara in Sílvia's office the night of the Christmas dinner. 'Did you tell her you both deserved something better? A tangible reward in exchange for your silence?'

Mar Ródenas shrugged.

'Why not?' she finally said. 'That was all they could give me.'

'But Sara couldn't do it. I don't think she was capable of betraying them; she didn't dare leave the photograph of the dogs in Sílvia's office.'

'Sara didn't have a shred of ambition!' Mar retorted.

'No,' said Héctor. 'Sara was loyal, but suddenly she saw her loyalties were divided. On the one hand she had the pact with her colleagues; on the other, her liking for you. In any case, her faithfulness to the pact won out. And you got angry, didn't you? She'd gone from being an ally to an obstacle: she knew too much.'

Inspector Salgado was putting the facts in order following reasoning that led him to the only conclusion possible.

'So the night before *Reyes* you decided to meet her to insist once more she tell you what you didn't know. And she flatly refused. You argued. By the way, you were blonde then, weren't you? You both had dyed hair: you blonde and she jet black.'

Mar turned to him. A slight trace of fury still shone in her eyes.

'She tried to dissuade me, and I knew she was just like the rest. And I told her so.' The fury in her eyes became rage. 'I blurted it all out, I insulted her. I reminded her

383

that any moment what she feared so much could happen again.'

'Sara Mahler had been the victim of sexual assault, hadn't she?' Given what he knew of Sara it was a reasonable possibility.

'Years ago,' she said scornfully. 'Sara was frigid and men terrified her. She couldn't even take a taxi; anything not to be alone with a man.'

'What did you do to her?' said Héctor quietly.

'I didn't do anything to her. I just told her my fiancé and his friends would take care of her. I'd decided: if Sara didn't respond to the easy way, we'd do it the hard way.'

Héctor shook his head, tried to piece it all together.

'I don't know how you arranged it – while she was in the bathroom, I suppose – but you took her mobile and deleted all the data to avoid, at least for that night, her being able to call anyone when you pursued her. And then it was also very convenient that we wouldn't find any trace of your friendship.' Héctor's tone changed. 'You called Iván, your fiancé. To wait for Sara in the station. Sara left upset and went to the metro. She felt awful: she'd betrayed her colleagues and you had disappointed her. What's more, she was terrified by your threats.'

Héctor had the projection ready.

'Neither of you anticipated that Sara would die. It was enough to frighten her. But things got out of hand,' he said, thinking of Fort's explanation, which had turned out half true. 'This morning the images recorded on the other platform arrived. I think you'll find your Iván in them. Your great hope was anonymity, that no one would link you to this. That they'd suspect each other. That we wouldn't know who to look for.'

384

Mar looked away from the screen and fixed her eyes on the inspector.

'No,' said Héctor. 'I want you to see how Sara died. You deserve to see it.'

He started the recording: the grey platform appeared before them. And Sara, anxious, looking behind her, with her mobile in her hand.

'Seeing her phone blank she must have realized you were plotting something,' Héctor continued. 'That your threats weren't a joke. Look at her!' he ordered. 'Have the decency to see what you did.'

Mar Ródenas obeyed. Then she really did become upset.

'Then you sent her the photo, from an internet café near the restaurant. It could have arrived later, but she received it on the platform. She became more afraid. And Iván, who'd seen her descend, only had to come out for a moment: call her, or show her a knife. And Sara was so desperate that she did the only thing she could think of to get away.'

The metro was arriving in the station. The Dominicans took up the foreground but Héctor could almost see what the images didn't show: poor Sara leaping on to the tracks to avoid something that in her mind was worse than death.

'You have no proof of this, Inspector,' Mar challenged him.

'Well, I'm sure your fiancé will confess when we put the other possibility to him: that he deliberately pushed her. I don't think he did, to be honest. Too risky, and also you need a real motive to kill someone in cold blood . . . No, Iván wanted to frighten her.'

385

Mar Ródenas hung her head. By then there was palpable fear in her expression.

'So once the rough patch was over you decided to go ahead with your plan and send the photo to everyone. They began to get nervous. Sara always had her computer on, so on a visit to her house you had obtained the email addresses. Not knowing all the details of the story didn't matter: there was no longer any way of finding them out and you weren't planning on giving up what you considered yours. What's more, you guessed Sara's death would have unsettled them all. But Sílvia didn't prove easy: she refused. You were so furious, I'm sure. Your threats weren't being taken seriously.'

Héctor saw the tears brimming in Mar's eyes. Of self-pity, rage or simply fear. He didn't care; he pressed on without a break, raising his voice, accusing this girl of the crime she had to have committed.

'By this point nothing mattered any more: Sara's death had made you both unwilling killers, so the next step wasn't so difficult. And Amanda was the perfect victim. Sara, scandalized by such practices, had told you about their games, and also told you where Amanda left the key every Sunday evening. Finding her half-asleep suited you: I don't know if you'd have been capable of killing her in any other circumstance.'

'This is no more than supposition, Inspector.'

'Come on, Mar! Don't try to fool me: you set up the blackmail, you threatened Sílvia with someone else dying if she didn't deliver the money. Amanda died to make your threats credible. Don't expect anyone to believe it was chance.' Héctor smiled. 'Right now one of my men is charging Iván, and however much he loves you he won't take the blame for this. You know it.'

Héctor lowered his voice and looked intently at Mar Ródenas.

'Just answer me one thing: why do you hate them so much?'

Mar held his gaze unblinkingly. Then she said, 'You paint me as a monster, Inspector, and you speak of poor Sara as if she were a saint. But they were the monsters. They'd killed two people and went on with their lives, with their money, with their jobs, with their partners. Even after my brother. I just wanted the same as them: work, a house, a future. Don't tell me I don't have a right to that. You know how all this will end? I'll go to prison and they'll still be free. Because no one will bother looking for the bodies of the wretches they killed. The poor men who don't matter to anyone.

'Read the note Gaspar left, Inspector. I carry it with me always. Read it and don't tell me those bastards don't deserve to die. Read it in front of me and I'll confess everything in writing.'

And Héctor read it to her.

Alba is crying. I can't make her stop. I had written a full confession, but I don't have the time or energy to repeat it now . . . what does it matter, anyway? This world doesn't let you do things properly. I told Susana everything, I said the only decent thing I could do was confess. I can't live with those deaths in my head. With the image of those dead dogs, the sound of that spade. With a promotion that is payment for the crime. A crime we hid among ourselves: Sílvia, Brais, Octavi, Sara, César, Manel and Amanda. I told Susana, I explained it to her, but she didn't understand.

Fuck, she won't stop crying . . . I told Susana and she didn't understand, she told me it was fine, I wasn't any more to blame than the others, she wouldn't let me throw it all away. It was like talking to Sílvia or Octavi . . .

I wrote my confession anyway. Tonight. While they were sleeping. I put everything in, without forgetting a single detail. And when I'd finally finished I felt like a new person. Calm, for the first time in months. I went into Alba's room . . . Her bedroom smells so good, of clean dreams, of sleeping baby. I gave her a kiss and left.

Susana was in the bathroom. She'd torn my confession into pieces, she was throwing it down the loo. I heard the water flushing away the truth, as if it were shit.

Alba won't stop. When she gets like this, Susana is the only one who can comfort her. I can't . . . I can't leave her crying now her mother's no longer here.

44

It was almost nine o'clock on Friday night and Héctor was still in his office, alone. The confession, which Mar had finally signed, was on his desk. He added it to the file, lacking the definitive report which fell to Agent Fort to write up, not able to get rid of the uncomfortable, uneasy feeling that usually overcame him at the end of cases as complex as this one, although never with such force.

You're getting old, Salgado, he said to himself. He wasn't sure it was just age. He was sure he'd done a good job. Mar Ródenas had killed Amanda Bonet and prompted the suicide of Sara Mahler. But she was right about one thing: the two dead boys in Garrigàs deserved justice. And he wouldn't rest until he'd achieved it.

He attached the note to the rest of the papers, not knowing whether it was rage, helplessness or grief, pure and simple, that was clouding his vision. The pain given off by that desperate letter was more than anyone should bear and he knew that in his hours of insomnia Gaspar Ródenas would haunt him. He needed something to restore the little faith in humanity he had left or nothing would be worth it any more.

He wondered how those four seemingly normal people had been able to live with it. He tried to think about how they would be feeling at that moment, but he couldn't put himself in their place.

Sílvia was lying on the sofa of her house, in the dark, listlessly watching the weather forecast announcing the possibility of heavy snowfall in Barcelona that night. She'd put her phone on silent so as not to hear César's calls, nor his messages pleading for forgiveness. If he'd really mattered to her, she'd still have been unable to forgive him. There was no pardon for César Calvo because it simply wasn't worth conceding it to him. Just as there would be none for any of them if the whole truth were discovered. She was ready to accept it. Live with it. Last thing that evening, her brother had told her that now the case seemed resolved, the sale of the company would go ahead, although he took the opportunity to hint that he couldn't promise her that the new owners would want to continue relying on her. Sílvia hadn't bothered to respond; she was too busy looking for a boarding school for Emma, not abroad, as they'd once discussed, but in Ávila: a religious school for children of good families, which her daughter would detest with all her heart. She'd even called the school to ask if they would admit her mid-term, as a special favour. Fortunately, money still opened doors and Emma would begin a new life, away from her, at the beginning of February. She had communicated this to her a while before, in a tone that brooked no argument.

At least that problem is solved, she thought, unable to face all the others. She leaned her head on the armrest and lay down fully, eyes fixed on the screen, where images of past snowfalls appeared, and closed her eyes out of weariness. The next thing she knew was a hand grabbing her hair and a rough voice, different to the one she knew as her daughter's, whispering in her ear: 'If you think I'm going to that convent you're crazy, you bitch.' Sílvia smothered a moan of pain and saw Emma, smiling, leaving as silently as she had come.

She remained still, curled up on the sofa trembling, more from fear than rage. Had it not been for the pain, she'd have thought what had happened was a nightmare. But no, it was real. As real as the music coming from Emma's room at a deafening volume. Not knowing what to do, Sílvia looked for César's number in her mobile contacts and called him: there was no one else to turn to. César was strong, he could protect her . . . After waiting a while she had to give in to the evidence that no one was going to answer and, still shaking, she switched off the television and shut herself in her room.

The music kept playing like a declaration of war. That night Sílvia decided to surrender without a fight and pretend not to hear it.

César would happily have answered if he'd received the call an hour before, while he was still at home, contemplating the fucking stained carpet that seemed to sum up his present and a large part of his future. Sílvia forgiving him seemed as impossible as forgetting the taste of Emma. So, when he'd smoked an entire packet of cigarettes waiting for an answer that didn't come, he decided to go out to do something he'd put aside for a long time. He didn't take his phone.

The girly bar on Muntaner embraced him with the kind of servile affection he was seeking. He was sure that for the price of a drink, even if it was absurdly high, this place of dark corners would offer him what he needed to calm his nerves. He realized he hadn't showered since the morning, but he didn't care. No one there was going to throw it back in his face. At the bar, glass in hand, he scrutinized the faces of the girls working in the place, looking for someone who would awaken enough desire for him to open his wallet. After a while he found them all old, faded, so different to what he had in mind that he didn't feel able to fuck them. Then, after draining the whisky in a gulp, he asked for another and took the opportunity to ask the waiter, in a very low voice: 'Listen, know where I can find a young girl? You know what I mean: young – really young.'

Octavi Pujades's wife died at dusk, when the snow was still only a threat. She simply fell asleep mid-afternoon and never woke up. Going in to see her before dinner, he realized her heart wasn't beating.

He closed her eyes and sat down on the bed beside her. He knew he should call his children and give them the news, start to prepare everything, but he needed to be alone with her for a while. He stroked her forehead and said a prayer in a low voice because it was the only thing that seemed appropriate. He'd already said goodbye on many nights when he'd believed it was all over, so now, the moment having come, he didn't have too much to say to her. Eugènia had died too many times for the definitive end really to affect him.

He went to the door of the house in an attempt to fill

his lungs with air that didn't smell of death and, unable to help it, he thought not of his wife, but of Gaspar, Sara, Amanda and the two dead boys. He told himself that he was the oldest of all, the one who logically should have gone first. And yet, there he was. Alive, smoking a cigarette that refused to kill him and with a relatively well-insured future before him. If everyone kept quiet, of course. He had to trust in that.

That night he didn't even hear the howls of the neighbouring dogs. The silence was absolute. It would have unsettled someone else, but for him it was already normal. Soon the house would fill with people, children, in-laws, friends, acquaintances, and this peace would end. He sighed: he'd have to go through it. It was the penultimate chapter before beginning a new story. A widower, about to take early retirement, and with enough money to face his twilight age with dignity. Ironic that, if nothing changed, he couldn't complain about how things had gone for him.

He had to force himself not to smile when he picked up the phone to call his son and tell him that his mother had died.

Manel didn't like storms, or rain. And snow even less, which according to the news was coming closer to the city. A snowfall which would conclude some horrible, shameful days in which he'd been treated like a criminal. He, who'd scarcely done anything except watch and agree. They'd locked him in a filthy place, with a couple of stinking prisoners, and then taken him to a public hospital where he had to wait to be attended amid a mountain of old, sick people. Bastards. It wasn't fair.

393

Hadn't it been Sílvia who was driving the van? And Gaspar who'd given that dirty North African the whack with a spade? And in the end it was this Mar Ródenas who had killed Amanda and pushed Sara to suicide. But only he, Manel, had had to suffer hell. He, who'd just followed the directives of the majority without hurting anybody.

Life is definitely unfair, he said to himself bitterly as he went to the kitchen to drink his usual glass of water. Cold water to clean him inside before taking a shower. His nightly routine was more necessary than ever after the experiences he'd suffered. Only for a moment he thought how horrible it would be if one of the others went back on their word and confessed what they'd done with the bodies: he didn't know if that would send him to prison, but the very idea that it could happen brought him out in a cold sweat and made the glass fall from his hand, breaking into pieces on the floor.

He interpreted the breakage as a bad omen. He gathered up the pieces, haunted by the terrible sensation that his life, his safety, lay in the hands of people who wouldn't mind letting him fall. Seeing him crushed.

Héctor was so absorbed in his thoughts that he didn't hear someone knocking at his door and he was startled when it suddenly opened.

'Inspector Salgado.'

'Yes?'

It was Brais Arjona.

'I know it's late, Inspector, but they told me that you were still here. And I don't want to wait until tomorrow to do this.'

Brais took a chair opposite the inspector.

'I've told my husband everything. Since I agreed to that damned pact, my only aim was hiding it. Now he's left, and the fear of losing him has gone with him. You know? I always thought that if this happened I'd be filled with remorse: for what we did there, for Gaspar, for Amanda, for Sara. For everything . . . But I felt nothing. Nothing. Not regret, not remorse, not even sadness. It's as if my emotions have frozen in this damned winter. That's why I'm here. Because either I came and confessed or I threw myself out the window. And I don't want to do that. I've always thought suicide was a bad solution.'

Two hours later the street received Héctor with the subdued liveliness of a Friday night in winter. It seemed wrong that outside there were normal people, people who didn't commit atrocious crimes. He took a deep breath and the cold pierced his lungs, and despite everything he took out a cigarette and lit it. Fucking tobacco.

Héctor smoked in silence for a few minutes, under an extraordinarily dark sky. He couldn't go home like this. Although he understood those who drank to forget, alcohol had never been a refuge for him. What he needed was air, people. To empty his mind of good and bad. It was too cold to stand still, so he decided to walk home.

He took Gran Vía, walking for only a few minutes when he remembered the dream he'd had the night before *Reyes*. There were no toy stalls, or coloured lights, or deafening Christmas carols. But he was the same, walking alone. He almost expected a damned glass globe to fall from the sky and trap him. And suddenly, as in the dream, the pedestrians stopped, surprised: they didn't disappear but just looked towards the sky. Héctor also raised his eyes on noticing it was beginning to rain. It wasn't rain; no, it was snow, just as they'd predicted.

Héctor was on the verge of smiling. There was something about snow that brought out the child in everyone. He went on, slowly, as he contemplated how, little by little, the street was being covered in an unusual white blanket. And he was near the Universitat Central when, cheered by this unusual weather that wasn't easing, he took out his mobile and called Lola, telling himself that that night everything was possible.

RUTH

45

In the superintendent's office, Martina Andreu was finishing her tale, in which she brought her boss up to date with everything that had happened after the removal of Ruth's file. For his part, Savall listened to her with an expression of concentration and a furrowed brow.

'Leire hasn't discovered a huge amount, although she didn't have much time,' the sergeant concluded.

They said it was snowing outside. Inside the office the atmosphere wasn't exactly warm either.

'Martina,' he said after a few moments of silence, 'you know if it weren't you telling me this I would have to take a series of measures.'

'And also even though it is me, Lluís. No problem, I'm ready to accept them.'

'Let me think about it. One is tired at the end of the week. I learned a long time ago that it's not a good time to decide anything.'

'In any case, everything is stamped, classified and added to Ruth Valldaura's file. It's not much: the contents of the file Castro took from Ruth's house, some hand-written notes, and the tapes she got from Fernández. This one, with the asterisk, is the one where Ruth appears.'

Savall nodded.

'Poor Ruth. Seeing that character up close can't have been a pleasant experience. I say it first hand.' He lowered his voice. 'I suppose Ruth went to intercede for Héctor. God, what naivety . . . as if that man could be persuaded of anything.'

'Yeah. But we're the same. Omar died and, between you and me, they should send that lawyer who did it to a spa instead of putting him in prison.'

'Of course no one will miss Omar,' Savall agreed. 'I swear, very few times have I dealt with someone so vile.'

'Yes, I remember him. Well, you have it all there.' Martina thought about her next sentence for a moment. 'Lluís, I know I'm not in a position to do so, but I want to ask something of you. Leire has done all this in her free time: leave her alone. If you have to open a case on me, do it.'

He brushed off this possibility with one of his typical gestures.

'You know I'm not going to do that. We've spent too many years together, Martina.'

'Thank you,' she said. Deep down she'd expected it, although one never knew for sure with something like that. 'Precisely because of the trust we share, I want you to know that neither Castro nor I would have become involved in this if the investigation were in other hands.'

She said it in all sincerity, but at the same time Martina knew that Ruth Valldaura's disappearance seemed condemned never to be solved. It wasn't the first time something like that had happened, nor would it be the last.

Savall shot her a reprimanding glance.

'I don't think you can permit yourself the luxury of criticizing Bellver. Not now, not in front of me. And,' he added, 'if you're referring to Salgado, I don't want him involved in that again. It was a mistake to allow it in the first place. It went against all logic, and you know it. As well as against every rule.'

'Rules . . . Good people have too many and bad people hardly any. You know that too.' Martina got ready to get up, but didn't. She looked at her boss and added in a low voice, 'At least put the case in someone else's hands, Lluís. If I were Héctor and Bellver was in charge of something concerning me personally . . . Well, it doesn't matter. Better I keep quiet.'

'Yes.' He took a deep breath and his large body appeared to swell. 'Leave it, it's Friday and it's already night. We superintendents shouldn't work these hours.'

'Neither should mothers,' she replied, going towards the door.

'Speaking of mothers, how is Castro?' asked Savall.

'Well. The birth was a few weeks early, but it all went off without too many problems.'

'It's not hard to believe Agent Castro's son was in a hurry to be born,' he joked. 'I've rarely had anyone so impatient in my charge.'

Martina smiled. It was everyone's first comment as soon as they met Leire Castro.

From her hospital room window, Leire was also contemplating that dense snowfall, so strange in Barcelona, and told herself: everything seems to be changing. Starting with herself. She had just been with Abel; only a short while, because the baby weighed very little and had to stay in the incubator like a defenceless guinea pig full of plastic tubes. When the nurse told her she had to return him to that tank Leire obeyed, but couldn't help a strange feeling. She would have stayed for hours observing him, checking that he was all right. Whole, healthy, perfect. The nurse must have read her mind because she calmed her with the efficiency of someone who has spent years handling premature babies and neurotic mothers. And with that same authority, she sent her to her room to rest. 'Don't worry,' she said to her, 'I'll be here all night, with these four little ones. Nothing will happen to Abel.'

And Leire believed her, although then, as she watched how those flakes were changing the city and converting it into a Christmas-card scene at the end of January, she thought about how terrible it would be if that nurse's friendly face hid someone capable of making the baby disappear, telling you that he'd died, and selling him as if he were an object. A baby like Abel, or like Ruth . . .

She told herself she still had something in her power that proved nothing and implied much, something that opened the door to a new enigma around Ruth Valldaura. If these suspicions were confirmed, Ruth's life had drawn a sadly perfect circle: she disappeared from a cradle at birth, and from her home, that loft she shared with her son, thirty-eight years later. All those who took pleasure in her as a daughter, mother, lover or spouse were now obliged to search for her as perhaps a woman had done many years before. A single woman who maybe had to face a whole world against her. A hierarchy of white robes and black habits, pieces aligned in this perverse chess, which, to be able to act with impunity, also counted on accomplices in other spheres.

She didn't hesitate to use the word 'perverse'. Leire thought that in this world, in this city disguising itself as pure, bad people existed. And she wasn't thinking of delinquents, or even killers, but of monsters without conscience like Dr Omar. The images of Ruth in that old man's clinic were still fresh in her memory and – she was convinced of it – were still part of that impossible jigsaw. She'd just managed to add new pieces to an incomplete puzzle. I'll have to accept that, she thought. Someone had told her once that to get older is to give in a little. Well then, she gave in, at least for a few months. And without feeling bad about it.

Leire stayed a little longer at the window, enjoying that white night, thinking about Abel. About her own parents, who were arriving the following day, caught by surprise first by a premature birth and then by adverse weather. About Tomás, who, disregarding everyone's advice, had started out on the journey and was now trapped on the train. And she remembered what her mother had said to her that day in the kitchen, the premonition that in fact seemed to have come true. 'In the end, when the moment comes, you'll be alone.'

But, as she watched the snow fall, Leire found she didn't feel like that at all. And with a smile she told herself, actually, it was the complete opposite. Since the previous day she'd never be really alone again.

SIX MONTHS EARLIER

It hadn't taken Ruth long to collect what she wanted to take. It would be two days, so she only needed a few things which she put in a small travel bag. The sun flooding the house made her want to go even more. In an hour she could be lying on the beach, reading a book. With no more obligations than using sunscreen and deciding where she wanted to eat. It was a good idea. She needed a couple of days for herself. Just that, a weekend of sea, calm and boredom. She deserved this small reward after a few complicated weeks, and some very unpleasant moments. She still hadn't got that sinister man out of her head, and the fact that he might have disappeared didn't calm her much either. Enough, she said to herself. She'd made a mistake going to see him, but beating herself up for it wouldn't do any good. She hadn't told anyone . . . Sometimes even she didn't understand why she got herself into these messes, which were really none of her business.

She was going, but beforehand, out of pure compulsion, she checked the taps in the bathroom and kitchen, and since she was there she put away the breakfast plates she had already washed. This is the behaviour of an old woman, she scolded herself as she did it. Then she grabbed her minimal luggage and made sure she put everything required in the bag: the keys of the house in Sitges, her mobile, the charger . . . She took out her sunglasses; that day she couldn't drive without them.

She was making towards the door when the bell rang and an annoyed expression crossed her face. She had no intention of being held up by anyone, but she was surprised to see who it was.

'Hello, Ruth. Forgive me for coming without calling. Do you have a moment?'

'Of course . . .' She tried to conceal her irritation as best she could and let him in, because she guessed that this temporary setback to her plans arose from something important.

Lluís Savall didn't usually make courtesy visits.

Acknowledgements

It's been about a year since *The Summer of Dead Toys* was published and it would be impossible to thank everyone who helped inspire the novel. From the commercial and publicity teams at Random House Mondadori to the booksellers who go on recommending titles to a faithful clientele, from the press to bloggers, everyone contributed an important grain of sand. I can't leave out the foreign editors who dared to bet on an unknown name and are now publishing Héctor Salgado's first case in their respective countries, nor Justina Rzewuska who made it possible.

Now, finishing my second novel, I'm absolutely aware that this wouldn't have come about without the contributions of many people who have put affection, intelligence and goodwill into it. I want to start by highlighting my editor, Jaume Bonfill: his patience and dedication have been vital in making *The Good Suicides* what it is. Neither can I forget María Casas and Gabriela Ellena, and they know perfectly well why; nor Juan Díaz, editorial director of Debolsillo, who continues to believe in me and Inspector Héctor Salgado.

Apart from them, and although I'm sure I'll leave

someone out, I want to give thanks to: my family, always there; Pedro and Jorge, Carlos, Yolanda and Guillermo, Sara, Carmen (and Leo), Jose, Hiro, Edu, Carmen Moreno (excellent poet), Anna, Xavi, Rebecca and her skulls, Sílvia and her spaghetti. And Ana Liarás for her understanding throughout this whole process.

To all and many more, thanks again.

The Summer of Dead Toys
Antonio Hill

SALGADO'S EX-WIFE GOES missing, and Salgado is removed from a human trafficking and voodoo case for beating someone up. As his personal life comes under scrutiny, he is sent to investigate a teenager's fall to his death in one of Barcelona's uptown areas.

What inconvenient truths lie behind the city's most powerful families? Salgado's wife is still not found, and two seemingly unsolvable cases are set to implode under the hot Barcelona sun.

'For all his storytelling skills, Hill's real achievement is in the creation of an idiosyncratic new character, Salgado . . . a series to watch'
INDEPENDENT

'A sympathetic and engaging protagonist and plenty of plot twists with a cliff hanger ending that sets things up nicely for the next in the series'
GUARDIAN

'A blast of hot air through the current frozen Nordic crime-writing landscape'
WEEKEND SPORT Book of the Week

'Evokes the master of Barcelona-set narrative, Carlos Ruiz Zafon'
INDEPENDENT

If I Close My Eyes Now
Edney Silvestre

A HORRIFYING DISCOVERY by two young boys while playing in some mango groves marks the end of their childhood. As they open their eyes to the adult world, they see a place where storybook heroes don't exist, but villains and lies do . . .

'Sadistic sexual politics, investigated by an unlikely trio of sleuths (two schoolboys and an elderly man); misogynistic murder, syncretic Christianity; municipal shenanigans, all fester beneath the raging Rio sun'
THE TABLET

'Silvestre's real subject is Brazil, "a country capable of advancing fifty years in only five of full democracy," as it lurches out of the developing world'
GUARDIAN

Happiness Is Easy
Edney Silvestre

OLAVO BETTENCOURT IS an important man, a man of spin. With Brazil adjusting to the new idea of democracy, his PR firm holds the balance of power in its hands. Which has also made Olavo very rich, if not very popular.

Loathed by his trophy wife and mired in a web of political corruption that spreads from Sao Paolo to Switzerland, Israel and New York, Olavo is an obvious target for extortion. And what better leverage can there be but the kidnapping of his only son?

Except that the child on his way home from school in Olavo's armour-plated car, absorbed in his colouring book as the gang closes in . . .

He's not Olavo's son.

The Unbearable Dreamworld of Champa The Driver

Chan Koonchung

LIFE IS SIMPLE FOR Champa. He has a good job as a chauffeur in his hometown of Lhasa, and if his Chinese boss Plum is a little domineering, well, he can understand that – she's a serious art-collector, after all. And he does get to drive her huge Toyota.

When he starts to sleep with his boss as well as drive her around, life becomes a whole lot more complicated. But not in a *bad* way. Suddenly Champa's sex life is beyond his wildest dreams.

But then Plum brings home a Tara statue – a statue that shines with exquisite feminine beauty – and suddenly life is not simple at all, as Champa finds himself on the long road to Beijing in search of its inspiration. And it's going to be a rough ride...

The Unbearable Dreamworld of Champa The Driver is a rollicking road novel brim-full of sensuality and danger. Underlying the optimism and humour of its hero is a darker picture of racism and rough justice in modern Beijing.

The Dangerous Game
Mari Jungstedt

THE PRICE OF FAME IS . . . DEATH

When Jenny is spotted by a high-profile modelling agency, she goes from ordinary schoolgirl to celebrity overnight.

Agnes used to be a model too – but now she lies in a hospital bed, slowly being destroyed by an eating disorder.

An attempted murder during a lavish photo-shoot means that Jenny's and Agnes's lives will soon intersect in the most terrifying of ways . . . Because someone is watching them. Someone with a plan.

Can Detective Anders Knutas figure out who it is in time to stop a terrible justice being served?

'One of the best writers of Scandinavian crime fiction'
Harlan Coben

'One of Scandinavia's best crime writers'
The Times

He Who Kills the Dragon
Leif G.W. Persson

IT SHOULD HAVE BEEN an open and shut case: Two drunks meet for a bite to eat and considerably more to drink, fall into an argument. And then one of them brings their evening together to a close by beating the other to death.

A strangely routine and yet puzzling scenario to Detective Superintendent Evert Bäckström, whose legendary poor temper not been improved by strict orders from his doctor to lead a healthier life. His gut feeling proves him right: within days, his team has another murder linked to the first on their hands.

Suddenly the nation needs a hero. Who better to save the day than Evert Bäckström, misanthropic, ostentatious, devoid of morals, Hawaii shirt-clad, and, latterly, armed? Once again an unholy combination of laziness, luck and an unbelievable sense of timing may yet rescue him from the perils of his fifteen minutes of fame . . .

'Bäckström is a character worthy of Joseph Wambaugh at his best . . . Underneath the humour, Persson shines a light on Swedes and their society, and in that broader sense may be the most interesting of the novelists in the current Swedish crime boom'
Barry Forshaw, CRIMETIME

'Just what fans of Jo Nesbo and Stieg Larsson are looking for'
BOOKLIST

'Excellent. . .There are so many levels and subtleties in the plot that there is only one way to read this book – at one sitting'
Borås Tidning

'Persson outperforms most of his competitors in the Swedish crime genre by miles . . . Hardboiled, clever, suspenseful'
Svenska Dagbladet